THE KA

One of the most powerful writers of adven[illegible] thriller fiction, Richard Cox is already known to thousands as the bestselling author of *Sam 7* and *Botticelli Madonna*.

Both a pilot and a Reserve Paratroop Major, he was Defence Correspondent for the *Daily Telegraph* for seven years, and before that was a Foreign Correspondent for the *Sunday Times* for twelve years, reporting wars, revolutions and other historic happenings at first hand – experience which has helped to make his fiction so authentic and convincingly detailed. In *The Katanga Run*, especially, his most ambitious novel to date, he has used his own on-the-spot observations of mercenaries in action and his first-hand knowledge of flying in Africa to make even more vivid this stunning story.

Also in Arrow by Richard Cox

Sam 7
Botticelli Madonna

Richard Cox

The Katanga Run

ARROW BOOKS

Arrow Books Limited
3 Fitzroy Square, London W1P 6JD

An imprint of the Hutchinson Publishing Group

London Melbourne Sydney Auckland
Wellington Johannesburg and agencies
throughout the world

First published by Hutchinson 1980
Arrow edition 1981

Made and printed in Great Britain
by The Anchor Press Ltd
Tiptree, Essex

ISBN 0 09 926530 3

Acknowledgements

I should like to thank
Peter Grose and Phillippa Harrison
who long encouraged me to write this book
and to others who helped,
most notably Bill Weston and
John and Barbara Latz

Prologue

The suspension bridge dominated the gorge. On each side stood high towers through the tops of which ran the massive chain links which held the roadway 200 feet above the river below and then curved down again to anchor points in the solid rock. The graceful silhouette of Frampton Bridge was a famous landmark in the Midlands.

The gorge itself was only a few miles long, a winding cleft through a range of hills where a river, exploiting a natural fault, had cut its way over millions of years. In places the sides were sheer cliffs and nowhere was the gorge more than 500 yards wide. The bridge, at the narrowest point between two outcrops of rock, spanned 700 feet.

On this raw Saturday in early February an east wind was whipping cloud low across the hills and rain spattered the cars as they crawled along the roadway. Six miles away at Frampton RAF station two jet pilots were talking in the oak-panelled Officers' Mess bar. They could drink before lunch because no one was flying today. Tomorrow, weather permitting, the squadron's disbandment flypast would be held.

The elder of the two men was about twenty-eight years old, thin, and with an intensity of manner which contrasted sharply with the open, suntanned face of his companion. Both men wore grey-blue service dress uniforms, RAF wings above the breast pocket, two thin rings indicating flying officer rank on their sleeves.

'You're wrong, you bloody African,' the elder was saying, hissing out the words as if afraid of being overheard, even though the barman had gone off to fetch something and they were alone. 'We're going to beat that bridge all ways. We climbed it. Now's our chance to fly under. And I shall lead.'

'It was pure accident that you were spotted and I got across first. Don't be so sensitive.' Mike Russell would never forget the night Jake had challenged him. Clad in black track suits and gym shoes they had crawled up the chains, one on each side, until they could edge into the towers and look out across the main span, the huge links sinking down like the track of some nightmare roller coaster, and the river water glinting dully hundreds of feet below. On the way down Jake had been caught in a car's headlights and had to freeze until it passed, giving Mike an advantage which he never lost and which Jake, as the instigator, never forgave. The bridge was an obsession with Jake Wildeblood, the ultimate challenge to nerve and daring.

'You came with me then,' Wildeblood insisted. 'You must come now.' There was a note of pleading in his voice which Mike had not heard before. 'It's our last chance. Every bloody pilot in the squadron's wanted to beat the bridge. We'll be the ones who do it.' His tone became more urgent. 'Listen, Mike, we're next on the roster for a weather flight. Bob Kane will have to order one before the flypast, at least if it's like today he will. It is the last chance. After that,' he snapped his fingers in Mike's face, '*finito*. Disbanded. *Kaput*. The show's over. What have we got to lose? Come on, boy. It's not even dangerous.'

Mike nodded warily. It was undeniable that at some time or another all seventeen of the pilots in 699 Squadron had discussed flying under Frampton Bridge and they had always agreed on one thing: it would be no problem. The twin-jet Meteor fighters they flew were manoeuvrable aircraft. The run-in over Frampton's industrial area would be dead simple. The distance between the cliffs of the gorge was more than twenty times the plane's wingspan. Once through, all you had to do was shove on full power, turn a little to allow for the first bend in the gorge, and pull up out of it. In RAF slang it was a piece of cake.

'The worst they can do is throw us out of the squadron,' urged Jake, 'and the bloody goverment's doing that anyway.' He turned and held his companion by the shoulders, looking fixedly into his eyes. 'You can't let me down. Not now.' Equally abruptly he let Mike go, his arms falling limp to his sides.

'All right,' said Mike, his mind suddenly made up. He had to give Jake a chance to even the score. 'We'll make it a stern—tail chase. You lead. I'll be half a mile behind.'

'We must go through together!' Having won the argument Jake immediately became insistent again. 'We must make a proper show of it.'

A shiver of unease whispered in Mike's stomach. To pass through flying as a pair, one alongside the other, would much more than double the problems. 'No,' he said firmly, 'if there's a wind like today's blowing it'll funnel down the gorge. Nothing will be predictable. I'm not formating on anyone down there. I'll follow.'

'Not half a mile behind, for Christ's sake!'

In fact at 350 knots, which was about the slowest they could fly to be sure of the rapid pull up they needed, half a mile was only four and a half seconds flying time. Mike deliberated. 'All right. I'll be two seconds behind.'

As he spoke the bar door swung open, and another pilot entered, an ascetic looking man of medium height with crewcut hair. The two others fell silent.

'You fellows planning something?' the newcomer asked with a marked North American accent. He tended to use college jargon which never failed to irritate Wildeblood. His name was Steve Barlow and he was a Canadian.

Wildeblood shrugged his shoulders. 'Just a touch of speculation. Wouldn't interest you, as you're not a risk-taker by nature.' The contempt in his voice was undisguised. He invariably went to the limit on principle, whereas Barlow flew by the book.

'Thinking about that bridge again?' Barlow laughed. 'Guess she's going to remain virgin as far as 699's concerned.' He saw Wildeblood's face flush and waved a hand at the bar. 'Forget about it. Have a beer.' He looked around. 'Where's that barman of ours?'

'Fixing a barrel or something,' said Mike. 'It ran out.'

Barlow leant over the bar and looked behind. 'No shortage of glasses. Have a whisky then?'

Wildeblood shook his head perversely. 'Time we were off,' he said curtly. 'Come on.' He gulped down what was left in his tankard and made for the door.

'See you later,' Mike said, in a more friendly tone. They were all civilians, all volunteer reserve pilots. The imminence of disbandment seemed to him no reason to break 699's camaraderie.

'I can't stand that man,' commented Wildeblood as they walked out of the Mess building to his car. 'No bloody guts.'

'He's a lawyer. All lawyers are cautious.'

'No he's not. He's chicken!' Wildeblood was shouting angrily into the wind. He had once suggested the bridge exploit to Barlow and received an unqualified refusal coupled with a more moralistic argument that he, Barlow, as a Canadian reserve officer attached to a British squadron while taking a post-graduate law degree at Oxford, was trebly obliged not to play the fool.

Back in the bar the Canadian poured himself a whisky, signed a chit for it, perched himself on a stool and surveyed the room. He doubted if he would ever come back after tomorrow's parade. What would happen to the row of visiting squadrons' emblazoned badges which hung above the bar? The pewter mugs? The framed cartoons and photographs? All the souvenirs an active squadron had collected over nearly thirty years which included five of full-time fighting. Barlow was honoured to belong to 699, but he couldn't feel quite the affection for its history which motivated the others. Nor the same bitterness at the bland announcement made by the Defence Ministry on 15 January to the effect that all twenty Royal Auxiliary Air Force Squadrons would be disbanded by 10 March.

This thought switched his mind back to the two others who had just left. 'I'll be two seconds behind,' Russell had said. They were planning something for sure. He reckoned Russell was influenced enough by Wildeblood to do some crazy final-fling act. He sipped his whisky. Should he tell the squadron commander, Robert Kane? A single overheard remark wasn't much to go on. Anyway Kane ought to know what was happening in his own squadron himself. It wasn't the one outsider's job to be an informer. Barlow drank down his whisky and decided to stay quiet. There might be nothing in it anyway.

Robert Kane was the only one of the pilots in 699 Squadron who was old enough to have served in the war, and he only just. He was thirty-one now. Stocky, thrusting, determined to make his squadron the best of the twenty. He was lucky that his civilian employers, a big metal-broking group in London, favoured this all-consuming leisure activity. They did so because their managing director had himself fought in the Battle of Britain, ending up as wing commander with a chestful of medals. A substantial number of 'The Few' had been auxiliary pilots and of them a high proportion had flown sorties from which they never returned. 699 Squadron had a heritage.

When Kane learnt that disbandment was inescapable

he decided to exploit the one lever of power the squadron possessed in order to secure his pilots a last few hours of jet flying. All the squadrons had honorary air commodores, who took a lively and personal interest in their affairs. Prince Philip, himself a pilot, was patron of 601 Squadron. The Queen Mother reigned over 600, the City of London one; and herself appointed new squadron commanders, only informing the Air Ministry afterwards. At Frampton the air commodore was a royal duke, whose awareness of tradition was intense. Kane had little trouble persuading the old boy that there should be a full disbandment parade before the squadron colours were laid up in Frampton Cathedral.

As the day of the parade approached, Kane noticed that a mood of light-hearted despair settled over the Mess. All other flying had long stopped and the pilots who came at weekends drank hugely more than normal, as though preparing for a wake, culminating in the last Saturday evening when after-dinner horseplay put one of them into hospital with a broken leg.

Sunday dawned as wet and windy as the day before.

After breakfast Kane called his pilots together in the briefing room, its walls lined with maps, and angrily spoke his mind. 'This squadron's had a damn fine record since it was formed in 1930,' he blazed, 'so let's sober up and concentrate on making the Duke's visit something we can be proud of.'

Standing by a blackboard on which he had chalked the flypast route diagrammatically, Kane briefed them on the day's programme. The Duke would arrive at 11.30. At 11.45 the squadron would take off, follow a short cross-country route, and fly in formation over the saluting base at 12.00 precisely, while the ground crew and the pilots not airborne marched past the saluting base. When the aircraft had landed the Duke would address all personnel. Then he and the officers would repair to the Mess for lunch.

There remained the question of who was chosen to fly and who not. Kane held off naming them until he had said what was on his mind, because it applied to all of them and he wanted full attention for his last talk to 699 as an operational fighter squadron. He paused, glancing round the assembled pilots who sat facing him on four lines of chairs. They wore flying overalls, the squadron's badge sewn on their right sleeves, the squadron's traditional bright orange scarves loosely knotted at their throats. Most were in their mid-twenties, one an architect, another a schoolmaster, Russell from Kenya was training in accountancy. Kane's eye rested on him. The Auxiliaries had always welcomed Commonwealth members. Mike had earned a place because he'd come back to Britain to volunteer for two years of National Service which he could easily have avoided. He stayed on, and joined 699, when the Mau Mau emergency persuaded his parents that he ought to learn a business in Britain, in case Kenya went bad. The other Commonwealth pilot, Barlow, was different. He had proved the kind of intellectual odd-man-out whom one ought to avoid recruiting. Yet how could one refuse a Rhodes scholar who was already a fully qualified jet fighter pilot and had a glowing recommendation from the Canadian authorities in London?

Kane's gaze flickered over the rest. They were a good bunch. He was proud of them. They did not deserve to be thrown on the scrap heap. If this had been 1939 these men would have been facing the Battle of Britain, not disbandment. There was no difference between their faces and the ones that gazed, enthusiastic and confident, from the old squadron photographs. They were the same breed and given a chance they would display the same fortitude, the same heroism. He was damned if he would follow the Tory Air Minister's degrading example and tell them they were not wanted.

'My advice is to swallow the insult,' he said at last,

'because it just might happen that the Government changes its mind. We have a lot of powerful friends and we're effective fighting squadrons. Suez may have been a bloody fiasco but there could still be a war in the Middle East. The Minister who thinks this is the time to throw away twenty fully trained operational squadrons for a saving of five million pounds a year and seventeen million gallons of aviation spirit needs his head examining. So my advice is not to give up hope yet. And meanwhile, let's make this parade and flypast the best the Duke has ever seen.' Kane paused again, changed his tone to a more relaxed key. 'Even though Jim breaking his leg cut one of you out, choosing twelve was damn difficult.'

Without further comment he read out the list. There were murmurs of both pleasure and disappointment. He grinned at Russell. 'Sorry, Mike,' he said. 'With two of you colonials around I spun a coin. Steve Barlow won.' He saw the Canadian freeze up at the joking use of 'colonial', but disregarded him. 'As for the others,' he went on, 'you'll just have to believe me it's no disgrace that you weren't chosen.'

As he said this his eyes flicked back to Russell and the pilot sitting beside him, Jake Wildeblood, who seemed unnecessarily tense. Again the question flashed through Kane's mind whether he should have thrown Wildeblood out of the squadron after he flew through that high tension wire. He was lucky to be alive. Frampton city had been without power for eight hours. The publicity had been appalling. Wildeblood was in many ways an accomplished pilot but now, in the split second of watching his expression, Kane regretted tolerating the accident, even though the man had flown on and landed safely. There was something wrong in his make-up. He took too many risks. Well, Kane thought, that's past history. It was all over bar the shouting now and Wildeblood wouldn't fly again. He turned to the met. officer. 'Let's have the weather then.'

The met. officer, a bespectacled regular who ran the

meteorological centre for all operations at Frampton, stepped forward and fussily pinned a chart to the blackboard. 'Gentlemen, as you may have guessed, there's a front going through.' He pointed at the isobars on the chart. 'No possible improvement before the afternoon. Nine-hundred-foot cloudbase, wind twenty-five knots gusting thirty, visibility three miles reducing to one in showers.' He turned with schoolmasterish formality to Kane. 'I would recommend a weather flight, sir.'

'Well, that's fifteen minutes' flying for a couple of you that the rest won't get.' Kane glanced at the adjutant, another career officer, 'Who are the lucky pair?'

'Russell and Wildeblood are next on the roster, sir.'

For a fraction of a second Kane thought of overruling the list. He could see the expectancy on Wildeblood's face and he didn't like it. But the need to be seen to be impartial was too great.

'Well,' he said harshly. 'You two know the route. Take off as soon as we're finished here. And keep it to quarter of an hour, right?'

At 9.45 the two Meteors rolled away from the dispersal, the low whine of their engines rising to an impetuous growl as the pilots taxied to the holding point. Then they lined up as a pair, one slightly behind the other, and roared down the wide tarmac runway, which glistened darkly from the rain, to lift off in a crescendo of noise. Jake led, banking almost immediately into a turn to follow the official route. Mike closed up to a mere wingspan away, keeping in tight formation. Three miles from the airfield Jake altered course, making hand signals in order not to reveal their intentions over the radio. Frampton was dimly visible in the distance, smoke from the factories merging into the leaden horizon. This is it, thought Mike, we're committed now. In fifty seconds it would be all over.

As they headed for the city Mike dropped behind. A

moment later they were over the Frampton factories, racing under the grey cloud. The suspension bridge was a dark outline in the murk, monotone, drained of colour. Beyond, the winding gorge disappeared in the rain. Drops of water smeared back over the perspex canopy. He kept one eye on the high tail of the aircraft ahead, the other on the bridge, swiftly checked the speed. 380 knots. Jake was going faster. His stomach tensed. They were a bare hundred feet up now. The last buildings flashed below. They were over the river, the hills closing in.

Jake was through, well clear of the span. Two seconds later Mike passed beneath the bridge himself. A man was staring down at him from the footpath. He banked a little for the right hand bend and was about to pull up when he realized that the cloud was on the hills and that ahead of him Jake was going into a victory roll, his left wing flipping down as the Meteor became inverted. Then the plane vanished in the murk.

'Christ alive, the bloody idiot.' Mike immediately throttled back, deciding to fly the winding gorge its whole brief length, instinctively bringing his speed down. The first curve was easy. A second later he faced a high white cliff with houses on its brow. He banked steeply round, making for a faint brightness under the dark line of cloud a mile away at the end of the gorge, and then saw Jake re-appear ahead of him, still half inverted and a full hundred yards left of the centre of the gorge. And too low. The roll was still not complete when the Meteor's wingtip caught a tree.

The plane disintegrated, exploding in a ball of fire, throwing up a cascade of metal fragments. As Mike flew past the blast rocked him. Then he was out of the gorge and conscious of only one thing. He had to call for help and he had to get back to Frampton.

The control tower's response was frigid, ordering him to return and land at once. When he taxied in Kane and the adjutant were standing on the tarmac. His explanations seemed pathetic even to himself.

Half an hour later he was under open arrest and sitting in the Officers' Mess. He sat because he could barely stand up. His knees were trembling as if he was diseased. There was no clear thought in his mind except the memory of Jake's Meteor crashing, the wing breaking off, the rest somersaulting and then that appalling flash of fire.

'It must have made a hell of a bang,' he said to himself, and laughed hysterically. A moment later he was crying.

'At midday a sloitary Meteor, flown by the adjutant, dipped its wings in salute to the Duke as the volunteer officers marched past, their long greatcoats flapping in the wind. That afternoon Kane, coldly furious, told Mike that the authorities had decided he could return to London and his studies, provided he came back immediately when required. The party was over.

The inquest was held at Frampton Coroner's Court two weeks later. Jake was described officially as a pilot who 'tended towards over-confidence and had been reprimanded for faults arising from this'. But the dry language lost its power to damp down the publicity when Steve Barlow unexpectedly stepped up to the witness box in the tiny courtroom, related how he had overheard the two men planning what might have been an illegal flight, but had not felt justified in interfering because he believed the squadron commander would know what was going on.

The silence which followed this apparent condemnation of Kane was broken by the coroner commenting harshly that it was not his business to examine personal relationships within the squadron, simply to establish the cause of death. Having dismissed the possibility of a deliberate crash, he recorded a verdict of 'accidental death'.

Meanwhile an RAF Court of Inquiry had taken a much tougher approach in the privacy of its hearings. It rapidly established that Mike's unauthorized low flying constituted an offence against Queen's Regulations. Shortly afterwards he learnt that he would be court-martialled.

The trial was held in an anteroom of the Mess at Frampton, presided over by a group captain. The case as outlined by the prosecutor was irrefutable. Among the witnesses he called was Barlow, to whom he gave a rough passage.

'You say you guessed this unauthorized action was in prospect and yet you did nothing, precisely nothing, to prevent it?'

'I did not feel the evidence was strong enough,' began Barlow. 'As a matter of conscience I could not make unproven accusations. I imagined the officer commanding the squadron probably knew, if anything . . . .'

He was cut short by the prosecutor, who demanded, 'In that case why have you come forward now?'

'In retrospect, sir, I consider what I overheard has a bearing on the case.'

'You are a lawyer by profession, are you not?'

'Which is why I was reluctant to interfere, sir.'

'I put it to you, Flying Officer,' snapped the prosecutor unpleasantly, 'that but for your pusillanimous behaviour the squadron would not be dishonoured. One of its members would still be alive, and we should not be assembled here.'

At this the president rapped the table and ruled the questioning out of order. Barlow was dismissed, scarlet-faced and trembling.

There was little Mike's defending counsel could plead beyond extenuating circumstances, which rested on assailing the dead Wildeblood's character as a malign and irresponsible influence. The damage imprisonment could cause to Mike's accountancy examinations and his civilian prospects was stressed.

The president sentenced Mike to be dismissed from the service subject to confirmation.

After the court adjourned, Mike had one inescapable request to make of Kane, before leaving Frampton for the last time. In the dragged-out days since the crash he had firmly decided that, whatever else happened, he would contrive to continue flying. For that he would need a civilian licence and his RAF flying logbook, which had been confiscated.

The two men walked in silence to the squadron office, where Kane unlocked the safe and removed the blue bound logbook.

'You realize this is Air Ministry property?'

'No, I didn't.'

'There are a damn sight too many things you don't know. Here, take the thing, make an extract of your flying on a separate sheet of paper, and I'll countersign that.' He handed Mike the book. 'And while you're about it, change your clothes. The sentence may be subject to confirmation but as far as I'm concerned you'll not be seen in uniform on this airfield again.'

An hour later Mike brought back the logbook and the extract, detailing the types of aircraft he had flown and the number of hours in each. Kane checked it carefully, pressed a squadron stamp beneath the totals, picked up a pen and wrote with a steady hand, 'Logbook closed in accordance with QR 775. Flying Officer M. V. Russell sentenced to be dismissed from the service by court-martial 18.3.1957.'

Then he signed it, handed it back, and said thickly, 'Now get out of here.'

The next day Kane himself was ordered to report to the Air Officer Commanding, Fighter Command, at headquarters near London. The AOC was in his mid-fifties, with greying hair, a lined face and deceptive benevolence.

'Come in and sit down, Squadron Leader,' he said as Kane was ushered in by the young woman officer who served as his personal assistant. 'Now, this has been an extremely unfortunate business. Please tell me about it.'

Half-way through Kane's account he interrupted curtly. 'I have read the summary of evidence, Kane. I want to know what really went wrong. Why wasn't Wildeblood taken off flying after the incident with the high tension wires?'

'He was an experienced ground attack pilot, sir. We had very few on the squadron. It's not an unheard-of accident.'

'It should be, Kane.'

'Some things have to be a matter of personal judgement, sir.'

'Agreed.' The Air Marshal paused for a second and then stared from beneath bushy white eyebrows, his forehead furrowed. 'You trusted this fellow even after he'd made a lunatic climb across the suspension bridge at night?'

'He did *what*, sir?' This was a genuine shock. Kane had heard nothing of the exploit. And as their commander he should have done.

'Did you not know that two of your pilots had scaled the Frampton Bridge from end to end one night last October? The same two, Russell and Wildeblood. You tell me you did not know?' The incredulity in the AOC's voice was unfeigned and cold.

'No, I did not, sir.' Kane felt sick. Why the hell had no one told him? What kind of loyalty had they all shown him, the bastards?

'Squadron Leader.' The Air Marshal spoke gently, the ice gone from his voice, and he played with a paperknife shaped like a sword, as if embarrassed. Had his assistant been in the room she would have immediately recognized that the moment of execution had come. Kane, being unfamiliar with the great man, did not, and relaxed a fraction. 'There is no greater honour the Royal Air Force can bestow on a civilian than the command of one of its auxiliary squadrons. It confers great privileges.' The Air Marshal's tone hardened minutely. 'And great responsibilities.' He twirled the paper knife. 'Your record shows that you possess exceptional flying skill. Unhappily I am not so confident in your judgement. Odious as the testimony of that Canadian was, it reveals a decided failure in man-management.' The paperknife was slammed down on the desktop and left spinning on its hilt. 'There is no room for failure in this Command, Squadron Leader. I should be grateful if you would tender your resignation to the Air Council.'

The Air Marshal rose and Kane hastily scrambled to his feet, completely lost for a reply.

'This is not an official reprimand, you understand, Kane. There will be nothing on your record.' The Air Marshal blinked as though regretting the whole unpleasant affair. 'I merely feel the time has come for you and the Air Force to part company. You understand?'

Kane came stiffly to attention, turned and left the room. Outside, the pretty woman officer handed him his peaked hat and his gloves. 'Don't take it to heart,' she said sympathetically. 'You'll live.'

1

The chief pilot of the charter company was a stocky sunburnt man of forty-five. He was standing outside the hangar at Wilson Airport, his khaki bush-shirt spotlessly clean, the silver metal wings glinting on his chest. It was eight in the morning. He glanced up at the sky. The patchy low cloud which so often covers Nairobi in the early hours was beginning to be burnt off by the sun. Soon this would be another of those peerless African days when the air was so clear that 1000 feet up you could see the snow-covered hump of Kilimanjaro 140 miles away. The chief pilot grunted, turned on his heel and strode back through the hangar to his office, calling out as he passed the pilot's briefing room, 'Mike, I have job for you.'

As Mike Russell entered, Zegintov was already surveying a route on the large-scale East African map which covered most of one wall.

'Yes, Captain Zog.' Mike had been with the company nearly three years now, but he remained respectful although, like everyone else in the flying business, he used the contraction which had come about because the African employees could never pronounce Zegintov. Captain Zog was a White Russian exile who had flown with the RAF in the war and come to Kenya in 1946. Originally he had found English grammar difficult, now he could no longer be bothered with it since his abbreviated, muscular use of the language proved forceful and effective.

'Yes,' he said, jabbing his finger at the contours of Mount Kenya on the map. 'Is nice job. There is Belgian family at Safari Club. You take two ten up there, fly to Crater, stay one night. Tomorrow afternoon you take to Seronera and come back. OK?'

'How many are they?'

'Three. Father, mother, daughter. Very pretty daughter.' Zog smiled. 'You behave yourself, OK?' It was a truism that the assistant hunters on safaris kept the clients' wives amused in camp and he didn't want his young pilots trying the same game, though it was not so often that they stayed out overnight, since the demurrage charges for keeping aircraft idle were high.

'Six hundred mile,' said Zog abruptly, tracing the route on the map with his finger up from Nairobi to the Mount Kenya Safari Club strip, down again past the city to the Great Rift Valley and over the Tanganyika border to the famous Ngorongoro Crater, then west to the Seronera camp in the middle of the Serengeti plains. 'In two ten you have plenty of fuel.' He consulted the big steel-cased watch on his wrist. 'Cloud is clearing. You leave in half-hour, you can make Crater midday easy, OK?'

Mike did not wait to be dismissed. As usual Zog was running things with the split-second timing of a bombing raid.

He hurried next door, did his calculations, filled in a flight plan and sent a messenger to the tower with it, gathered together his maps and stuffed them in a briefcase, picked up the overnight grip which Zog had warned him to bring, and walked out to the tarmac.

The Cessna 210 was a sleek, white-and-red-painted aircraft with a three-bladed propeller and a retractable undercarriage. Though only single-engined, it cruised at a steady 140 knots and was one of the workhorse planes which had enabled Zog to build up his fleet from one to twenty-three in the five short years since he had launched his own firm.

As Mike walked round doing the external checks on the 210, he reflected that even Zog couldn't have done that in Britain. People weren't air-minded enough. But here, where the roads were made of the local red murram soil, rutted and dusty in the dry season turning to greasy mud in the rains, flying was the natural way to get about. The trip he would complete by lunchtime today would have taken nine or ten exhausting hours by road.

Opportunity was one reason Mike had come home in 1957, abandoning accountancy and surrendering to the fact that flying had got into his blood. He had the bug. But although his RAF wings gave him the basic qualification for airline flying, no British airline or charter firm would overlook the disgrace of the court-martial. By contrast Zog had merely shrugged his shoulders and remarked, 'I need pilot who know this country. You take commercial licence and come back, OK?'

Three years later Mike had another 1150 hours flying in his logbook, and no regrets, though he still sorely missed the surging power of the jet fighters and the split-second reactions they demanded. Nor could you throw Zog's Cessnas around the sky, with or without passengers aboard. But at least each day was different. He glanced up. The cloud was thinning fast. It was time to go.

The Safari Club faced Mount Kenya, though there was cloud up here which concealed its summit's ice and snow and lay in tendrils above the densely forested lower slopes. Mike flew over the club, announcing his arrival with a couple of tight turns over the white building with its swimming pool and wide lawns, on which crested cranes and other exotic birds wandered, tamely amusing the rich. Mike smiled as the noise of his engine made some of them flap for cover. The club was altogether too lush for his tastes, too far removed from any kind of real safari, and he was always faintly suspicious of people who stayed here. As he swung the plane round into a conventional circuit and then lined up to land on the grass strip he wondered what these Belgians would be like.

When he taxied clear of the strip to the parking area, a Land-Rover roared up, shuddered to a halt, and an African driver leapt out to open the doors for the clients. Typical Safari Club drama, thought Mike, methodically shutting down the engine. By the time he was out of the plane, the Belgians were walking across: a middle-aged man, slightly bald, in a white short-sleeved shirt which hung outside his trousers; his wife, a tidy woman in a print dress; and the daughter.

Mike agreed immediately with Zog's description of the girl, though as they shook hands he decided she was as much elegant as pretty. She was tall and her blonde hair was swept up into a chignon, accentuating high cheekbones, but a slightly aquiline nose made her something other than a conventional beauty. She had grey-blue eyes and a generous mouth.

'So you are our intrepid bush pilot,' she said, smiling. 'I am pleased to meet you.' Her English was near perfect.

'Take no notice, M'sieur,' interrupted the mother, who spoke with a heavy French accent. 'As you can guess, I am Mme Berthoud and this is my husband.'

The man shook hands, muttered a few faltering words in English, then lapsed into French: '*Je m'excuse ...mon Anglais*' – he made a gesture of despair – 'I am not speaking so much.'

Mike did his best to show willing with his schoolboy French and helped them into the aircraft. Chantal decided to sit in the front.

'I always wanted to learn flying,' she said enthusiastically. 'Now you can show me.'

Mike grinned. He liked the girl immediately and, as the

aim was always to please the client, within the limits of safety, he handed her a pair of headphones. 'The engine's a bit noisy. We can talk on the intercom.' He helped her adjust the tiny microphone, then flipped quickly through his checks and started up.

Flying back down towards Nairobi, over the densely cultivated ridges of the Kikuyu country, he let her try the controls, and found she handled them with a light and responsive touch.

'You've got the right idea,' he smiled encouragingly. 'Some women have a better instinctive feel for flying than men.'

But over the thirty-mile-wide, barren, lava-rock chasm of the Rift Valley, where hot air currents were liable to rock the plane, he took over again, contenting himself with pointing out such sights as the Magadi soda lake and Kilimanjaro's snow-cap away to the left, until they came over the ten-mile-wide volcanic crater of Ngorongoro and landed near the lodge on its forested lip, from which you could look down on the herds of game 2000 feet below.

The Berthouds generously insisted that he accompany them on their expedition down into the crater that afternoon and somewhat annoyed the official guide by frequently referring to Mike for information as they stopped to gaze at wildebeest and zebra in the grassland of the crater's floor, took excited photographs of rhino and elephant and constantly expressed the hope, in voluble French, of seeing lion. They were not disappointed. As the Land-Rover ground its way back up the precipitious track, Chantal said enchantedly, 'People told me and I never believed them. You know in Katanga there is so little left. Once upon a time there I suppose were animals, but now only up in the north. Of course, there are some, but nothing like this.'

That evening, the Berthouds again insisted on Mike being with them.

'After all,' said M. Berthoud in his laborious English, 'we pay for you, you must be like our guest.'

After dinner they sat around a log fire in the big lounge – at more than 7000 feet above sea level it was cold at night – and as they chatted Mike gradually discovered the family's background. They lived in Elisabethville, the capital city of the Katanga province of the Belgian Congo, where M. Berthoud had established a profitable printing business. Chantal had been sent back to Belgium to complete her education, and to take a secretarial course in Liège. 'It's a dreadful town,' she commented. 'I was so glad to be back.' Now she was employed as personal secretary to the recently elected provincial President, Moisé Tshombe.

'Aren't you giving them independence this week?' asked Mike. This was the year of the 'wind of change' and he had lost count of the number of colonies scheduled to throw off their British or French tutelage.

There was an awkward pause, which the mother broke. 'Yes, M. Russell. You are right. It will be on the thirtieth. That is why we decide to have a little 'oliday.' She glanced at her daughter. 'Chantal does not agree. She thinks we should fear nothing. But I cannot forget the terrible riots in January last year. I prefer we return when the celebrations are finished.'

'*Mama*—', Chantal cut in. 'You think that man Lumumba is an ogre, but don't you see, they are getting what they wanted. They will all be happy.'

'You are too loyal to your M. Tshombe.' She spread out her hands expressevely. 'It's true we all like him. He is a Christian. He is *evolué*. But he is only one. The rest are unpredictable'. She stretched out the word and repeated, 'Completely unpredictable.' Then, neatly turning the conversation away from a subject they had clearly argued about *ad nauseam*, she looked at Mike. 'What has happened to you and this Mau Mau you have in Kenya? That was a terrible thing, was it not?'

'That's all over,' said Mike cheerfully. 'What matters now is mending fences. We're obviously going to have an African Prime Minister and the sooner we come to terms with the idea, the better.' He shook his head 'Not that either the Governor or most of the settlers are willing to see it.' As he spoke, he became aware of Chantal's eyes watching his intently as the firelight flickered on her face.

'Do you truly believe that?' she asked warmly.

'I was born here – my father's a hunter and he also has a farm. He was heavily involved in fighting the Mau Mau. Neither he nor my mother is convinced there's a future here. So they made me go to Britain, do my military service in the RAF, learn a business.' He grinned. 'I hated it. The only good thing was the flying. But I realized one thing. Britain's going to get shot of her empire fast, so anyone who wants to go on living here had better get used to the idea of a black government.'

Suddenly he became aware that conversation around them had died. Everyone else in the lounge was listening. He lowered his voice and changed the subject slightly. 'I qualified as an accountant in London. But the thought of sitting at a desk for the rest of my life was too much.' He grinned at Chantal. 'Flying gets into you system as badly as Africa does. So I came back here.'

Within seconds he regretted this confidence. She immediately asked him why he had not joined an airline. He flushed and tried to pass it off lightly. 'Who'd want to be a second pilot with BOAC, spending the next fifteen years winding up the undercarriage and sending the stewardess to fetch coffee for the captain? This is real flying out here.'

He felt a sudden impulse to tell her about the court-martial which had wrecked any possibility of airline flying, but choked it back. Mike would never unburden himself in front of clients. His father had drilled the etiquette of the safari into him when he was a boy. 'There's nothing to beat bush flying,' he added, 'especially with a man like Captain Zog.'

'Which means you have been happy.' She knew he had and was glad.

'Pretty well. I'm not sure I want to go on safari flying for ever, though. The scope's a bit limited.'

M. Berthoud muttered something to his wife in French and Mike abruptly realized how completely he was dominating their evening. He rose to his feet and said apologetically, 'I've been talking too much. Time for bed.' He shook hands with them in turn, feeling a decided extra warmth as he took Chantal's. 'You ought to be off as well, if you're going on the six o'clock game run tomorrow morning.' Thanking the parents for their hospitality, he left the room. Attractive as Chantal was, and responsive, he wasn't going to press his luck with a girl he would probably never see again. Quite apart from Zog's warning, one-night stands were not Mike's line.

'What a nice young man,' remarked Mme Berthoud after he had gone. '*Il est très, très sympathique*.'

'Yes,' agreed Chantal abstractedly, still pondering Mike's undisguised affection for Africa. 'He is not only out for himself.'

The next morning the family decided they had seen enough of the Crater. They would leave for the camp Seronera in the Serengeti earlier than previously planned.

'After all,' remarked the father, 'we pay for the plane and the pilot. We can make the programme.' M. Berthoud was nothing if not a businessman.

An hour later they were over the endless landscape of the Serengeti Plains, where at this time of year the great herds of wildebeest and zebra were migrating westwards to the permanent water of the western corridor. Mike flew low so that they could watch the columns of animals, six or seven abreast and several miles long, raising trails of dust as they moved steadily across the dry savannah.

'If the lame or the old fall behind, they've had it.' Mike commented, banking the wings gently and pointing down so that they could see what he meant. 'If the lion don't get them, the jackals and hyenas will. That's nature's version of the health service.'

'Do you ever hunt?' asked Chantal. She was in the front as before and wearing the headphones.

'No, not professionally. I shoot occasionally on the farm. For the pot mainly, not for trophies. Why kill if you don't need to?' It seemed unnecessary to explain more. 'Wildlife is my hobby,' he added.

After they had landed on the strip near the camp at Seronera, and the luggage had been loaded on to the truck which came out to meet them, the Berthouds thanked him warmly yet again and exchanged addresses.

'If you ever come to Katanga,' said Chantal, 'please stay with us. I mean it. We have enjoyed meeting you very much.'

They shook hands with continental formality before Mike climbed back into the Cessna. When he had taken off he circled once and dipped his wings, but the truck was already speeding off and no one waved. He did not expect to come across them again. Captain Zog's domain was East Africa, not the Congo. Philosophically he set course for Nairobi. Life was like that. The best girls always seemed to be snatched away before one could get to know them.

A week later Mike went to spend a few days leave at his parents' home up-country. His father was away with a party of American clients on a three-week safari and his mother was looking after the ranch.

The land was only half tamed despite their efforts. Camphor-scented eleshwa and thorn scrub encroached relentlessly on the grass, which their own herds shared with zebra, impala and waterbuck. Low rainfall made it a struggle to fatten 1000 head of cattle on the 4000 acres, while the house had a simplicity in keeping with the environment. Originally not much more than a cedar log cabin on stone foundations, it had been enlarged piecemeal as need arose, so that now it was a sprawling, corrugated-iron-roofed bungalow, surrounded by a garden which Mary Russell cherished. They had built the whole place themselves, even quarrying the stone from a hill on the farm. Naitolia was their home in the deepest sense of the word.

Every evening, when the day's work was over, they would sit on the verandah while the sun sank towards the mountains on the further side of the Rift. Mike considered this the most beautiful view in the world. In the far distance a huge lake turned silver, while the slanting light caught the velvet yellow bark of the thorn trees and cast long shadows on the grass. There was a smell of woodsmoke. Then, with a rapidity unknown away from the equator, the sun disappeared behind the mountain ridges, the colour ebbed from the landscape and the crickets began the rasping chorus of the African night.

This was always the signal for the same request. 'Bring the drinks tray, will you, dear?' asked his mother. 'And the radio.' She liked to hear the world news and the reception was better outside than in. A few minutes later Mike returned and they heard the announcer start the headlines, his voice distorted by static.

'In the former Belgian Congo the army has mutinied. Europeans are reported fleeing from the capital, Leopoldville.'

Mike sat stunned. 'I wonder if they went back,' he muttered apprehensively.

'Shush, dear. I want to listen.'

The announcer's measured BBC accent droned on. 'Soldiers demanding more pay have rejected their Belgian officers, beating some up and raping their wives. Prime Minister Patrice Lumumba has visited Camp Leopold near the city in an attempt to restore order. But already the mutiny is reported spreading to other towns.'

When the news was over Mike leant forward in his

cane chair and switched the set off. 'God, I do hope they're all right,' he said.

'You're worried about that family you took to the Serengeti?'

Mike nodded. 'They were afraid things would go wrong.'

'It could never happen here.' Mary Russell was confident. 'We know how to train African soldiers.'

'Chantal is concerned about the communists. She thinks they'll try to get us all out: British, French and Belgians alike.'

'They say that man Lumumba is a communist.' Mary Russell paused; she had only a vague idea what being a communist meant, apart from being something to do with the Russians and altogether bad. Taking people's property, that was it. Satisfied, she turned without preamble to what was really on her mind. 'Are you in love with this girl?' she asked.

Mike blushed, glad of the dusk. 'I liked her a lot,' he admitted. 'I think she felt the same.'

'Well, dear, you must ask her to stay sometime.' Mary Russell sat up in her chair as though the matter was settled. 'It's time we went indoors,' she said. 'It's getting quite chilly.'

Over the next few days the news from the Congo grew dramatically worse; the whole structure of the Belgian colonial system there was collapsing. Army mutinies broke out in more cities, including Elisabethville, the Berthouds' home town.

By this time, Mike's brief leave was over and he was back at Wilson Airport, able to make inquiries. But the most anyone knew was that the Berthouds had completed their safari and left. Meanwhile Belgian refugees began arriving in Nairobi. Whole families had abandoned houses and possessions in the eastern Congo, fled by road into Uganda and were now being flown back to Brussels. Rumour had it that if you went to Uganda you could pick up a Mercedes for a couple of hundred pounds, so desperate were these refugees for funds. On 10 July the radio announced that Tshombe had called in Belgian troops to put down the mutiny in Elisabethville.

Mike heard about it in the briefing room, and was so unaffectedly pleased that the other pilots, always quick to rib a colleague, started asking him the date of the wedding. They were interrupted by a guttural shout from Zog.

'Mike. Come to office.'

When he hurried next door, Zog was holding one hand over the telephone. 'Is Belgian consul. He want pilot to fetch people from Congo. You are only one who speak French. Will you go?'

'Is it the Berthoud family?' As he put the question Mike realized he was being stupid. However, Zog asked the consul briefly, then replied. 'No. Is coffee farmer and his wife. They are cut off by army.'

'All right. I'll go.'

Zog spoke into the telephone some more, then demanded bluntly, 'Who pays? Belgian government? OK. We try. But I am not promising, understand? Yes, right away.' He put the instrument down, then moved to examine the map. 'Will not be so easy this one. Consul says farm had only short strip and he has no map reference.'

Together they surveyed the area on the map. A chain of lakes ran almost the whole tremendous length of the Congo's eastern frontier. In the north, bordering Uganda, was Lake Albert, south of that Edward, next Lake Kivu, then the 400-mile-long strip of Lake Tanganyika, the second deepest in the world, dividing Tanganyika on its east from the Congo province of Katanga.

'Is there,' said Zog, jabbing his finger at the steep contours of the hills on the western side of Lake Tanganyika. They studied the detail. There was nothing to indicate an airfield within sixty or seventy miles of the small town which the consul had mentioned as being the nearest.

'There's only one way,' said Mike. 'I shall have to fly from the town along the lake shore road.'

'You can try,' said Zog. 'He says strip is near farm on hillside. Family are waiting all through daylight hours. They have ham radio, consul thinks on short wave only. So you cannot call with aircraft radio. Better take transistor.' Zog raised his sunburnt forearm and studied his watch as though it could give some magic answer to the problem. 'Is nine o'clock,' he said. 'You take one eighty, is best for short take off. Take four cans extra petrol. Go straight away, refuel Tabora, we will do flight plan.' He grunted. 'Maybe you get there two hours before dark.'

'Do I have to take the one eighty?' Mike pleaded. 'It's bloody slow.'

'Altogether is seven hundred miles. Even with stop you can do in six and half hours.' He turned to Mike. 'You better go. And mind,' he wagged a finger, 'insurance does not cover risks of war, so don't lose my damn plane, OK?' He grunted. 'Pilots I can find, aeroplane is more difficult.'

The flight across the endless bush of Tanganyika was slowed down by a headwind. At Tabora they asked him to file a flight plan. Not wanting to waste time with the customs, he made one for Kigoma, the small Tanganyikan lake port near Stanley's famous meeting place with the 'lost' Dr Livingstone in 1871. An hour and fifty minutes later he was over the lake, his eyes scanning the mountains on the far side, already falling into shadow. He had barely two hours left to sunset.

The hills rose steeply from the lake, rearing up to over 10,000 feet, and thickly forested. On the far northern horizon a great mass of cloud presaged storms and a change in the weather. Mike flew with the transistor on the seat beside him, the volume full on. Occasionally he reached out and twirled the tuning knob through the band of frequencies he had been given. All he received was intense, crackling static.

Below him a dirt road twisted along the contours of the lake until it came to a small town. Mike could see military vehicles in the dusty main street. African soldiers standing by them craned their heads to look up at him. Then, quite distinctly, he saw one heft a rifle into his shoulder and take aim. With sudden realization of the danger, he slammed on full throttle and pulled up into a climbing turn away from the town. If the soldier did fire, he must have missed. But the incident reminded Mike forcefully that his own detachment from events on the ground was delusory. It also confirmed that the mutineers held the town. But where the hell was the farm? Still climbing, he circled warily out over the lake, noting that two roads ran north, one along the shore, the other twisting up into the mountains. The lake was 2534 feet above sea level. Coffee grew best higher up, around 5000 to 7000 feet.

He followed the hill road, which soon became detectable only as a narrow gully in the forest. The trees were so tall that if he deviated at all he lost sight of it. Rain began to fall, heavy drops spattering on the windscreen. Automatically he checked the carburettor heat, pulling a knob which cleared any ice in the intake by letting in warm air from the engine. Strange as it seemed, tropical thunderstorms could bring on acute icing conditions. He pushed the knob home again, with the mild relief he always felt when a routine check proved satisfactory. At exactly the same moment the transistor came to life. For a second he thought the two things must be related, then reason prevailed and he reached out to tune the radio. A distorted voice came across, pathetically anxious.

'Allo, allo. Nous sommes à la piste.'

Mike swore. So they were on the strip. But where was it? Obviously they could either see him or hear him. He banked hard into a right-hand turn, scouring the forest.

'*Non, non!*' came the voice, high pitched with worry.

Resisting an instinctive reaction to reverse the direction of his turn, which could result in losing his bearings relative to the all-important road, Mike continued slowly round. Then suddenly he saw that a couple of miles beyond the road the forest ended and there were lines of dark green bushes just visible through the rain. It must be the coffee estate. He straightened up, peering down.

'*Nous sommes ici!*' screamed the voice, idiotically self-concerned.

At last he saw the strip, a reddish-brown scar on the green which seemed to have been more excavated than levelled. One end was cut into the hillside. So impossible would an approach or take-off be from that end that the trees above had not been felled. Irrespective of wind direction there was only one way in. He pulled into a tight turn, the wings nearly vertical, and circled above. On the ground were four people, waving frantically. There was a pile of luggage, too. He swore again. The 180 could carry four including the pilot, plus a small amount of baggage. An overweight aircraft would never get off such a short strip at this altitude. He straightened out again, forcing himself to relax, and prepared to land. The rain was driving down now and cloud was beginning to envelop the mountain tops above in an ominous grey shroud.

With the speed right back, full flap on, and plenty of power, he settled down to the approach, buffeted by the wind which appeared to be straight behind him. In these conditions there could be no allowance for error. Even with the airspeed wavering just above the stall the wind added horribly to his speed over the ground. As the wet earth came up towards him he hauled back on the controls, cut the throttle and thumped her down, braking as hard as he dared. The Cessna stopped with perhaps fifty yards to spare. Wiping the sweat off his forehead with the back of his hand, he taxied back to where the group was waiting. It could be worse, he thought, at least the wind would help the take-off. Now for the arguments over weight and destination. It would be dark in an hour. Why the hell did Zog always insist on cutting things so fine?

His passengers proved to be two men and two women, all soaked to the skin. The older of the men held a small radio transmitter with a stubby black aerial. He greeted Mike in French.

'We are so glad you have come. The army have blocked the roads. We did not know if our message would be received.'

Mike bit back an acid comment on the man's failure to give any sensible directions and looked the four of them over. 'What do you each weigh?' he demanded curtly.

'Weigh?'

'Yes, your weight. In kilos. Come on, we've no time.'

At last he extracted the information, the fatter of the two wives displaying an absurd coyness which made him automatically add ten kilos to her figure. He did some mental calculations, then faced them.

'My aircraft has only four seats. One is mine. It's a risk taking three in the back. The third can't be strapped in. If I take you all, it's without any baggage.'

'Without my clothes!' screamed the fat woman, as his words sank in.

'Allez vite,' Mike ordered, then turned to the men, disregarding her. 'We have to refuel.' He stepped across to the plane, opened the door and began heaving out the four jerricans from the back. Then, directing the men to help him, he hoisted himself on to the high wing, using the wingstrut as a foothold, and filled the tanks through a funnel.

Some rain would get in too, but that was a chance he had to take. Better a risk of engine failure than the certainty of running out of petrol. As he emptied the cans he could see the fat woman frantically burrowing in her suitcase, kneeling by it in the mud, trying to extract her valuables and stuff them into her handbag, her sodden dress clinging to her body. He felt acutely guilty at so humiliating her.

The younger man read his thoughts. 'Is it truly necessary?'

'If we're going to take off, it is.' Zog's words about not losing the aeroplane echoed in his mind. Jesus, he didn't want to kill himself either. Once you reached the end of this strip; that was it. There was no safety margin. Either you would be airborne or you'd topple off the end into the trees below. The drop must be a sheer thirty feet.

'*Mon Dieu! Regardez là!*' The younger man was pointing at something underneath the wing, shouting agitatedly at him.

Mike finished emptying the last jerrican and climbed down to see where the man was gesturing. A thin stream of liquid was dribbling off the underside of the starboard wing. Was it just rainwater or had he overfilled the tank? He ran round, put a finger underneath, smelt it. Petrol. Then he saw the bullet hole.

His first reaction was simple anger that the bastards had shot at a defenceless civil aircraft. Then he examined the hole carefully and asked the two men if they had seen anything dribbling out before he began refuelling. They thought not. The bullet had entered the aluminium skin at an angle, presumably as he was banking away from the town. It might have only pierced the tank near the top. Anyway there was no means of finding out now.

'Get in,' he said. 'We're going.' He carried the empty jerricans to the side of the strip, put the funnel in the plane and helped the women in. The fat one was weeping, tears mingling with the rain running down her face. He made her sit in front, reckoning she was heavier than the others, and told her to keep her hands and feet away from the controls. She didn't answer, but drew her feet back as though she was contaminated. He felt even more sorry for her.

When they were all in, the other woman more on the men's knees than on the back seat, he started up, pivoted the plane as close as he could to the wall of earth which was the hillside end of the strip, then thrust the throttle forward, his toes straining on the brakes to hold the plane as the power built up. When the engine hit 2300 revs he let go and she surged forward, mud splashing up from the wheels. Cautiously he allowed the tail to lift. To his relief she came unstuck half-way down the length, wobbling into the air and then rising sharply as he caught the full benefit of the wind. As soon as he was in a steady climb, heading out towards the lake for safety, he looked sideways to see if the petrol leak had stopped, but it was impossible to tell because the slipstream was whipping too much spray off the wing.

'Now,' he shouted above the roar of the engine. 'We can just make Kigoma before dark. Is that OK?'

There were immediate protests. They wanted to be taken to the neighbouring Belgian territory of Ruanda Urundi, whose capital Usumbura was at the head of the lake. When they assured Mike that no one would bother over the customs formalities, he agreed and set course north. Although the fuel gauge showed the starboard tank's fuel was going down rapidly, there was more than enough in the port one. He landed at Usumbura shortly after dark without further problems, except that he had no francs.

'Please don't worry,' the older man assured him. 'A friend of mine runs the Hotel Paguidas. He will arrange everything.'

A more immediate task was to telephone Captain Zog. Mike persuaded the air traffic control to send a telex reporting his arrival to Nairobi, but he had to wait an hour for the phone call and Zog's initial reactions were furious.

'What you say? You have bullet hole in tank! Are you crazy? I tell you I want my airplane safe.'

'You also told me to use my discretion. These people were completely cut off.'

There was a short silence. Then Zog appeared to have calmed down. 'OK. There is Cessna agent in Usumbura. You make repair and come back tomorrow.'

His duty done, Mike allowed the Belgians to buy him dinner. They went by taxi to a lakeside restaurant and ate in the open air. The fish was excellent. It seemed unbelievable that twenty miles away the population of a country the size of Western Europe was in panic, African and European alike.

'You know something?' said the younger man. 'We made a mistake with the Force Publique. We never educated any Africans to be officers. Now we are reaping the storm.'

'Only Katanga is safe,' commented the fat wife. 'In Elisabethville the Colonel Crevecoeur has stopped the mutiny single-handed, we heard.'

'I was flying a family from there recently.' Mike tried to sound unconcerned. 'The Berthouds. I hope they're safe.'

'Indeed,' replied the woman warmly. 'Did you not realize Charles Berthoud is my brother?'

Mike gazed at her in amazement. Could Chantal be this dumpy, frowzy woman's niece? 'That's an extraordinary coincidence,' he managed to say.

'Oh no, it is not.' The woman's calmness was in total contrast to her earlier tears. 'By a miracle we spoke to Chantal on the telephone yesterday. She was sure she could find a plane. So we packed and waited.' She smiled at Mike's surprise. 'My niece swore she knew a pilot who could be relied on.' She chuckled happily. 'And here we are!'

Still astonished, Mike tried to piece together events in his mind. Chantal must have sent a message to the

Belgian consul. And Zog, the old bastard, had kept quiet about its origin. 'Well,' he said at last, 'if you see her, please give her my regards.'

The woman shrugged her shoulders eloquently. 'Some time, I am sure. But now we shall go to Brussels. The Congo must manage without us for a while.' She seemed very matter of fact about the whole business.

The rest of the evening was dominated by reminiscences of life in the Congo. Chantal's aunt and uncle were called Martiny. They originated from Liège, as Chantal did, had carved a prosperous coffee farm out of the bush, and intended one day to sell up and retire to Belgium. Mike listened politely, often missing the nuances of their speech, yet conscious of a gulf between their attitudes and his own family's. They were here relatively briefly for the money, whereas his own father had adopted Africa as his home and intended to stay. Eventually he made a discreet comment on this.

'Ah,' remarked Mme Martiny knowingly, 'Africa is fine. But not for ever. Now Chantal, she thinks differently. Like you, she was born here. She will stay to the end.'

'The end?'

'Listen, my friend,' interrupted her husband. 'We have given power to the Africans and who ends up Prime Minister of the whole Congo? A madman, a revolutionary called Lumumba who's in the pockets of the Russians.' He made a gesture of despair. 'He even insulted our King in his independence day speech.'

'The only sensible one is that Tshombe who Chantal works for,' said Mme Martiny.

'I get confused,' said Mike. 'Is he a Prime Minister as well?'

'The President of Katanga province. But,' Mme Martiny remonstrated with her finger, 'remember one thing. Katanga has the copper. It's the treasury of the whole country. The rest you can forget about. By comparison the other five provinces are nothing. And Tshombe understands he must work with us Belgians if he is to stay rich. Yes, he understands. He is what we call *évolué*: civilized, educated. Not like that savage Lumumba.'

'Without Belgian administration everything will collapse,' said her husband. 'You'll see.'

Finding such self-inflicted pessimism incomprehensible, Mike excused himself and went to bed.

The next day the two families left on the Sabena flight for Brussels and Mike spent all morning stripping panels off the Cessna's wing with the help of an engineer, only to discover that the bullet had penetrated the fuel tank at an angle, channelling away the thin metal and making it hard to repair.

'You need a new tank,' insisted the engineer. 'We have one. Can you wait?'

There was no option. That evening, when they had completed the job by working flat out, he was called to the airport commandant's office. The commandant was a stocky, former air force officer who came straight to the point. He wanted Mike to stay on and carry out more rescues.

'We need all the planes we can lay our hands on,' he said. 'You probably heard there's a woman pilot from Nairobi with a Comanche up at Paulis in the north, and there are a couple of Australians taking a Dakota in and out of proper airfields. But we're still receiving calls for help from mission stations and farms to which we cannot respond. We need your Cessna, Mr Russell, and you with it.'

'Captain Zog will go berserk,' protested Mike. 'It's bad enough to have one bullet hole.'

The commandant smiled. 'I know the old devil. So long as he trusts you he'll agree.'

The telex answer from Zog was a masterpiece of terseness. It read: 'OK who do we charge?'

For a whole week Mike flew with the transistor on the

seat beside him, tracking his way along twisting roads to emergency landing strips cut in the forest and bringing out a variety of Belgians. The weather was appalling. The cloud when he rescued the Martiny family had been the precursor of a frontal system passing slowly across the eastern Congo, which brought deluging rain. Often the low cloud only cleared in the late afternoon and on several occasions he found himself trying to calm down violently agitated people, who refused to understand the perils of the bad weather. The whole European population seemed seized by hysteria, except, he observed, the missionaries. The White Fathers and the Benedictines gathered together groups of refugees, because their mission stations usually had airstrips, but they invariably refused to quit themselves. Our work is here, they said, the Africans depend on us. And they would gently remonstrate with lay friends who urged them to leave too.

Then, as suddenly as it had begun, the panic subsided. Mike learnt much later that 25,000 Belgians had fled the country in the two weeks since the mutiny and that the Belgian troops had begun to be replaced by a United Nations force of various nationalities. Rumours of this reached him, and so did garbled stories of Tshombe declaring Katanga an independent state. But he no longer cared. He was dog-tired, longing for home, and uncomfortably aware that the feed from the Cessna's new fuel tank was not operating correctly. When on 18 July, the airport commandant thanked him profusely and allowed him to leave, promising that his courage would be rewarded, his only feeling was relief that he would soon be back in a stable country.

Late that afternoon he landed back in the dry warmth of Nairobi with a sense of overwhelming gratitude for the calm voice of the air traffic control, the lines of parked aircraft shining in the sun, the greetings from the mechanics, Zog clapping him on the shoulder, his car standing where he had left it by the hangar, everything that was the opposite of the chaos he had left.

In the evening, back at the small house which he shared with another pilot, he rang his parents. 'You know,' he said, after relating a modified version of his adventures, 'we're bloody lucky here.'

Two weeks later, at the beginning of August, a typed letter came from Chantal, on official writing paper. She thanked him profusely, told him her parents were well and explained why Tshombe had declared the Katanga province unilaterally independent. 'You understand, he does not want a country poisoned by the communism of Lumumba. He only ever wished for a federal system. The mutiny was for him the final straw. Most of the wealth of the Congo is here and he believes with passion it can only be safeguarded by black and white co-operating as equals. By law and order.'

Mike had no quarrel with this sentiment. But the final paragraph took him aback.

'The President has heard about your flying. He is looking for a pilot. The pay will be generous and free of tax, much more, I think, than you earn from your Captain Zog. At this time we have a Cessna. Soon we will have a jet. In fact, I can tell you in confidence, M. le President Tshombe hopes to create an air force. It will provide a fantastic chance for someone with your experience. Please cable yes or no.' In a postscript she added: 'Personally I must say it would be very agreeable to see you here in Elisabethville.'

Mike sat down and re-read her words carefully, then went and knocked on Captain Zog's door. There was no point in trying to fool Zog, so he simply handed him the letter.

Zog went through it slowly and gestured to a chair. 'Tell me,' he said, 'what you think about this Congo business? They sit there with all the bloody riches in the world. And what they do? They talk politics. This Prime

Minister Lumumba, he call in United Nations for assistance. United Nations, they order Belgians out. Belgians they back this President Tshombe. Now Tshombe wants air force. Crazy. You know what that means? Sooner or later they fight.' He glanced shrewdly at Mike, his eyes narrowing. 'You want to go, huh? I see it.'

'I'd like to. Not just for the money.'

'For this girl you meet once, twice? Then you *are* crazy.'

'She believes in what they're doing. Katanga's the only part of the Congo that isn't in chaos. They deserve help.'

'Maybe.' Zog appeared to accept the point, then he suddenly slammed the table. 'Since when you become bloody philanthropist? Tell me that, OK? Since when?'

'You didn't see what it was like in rest of the Congo.'

'Who cares about bloody Congo?' Zog leant across the desk, a sly smile spreading across the face. 'Don't tell me, I know. They kick you out of RAF. Now you can start your own bloody air force. *That* is what you like about Congo.'

'It's an incentive. I would enjoy it. I admit that. Mike clenched his fists like a boxer. 'Listen, Zog, there's an exciting job to do down there. I'd like to have a go.'

Zog sat upright, the grin gone, a serious expression on his face. 'OK, Mike, I was bomber pilot, but I understand. Maybe you get something out of system, huh? I keep job for you here. How long you want? One year?'

'How can I tell, Zog? You've seen the letter.'

'Then come back when you finish.' Zog stood up. 'Some safaris you can only do in time it takes.'

2

Robert Kane's thirty-second birthday proved no occasion for rejoicing. By a seemingly deliberate piece of timing the post brought a dry official letter from the Air Ministry accepting his resignation from the Royal Auxiliary Air Force, but reminding him of his liability to call-up under certain conditions of national emergency. There was not even a perfunctory acknowledgement of long and devoted service. He almost tore the thin sheet of paper up in disgust, then thought better of the idea. There was at least one man who would understand how he felt. He took the letter with him to the office and asked for an interview with the Managing Director.

James Skinner, the former fighter ace who ran International Metal Exports Limited, usually known by its acronym IMEX, owed his position primarily to having flown in the war alongside the heir to the company, Sir John Gravesand, who enjoyed the title his father had earned, chaired board meetings with reasonable competence, and received an enviable income from his majority shareholding. None the less he devoted far too much of his time and capital to ocean racing. His overriding ambition was one of the most expensive a man can have: to win the America's Cup, albeit in a consortium with several others. In consequence he was happy to leave the day-to-day running of IMEX to the determined and efficient wing commander he had served with in the war, who understood his passion for sport, and who was steadfastly honest. The only snag about James Skinner was that he lacked a strong enough instinct for making money. He was a manager, not a merchant, and quite often when he felt he ought to refer to the owner, he could only do so over a crackling and distorted radio link to whichever yacht Sir John was on.

Robert Kane did not know, as he knocked on Skinner's mahogany-panelled door on his birthday morning, that IMEX was ripe for a takeover and about to fall into the hands of an American mining conglomerate.

Skinner welcomed Kane into the big, deeply carpeted office and waved him to a chair with his usual breezy informality, though he looked unusually tired.

'So what can I do for you, Robert?' His broad face creased into a smile. 'Want a raise for your birthday?' Skinner was a good commanding officer and made certain his secretary kept records of all his staff's family backgrounds.

'No. It's not money. I want advice.'

Skinner saw the troubled look in his eyes. 'To do with that bloody idiot killing himself?' he asked.

Kane nodded, rose to his feet and handed the Air Ministry letter across the wide partner's desk. 'This was my birthday present from the RAF,' he said bitterly.

There was a brief pause as Skinner read it. Then he leant forward, his arms on the desk. 'You want my advice? Just file this away with your other papers and forget it. We all come to the end of the road sometime. If some tinpot Air Marshal decides he doesn't like you, there's damn all you can do .'

'I lived for 699,' said Kane shortly.

Skinner leant back again and considered the man facing him. Kane had shrewd blue eyes, a strong chin, a thick thatch of hair cut short. There was an aggressiveness about him of which Skinner approved. No one rose to command an auciliary squadron without considerable ability, because it meant leading two lives; one service, one civilian here in the City. In the war, thought Skinner, Robert Kane might have been killed early, but more likely he would have learnt the realities of fighting fast, survived, and ended up highly decorated, as Skinner himself had been. Now, in a world at peace where even squabbles over the Suez Canal seemed unlikely to upset the fundamental balance of the two great power blocs, and the Korean War had limited the expansion of communism in Asia, there was no such outlet for the energies of a man like Kane.

'I suppose you thought of trying to sign on?' remarked Skinner casually. Kane must have thought of quitting IMEX for full-time flying.

Coming from anyone except Skinner, with his DSO and his Air Force Cross, this would have been an accusation of disloyalty. Kane took it as the honest question it was.

'Briefly,' he admitted. 'Though even with my experience I'm probably too old.' It was more a question than a statement, in fact, he suddenly realized, it was the crucial question that would decide the direction of his life. Skinner grunted.

Twenty-six was the upper age limit for pilot recruitment. On the other hand the cost of training a jet pilot was astronomical. Only the air force run by civil servants would throw away the kind of investment Robert Kane represented. But after the reprimand? Skinner glanced down at the letter. There was no point in letting this man fool himself. In any case, which should come first: the service which had let them both go, or the company they both now worked for? To hell with sentiment. IMEX was in trouble. It could use Kane.

'If I were you,' he said, pushing the letter back across the desk, 'I'd pack your uniform in mothballs, hang the squadron photos in the john, and start giving us one hundred per cent of your time.'

Kane flushed, though it was fair comment. Most other employers would have said as much years ago. He sat silent for a moment, then spoke with a firmness which made his decision clear.

'All right, sir. But I'd like to get abroad a bit.' He felt this was a reasonable request. IMEX negotiated worldwide. Hitherto he had avoided travel because of the squadron, becoming a proficient dealer on the London Metal Exchange.

'How about the States for a few years?' asked Skinner abruptly, an idea formulating in his mind. 'If you'd like a challenge I can give you one. Tough. Make or break. If you fail, you'll be out. How would that suit you?'

'Are we expanding over there?' asked Kane, surprised.

'No. We're being taken over.' Skinner's voice was subdued and angry. Kane realized why he looked tired. 'Officially it's still a secret, but we can't stop it. Western Mining want an established metal trading subsidiary. Why, I'm not sure I know. They're hardly strangers to selling.' He shrugged his shoulders. 'Anyway they offered the owner more than he could refuse for a stake in us. Then, while they were doing that the bastards went behind our backs and picked up a lot more shares privately. This week they informed us they had control.'

'And how do I fit in?' demanded Kane.

'Very simply, if you're willing. They want one of our best middle managers trained in their methods of operating.' Skinner leant across the desk again, confident that his sudden hunch in making the offer was justified. 'Listen, Bob, you won't get a chance like this again. Forget about flying. Start making a future for yourself. You'll be doing us a good turn at the same time. We need to send a first-class bloke.' He paused, wondering if Kane would really prove to be ambitious enough. 'Let me warn you. They're a ruthless bunch. May not look it at first. But they are and you won't survive unless you're as tough as them.'

Kane considered this for a moment, liking the sound of it. 'And the money?' he asked bluntly.

'No commission, but twice the salary as a start. Put it this way. The money will very rapidly become as good as you are. And if you're bad, you'll be out on your neck. There's no old boy net to protect you there. No paternalism like the City has here. If you succeed you'll very shortly be able to buy your own plane and tell the Air Ministry where they can put theirs.'

Skinner leant back, reading the enthusiasm in his subordinate's face.

Thank you, sir,' Kane said without hesitation. 'I'll take the job.' He stood up to go. 'And thanks for the advice. If I'm going to stay in this business it's time I started getting a sense of direction.' He hesitated. 'May I ask you a personal question?'

'Fire ahead.'

'Didn't you miss the flying?'

'I can truthfully say I never touched an aircraft again,' Skinner laughed. 'As a matter of fact my wife made me promise not to. She was always scared. Far be it for me to decry the married state but if I were you I'd keep off it a while longer. You're going to need all your energy keeping your end up with the Americans.'

Two weeks later Robert Kane reported to the Western Mining offices off Wall Street in New York. His introductory weeks at the huge mining conglomerate were deceptively gentle. Western Mining was primarily in copper, with its main stake in Arizona and Utah, substantial holdings in Chilean companies, and growing investments in Canada and Australia. The United States was the world's largest producer, and from his years of broking Kane knew the basic structure of the American industry, dominated by big corporations like Anaconda, Magna, Newman Cooper, AMAX and, of course, Western Mining itself. The corporation was huge enough, rich enough and abundantly self-assured enough to allow time for a newcomer to learn about its business at relatively slow speed. Under the tutelage of a junior Vice President, Kane became familiar with the structure of this multi-billion dollar empire, and its management philosophy.

Then, with no warning, the silken mood changed. At the end of his fifth week Kane was called in to the Vice President.

'I guess we've given you a pretty good rundown on Western,' he said. 'Now you tell me something.' He was watching Kane closely. 'Suppose you had to explain to a Congressional Committee how we operated, what would you say?' He sat back behind his desk, pulled on a cigar, waited a few seconds and added, 'In two sentences.' Hell, thought Kane, that's a fast one. He meditated a moment, remembered someone's remark about witnesses being able to sucker a Congressional Committee only so far, and took the plunge.

'I should say, sir, that Western Mining's output is crucial to the economies and defence of the free world, vital to employment in the States of Arizona and Utah and that you operate primarily for the benefit of your shareholders, the majority of whom are United States citizens.'

'That's a helluva long sentence,' the Vice President chuckled, 'OK, you're allowed one more. Let me give you a clue. What's our motivation?'

'Profit,' said Kane confidently. 'And exploiting the recources of the earth to that end.'

'Not bad. You pass. A lot of young college men I know would have smart-arsed around talking about in-house managerial objectives, obligations to society and all the rest of the junk. Sure we depend on government for many of our contracts so we have to humour Congressmen. But we don't kid ourselves. Our aim is to get minerals out of the ground, sell them profitably and screw the competition. That's one reason we wanted an independent London metal-broking firm under our control.'

'I had wondered,' Kane ventured.

'It's not the only reason. But you'll learn. We can use you, Bob. You're the kind we need. And right now we want you to get to know the guts of the business. "Exploiting the resources of the earth." He chuckled again, 'Too damned right. In Arizona, as of Monday, you're named Assistant to the Mine Manager at Delphi Ridge. OK? They'll meet you off the Monday afternoon plane at Tucson.'

Tucson proved to be a resort city, close to the Mexican border and attractively influenced by the Spanish heritage of its neighbours. However, Kane soon discovered that most of Arizona was semi-desert and the mining community on which his life was to be centred, seventy miles out of Tucson, was in an area rich in minerals but little else. Delphi Ridge, where a company township was rapidly springing up to meet the needs of a new copper mine, might just as well have been on the face of the moon. The landscape was spiked with cacti and as far as vegetation went that was about all, apart from tumbleweed sprouting here and there among the sunbleached rocks.

This harshness seemed to have communicated itself to the mine manager, a deep-voiced Californian whose spartan office was decorated only with charts of forecast production and plans of the shafts being sunk. Kane was taken straight there on his arrival.

'The name's Rick Croft,' he said, rising to shake hands and then staying on his feet. 'Well, I guess we don't want to sit around in here. If you're going to work for me the first thing is to know your way around the plant.' He gestured at a row of bright yellow protective helmets hanging near the door. 'Never move without one of these. Just about all of Delphi Ridge is a hard hat area.' He strode across the room, took one and gave another to Kane. 'Your name's Robert, right? OK, Bob, let's go.'

As they walked through a *mêlée* of cranes, half-completed sheds and groups of workers towards the No 1 shaft, Croft made staccato comments.

'Most of the labour here's Mex. Ever hear the name "spiks"? That's them.'

'And what do they call you?' Kane asked without thinking.

'Boss.' His tone was hard and without humour.

Passing another group he added 'There's Indians too, and niggers. Pretty few whites except in management.' Then he suddenly laughed, surprising Kane. 'Guess they call us "honkies". But not when I'm around. I'd bust them.'

They reached the shaft, the wide-legged framework of its hoist towering above. Kane commented that it looked no different from a coal mine.

'One headgear's pretty much like another.' Croft waved towards the lift cage, the gate clanged shut and they went down.

Two hours later Kane had begun to understand what opening up a mine involved, quite apart from the 20 million dollars this one was costing. He had descended Delphi's first shaft in a lift cage to 600 feet below the surface, the atmosphere becoming noticeably hotter all the time. Then, the hard hat firmly on his head, he had ridden the open trucks of a tiny electric train along the rough-hewn gallery which led to the face. There, rubber boots ankle deep in water, thick electric cables snaking out behind them, stood three young Mexican workers steadying themselves with their legs apart, their muscular arms guiding the most massive drills he had ever seen. The noise was deafening. Sweat coursed down the men's faces and backs. Their hands, in protective gloves, were thick with oil, and oil was spattered on their forearms and overalls. Each man had a lamp on his helmet, illuminating the rock as it splintered and fell away under the thundering blows of the machinery.

'Jack hammer drills,' Croft shouted in his ear. 'Takes real men to handle 'em.'

They backed away a yard, splashing in the water. The heat and humidity were overwhelming.

'Ever been down a mine before?' yelled Croft.

Kane shook his head. For nine years he had dealt in metal, helping make and lose fortunes for others, but the nearest he'd got to the raw substance was a polished malachite desk ornament sent him one Christmas.

Croft bent down and picked up a chunk of rock. 'This is what it's about. This is the orebody.' He was still shouting above the din of the drills. 'See that?' He pointed to a stratified pattern of iridescent green which ran through the otherwise whitish lump. Along with the green was another speckled biscuit-coloured stratum and a few threads of dark that could have been copper itself. 'That's what the spiks are slaving for. To get two point seven tons of refined copper we have to shift one hundred tons of orebody.' He gestured at the piles of rock being loaded into trucks. 'And to reach that orebody we have to blast out thousands on thousands of tons of goddamn useless rock.' Kane nodded appreciatively. There seemed no point in trying to speak. 'People who just pick up a telephone or plug a hoover in,' Croft went on determinedly, 'they don't ever know what it takes to make those wires.' He turned, yelled a few words of encouragement to the foreman driller, then gestured Kane back to the truck.

On the surface, blinking in the sunlight, Kane wiped the dust and sweat off his face. His shirt was sodden. 'Jesus, what a life,' he muttered. 'Why do they do it?'

'For money. Like we all do.' Croft eyed the Englishman suspiciously. 'I always wondered if you guys who sit in plush offices selling the stuff understand what it takes to run a mine.' He laughed shortly. 'Well, you'll learn. You'll be down there plenty more. Now let's see the rest of the site.'

The seven months Robert Kane spent at Delphi Ridge were the hardest of his life. There were few breaks in the unremitting work. Nor was it easy to be accepted. However the hositility subsided after a troublemaker, who had been drinking, picked a fight with him over a triviality. Kane, who was no weakling, responded by knocking the man half unconscious and then frog-marching him to Croft's office, where he was sacked on the spot. The union officials conceded the man had been drunk and were privately glad to be rid of him. From then on they collaborated fully with Kane, whose stock rose further when Croft leaked word of his being an ex-fighter pilot.

Occasionally Croft invited him for an afternoon's bird shooting, which was the manager's one passion outside mining. A scrub-grown ravine a few miles away supported a number of sand grouse and the two men developed an easy-going comradeship trekking in pursuit of them.

One evening in November the two men repaired to the Delphi Diner – the Ridge's only restaurant – for a beer after one of these excursions and Croft casually raised the question of Kane's future.

'Guess you must be wondering what happens next?' he remarked.

Kane nodded.

'As far as I'm concerned you've done OK. I reckon they'll call you back east pretty soon. If you don't understand what a mine's about by now, you never will do.'

The forecast was accurate. Western Mining's summons came shortly before Christmas. When Kane said farewell to Croft it was with sincere regret: the manager was one of a breed one could not fail to respect. But, Kane reflected as the airliner climbed away over the harsh landscape, the managers were not the ones who made the real money. He was set to join the financiers.

There could hardly be an eating place more different from the Delphi Diner than the New York Yacht Club on West 44th Street, built on a site donated by Commodore Vanderbilt, ornate, spacious, patrician. This was where Robert Kane was summoned to meet his employers from IMEX one evening early in January 1958. He was now back at Western Mining's New York offices, staying temporarily in a hotel at the company's expense, and, though pleased at receiving a substantial raise, he was restless. He was a man who liked to know precisely where he was going.

The weather in New York was bitter, an east wind driving showers of sleet, catching one unawares on street corners. Kane ran up the wide steps of the club with relief, handed his coat to the hall porter, and was shown up the marble staircase to the first floor, where both James Skinner and Sir John were waiting. The club lounge was long and high-ceilinged and his two hosts were seated in deep armchairs. But what caught Kane's attention first were the many large glass display cases of yacht models, ranged around the far end of the room.

Sir John noticed this with immediate approval. 'All the America's Cup contenders,' he explained, shaking hands warmly. 'Unique collection. We'll have a look at them before dinner. Meanwhile, what's your poison?' He waved a hand at an elderly white-coated waiter hovering near the door, who now shuffled slowly towards them. Kane suppressed a laugh. The man might have been an ancient retainer in an English country house. The club was a world away from the city streets outside.

Over the drinks Kane learnt that he had made his mark at Western Mining.

'They sent you to the toughest spot they could think of,' commented Skinner, 'reckoning that if you were no good you'd be found out pretty fast.' In fact the manager down there gave you a thoroughly good chit. Congratulations.'

'So what's next, sir?'

'We'll discuss that over dinner. First tell us a bit about your experiences.'

Whether this was mere politeness, Kane was not certain at first. But that he had shifted into an altogether higher stratum at IMEX became clear when they showed him the ship models, all breathtakingly detailed scale replicas of the world's most prestigious racing yachts, and Sir John remarked casually. 'If you can arrange leave at the right time, I'd be glad to have you along to see what ocean racing's like. Have you crewed at all before?' He smiled. 'Even the most distinguished guests have to lend a hand aboard *Clementine*.'

Then they ushered him downstairs again to the dining room, oak-beamed and panelled in a way Kane thought he recognized but couldn't place until Sir John explained.

'Believe it or not,' he said, 'this is a replica of Lord Nelson's cabin on the *Victory*. Hugely bigger, of course. You can see why the club is considered an historic building.'

Sir John recommended the grilled swordfish steak, ordered wine, and the real business of the evening began.

'You must have been wondering what's in store for you,' Skinner remarked. 'Frankly we've been somewhat in the dark, too, which is why we came across. In fact IMEX is to continue its traditional metal broking, but it's also acquiring a new role.'

'This is strictly confidential,' put in Sir John, 'you understand that, Robert?'

'The President of Western Mining has a theory,' continued Skinner, leaning forward across the table and lowering his voice. 'It's very simple. The colonial empires are breaking up. When they collapse, all the mining concessions they hold will be, as he puts it, up for grabs.'

'Foul expression,' commented Sir John. 'But he has a point. I never realized how things were going until Jimmy briefed me.'

'It's obvious,' went on Skinner, 'except that people at home can't comprehend what's happening. We've been in full retreat since we lost our nerve at Suez and Nasser trounced our reputation. The French pulled out of Indo-China after Dien Bien Phu in 1956 and now they're locked in a vicious war in Algeria, which I personally don't think they can win.' He held up his hand, the fingers spread wide. 'Let's tick off the colonies worth having. Ghana, independent last year: gold.' He flipped one finger down, following through with the others, one by one. 'Sierra Leone, on the way: diamonds. Nigeria, self-governing already: tin and oil – huge quantities of oil, British Petroleum believes. French Guinea, approaching independence: bauxite.'

'I think I see what you mean,' said Kane. 'Are we interested in oil, too?'

'I think Western will be after Nigerian oil exploration rights. But as far as we're concerned, minerals are the target. So Ghana could be promising. So would the Sierra Leone diamonds, if the South Africans didn't have such a stranglehold on the place. However, the biggest opportunity may come somewhere else. Did you read that the Belgians have been forced to allow local elections in the Congo?'

'I missed that, I'm afraid,' Kane admitted. 'The local paper at Tucson wasn't overburdened with foreign news.'

'It's not the kind of item you can afford to miss from now on,' said Skinner, with surprising sharpness. 'God knows African politics couldn't interest me less, but we're going to need to sense the way the wind's blowing before everyone else does.'

At this moment they were interrupted by the arrival of the first course, then the wine waiter began fussing around, and the conversation died, leaving Kane a chance to think. His immediate reaction was that the mood of nine months ago in London had vanished. Even though his own status was higher now, whatever they wanted him to do was not going to be a walkover.

At last the waiters bustled away, and Skinner resumed his monologue. 'The Congo is the place,' he said, between mouthfuls of pâté. 'Christ alive, look at a map. It's the size of Western Europe. Down there the Belgians hold one-sixth of the world's copper, half its uranium. They've got tin, manganese, diamonds, silver, zinc, cadmium, cobalt. The Congo's output is worth one thousand million pounds a year. And the whole bloody lot is controlled from Brussels, mined by Belgians, refined by them, sold by them, shipped by them. The Congolese don't feature, except as labourers. If Western Mining could horn in there, the rewards would be colossal.'

'Are the Belgians discussing independence?' queried Kane.

'No, but the Africans are! And anyone who encourages them to see how they're being exploited is going to be their good friend. You speak French, don't you?'

'Passably.' Kane was beginning to understand now.

Skinner glanced at Sir John. 'We'd better send him to Berlitz for a brush-up course, hadn't we?'

'Frankly, Robert,' remarked Sir John, 'this game of smelling out concessions and takeovers when you're pretending to be buying metal is, hmm, foreign to us. However, if Western Mining plays a tune, we dance to it. I'm afraid though,' he murmured, stroking his moustache with a forefinger, 'that it's bad form.'

Kane considered this for a few moments, making use of the excellent fish to delay replying, and wondering if Sir John could be as much a caricature of a gentleman as he appeared. 'There's one thing, I don't follow,' he said at last. 'Why doesn't Western Mining send in its own men? Why use me?'

'Ah,' Skinner chuckled, 'I have to grant their President one thing. He has a damn subtle mind. Part two of his theory is that the ex-colonies will end up trusting their former masters more than anyone else. The devil you know is better than the devil you don't, sort of thing. For example, if a British expert advised an African leader to turn to a US company for a development project, he might do so more readily than if the Yanks simply went straight in after the business themselves.'

'Fair enough in Ghana or Nigeria. But why should the Congolese take any notice of us?'

Skinner sighed. 'As Sir John says, it does go against the grain a little. But Western Mining have one further concept. A very, very simple one. They believe money can buy anything, especially politicians. And with characteristic prudence, they would far rather see one of us compromised than one of their own men if things go wrong.'

'When you say "us" you mean me?' With an effort Kane stopped himself swearing out loud. Bloody hell, these two had a nerve. Laying it on about the British approach, not liking American ways, all the rest of the bullshit, and then calmly asking him to start getting his hands extremely dirty on their behalf.

If Skinner felt any embarrassment he did not show it. 'You'll be handling a lot of money, Bob, and you'll have to be careful. In return you'll get a very high salary, a very generous expense account, and a substantial bonus whenever a contract is signed. Plus, of course, normal commission on any genuine metal-broking deals.' He smiled comfortably 'I did promise you the chance to make a lot, remember?'

'How much, roughly?' If they were going to buy his integrity, they could damn well come up with figures.

'Ten thousand pounds basic.' Skinner paused to let the amount sink in. A third of that was a good salary for a man Kane's age in London. 'A normal bonus would be point one per cent of the contract's annual value. Put simply, if you land Western a concession worth ten million a year, you'll pocket an extra ten thousand. Almost free of tax, too. Western have an office in the

Bahamas and we'll make you resident there.'

'To whom will I be responsible?'

'Nominally to us in London. You'll carry our visiting cards and all your telexes will come through us. But in practice you'll be reporting to the Vice President of Western here in New York. It's him you'll fly across to see when a deal needs clinching.'

Kane sipped some wine and carefully finished his fish. He had made up his mind. To hell with the risks. This chance would not be repeated. But he wanted more money. He could envisage unpleasant scenes if his mission became known to the colonial governments. 'I must say, sir, that's a very decent offer,' he said to Sir John, deliberately playing the typical Englishman himself. 'There's only one thing. I do feel that if I'm to be based in the dollar area my pay should be aligned with American levels. I hope that's not unreasonable.'

'Sounds fair,' commented Sir John, 'although ten thousand is a pretty good whack, eh? As much as the Prime Minister gets, isn't it?'

'Exactly.' Skinner was uncompromising. His room for manoeuvre was limited by the rather larger slice of the profits he and Sir John intended to take, and out of which Kane would be paid.

'I agree the salary is generous,' said Kane coolly, determined not to back down completely. 'But I believe in gambling on my own judgement. If you can make the bonus point two of one per cent I'll accept.'

There was a short silence.

'All right,' said Skinner reluctantly 'We'll double the bonus. God knows you'll earn it.'

'So that's settled?' inquired Sir John, with evident relief, 'Excellent. Now how about some dessert? I can recommend the sorbet.'

The yellow cab driver deposited Robert Kane on the United Nations Plaza with a scowl. 'Bunch of goddamn commies in there,' he said, looking suspiciously at the dollar bill given him for the fare. 'Me, I guess McCarthy was right all along.' He accelerated away into the traffic.

Kane glanced up at the slab-sided Secretariat building, its thirty-nine-storey-high wall of windows tinted faintly green, the contrastingly low white bulk of the General Assembly hall crouched alongside. Somewhere up there, meeting a UN official, was the man whose signature could ratify a 1000 million pound mineral contract. Kane instinctively crossed his fingers as he stood on the kerb. His 0.2 per cent commission on that contract would be 2 million pounds. 2 million pounds. An unimaginable amount. Unimaginable in one's own bank balance, that was, as opposed to the fairy-tale world of financial news headlines. The deal would make headlines too, though his own name would not feature in them. More than two years had gone into preparing the ground for a contract which would undoubtedly be the mining coup of the decade. It was now August 1960. In the two and a half years since his terms of employment had been agreed over dinner at the Yacht Club he had often wondered if IMEX regretted that rate of commission. There had been something less than a generous smile on Sir John's face when he had handed over the cheque for 32,000 pounds accruing from the Ghana deal last year. Kane doubted if the Chairman would be able to force a smile at all when saying goodbye to 2 million. He'd probably want to pay by instalments.

Kane's brief reverie was interrupted by a passer-by jostling him. He immediately broke into a quick walk, his grip tightening on his briefcase. Africa had taught him a lot about pickpockets. He was still convinced that the man who filched his wallet during dinner at the Ambassador Hotel in Accra had been one of the Ghanaian officials he was negotiating with. His American Express card had subsequently gone half-way round the world, finally being recovered by the police from an Asian trader in Northampton.

Kane walked through an ornamental garden, set with flowers and shrubs, to the visitors' entrance. Inside the long lobby stood a circular reception desk. One of the three girls behind it looked up as he approached and asked coolly what she could do for him.

'I have come to see the Congolese Prime Minister,' he said. 'Mr Lumumba.'

'The delegations are not in this building. You'll have to call at their offices.' She began to flip through a book of addresses. 'The Congo?' She evidently failed to find an entry and turned to one of her colleagues for advice.

'He is with Mr Cordier,' said Kane.

'Please.' The girl disliked being told. 'We are finding the address.'

'I arranged to see him after his meeting,' Kane insisted. 'Can't you telephone Mr Cordier's office?'

'Today?'

'Yes. Today. August the first.'

With extreme reluctance she scanned through an internal telephone directory. Kane decided she must be either Swedish or Norwegian, she had that glacial northern self-assurance. 'You mean Mr Andrew Cordier?' She demanded in apparent disbelief. 'The executive assistant to the Secretary General?'

He nodded.

'What is your name, please?' She dialled a number, spoke briefly, then announced flatly, 'The meeting finished early. The Congolese have gone to the delegates' dining room.' She inclined her head. 'Through there.'

Kane spotted Lumumba the moment he entered the room. The Congolese leader was tall and thin, with heavy spectacles and a tiny goatee beard. He was talking volubly to a group of Africans clustered at two tables pushed together.

Kane approached and to his relief was recognized. 'Find our English friend a chair.' Lumumba waved one of his assistants into action and Kane quickly found himself squeezed between two of them listening to an impassioned denunciation of the United Nations in heavily accented French.

'We ask for military assistance and now they are disbanding our army, our own Force Publique.' He gestured like a demagogue on a platform. 'We ask them to go into Katanga to subdue the rebel Tshombe and they refuse. They are not impartial at all, any idiot can see they are siding with the Belgians against us.' Lumumba was obviously furious at the outcome of his meeting and spoke with passionate vehemence. 'If this is all they can do, I shall go elsewhere for aid. There are countries ready to help us.' Kane guessed this must be a reference to Russia and was caught unawares when the Prime Minister turned on him. 'I shall fly to London tomorrow. Why don't you British help us? Or are you on the Belgians' side too?'

'Emphatically not.' Kane spoke quietly. 'As you know, Prime Minister, my company has a plan to help you.' Kane hesitated to mention money in front of so many others. 'The plan I told you about in Leopoldville last month. I was hoping we could discuss it.

'Last month!' Lumumba looked at him amazed. 'What has last month to do with today? Today we are under attack by the Belgian colonialists. We need troops, guns, planes. We must destroy the Katangan rebels and their Belgian advisers. That is what I told Cordier and all he talked about was negotiation, not force. The Secretary General is in our country now, at this moment. Why is he not taking action? If he continues to do nothing our people will rise up against the United Nations intruders. We will expel them.'

After listening to a further ten minutes of over-excited diatribe against the UN, from which Lumumba had first demanded assistance only a fortnight before, Kane concluded that he was wasting his time. Nothing could be achieved when the man was in such a volatile mood. What he needed was a *tête à tête* negotiation with at the most a couple of advisers present. This was what he had achieved in Leopoldville at Lumumba's villa shortly before the independence. He had no doubt the Prime Minister would listen when he pointed out that 1000 million could buy a hell of a lot of armament. But this was hardly the place, not with that damn great inscription on the wall outside the UN about beating swords into plowshares and spears into pruning hooks. 'Nation shall not lift up sword against nation. Neither shall they learn war any more.' No doubt plenty of arms deals had been discussed in privacy here, but Kane wasn't prepared to risk it in public in the delegates' dining room.

He arranged with one of Lumumba's aides to call at their hotel later and excused himself. As he threaded his way back towards the entrance a spare, ascetic man in a grey suit rose up from one of the tables and caught at his arm.

'Hey, aren't you Bob Kane?'

Kane swung round, taken by surprise.

'Remember me?' said the man in a Canadian accent. 'Barlow. Steve Barlow. I was in your squadron.'

Kane stopped dead still, recollections swirling the image of the man facing him into that of the witness at the court-martial, uniform distinctive because of its Canadian badges, giving the hesitant evidence which had damned him. 'Yes,' he said tightly, 'I do remember you.'

'I saw you were with Lumumba. He's been giving us problems today.' Barlow seemed determined to create a conversation. 'We're working on the Congo operation.' He indicated the two other men sitting at the table, who were embarrassedly uncertain whether to stand up for an introduction or not. 'Won't you join us?'

The references to the Congo jolted Kane back into the present, stifling his instinct to let fly at Barlow, demolish him before his colleagues and then walk away, the court-martial evidence at least partially avenged. That was what the bastard deserved. But if the man could be used, why not? He need have no scruples over exploiting anything Barlow told him and more information on Lumumba would be valuable. 'Thanks,' he answered, 'I haven't eaten.' He shook hands with the others and took the empty fourth chair at the table. 'How long have you been with the UN?'

'Since last week.' Barlow was relieved, having seen in Kane's expression that he was about to be cold-shouldered. The court-martial still lay on his conscience, an aching example of how to do the wrong thing for the right reasons and one which had conditioned much of his thinking since. 'We've all recently joined the team the Secretary General is building up,' he explained enthusiastically. 'You know, Mr Hammarskjold has moved pretty fast.' He began enumerating dates, ticking them off on the fingers of his outstretched hand. '7 July the Congo was accepted as a UN member state, a couple of days after the army mutinies began. 11 July Katanga seceded. 12 July an ordinary commercial cable landed here asking for military aid. 13 July Hammarskjold convened a special meeting of the Security Council. It began in the evening and lasted most of the night. The resolution early in the morning of 14 July called on the Belgians to withdraw their troops and authorized the UN to provide military assistance.'

The man on Kane's right, an Irishman, cut in. 'The amazing thing was, the Russians and the Americans both agreed something had to be done. And it's the more extraordinary because Lumumba had also asked both of them for help direct. Mind you, there are still two ways of looking at it. Lumumba originally asked us in to restore order and then shifted to wanting the Belgians expelled as aggressors. So the United States support the order part and the Russians want to see the Belgians kicked out.' He laughed, 'It's scarcely a marriage of true minds.'

'Perhaps,' admitted Barlow. 'But it is preferable to an East-West conflict and legally the situation is clear.' He allowed himself a thin-lipped smile. 'The Belgians sent in troops to put down the mutinies without the consent of the newly independent Congo Government. The Security Council decided there was a threat to international peace.' He turned to Kane 'This may not mean so much to you, Bob, but it's the first time in the history of the UN that article ninety-nine of the charter has been invoked.'

Kane nodded. He didn't give a damn about the charter. What he wanted to know was whether the UN really was going to expel the Belgians. If it was, then the chances for his deal were immeasurably improved. Someone would have to run the mines. 'And are the Belgians going?' he asked.

'The troops: slowly. Yes, we're replacing them. We brought Tunisians in on 15 July, then Ghanaians, Ethiopians, Moroccans.'

'And Irish,' the Irishman laughed. 'Looking for all the world as if they'd come to fight the Great War. Thick khaki, puttees, peaked hats. The poor devils, they must be sweating something terrible.'

'The question is,' Barlow continued, 'if the Belgians refuse to withdraw their military from Katanga, do we throw them out by force? Mr Hammarskjold refuses to. I'm sure he's right. To do so would be counter-productive, definitely counter-productive. But, of course, Lumumba insists we should.'

'So?' Kane kept his tone light, though Barlow's explanation had reached the crucial point. 'Will the Belgians be persuaded?'

'Mr Hammarskjold is out there now. He's determined to succeed by negotiation.'

'And the Belgian civilians, the administrators, the engineers – the whole infra-structure – what about them?'

'Many have quit,' commented the third man, a swarthy-faced slightly fat individual who Kane later learnt was a Bolivian. 'We are providing technical aid as fast as we can arrange it.' He gave Kane a sharp look. 'May I ask what is your interest?'

Kane chuckled. A laugh was always worth a hundred earnest explanations. 'Much the same. Technical assistance. I work for a mining group, specializing in the sale of minerals. We were asked by Lumumba to give him an independent assessment of the Congo's potential.' It was a lie, but a passable one. He was offering the Africans a contract, not a report.

The Irishman shook his head resignedly. 'He'll be the death of us yet, that man. I truly believe he'd ask the fairies at the bottom of the garden for help, if he met one.' Suddenly he realized this sounded insulting and added hastily, 'No offence taken, I hope. It's merely that we're trying to channel aid through the UN if we can.' He sighed and turned to the Bolivian. 'Manuel, it's time we were back upstairs.'

Their move to depart acted as a signal to the waiter, who arrived hurriedly with their bill and then took Kane's order.

'Well, Steve,' said Kane when the waiter had gone, 'I'm still in the same business. What made you change yours?' He did his best to be friendly, though it cost him an effort. It looked as though the Canadian was of some consequence in the UN.

Barlow toyed with a fork, giving the question much more consideration than Kane had intended.

'It's a long story. After I left Oxford, when my time as a Rhodes scholar was finished, I went back home . . . .' As he unfolded this period Barlow wondered if he could ever explain the turning point in his whole view of life. Yet he knew precisely when the moment had been.

Steve Barlow's home was a rambling, four-storey nineteenth-century house along the shore of Lake

Ontario, half an hour's drive from downtown Toronto, where his father worked as a feature writer on the *Globe* newspaper. His father was a big, loose-limbed, shambling man, of profound liberal convictions, who had refused more lucrative jobs because of the freedom the paper gave him to explore social problems and causes in his articles. But neither his, nor his readers' interest in any one cause lasted overlong. Equally the house, crammed from cellars to attics with memorabilia, had never achieved an overall decorative scheme, despite his mother's occasional bursts of domestic energy. Like his father's mind, it was a treasure trove of unrelated objects: as comfortable in places as its old chesterfields, as unexpected as the huge bronze Burmese gong which stood in the hall and which was never struck because they had no fixed mealtimes. Life drifted in and out of the house with a constant passage of people. Neighbours' children came to play table tennis or borrow roller skates; fishing friends of his father's drank beer and planned trips; his mother's fellow school governors called for coffee. Always there were visitors, often politicians or academics, who canvassed old man Barlow's views and editorial support. How their entertainment was afforded remained a mystery, though Steve knew the newspaper contributed, because with three boys and a girl to educate the family were perennially broke.

Possibly as the result of being the youngest, Steve grew up determined both to follow his father's ideals and to improve on their effectiveness. In time this matured into a belief that principles were better enshrined in law than in leader articles. At seventeen he decided to become a lawyer and a year later, when he was almost through upper school, he discovered that one way of paying for the legal studies was to enrol as an officer cadet in the Royal Canadian Air Force under the reserve training scheme for university students. During the subsequent three years at the University of Toronto he flew five months of the year, supporting himself in better style than many who worked their way through college by other means. He emerged with both an excellent degree and his pilot's wings. There followed three years at the Law School, culminating in his master's degree, the LLB, and then the summit accolade, a Rhodes scholarship to Oxford. There was little doubt that his flying contributed to the award. He was now on jets and the selection panel liked applicants who showed a sense of citizenship as well as academic brilliance. After all, they were choosing future Commonwealth leaders.

On his return to Canada, untainted by the 699 Squadron debacle, Steve Barlow found himself in demand. But he had already been approached by Canadian diplomats in London as a possible Foreign Service Officer and it took him little time to decide to join the Department of External Affairs. He was now twenty-six, highly qualified, and could reasonably expect to go to the top. After a year in Ottawa, he was posted to the Canadian delegation to the United Nations, a move on which his father congratulated him with real warmth. Canada had international commitments of a particularly interesting kind to a young man with liberal ideals. She had participated in the UN Emergency Force, established in Egypt after the Suez Canal affair, and she was a member of the International Control Commissions for both Laos and Vietnam.

It was Laotian problems that brought Steve Barlow to the attention of the UN Secretary General. In 1959 Dag Hammarskjold was trying to persuade Canada to resume her seat on the Laos Commission. As was his habit, he gave a small party for the negotiators, moving round the room, chatting to each official in turn. Fifty years old, he was a slightly built man of only average height, wearing a well-cut double-breasted suit and a mildly extravagant spotted bow tie. Hammarskjold had typically Swedish fair hair brushed back from a high forehead, but his rather protuberant nose, dimpled chin and smiling mouth gave his face a puckish quality, though the deep-set blue eyes missed little. When he was introduced Steve felt every detail of his character was being examined.

'So you are the young lawyer turned diplomat I've heard about,' remarked Hammarskjold amiably. He was always meticulously briefed. 'You were a Rhodes scholar. A beautiful city, Oxford.'

'Unfortunately being over there I missed your speech at Mcgill.'

'About OPEX? Ah, that is my favourite child. The scheme interests you?'

'It does, sir. It seems to me one of the least colonial ways of giving help to under-developed countries. If that's the right word for them.'

The sentiment struck an immediate chord with the Swede. His eyes twinkled appreciatively. 'It is indeed a curious term.' he exclaimed, 'if you realize that a few of them have civilizations dating back far beyond anything we know of. They are under-developed only in the economic sense.'

'I agree, sir.' Never before had Steve felt so inspired by someone's individuality and presence.

'It's a pity assignments in them are so unrewarding in terms of money. We have to build on the idealism of people. Finding ones with this kind of pioneer spirit is a somewhat tough job,' he smiled again, 'but we try.'

At this moment an aide caught his attention and he turned away, though not before adding, 'I hope we shall meet again one day.'

Coming from a man of Hammarskjold's idiosyncratic determination, Steve knew the wish would be realized. However, more than a year passed before anything happened. Then one day in July 1960, when he was back on a desk job at the Department of External Affairs in Ottawa, he was summoned by the Director of the Personnel Operations Division. Reckoning that this interview would be about a long-anticipated overseas posting, he went to the office in a state of some apprehension.

The Director, a small tubby man who prided himself on being more outspoken than most government servants dared to be, surprised him. 'You know there's a United Nations operation being mounted in the Congo?'

'Naturally, sir.'

'The Secretary General has personally asked the Under Secretary of State if we'll release you to join the civil side of it.' The Director leant forward and relaxed. 'Say, Steve, don't think me rude but how the hell did you make that kind of impression on him? You can hardly have met him in New York.'

'Only once.'

'Well, he's getting quite a reputation for asking governments for particular men, rather than merely accepting whoever they might nominate. I guess it's a high compliment. We'll release you on secondment if you want to go. Maybe you'd like to think it over.'

Steve went off and took a solitary lunch in a quiet Ottawa restaurant while he meditated the pros and cons. There was nothing to stop him. Both his parents were in good health and anyway his elder brothers could cope with any emergency. He had no female attachments. Morality had been pretty strict in college. Two years at Oxford had broken the only potential attachment and since then his work had kept him totally absorbed. In any case, as he had begun to admit to himself, he was shy with women and felt no urge to share his life, either for sex or simple companionship.

What were the advantages? he reflected, sipping a beer and gazing out of the window at the sunshine on the street. The main possibility was that the move might damage his career rather than advance it. He pondered this, thought of consulting his father, then decided no, his father was certain to support an international rescue operation. Better come straight to the point with the

Director after lunch.

'You reckon it's a productive exercise, sir?' Steve asked. 'I mean, from the Department's viewpoint it would be good experience?'

'It sure would. Believe me, Canada will go all the way with Hammarskjold on this one, just as we did with UNEF. We've already agreed to send army signallers to provide communications for the UN force. They'll be airlifted out any day. The Congo could be the most tricky operation ever undertaken by the UN. We can help because we're one of the few white countries that can adopt an independent, neutral stance. All right, we do belong to NATO and the British Commonwealth.' He made a gesture as though brushing away a fly. 'But no way do we have any colonialist taint. We have a role in the third world such as no great power can ever play, the United States included, and which it's our duty to fulfil. We want to see the cold war kept out of Africa. I would recommend acceptance.'

'So here I am.' Barlow smiled in his rather formal way at Kane, who had finished his lunch. 'I warned you it would be a long story. And next week they post me to Leopoldville.'

'Where the action is.' Kane's attention might have appeared to drift during the Canadian's monologue, but he had not missed a word of significance, and he saw one thing with particular clarity. Barlow was an idealist as well as ambitious in his straight-laced, lawyer's way. He would pursue the fulfilment of the United Nations resolutions to the letter. For so long as the UN supported Lumumba and wanted the Belgian troops and advisers out of Katanga, Barlow would be a convenient friend to have. The destruction of Belgian influence was a crucial factor in gaining acceptance of Western Mining's contract. 'Well,' Kane added cheerfully, 'the Congo can hardly be hotter than New York in August. I'll probably see you there.'

'I hope so.' A spasm of worry passed across Barlow's face. 'Bob,' he said, 'I want to apologize for my failure over that crash. I've thought about it a lot since.'

'Forget it. The past is the past.'

'No. I need to tell you, I sincerely regret not informing you about the conversation in the bar.' His tone was urgent now, the sinner in the confessional. 'Failure to act is a moral crime. You can kill by inaction as easily as by deeds. I learnt that at Frampton, Bob. I could have prevented that fatality. I regret most profoundly that I did not.'

'For Christ's sake, forget it.' Kane was angered by this assumption that only the dead Wildeblood mattered. The dead should wait on the living. Barlow seemed to have no appreciation of how damaging his evidence had been.

'It's decent of you to say that. But I can tell you, Bob, I've learnt the lesson.' He sounded like a penitent reluctant to take off his hair shirt. 'You know what Dag Hammarskjold told me? "It is more important to be aware of the grounds for your own behaviour than to understand the motives of another." A profound remark. Never again shall I evade taking action if I'm morally in the right.' He paused. 'And legally within my powers, of course.'

Kane restrained himself from comment, reflecting that the Canadian was still as impracticably high-minded as he had always been. Instead he said, 'I must go. Thanks for the lunch. I'll look you up in Leopoldville.' He shook hands, then shot out one last query. 'I heard a rumour about Tshombe hiring mercenaries to fight for him. Do you reckon it's true?'

'We had a report of recruitment starting in Brussels. It's not substantiated.' Barlow's face became even more set. 'If it were, the United Nations would condemn such action unreservedly.'

As Kane left the building he wondered cynically if

Barlow counted condemnation as a form of action. If so, then Africa would swallow him whole and spit out his bones after breakfast.

An hour and a half later Kane reached the Congolese delegation's hotel, where Lumumba occupied a suite. He was announced from the lobby and told to go up. Apart from the furnishings, the scene was like many other occasions on which he had paid court to African politicians. A sleepy-eyed guard sat in the tiny hall of the suite and nodded him into the sitting room, where nine or ten minions lounged, some chattering, some listening. The tables were strewn with beer glasses. Thick cigarette smoke drifted above, eddying towards the air-conditioning vents. The difference was the tall, restless figure of Lumumba himself, pacing the room, jabbing out excited comments, gesturing with his whole body. He was a born demagogue. He greeted Kane emotionally, 'Ah, my friend, now we can talk. What have you brought? Have a drink.'

Kane fished into his briefcase and produced a gold-tooled leather folder in which reposed a Letter of Intent carefully worded earlier that afternoon. 'An outline proposal, Prime Minister, the same as we discussed before.'

'We must have space!' Lumumba motioned two Africans out their armchairs and told them to clear the adjacent table. He did not relax but sat on the edge of the deep armchair, poring over the document through his thick lenses. 'Yes,' he muttered. 'Until now we have been exploited. We have known ironies, insults and blows which we had to undergo morning, noon and night because we were blacks! Now we call the tune.' He pointed suddenly at a phrase in the letter. 'What does this mean "conditional upon world prices prevailing at"?' He looked up at Kane, mistrust in his dark eyes. 'We must set the price for our products, not the capitalist exploiters! They cannot control our inheritance.'

'Often prices can be set by contract in advance,' Kane tried to temporize. 'Not always, though. The London Metal Exchange is internationally accepted.'

'By the old order. Not by us. You realize we have been offered seven hundred and fifty million pounds for our mines?'

'You're being sold short.'

'Explain.'

'That is too little.' Kane marvelled at the African's simplicity. The Congo's annual output was worth 1000 million. 'Prime Minister,' he said, 'our company is offering you a thousand million pounds – two thousand four hundred million dollars – plus a royalty on sales. We don't even want to interfere with the running of the mines. We will simply get you the best prices the world can offer.'

'We shall expel the Belgians!' Abruptly Lumumba was back on his lunchtime tack. 'If the West will not help us then the Russians will.'

'If you want technical assistance Western Mining can give it.' Kane chanced his arm. 'You came asking for American aid. On behalf of one of the biggest mining groups in America I am offering it. Without strings, Prime Minister, with no strings. Whatever you ask, they will provide. If you prefer the Russians, that is your affair. We will nonetheless market the metals and pay two thousand four hundred million dollars for the concession.'

Lumumba appeared confused by this. He turned to one of the aides who were crowding round, standing behind him and Kane. 'We will need lawyers, won't we?'

Kane caught the assistant's eye, gave the tiniest shake of his head, then said 'For the full contract, of course. Hardly for this, Prime Minister.'

'I am in agreement,' stated the assistant blandly. Kane had told him back in Leopoldville what his support would be worth. It was a substantial sum, a lifetime's normal earnings for a civil servant.

'Very well.' Lumumba had made up his mind and was characteristically all impatience. 'Give me a pen, who has a pen? We cannot waste time.' He seized the gold Schaeffer which Kane proffered and scrawled his signature on the document with a flourish. Then with sudden formality he rose, shook hands warmly as if before a possé of photographers and announced, 'This is an historic occasion. A new era of co-operation has begun for the Congo.'

The phone rang. 'For you, Chief,' said another aide. As instantly as the solemnity had began, it ended. Kane stood clutching the folder while Lumumba erupted into an emotional tirade down the telephone on another subject. The official who had been bribed sidled up. 'I will show you out.'

On the way down in the lift the official said, 'Come to Leopoldville with the full contract. All will be well. We shall be back in a week, after London and Accra.'

'I hope so,' said Kane. 'Twenty per cent will be in your account tomorrow. The rest comes with the contract.'

'Half. I should have half.'

The lift was almost down to the lobby level. 'Twenty-five per cent, then,' Kane conceded. 'A Letter of Intent is no more than it says. I want a fully binding agreement.' As the doors slid open, he shook the man's hand. 'Thank you for seeing me down. *Au revoir*.' He walked off, turning to wave as the lift doors closed again. The balance between keeping corrupt officials sweet and keeping them in order was a delicate one.

After the Vice President of Western Mining had finished talking to Kane on the telephone, congratulating him and agreeing his departure to Leopoldville, he buzzed the President's office on the internal phone and a booming voice from the small loudspeaker told him to come along.

The President, whose sanctum lay along the same thickly carpeted corridor, was in some ways more familiar to readers of *Time* or the *Wall Street Journal* than to the bulk of his employees. His broad, full face, stubborn chin and thick white hair made his photograph a stock item for financial editors. He had close links with both the great financial institutions of Wall Street and with government. His brain worked fast, forming conclusions while he listened to the Vice President's summary of events.

'So far so good,' he commented. 'You know, Bill, if we land this contract, fine. But let's not be too precipitate. We're already in the run-up to the presidential election. Suppose Kennedy gets the nomination and wins, our foreign relations could be a whole new ball game. Besides,' he rubbed the side of his fleshy nose reflectively, 'copper prices haven't been any too good of late. Two hundred and thirty-one pounds on the LME is nothing to go wild about. If things don't improve, our production from Arizona and Chile could be more in need of support than competition.'

'You mean would we make more profit by handling the Katangan copper through IMEX or by keeping it off the market?' The Vice President assimilated this idea. Constraint of trade was nothing new to him, but he had become so thoroughly imbued with the excitement of snatching what amounted to a private empire from the Belgians that this took him aback. 'Could we get away with it? The Union Minière is a damn powerful organization.'

The President raised one bushy eyebrow in mock surprise. 'Circumstances could inhibit Katangan exports, surely. Even if the Congo central government doesn't go to war with this guy Tshombe, there can still be problems. Transport. Labour troubles. I'd like an analysis of the situation on my desk next week.'

3

To Mike Russell's surprise the cable from Chantal, welcoming him to Katanga, instructed him to fly via Salisbury to the mining town of Ndola, on the Northern Rhodesian copper belt, and go to the Savoy Hotel, where a room would be booked for him. A quick check with the map showed that Ndola was only just across the border from Katanga. Presumably he would be driven the rest of the way. When he spoke to a travel agent he understood rather more: the only airline flights to Elisabethville were via other parts of the Congo. It was an intimation that being a pilot for Tshombe might have disadvantages.

As the Viscount airliner circled to land, Mike caught his first sight of the mines: tall chimneys belching smoke, huge mounds of grey tailings, rising like low hills in the wide, flattish landscape of African bush. Then the plane bumped down and he was jostling his way into a large corrugated-iron-roofed Nissen hut which served as the airport terminal. He found a taxi and headed for the town, only three miles distant.

Ndola was much as he had expected: prosperous, spaciously laid out, with mining executives' verandahed bungalows in large gardens with trees and flowers. However, the Savoy Hotel, in the town centre, was a drab, modern building. After he had checked in the assistant manager, a European, came up behind the reception desk, glanced at his name in the register, then gave him a curious look, half inquisitive, half suspicious.

'You'll be picked up in the morning. Eight o'clock.' His voice was rasping, a barrack-room corporal's.

'Would you like me to settle the bill now?'

'It's been taken care of.' The manager nodded towards the bar. 'There's another of you through there. Were there any others on the plane?'

'How the hell should I know?' Mike erupted against this man's attitude. It had not occurred to him that the Savoy might be a rendezvous for people going to Katanga.

'Birds of a feather.' The manager backed away slightly from the desk, adding more to himself than to Mike, 'They'd be here by now anyway.' He retreated to the office.

When his case had been taken upstairs by an African porter, Mike went down to the bar. It was an unprepossessing room, the counter stained by frequent rowdy drinking sessions. At the far end a thick-set man sat on a stool, gazing morosely at a glass tankard of beer.

'Are you going to Elisabethville too?' Mike asked.

The man swivelled on the stool, sized Mike up briefly, then nodded and stuck out a strongly muscled forearm to shake hands. 'Herman,' he said with a South African accent. 'Herman Schmidt. They call me Herman the German.' He chuckled, his broad fair-complexioned face creasing with a kind of inner pleasure. 'I don't mind, man. Why should I?' He lapsed into apparent consideration of this thought, re-emerged slowly and shouted at the barman, 'Another beer, boy.'

Mike hoisted himself to a stool and looked the German over while they waited for the beer. Even hunched up on the stool, he was an ox of a man. His broad torso, bulging through a check shirt, seemed part of the same solid structure as his arms, as though the whole body had been carved out of a single chunk of rock. His bullet head grew out of this mass without much sign of a neck between. He had had closely cropped curly blonde hair and pale blue eyes. His skin was pinkish and freckled; obviously the sun burnt rather than tanned him.

When the beer came, Herman pushed it across, raised his own glass and said, 'Cheers, man.' But to Mike's surprise, he didn't swill back a huge gulp. He drank cautiously, as though disciplined to making it last. Then, after a pause, he asked, 'What's your normal business then?'

'The same as I'm being hired to do here. Fly. I'm a pilot.'

The German's eyes widened a fraction. 'Man, that must be well paid!' A regretful expression came over his face. 'That would be good. A pilot. Tell me,' his accent flattened and drew out the vowels. He spoke with deliberation, articulating each word. 'Is that a difficult thing to learn?'

'Not so much.' Mike didn't want to hurt his feelings. 'It's more a matter of time and study.'

Herman nodded ponderously. 'Study is the thing, man. You need to study. Then you can make money. It's my problem. I have this little farm down near Bulawayo and I carved it out of the bush myself, man, but it's too small. That is the problem, however much I work.' He spread his huge hands out, palms uppermost, and Mike could see he wasn't lying. The strong stubby fingers were calloused and ingrained with dirt. 'So when I met this man in Bulawayo,' Herman continued, 'and he said I could earn one hundred and forty pounds a month and danger money as well, you can imagine, man, I didn't take long to think about that. I arranged with my friend Joe for him to sell the vegetables and to pay the boys at the end of each month and I told them to expect me when they see me.'

'You're not married?'

Again the sadness crept into the German's eyes. 'You

know, man, I am not too attractive to the ladies and what can I offer them? Twenty acres and a small house I built myself. Oh, you would like my house. It has a little bar I made in the corner of the living room and I can stand behind and give drinks to my friends. It's nice. But there are all kind of things ladies want besides, eh? Perhaps if I can save some money in Katanga things will be different. The man in Bulawayo gave me not only the air ticket but one hundred pounds. Straight away. Advance of salary, he said. "You won't spend it", he said. "You'll be too busy fighting those Baluba." ' Herman shook his head reflectively. 'As a pilot, I reckon you must get more than me, man.'

'I'm supposed to be Tshombe's pilot.' Mike was faintly uneasy. The man in Bulawayo sounded like a recruiting officer. 'Are they taking on a lot of people?' he asked.

'Maybe. I think I am one of the first from Bulawayo. It's good money. I don't mind fighting these Baluba.' He grinned with sudden enthusiasm. 'Any munt who is not frightened of me is a very stupid person, I can tell you that, man. There is no need to study to know that.' Having delivered this dictum, he lapsed into silence. Later, when Mike knew him better, he would realize that for Herman this had been an exceptionally long speech.

The Chevrolet Impala sent to fetch the two men confirmed Herman's belief in his companion's importance. The African driver set off at terrifying speed down the main road to Kitwe and then on to the border, through wooded country with occasional streams and open grassy spaces.

'We call them "dambos". There's always water in a dambo,' Herman explained.

The other characteristic of the area were enormous anthills, ten to fifteen foot high mounds of red earth, sometimes rounded and overgrown with bushes, sometimes new and naked in weird jagged pinnacles. Mike estimated some were more than twenty feet broad at the base.

'Hard as hell, man,' Herman said. 'You try to shift one of those, eh!'

At the frontier post they were given the same curious looks, though the Rhodesian officer, in the stiffly ironed grey shirt and khaki shorts of the British South Africa Police, wished them luck when he saw their colonial passports. 'You'll be up and down through the pedicle quite a bit, I suppose?'

Herman grunted non-committally. He never gavc a policeman information unnecessarily.

After they were let through, Mike consulted the road map and saw that the pedicle was a projection of Congolese territory perhaps fifty miles wide and 150 long, which cut an incongruous slice out of Northern Rhodesia. Elisabethville was situated at the head of it. Immediately this turned Mike's thoughts to Chantal and he wondered if she would be waiting to meet them. His inner excitement grew as they raced towards the city's outskirts, through an area of African mineworkers' housing. In the distance a tall chimney trailed smoke.

'Fonderie de Lubumbashi,' said the driver, reminding Mike that from now on his French was going to be exercised.

A few minutes later they were in the heart of Elisabethville. The jacaranda trees were in bloom, their blossom stretching down the avenue in a mauve mist. Colonnaded white buildings, well-filled shops and continental style restaurants all testified not only to a high standard of living, but to a sophistication which Ndola had completely lacked. Mike thought how odd it was that the same stretch of bush could be imprinted side by side with two such different civilizations.

The car passed the town centre, down a long street and then screeched to a halt outside a building hung with what was evidently the new Katanga flag: red and white divided by a slanting green bar, with, on the white three copper crosses, the traditional shape in which native copper was cast before the European came. The driver swung out of his seat and went inside. But a white-helmeted African policeman stopped them following. 'No entry to the President's office without a pass,' he said firmly. Then Chantal appeared, elegant in a light blue dress, the sun catching her hair, her figure framed against the dark shadows of the entrance hall. Mike would never forget this moment. She came down the steps, smiled at him and held out her hands. 'Welcome,' she said simply. 'It's good to see you here.'

They shook hands warmly. His instinct was to kiss her, but he felt embarrassed by the sentry and by Herman. He introduced them, adding quickly, in case she disliked Germans, 'Actually he's a Rhodesian.'

'Ah,' she was intrigued. 'You must be one of the new volunteers.' She emphasized the word as if it were a rank, like sergeant or corporal. 'The driver will take you on to Major Weber at the *gendarmerie* headquarters.'

Herman recognized this as his dismissal, and clapped Mike on the shoulder. 'See you again, man.' He glanced at Chantal. 'Some fellows do have all the luck.' He got back in the car.

Chantal led Mike into the building. 'The President wants to meet you straightaway.' She gave him an encouraging look. 'I think you'll see that he is a remarkable man.'

The presidential office was large and opulently furnished. As they entered Tshombe rose from behind his wide desk. In his dark suit and white shirt he seemed more like a successful businessman that a politician. He was tall, broad shouldered and altogether an imposing person, though the most striking thing about him was an enormous smile, which enveloped his whole face. His accent was cultivated. After a few conventional remarks, during which coffee was brought, he became serious. 'I want you to appreciate what we are doing here,' he said, his shoulders hunched, facing Mike across the coffee cups. 'We have restored order. *Mon dieu*, you have seen what it is like elsewhere. Here we have an island of sanity.' He raised a finger dramatically. 'But we are threatened. Not from one side. From three. In the north we are trying to pacify the Baluba rebels. On top of that the Lumumba government is preparing to invade our territory. Our sovereign territory. Now, the United Nations is demanding to send in troops.' He began to speak more emotionally, and Mike realized that underneath the quiet joviality lay a potentially tempestuous character. 'We are determined to resist the Lumumba government's illegal representatives. And we will not allow the United Nations into Katanga.' He clenched his fist, repeating, 'We are all determined to resist. As our national anthem says, "With our arms and our blood, with our teeth." As for Lumumba! He is dangerous and mad. He will destroy the Congo.'

Gradually he relaxed again, revealing that with some of the Belgians going, he had begun to recruit replacements. 'If my Belgian officers are forced to leave, I shall rely on men like you.' He paused, the amazing smile flickering over his face. 'We want Europeans, but we want them in the service of Africa. That is what the United Nations is unable to comprehend. If you work for us on that basis, then we can be friends. It is impossible for us to develop Africa without an important contribution from abroad. I tell you, I am a realist.' He shook his head. 'There is so much to do.' Then his face brightened. 'Fortunately we have the natural resources. Katanga will be an example to the whole continent. Can I depend on you to support our cause?'

'Yes, sir. You can.' Mike had decided Chantal was right. Not only was Tshombe persuasive, he had put into words much that Mike already felt. 'I was born in Africa,' he said.

'Excellent.' Tshombe stood up, extending his hand. The

interview was over.

Outside the room, he asked Chantal when he would start flying the President around.

'Not so fast. Things have changed since I wrote to you, they are still changing. Let us go home to my parents for lunch and I will tell you.'

Chantal drove a small white Citroën, a car so basic that it had no pretension to style at all. 'Don't laugh,' she remarked. 'If you don't know these, you're missing something. They can go anywhere.'

'I believe you.' He had imagined her in a sleek little sports car and was agreeably surprised at this practicality. The house, however, was precisely what he had anticipated, a low-built stuccoed villa in a neat walled garden, with a Mercedes parked in the driveway and several African servants in white uniforms. They could have been in an expensive Brussels suburb, were it not for the strong sun and the riotous orange-red blossom of a flame tree in the garden.

'We hope you will stay with us for the first few days,' said Mme Berthoud. 'Until you are settled in to the job.' She liked Mike and thought him agreeably good-looking. She showed him to the guest wing, fussing over him appropriately.

Lunch was not protracted, since M. Berthoud had afternoon appointments. None the less Mike assimilated much of what had happened. Many Belgians had fled at the time of the mutiny and only about half had returned. Tshombe's political party, called Conakat, had only a slender majority in the Assembly and the other main one, led by Jason Sendwe, representing the Baluba tribe of the north, was fiercely opposed to the secession.

'Those terrible Baluba,' sighed Mme Berthoud. 'They are real savages; cannibals, some of them.' She forked up the last mouthful of steak, consumed it happily and then added, 'There'll be trouble with them.' She turned to Chantal. 'How could your M. Tshombe possibly manage without Belgian officers and advisers? The mere idea is ridiculous.' She reached for the salad bowl, tossed its contents quickly and passed it to Mike.

Chantal looked across at him. 'My mother has a wonderful way of making everything sound like a domestic problem. But it's not. Yesterday the United Nations Security Council passed yet another resolution. At 4.25 in the morning. They'd debated all night.'

'Can an international talking shop thousands of miles away in New York really do anything?'

'They called on the Belgian authorities to withdraw immediately from Katanga. They want to replace our Belgian soldiers with a UN Force. How it's done is to be determined by the Secretary General.' She made a moue of annoyance. 'He hasn't wasted any time either. Today we had a message from him asking if M. Tshombe accepted "The duty of co-operation". Later he announced that he proposed to fly here with two companies of Swedish troops on Friday.'

'The day after tomorrow?' At last Mike understood the emotional mood Tshombe had been in. 'Why don't you simply close the airport?'

'Your bluff succeeded last week,' remarked M. Berthoud, in one of his rare contributions to the tabletalk.

'Papa, I agree we persuaded the UN man Bunche that if he brought in soldiers there would be riots and bloodshed.' Chantal turned back to Mike. 'There would have been, as a matter of fact. Just as there would be if Lumumba came. People here are truly frightened of Lumumba, terrified. He may not legally be certified as insane, but he is irrational and violent. He is an expert at making trouble.' She sounded very worried. 'Until June it was only the Belgian government which had to bear the brunt of it. Now we all do. Seriously, Mike, if he came here there would be bloodshed. And we are afraid the arrival of UN troops would be a prelude to his coming.'

'Surely you can hold off this attempt, if you succeeded

last week?'

Chantal shook her head. 'Last week it was only the Secretary General's representive. Now it will be the big man himself. Our M. Tshombe is a complex person. He respects the UN in a way. As he told Hammarskjold, he doesn't want to cause an armed conflict. He prefers to negotiate. Actually he would like the Congo to be a confederation of independent states and he still hopes Hammarskjold might help bring that about.'

'Well,' said Mike, 'politics are not my game. I'm here to fly. When do I start?' Suddenly a thought occurred to him. 'What happens if the UN take the airport over?'

Chantal had finished her meal. 'Mother,' she said, 'would you mind if Mike and I take our coffee in the living room? There are things I want to tell him.' She folded her napkin carefully, and led Mike through. One of the servants brought coffee cups on a tray.

'Listen,' said Mike. 'If there's going to be any kind of a fight I'd better take that Cessna somewhere safe. I don't want another one full of holes. Nor, I'm sure, does your boss.'

When the servant had gone Chantal sat forward on the edge of the sofa and looked appealingly at Mike. He had one of the most open, honest faces she had ever seen, but there were crinkles of worry round his eyes. There was no point in deceiving him. 'Things have changed a lot since I wrote. You won't be flying the President, except in emergency. We only have one aeroplane and there are more urgent uses for it supporting the gendarmerie.'

'I thought you said there was going to be an air force!'

'Please, Mike don't be angry with me. M. Tshombe genuinely did want a personal pilot a few weeks ago. Since then the trouble has flared up with the Baluba. The gendarmerie who have to pacify them are African soldiers with Belgian officers. If the Belgians go, other leaders must be found. Last week we appointed recruiting agents in Brussels, Johannesburg and Bulawayo. The German

Rhodesian you arrived with was one of the first mercenaries they hired. More are coming.'

'Mercenaries?' The word had an ugly ring to it.

'We call them volunteers, but why bother?'

'So that's what I am?'

'You can remain a civilian pilot if you want. The plane is still painted blue and white with a civilian registration.'

Mike remembered Zog's parting words, 'Sooner or later they fight .... Now you can start your own bloody air force.' He should have recognized what the situation here implied. 'It's partly my fault,' he said. 'It's just that when you said Tshombe was getting a jet, I thought you meant an executive plane.'

'He was thinking about that. But Major Weber and the others have pointed out he needs fighters, not personal transport.' She held out her hands and touched his. 'I owe you an apology. There is only one compensation. If you stay they will make you a captain.'

'In the gendarmerie?' The idea took some getting used to.

'Mike.' She spoke his name softly and with affection. 'There is no air force. Not until someone creates it. We just have five thousand soldiers whom we call gendarmes. Please understand.' She drew back her hand. 'If you don't like this, I can promise M. Tshombe will release you from any obligation and pay your fare back to Nairobi.'

Mike shook his head. 'I think I'd better go and see your Major Weber.' He grinned. 'Meanwhile, why don't you start designing an air force uniform? We can always get the planes later.'

The gendarmerie headquarters brought two surprises. The first was the uniform: khaki trousers, bush jacket with blazing red shoulder badges for officers and a South African style wide-brimmed hat, one side pinned up against the crown and bearing the new Katanga badge. Mike hated to think what Captain Zog would say if he saw it. The second shock was that Major Guy Weber immediately introduced him to a Belgian air force officer in conventional blue shirt and trousers, Belgian badges of rank on his shoulder straps and an RAF style peaked hat.

'May I present Wing Commander Jacques Duclair?' said Weber formally. 'He will discuss the modalities of your employment.' He gave Mike a small smile. 'Since the famous Cessna is unserviceable you must be prepared to defend it from the Swedes. But the danger should not be acute: they haven't fought a war for an hundred and fifty years, after all. They are badly out of practice.'

'Let us hope so,' said the air force officer warily. He was a lean, languid man whose expression seemed to Mike to lack both confidence and probity. Not the sort you would lend money to. He led Mike to his own office.

'I imagine you are wondering why we recruit pilots when I am here,' he began. 'Well, my position is slightly equivocal.' He perched himself on the side of his desk and threw his hat neatly up to a hook on the wall, as if it were a quoit. The hat swung, but remained aloft. 'The day I miss, I shall leave,' he remarked. 'We all have our private omens. The hat is mine.' He pulled a cigarette pack out of his shirt pocket. 'Smoke? No? Forgive me if I do.' He lit up urbanely, then contemplated Mike. 'Of course I am a most experienced pilot. I began with the RAF in the war. However, here I am strictly speaking an adviser. Whether advisers should take an active part in military operations is a most interesting question.'

'Who would know if you did?'

'In a place like this? My dear fellow, everyone. It's a rabbit warren of rumour. With a Belgian unit, of course, I could fly. The whole question is whether my government would approve of a fighting role with the gendarmerie should the UN learn of it.' He blew a lazy smoke ring. 'We support Katanga. We must also appear to be collaborating with the Security Council resolutions. It is what we call "*une situation très nette*". On balance, I do not wish to chance becoming a scapegoat, to lose my career, my pension. I am content for others to fight the Congo's war. *Vive les mercenaires.*' He smiled and slid off the desk. 'But at least I can show you the plane.'

The airfield was north-east of the city. At the gate an African gendarme stood by a white sentry box. He saluted ponderously as the jeep drew up. The wing commander waved a casual acknowledgement, then drove past the impressive white terminal building, where a long viewing terrace was set with café tables and big red and white umbrellas, like a café in the south of France. 'The arrival of the Boeing from Brussels is quite a social event,' he remarked. 'Half the town comes to watch.' A couple of minutes later they reached a guarded hangar, the high doors open. Inside stood a couple of DC3s, each emblazoned with the legend AIR KATANGA, and the Cessna, on which a Belgian mechanic was working. He straightened up as the wing commander approached.

'We haven't cured the mag drop yet, I'm afraid, sir.'

'Is it bad?' Mike asked.

'Three hundred and fifty r.p.m on the left magneto. The right's OK.'

'Way outside the permitted limit,' Duclair observed. 'Of course, if you don't mind risking an engine failure ....' He left the sentence unfinished.

Mike looked at him. 'If it meant the difference between the UN seizing the aircraft and our keeping it, I'd have a go.'

'Then I suggest you come out here on Friday. If Hammarskjold lands and the Swedes do anything stupid, we can probably enable you to take off before they realize what's happened. Especially with civilian markings. You could go to Kipushi. It's barley fifty kilometres down the road.

'What's the road itself like?'

'Not bad. Quite a decent surface. And straight. You could put down on it in emergency, no problem.' He shrugged his shoulders. 'Unless you hit a tree or a pole.'

'All right. That's what we'll reckon. But I'd like an escort.'

'You show commendable spirit, my dear fellow. I have no doubt Guy can provide a gendarme.' Duclair arched an eyebrow. 'Perhaps not in that rather fancy uniform, however. Do you prefer your escorts white or black?'

'I don't give a damn as long as he can shoot straight.'

'White then. Shall we go? I feel we have earned a little refreshment.'

In the evening Mike took Chantal out to dinner. They went to the Hotel Leopold II in the town centre which everyone knew colloquially as the 'Leo Deux'.

'There are a lot of newspaper reporters here,' she said. 'But the food's good. And you'll see a cross section of society.'

They sat discreetly in a corner, while she pointed out local celebrities: one of the Union Minière managers; the bank director; a tall Belgian colonel in uniform. 'Crevecoeur, he's the one who put down the mutiny. But I'm afraid he'll be gone soon. A lot of the good ones are leaving.'

'I wasn't over-impressed this afternoon.' Mike confessed. 'It all seemed a bit amateurish.'

'In a way, perhaps.' She meditated for a moment. 'Some of them, yes. But make no mistake about Weber. He has a head on his shoulders, that man. And remember, it's only a month since the mutiny. They have to rebuild an army. None of the mutineers are being re-employed. In the rest of the Congo they simply took the rabble back. The Congolese National Army, we call it the ANC, has no discipline. They are permanently mutinous. They've hardly been paid since the Independence. The UN should have disarmed them. Even the UN's General Alexander said so. Here it's a different situation. Tshombe refused to re-instate mutineers. Our gendarmerie is loyal.'

A trio of photographers entered the dining room,

causing a momentary stir. They were in shirt sleeves, cameras hung around their necks, carrying extra equipment in squat black boxes. They found a table and began talking in loud voices about the possibility of shooting Hammarskjold's arrival. One was American and two were British. 'According to Reuter his take-off from Leopoldville is scheduled for eight,' said the American. 'We should be in position at the airfield by eleven at the latest.'

'I heard Lumumba wants to come with him,' said one of the Britons. 'And Lumumba's declared a state of National Emergency.'

'Boy, there could be a bust-up tomorrow.'

'Are they right? Will things blow up?' asked Mike.

'As I told you, if Lumumba or any of the central government come, it will. Otherwise Tshombe might just outwit them. I shall be with him at the airfield.'

'I wish I could be, too.'

She smiled gently. 'So do I, but your task is to safeguard the Cessna. I'd rather you did that.'

Mike was at the airport early. He went straight to the hangar. There, standing nonchalantly just inside the door, was Herman, dressed in his check shirt and slacks, a small machine-gun in his hand. He stepped forward.

'Jesus, you gave me a fright,' said Mike. 'What the hell are you doing here and whatever is that?'

'Too many questions, man.' He rocked with suppressed laughter. 'Today, I am your bodyguard. It should be quite obvious even to an idiot, eh? And this thing,' he lifted up the small weapon. 'This is the new toy they have given me. It's Italian, nine millimetre, a Luigi Franchi.' He admired its pearly grey finish. 'They call it a machine pistol. Very convenient and lethal to thirty yards. Not bad, eh, man?'

'Well, let's get the Cessna out. We might as well be ready.'

Together they pushed the high-winged blue and white

plane on to the hard standing in front of the hangar. Mike checked it over thoroughly. Then he started the engine. It ran slightly rough. He called the control tower on the radio and agreed that if shooting started he would not ask for clearance, but would taxi straight out to the runway. Then he closed down the engine and they settled into their long wait.

As the minutes passed the airfield filled with troops, who took up positions around the buildings and the control tower. Two armoured cars arrived. Near another hangar stood a large stack of empty oil drums. When trucks roared up and the drums were loaded Mike guessed they were for blocking the runway if necessary. Then, to his amazement, shortly after ten thirty, a military band marched on and were paraded near a dias, behind which flew the Katanga flag on a small pole. Tshombe was obviously keeping his options wide open. He wondered what was going on in the control tower. Then, the noise slowly swelling, he heard the engines of a large aircraft approaching. Out of the distant blue, among a scattering of clouds, a white Convair airliner came into sight. Everyone on the airfield stiffened. Even Herman stayed in the shadows as he stared upwards. The airliner came overhead and then, instead of going into a conventional landing procedure, began to describe a wide turn, completing first one circle, then another, then another, continuing on and on. The troops fidgeted with their weapons. The tension heightened. Something must have gone wrong.

In the tower Tshombe sat at the controller's desk, the microphone in his hand, surrounded by aides and advisers, both African and Belgian. He was talking direct to Hammarskjold on the plane's flight deck. Chantal listened, a shorthand pad on her knee. Although she knew everything the President said on the radio was being tape-recorded automatically, she took down every word. The plane had been circling now for over fifteen minutes.

The Secretary General's dry voice came over the small loudspeaker. Everyone in the room could hear it clearly. 'If permission to land is not received for all my five aircraft within five minutes, they will all return to Leopoldville.'

'There has been a misunderstanding.' Tshombe was trembling slightly. 'Please wait one moment longer.'

A hurried confabulation took place with his aides. Chantal heard one say, 'Is it certain that none of the central government are on board?'

'I think so.' Tshombe held the microphone again. 'The order forbidding the Swedish troops was a mistake. If you assure us the aircraft have no one other than your staff and the two companies of Swedes, then I personally authorize the landing.'

Above, awkward on the Convair's flight deck, the Secretary General spoke quietly to the captain. 'There is somewhat of a risk with so much military preparation down there. However, we must take it.'

The captain assented and as Hammarskjold accepted Tshombe's permission, he swung the airliner out of its orbit, which had now lasted twenty-five agonizing minutes, and began preparations for an approach to land. Calmly Hammarskjold walked back to the passenger cabin and rejoined his anxious staff.

On the ground Mike saw the maneouvre. After a few minutes the white Convair appeared far away, lined up with the runway. It made a perfect landing. After it came four more planes, carefully spaced out. By the time the Convair had taxied to the terminal, its two prop-jet engines whining shrilly, Tshombe was outside by the dais, a beaming smile on his face. The band was preparing to strike up. The flag fluttered. A crowd of photographers were held back by white-helmeted police, while more scrambled for vantage points on the terrace.

Chantal stayed in the control tower, now deserted by all but the normal staff, and watched as Hammarskjold descended the steps from the plane's door, followed by two generals, one visibly an African. She heard the band launch into the Katanga national anthem with its melodramatic phrases, and as the Secretary General walked towards Tshombe she realized with a surge of relief that her boss had scored a significant public relations victory. Here was the Secretary General, pledged to end Katanga's secession, shaking hands with the Katangan President in front of the Katangan flag, with the band playing the anthem and the whole free world's press watching. Tomorrow the photos would be on the front pages of newspapers in every capital. She laughed delightedly and when she saw the sour expression on Hammarskjold's face, she laughed again. She was in no doubt that Tshombe had put one over on him, and very neatly at that.

The radio came to life. Mike's voice gave the Cessna's registration and asked, 'Please advise if take-off required.'

Startled, Chantal turned towards the controller. Across the tarmac she could see the Cessna and the dark shape of Mike inside.

'What do we say?' demanded the controller impatiently. 'Everyone's forgotten him. Typical.'

Chantal scanned the airfield carefully. The Swedish soldiers were all disembarked, forming up into their two companies, their officers in front, apparently waiting to be inspected. The band was blaring out an unintentional parody of the Swedish national anthem. Tshombe was still smiling broadly. The gendarmes were lounging about, relieved not to be alert any longer.

'I don't think there will be any fighting today,' she said.

The controller pressed his microphone switch. 'Negative. Hold position. Report to tower.'

As Mike climbed out of the Cessna, Herman asked what was going on.

'False alarm. Nothing's happening today. At least that's my guess.'

‘This is a crazy place, man.’ Herman was cradling the Luigi Franchi almost lovingly in the crook of his arm. ‘How can it last, I ask you?’

‘I’m damn glad things didn’t go bang today. Faulty magnetos have a habit of failing on take-off, or just after. We might never have reached the Kipushi road.’

‘Is that so?’ Herman shrugged his massive shoulders and fondled the machine pistol with regret. ‘They have told me I will be going north in the column against the Baluba next week. I would like to have seen the Kipushi road.’

‘Let’s go, Herman,’ said Mike. ‘I’m wanted at the tower.’ They walked back to where their jeep was parked. Unknown to him, Mike would make more take-offs and landings from the Kipushi road than he ever would from Elisabethville airport.

The next day, on 13 August, Hammarskjold and Tshombe jointly announced that discussions were proceeding on the relief of Belgian troops by the UN Force. In due course Moroccans and Ethiopians would arrive. Meanwhile as a first step the Swedish companies would take over the protection of the airport. In the afternoon Mike flew the repaired Cessna down to the grass field near the mine at Kipushi, his freshly issued gendarmerie uniform in a suitcase. With it was a Luigi Franchi like Herman’s. For all Chantal’s optimism he now knew the Belgian regulars like Duclair would leave and Katanga would need an air force.

Robert Kane’s arrival in Leopoldville, the sprawling capital city on the Congo river, coincided with Hammarskjold’s bold flight to the Katanga province. Despite the newspaper headlines, as far as Kane was concerned the most immediate effect of the crisis was that all the hotels were full. He eventually obtained a suite on the fifth floor of Memling, the city’s best establishment, deciding that the expense of having a spacious, grey-carpeted sitting room in addition to a large double bedroom could be justified by the size of the impending deal. The suite was to prove a useful asset during his stay.

Making contact with Lumumba proved difficult. He never seemed to be at his office, so Kane took a taxi to his villa, guarded by Ghanaian soldiers of the UN, as apparently he did not trust the Congolese National Army to protect him. Gaining entrance took time and much talk and, when Kane did get inside, he discovered he was merely one of an endless retinue of hangers on and advisers from all over Africa. There were Guinean diplomats, politicians, even a French born press officer. The place was a maelstrom of argument, pleading and denunciations, at the centre of which Lumumba himself, moody and excitable, weathervaned from one idea to the next. Wandering around, Kane found the aide he had bribed in New York, slipped into a corner with him, and was promised an audience 'as soon as his Excellency is free'.

After interminable waiting, Kane was ushered into the presence. Lumumba recognized him at once and pumped his hand. 'Ah, our English friend. Have you heard the iniquities those UN people have been up to? They fail to assist us to enter Katanga. Instead of overthrowing the rebels they recognize them. His voice became shrill and looking into his eyes Kane wondered if he was on some kind of drug or stimulant, the pupils were so distended. 'Those Swedes are nothing better than Belgians in disguise!' he shouted. 'The Russians are right. Hammarskjold is a traitor to the cause of African freedom. I shall refuse to meet him again.'

The tirade lasted half an hour. Then, as suddenly as he had flared up, Lumumba became listless, his voice quietened and he said wearily, 'Our country needs help. Independent help.'

The aide took the unexpected cue beautifully. 'It is

exactly such assistance as Mr Kane's company is offering, Prime Minister. Our lawyers have approved the mining contract. They advise acceptance.'

'Are all the details correct?' Lumumba sounded far away, then seemed to pull himself together momentarily and challenged Kane. 'You realize even the Belgian colonialists spent ninety per cent of the taxes from metal production here in the Congo?'

'But what of the profits? How much of those went overseas?'

'Yes, you are right. We were always swindled. But not any more. Never again.'

'You think the Belgians will change their ways, Prime Minister?' Kane asked. 'I assure you our contract will outdo the best they would offer even at the Last Judgement.'

Lumumba laughed. The irreligious joke appealed to him. 'Very well. If the lawyers agree, we will sign.' He turned to the aide. 'There must be a proper ceremony. Arrange it. These occasions require dignity. The whole Cabinet must be there, even Kasavubu, if the old fool will leave his house.' Kasavubu was the President of the Democratic Republic of the Congo and famous for staying at home.

When Kane left the villa, watched suspiciously by others in Lumumba's entourage, he was convinced he had won. That evening in the privacy of the hotel suite he paid a further 10,000 dollars to the aide, though he was taken aback when the man demanded money for the lawyers, too.

The next day Kane decided to make his acquaintance with the UN headquarters, a miserably inadequate building called Le Royale, whose only redeeming feature was a Greek restaurant on the ground floor, where many of the staff ate. Upstairs the flurry of activity accompanying Operation Simba, as the Secretary General's mission had been codenamed, still continued. 'Simba', he learnt, meant 'lion', which seemed a somewhat aggressive title for a peacekeeping operation. It was about all he did learn until, deciding to lunch downstairs, he joined a table crowded with UN staff and found himself next to an attractive Swiss-born girl of about twenty-three.

Suzy had chestnut hair, a small, piquant face with an upturned nose, sexy hazel eyes and an immediate readiness to talk to strangers. Kane noticed a smile flicker over the mouth of one of the men as he introduced himself to her, a smile which said quite clearly, here we go again'.

'Do you by any chance know a friend of mine called Steve Barlow, a Canadian?' he asked, stoically disregarding the man opposite. 'He was coming out.'

'How funny!' Suzy giggled, more with relief at the easy passage she was going to have than at anything humorous. 'He's joining Mr Cordier's staff and I am Mr Cordier's secretary. What a strange coincidence.'

'Isn't it?' Kane agreed, remembering from New York that Cordier was Hammarskjold's special assistant, and appreciating how useful Suzy could be. 'Well, I'll be damned! When does Steve arrive?'

'Any day now. Have you known him long?'

Her obvious desire to keep the conversation going made it simple for Kane to monopolize her. After fifteen minutes of banal exchanges, he suggested they meet for dinner in the evening.

'Oh, I should love to, but we are giving a party.' She glanced at two of the others, saw no discouragement and made her decision prettily. 'I know what,' she exclaimed, 'You must come too, and then we can go out afterwards. What fun!'

The party was held in the flat of a Ghanaian diplomat, whose supply of duty-free liquor was matched by an exuberant sense of hospitality. As the evening grew merrier he jokingly ordered Suzy to be responsible for the English visitor's entertainment. She acquiesced with a slyness which left Kane in little doubt of her mood.

The guests began to filter out around 9.30 p.m. and, when he suggested the undeniably first-class restaurant in the Memling, she agreed and drove him in there in a white Volkswagen Beetle, emblazoned with blue UN signs, which he discovered was one of her perks, along with a small apartment and generous allowances. 'Why else would anyone come to the Congo?' she explained, grimacing at the mere thought. During dinner he realized that, though the Secretary General might be an idealist, he and Steve Barlow were in a minority. Most of the lesser mortals were there for the money and the money in the United Nations Operation Congo, or ONUC as it abbreviated from the French, was good.

It was close on midnight when they finished dinner. They had danced, drunk liqueurs, altogether cost IMEX a fair sum. As they walked out into the hotel lobby Kane was wondering how bluntly to invite her upstairs when she saved him the trouble.

'Bob,' she said, glancing at the clock, 'I quite forgot something. There's been a lot of hostility against the UN in the last two days. Yesterday the Congolese forced their way on to one of our planes and attacked some Canadian soldiers. We were warned not to drive around after midnight, at least not in a UN vehicle.

'I have a suite here. You could always stay.'

'I think it would be better,' she said and took his arm as they went to the lift. At the reception desk the clerk watching them smiled happily to himself. The lady would be worth a substantial tip tomorrow.

Kane always remembered that evening of 19 August. Suzy was possessed of an uninhibited lust such as he had never before encountered. She clung to him in bed, urging him on, digging her nails into his back, finally crying in ecstasy. Then she fell sound asleep, while he lay on his back, delighted at having found a mistress. What was more, in the morning, over breakfast, which she ate clad in his silk dressing gown, she talked. She confessed to three passions: bed, clothes and chattering away. Kane encouraged her in the last to the point where she was late for work.

Nine days later, when he had slept several nights at her apartment in the Residence Mayumbe, and she had equally earned the night clerk at the Memling a full 1000 francs, she was dipping her croissants in the coffee and muttering about how good they were, when she suddenly remarked, 'Did you say your important interview with Lumumba had been postponed until 5 September?'

'I was a bit puzzled. They told me he'd gone to Stanleyville.' The signing ceremony had been put off only at the last moment and in fact he was more than puzzled, he was damned worried.

Suzy giggled. 'Really! How do they think they can keep things quiet?'

'What do you mean?'

'Well, yes, he did fly to Stanleyville, but only because the Russians have sent him fourteen transport planes and a hundred trucks there. What he's actually doing is sending in the ANC to invade Katanga. We heard about it yesterday afternoon.

'You mean there's going to be civil war?' Kane put his cup down abruptly. He had 2 million pounds at stake on Lumumba. This added a dangerous new dimension to the contract.

'He can hardly join up with the Baluba to overthrow Tshombe and not have a battle, can he?'

'Will he win?'

Suzy smiled. 'Our people will be delighted if he does. It'll save us from having to deal with Tshombe ourselves.'

'Yes, but will Lumumba win?' Kane reiterated.

'He thinks it will be over in a week. It all depends if you believe what he says, doesn't it?'

4

The Baluba were in full revolt against Tshombe now and the gendarmerie were slogging their way north in small groups to establish control of the plateau which the Belgians had named High Katanga. Numerous rivers drained down out of the plateau's rolling bushland. Word had got back to Elisabethville that an important river bridge had been damaged.

Duclair had allocated Mike to fly the Cessna in support of the advance, reconnoitring ahead and acting as the eyes of the Belgian major in command. As a result, although theoretically based in the capital, in practice he operated the Cessna out of any available strip within striking distance of the gendarmerie columns. The flying was exciting and dangerous, but he was becoming frustrated with it on two counts. It separated him from Chantal and it kept him out of the planning for a Katanga air force which he had looked forward to when he originally left Nairobi.

Yesterday he had taken the plane down to Elisabethville to pick up supplies for repairing the river bridge. This morning he asked Duclair when they were going to receive more aircraft, in particular any jets.

'My dear fellow,' Duclair had said in his habitual languid tone, 'There is no need for you to trouble yourself with these matters. Everything is in hand, I assure you.

What matters for the moment is giving maximum support to the gendarmerie with the planes we have.'

Mike had bitten back an angry reply about the Cessna's limitations and left again for the bush. Now he was searching for the column.

From the air the gendarmerie trucks were first discernible as a plume of dust trailing lazily above the bush and the high, tawny elephant grass. If they hadn't been moving, Mike doubted if he would have located them. There were only four African soldiers crouched in their open backs clutching rifles, swaying as the vehicles bumped on the rutted track. A solitary jeep, its top also down, headed the small convoy. He glided the Cessna down, then dived off the last 500 feet, gunned the engine, roared over them and pulled up into a climbing turn. The Cessna was a long way from being a stunt plane, but he had already learned that the boys on the ground enjoyed a bit of a performance. As he continued the turn steeply above them, the Africans waved and so did a thick-set figure in the jeep, recognizable at once as Herman.

'Where do you want the drop?' he asked over the radio. A Belgian voice answered, guttural and difficult to understand.

'At the bridge, if there is space.'

'Roger. Wait.'

Mike levelled out and flew ahead of them along the road. Beside and behind him on the aircraft's floor were a pile of boxes and canvas bags. They contained six-inch nails, hammers, saws and other tools for repairing the bridge, plus a resupply of food for the Europeans and a quantity of nine-millimetre ammunition. To make room for this cargo, he had removed all the seats except his own and taken off the passenger door opposite him. When the moment came he would heave the containers out with one hand, holding the plane as low as possible, but first he had to find a suitable clearing.

Ten miles ahead of the trucks Mike came to the river,

trees thick along its banks. A village was situated a mile away. From the air all looked peaceful. Women in brightly coloured dresses were carrying bundles on their heads as they sat by the roadside. There were children playing in the dust, a boy herding a straggling group of goats, men on bicycles: all the normal activity of an African village.

Yet the bridge itself was broken. He pulled into a tight turn, as though pivoting on the left wingtip, and assessed the damage, making mental notes. The pontoons of the bridge had been severed near the far side and now its two uneven parts were swung back towards the banks by the current, like sections of a broken bracelet. None the less it looked repairable, given enough wood and rope and the manpower to haul the pontoon straight again against the flow of water. After scribbling a few notes on a pad strapped to his thigh, he flew back to the column and reported.

'Is there a place to make the drop?' the Belgian major's guttural voice demanded.

'Affirmative. There's a clear stretch of road close to the village.'

'Patrol up and down the road ahead of us until we reach it. Understood?'

Mike obeyed, watching the trucks rumbling along below, the jeep leading. Although the Cessna had a high wing, giving him a view interrupted only by the white-painted wing strut, he still could not see directly below, except by tilting the plane. The bush and elephant grass bordering the road was so thick that a slant view would not reveal men hiding in it. He was puzzled at the apparent normality of the village, when the bridge had been destroyed. The people must derive at least part of their livelihood from passing traffic. A faint shiver of unease told him something was wrong, the sixth sense of a man born and brought up in this continent. So he scanned the area near the road with great care, weaving to and fro above it.

Even so, he only spotted the ambush moments before the jeep reached it. The high grass along the roadside swayed, catching his attention, and he suddenly realized there were at least twenty rebels concealed there.

'Ambush ahead!' He had to restrain himself from shouting. 'On your right.'

The jeep skidded to a halt, raising a cloud of dust. The trucks behind followed suit. He swung the Cessna into a tight turn, trying to keep the scene under observation. One European ran back to the trucks as the soldiers jumped out. In the jeep Herman was heaving round a machine-gun mounted on the vehicle's wing. The first Baluba emerged on the road, ragtag figures in tattered clothing, armed with spears and long knives as well as guns.

The Belgian major was keeping his nerve. Mike could see him leaning over the side of the jeep, the microphone in on hand, his sub-machine-gun in the other, calmly watching the Baluba approach. 'Are they on both sides?' he asked.

'Negative.'

They were running towards the jeep now, and only 100 yards off.

In an attempt to harass them he dived the Cessna straight at them, regardless of the danger. Some were armed with spears. The leader, in a khaki uniform, was waving a rifle and incongruously had a pair of binoculars round his neck. Mike roared down as low as the trees permitted but it had no effect. He pulled the plane up into a climbing turn and resigned himself to being an impotent spectator. There was not even anything he could say, because no one was manning the radio. The major was crouching by the roadside, his sub-machine-gun on his shoulder, taking carefully aimed shots. An African soldier, prone beside him, was doing the same with a rifle. By the time the Baluba had covered half the distance at least ten of them were down, but there were dead gendarmerie sprawled in the road, too. One platoon had rallied and was advancing in skirmishing order along the other side of the road from the major, while another appeared to be attempting an encircling movement through the bush to get behind the rebels.

As if watching a silent movie, he saw the brief battle reach its crescendo. The remaining Baluba charged towards the jeep, firing their weapons dementedly as they ran. They were a few yards from the jeep when Herman stood up, swung back his right arm and lobbed a grenade forward, immediately ducking down. It exploded square in the path of the Baluba, throwing up a fountain of smoke and dust. A few emerged, stumbling, and were felled in hand to hand combat beside the vehicles.

Mike continued circling, agonized at his inability to help, until the Belgian major's voice came over the air.

'Can you land to take wounded?'

Mike had already considered this. 'A couple of kilometres further on it's possible.'

'Land as soon as we are there to give you cover.'

Five minutes later he was ordering them to halt at a straight stretch with no trees close to it, on which he reckoned he could make a successful if bumpy landing. He was taking a considerable chance. They would have to clear a much longer stretch before he could take off again and, if there were more Baluba in the area, they would be in trouble. He made an approach with full flap on, keeping the speed as low as he dared. Even so, it was a tricky business. He had only a few feet clearance from the bushes and high grass on either side of the road. The wheels bounced, then the plane settled down and jolted to a halt as he clamped on the brakes. As he climbed out, his shirt soaked with sweat, the jeep roared up. Herman was sitting in the front passenger seat grinning contentedly, one muscular arm resting on the butt of the heavy machine-gun. The windscreen had been removed to make way for it and Herman's face was pinker than usual from the effects of the wind and sun. There were several bullet holes in the jeep's body, and it was scored by grenade fragments.

'They nearly had us then, eh?' said Herman, his sentences as slow and ponderous as ever. 'It was very lucky you were up there, I can tell you that, man. Here on the ground you cannot see two yards into that grass.'

A European sergeant was in the back of the jeep, clasping his knee. 'They got me through the leg,' he explained, teeth gritted, and began cutting away his trouser leg to examine the wound. 'They're bloody possessed, those Baluba. Did you see their eyes?'

'It's the dawa,' said Mike. 'Hemp, if you like. They are possessed. They're doped to the eyeballs.'

'If it weren't for us, half the gendarmes would have run.' The sergeant was contemptuous.

'I could see some who didn't. Anyway, can you blame them? The attack looked bloody frightening to me.' He fell silent. Africa was more complicated than this man knew. If you had grown up here, played as a kid with African children, shivered at the loneliness of the bush at night, had seen a generation trying painfully to grow away from the power of the witch doctors, then you could understand. You wouldn't expect a few months' military discipline to be any match for centuries of terrifying superstition. In the Congo the Belgians had educated Africans only at the lowest level in a country where appalling atrocities were associated with power. The Baluba didn't merely kill a locally important man, like a village chief. They cut his entrails out and ate the liver hot from his body before he died. The more important the person, the worse the mutilation. It was small wonder the soldiers were scared.

'This isn't a European war,' he said to the sergeant. 'Africa has its own rules.'

'We ought to fight as a mercenary group, not try to

lead these buggers,' commented the sergeant, tying a dressing round his bleeding knee.

'And you need air support,' said Mike.

'You are right,' interjected Herman. 'What we need is fighters up there with guns and bombs.'

At this moment one of the two big trucks came backing down the road towards them, its engine roaring. As it halted the Belgian major jumped out.

'Is the aircraft damaged?' he demanded.

'I haven't had time to see yet.'

'Then we had better look.'

The two men walked briskly back the few yards to the Cessna, Mike reflecting that the Belgian was in fact a much tougher character than he had thought at first.

They walked around the plane slowly, examining the fuselage. There were three bullet holes in it – neat holes in the aluminium skin, except for one which had shattered the Perspex of the rear window. Mike opened the door, crawled on his hands and knees down the fuselage and checked the internal damage. Then he tried the controls. They all appeared to be working satisfactorily. When they had inspected the wings and the engine he turned to the Belgian, grinning.

'Well,' he said. 'That's some kind of miracle. Not one seems to have done any serious harm. The holes can be repaired back at Elisabethville. They won't stop me flying.'

'How many can you take in the plane?'

'Three plus myself.'

'Then you will take the sergeant and the worst injured Africans.'

Two hours later Mike was satisfied with the way the elephant grass had been scythed down. The sergeant and the wounded Africans were loaded in, squatting awkwardly on the floor since they couldn't be strapped in. Mike went through his usual checks, ran up the engine, thrust his feet hard on the brakes while he got full power, then let the Cessna go. One of the Africans was sobbing, whether with fear or pain he couldn't tell. The plane bumped along the road, wingtips just clear of the grass. In order to keep straight, he held her down until he had full flying speed, then hauled back on the controls and prayed. The Cessna lumbered into the air, was caught by the wind ten feet up and veered sideways towards a tree. He kicked her straight again with the rudder, missed the tree by a couple of feet and was safe. As he circled above before setting course, he saw the Belgian hustling the soldiers back into the trucks. Already the framework of the report he would make was in his mind. Air, air and yet more air support was what was needed.

On the outskirts of Elisabethville, half-way to the international airport which the United Nations were still guarding, there was a disused military airfield. This was where the Cessna was now based. He had radioed ahead for an ambulance and as he taxied up to the hangar there was one waiting, a long Ford station wagon, painted duck-egg blue with a prominent red cross on its doors and stretchers inside. The wounded sergeant and the two Africans were carried to this car, which immediately drove off, siren wailing. There was one thing about that flight, he thought grimly, it was good for morale. At least the gendarmerie would know that it wasn't only whites who were given preferential treatment.

Next he gave instructions for the bloodstreaked floor of the Cessna to be cleaned up, spoke to the mechanic about the damage and then went in search of a telephone. He had not seen Chantal for eight days and felt disconsolately out of touch. There was no reply from her office. It was already six, so she would probably be on her way home by now. He decided to drive straight there.

Mike's stay at the Berthouds' home had been brief. He had soon been found a villa which he shared with the DC3 pilots, a move that had precipitated a minor rift with Chantal. As more mercenaries arrived, some of them undiguised riff-raff, the Berthouds became less happy at having one around their house. At first he had been annoyed with her. Then, as he realized that she had quarrelled with her parents over the question, he accepted their attitude as one more facet of a situation that was never as clear-cut as it appeared. There were quite a few business people in Katanga whose support for Tshombe was less strong than the desire to hedge their bets.

When he drove up to the Berthouds' house and saw Chantal's white Citroën parked outside he felt an illogical surge of relief. Chantal herself came to the door. She was wearing a silk cocktail dress and was obviously preparing to go out. She looked at him almost embarrassedly.

'Mike, I never expected you. Why didn't you say?'

'I didn't know. They're keeping me busy.'

Suddenly she noticed bloodstains on his trousers. 'Have you been hurt?'

'No.' He smiled, secretly pleased at her concern, then became serious again. 'Some of the soldiers were wounded. I brought them back. You know, Chantal, those boys out with the gendarmerie earn their danger money. I'm not sure that people down here appreciate it.'

Chantal was about to assure him that she did, when an idea came to her. 'How soon can you be changed and clean?' she asked. 'I'm going to a reception where you can meet them all: Tshombe, Munongo, their advisers.' She stood back and looked him over. 'It would be nice to take you as you are, just for the effect.' She thought this over for a moment. 'But they might not like the bloodstains,' she laughed, 'they are very correct at their parties.'

'I don't think it's so funny.' Mike shook his head vexedly. 'It just proves my point.'

'We're not having an argument now. Do you want to come or not?' She added an inducement. 'You can take me out to dinner afterwards.'

Half an hour later she drove him through the gates of the presidential palace, the sentry recognizing her and saluting with a flourish, and they were ushered into an official reception. Mike never did discover who or what the affair was in honour of, but Chantal steered him skilfully into the circle around Tshombe, and after a few minutes he was being encouraged to relate his experiences.

'You must have fighter aircraft, sir,' he concluded. 'Good, solid, workhorse planes which can back up the men on the ground.'

'What kind should we buy?' Tshombe was intrigued. He enjoyed obtaining new opinions.

'T6s would be good, sir.'

'Write us a report, will you?' He turned to Duclair, who had unobtrusively joined the small group. 'I want you to act on what this young man suggests, Wing Commander. If he is doing the fighting, his ideas must be worth hearing.' The President smiled and moved on.

'So you want to become an adviser,' Duclair remarked to Mike. There was unconcealed enmity in his expression, though his tone remained as urbane as ever. 'If the President insists, then of course you will be consulted. But be warned, my friend, it is a much more comfortable game than fighting and therefore more competitive.'

Mike had barely absorbed the significance of this oblique threat when they were interrupted by a phenomenon which he had never experienced before. Like a gust of wind rustling through a cornfield, an excited murmur of talk swept through the room. Conversations stopped, small groups of people turned to each other, unbelieving, questioning, then exclaiming in astonishment and passing the news on to their neighbours. When Duclair caught it even his habitual sang-froid broke.

'My God,' he said. 'You hear that? General Mobutu had brought off a military coup in Leo. Lumumba is under arrest. Damn me, that's one for the book.' He grinned at Chantal and laughed uproariously. 'Now let the United Nations sort that out.'

The next day Mike resumed his routine flying in better spirits: Duclair would now be forced to employ him more fruitfully. As for Lumumba's arrest, he did not share the Belgian's delight. If African characteristics ran true to form, the soldiers who had detained him yesterday could easily be releasing him tomorrow.

When he reached the bridge the gendarmes were swarming around the anchor points of the pontoons, slowly bringing them back into position. He made his supply drop and then passed over the village. It seemed to be extraordinarily inactive. There were no people around at all. As he came directly overhead he understood why. The group of mud and thatch houses had been burnt out and the fire-blackened walls smashed down. Little eddies of smoke still curled up from several of them. Stretched out on the beaten earth of the village meeting place lay a group of bodies. Others nearby had obviously tried to escape and been shot down as they ran. With a sick feeling in his stomach Mike realized this could only be the work of the gendarmerie, exacting instant revenge for the ambush. It differed only in degree from the atrocities of the Baluba rebels themselves. He wondered dully if Herman had taken part and hoped not. They had come to fight, but he had thought to fight cleanly.

The glaring daylight filtered through the venetian blinds and crept beneath the bedroom curtains. Nothing could keep out the African sun. Robert Kane woke from his stupor, yawned, rolled over and felt Suzy's body inert beside him. He lay quite still for a moment, staring at the ceiling, listening to the rasping hum of the air-conditioner. At least it was cool in here. He had drunk too much last night at a UN party, whisky for whisky with a Ghanaian diplomat whose capacity had proved greater than his own. He had done it because he urgently needed information.

More than three months had passed since Lumumba's signing of the Letter of Intent in New York; three months of mounting political confusion. Today he had to report to Skinner on what might happen next to the unpredictable Congolese Prime Minister and he was desperate for a lead.

He lay, struggling to recover from his hangover, brooding on a situation which would have been farcical if there had not been so much at stake, both commercially and internationally. The military coup of 17 September had led to a couple of days' imprisonment for Lumumba, after which the UN had rescued him. But effectively he was under house arrest, because, although the UN still recognized him as Prime Minister and UN soldiers guarded his villa, an outer ring of the Congolese army stood ready to seize him if he left. So for two months he had conducted his political business by telephone, unable to move. Meanwhile a serious East–West confrontation had developed over the Congo. The Soviet Union backed Lumumba, while the West and – more importantly – the Congolese army leaders supported the President, Kasavubu. Defying each other, both sides sent delegations to occupy the Congo's place at the United Nations. After endless arguments the General Assembly was forced to make a choice. Yesterday, 22 November, it had voted fifty-three to twenty-four in favour of accepting Kasavubu's delegation, which meant that the UN now recognized Kasavabu as the legitimate Head of State, not Lumumba. For Kane it spelt disaster, unless by some miracle Lumumba regained power, as the Ghanaian diplomat suggested he would.

God, those whiskies! In trying to pump the Ghanaian he had drunk so much that he had been unable to make love afterwards. His hand felt Suzy's thigh, firm and warm. Longing swept through him and he rolled over towards her, kissed her face, reached for her breasts. She shifted, muttered inaudibly and then, slowly responding, began to cling to him. For a few minutes he forgot the problems ahead.

'What a nice way to be woken up,' she said eventually, stretching her body lazily. 'What a very nice way.'

Kane, his flesh satisfied, now wanted to start the day. He reached out one arm, felt for the telephone and ordered breakfast. Orange juice, coffee, croissants.

'Tea, darling,' she protested. 'If you loved me you'd remember.'

The half-joke caught him unawares. He asked for the tea, then sat up and evaded the question of affection by turning to the subject on his mind.

'How long will the UN go on protecting Lumumba? That man last night said the Ghanaian guard would stay until he was back in power.'

'I'm surprised you can remember what anyone said. Suzy knew she was being used and she put up with it because she enjoyed making love to Robert and he gave her generous presents. But since he had been incapable last night, she was going to tease him a little. 'Darling, what's the hurry? I have the morning off. We're two hours ahead of London. You needn't answer their cable until the afternoon.' She began caressing the inside of his leg.

'Suzy, my love.' He reciprocated a little by stroking her hair. 'Surely Hammarskjold must have given a directive.'

'Darling, the Congo is a match for anyone, however clever they are.'

'Sweetheart, can't you help me?' Kane kissed her hair. 'I have to know if your people are going to continue protecting the man.' He glanced at the telegram lying on the table, thought of reaching out to read it once more, then rejected the idea. Suzy was obviously in a contrary mood. He kept his arm round her, his mind on the message. James Skinner had not wasted words.

'WHAT PRICE CONGO CONTRACT NOW?' it said and was signed IMEX. Evidently Western Mining had brought them in on the act again. Kane wondered at the several ways of interpreting this brief text. None, so far as he could reason it out, were complimentary. Especially in view of the bribes and other expenses he had incurred. Suzy began stroking him softly again, very distractingly. Hell, he thought savagely, I don't regret the item with me now. But he still wanted more than just sex for his money.

'Hammarskjold must have given new instructions,' he repeated.

'Why don't you ask your friend Steve?' She was still baiting him.

'Because I trust you more.' At least he could say that with sincerity.

Suzy nuzzled her head against his chest. 'If you promise not to get up yet, I'll find out for you before lunch.'

'That's a deal.'

He felt no enthusiasm. Every hour was precious, every minute. Yet he had to know. When Suzy pulled him down on to her again, he stifled his impatience and complied. If satisfying her was the way to what he wanted, then satisfy her he would. Five minutes later the hotel servant left the breakfast tray outside the door because he could get no answer.

By lunchtime Kane had received another cable instructing him to report immediately to London. Happily Suzy kept her word. When she met him at a café near the Royale he could sense her elation before she spoke. She walked up to the table with such flouncing jauntiness that most of the men's heads turned to watch her.

'Well,' said Kane, 'you look like the cat that's found the cream.'

'Sweetheart, I have two pieces of gossip for you, not one.'

'Keep them for me, please, not the whole room.'

Suzy lowered her voice. ' "You know who" has warned the government that any attempt to break in and arrest

Lumumba will be met with force. But they call him "the drowning man".'

'You mean he's finished?'

'Your friend Steve Barlow doesn't think so. He thinks he'll stage a come-back.'

Kane pursed his lips, thinking. He had been avoiding direct contact with Steve, reserving the possibility for emergencies. Since Suzy worked in the same section of the UN staff it was hardly necessary. Anyway Steve had only been in the Congo a few weeks.

'And how is Steve?' he asked.

Suzy smiled secretively. 'That's my second little snippet. He's being sent to Katanga.'

'The devil he is. Complete with his ideals?'

'As far as I can tell,' remarked Suzy pointedly. 'They are rather more intact than yours.'

Despite the easy flight connection made in Brussels, and his being accustomed to constant travelling at his employers' behest, Kane was dog-tired when he reached IMEX's offices the next morning. His eyes felt inflamed, as though pepper had been thrown in them. His back bore the scratches of Suzy's enthusiasm. His joints ached. It was just not possible to pile a sleepless night in an airliner seat on top of a session with Suzy and feel ready to meet one's boss. When Skinner greeted him it was with an immediate question.

'You look pretty jaded. What have you been up to?'

Kane tried to laugh it off. 'Chasing information, that's all.'

'Well, sit down. Would you like a drink? It is midday.'

Gratefully Kane accepted a gin and tonic in a heavy cut-glass tumbler.

'Now,' Skinner went on, settling himself down. 'Is Lumumba finished or not?'

'The UN is still protecting him . . . .'

'Bob, Mr Dillon at Western has asked me to remind you

of your disbursements on that man and his entourage. The total is running pretty high. More than a hundred thousand dollars this year. Do we have to write it off?

'African politics are a very up and down affair, sir. We could still get the contract.'

'And suppose we don't?'

This was precisely what had kept Kane awake on the plane in spite of an excellent dinner and plenty to drink.

'There is one alternative,' he said. 'We could play for concessions in Katanga alone. If we assume Tshombe will be overthrown, then we could do a deal with the provisional government that replaces him.'

'That would not be a Congo-wide contract?'

'No, sir, it would not, it would be limited to Katanga.'

'And with whom would we be dealing there?' If there was interest in Skinner's voice, there was also a sense of resignation at starting the routine again.

'Tshombe's opponents,' said Kane, 'they're associated with Lumumba. I know some of them quite well.'

'You mean the rebels' leaders?'

'I mean anyone who can deliver up mining concessions.'

Skinner leant forward, elbows on the desk, interlacing his fingers, an attitude he sometimes adopted with senior employees when he wanted to be blunt yet relatively cordial. 'I met a diplomat the other day, who has been out where you are. He made a remark which stuck in my mind. It was "You cannot buy a Congolese Minister, you can only hire him for the afternoon." Is that true?'

Kane did not reply at once. If anyone knew he should. He remembered the endless waiting for meetings with Lumumba, the incessant paying out. Had all his efforts been wasted? 'It's a very clever witticism,' he said defensively. 'None the less a contract is a contract.'

'When you get it.' Skinner pulled at his chin. 'I suppose if you've spent one hundred thousand dollars encouraging local politicians, then you must have a few aces up your sleeve. You'd better get back there and start playing them.' He paused. 'We'll give you three months longer. If you do succeed with Lumumba, magnificent. If not, we want viable alternatives. Not on the same scale, I appreciate that. But alternatives.'

After Kane had left, Skinner rang Western Mining in New York and spoke to the Vice President. 'I've given Kane three months.'

'Who's his money on this time?' Dillon was becoming cynical about the whole business.

'Friends of Lumumba's who are Tshombe's opponents. By which he can only mean the political leaders of the rebellion in Katanga.'

'The hell he does!' Dillon's interest quickened. 'Would you get chapter and verse for me, James? That might just fit with the scheme we discussed.'

'It might well.'

When Skinner put the telephone down he poured himself another drink, then meditated for a while. He wasn't sure he approved of Western's methods of playing power politics. In fact they were plain immoral. On the other hand, as Sir John had pointed out to him in an unusually perspicacious analysis of the two companies' relationships, IMEX was used to observing international trends, while Western, like other giant American corporations, manipulated governments in order to create the trends it wanted.

'So,' said Duclair, 'we can combine this trip with a little Christmas shopping.'

The Belgian wing commander in a well-cut overcoat, only his suntan betraying that he might be a visitor to Paris and not a resident, was walking up the Champs Elysées with Mike Russell. It was early December and cold.

'I imagine you will want to buy something for the lovely Chantal?' suggested Duclair.

Mike replied non-committally, uncertain whether he was being mocked. 'Let's deal with the business first,' he said.

'As you wish. The office is not far away.'

Mike did not reply. He did not trust Duclair. When, as a result of his report to Tshombe, he had been told he would be sent as part of a purchasing team, he had imagined going to New York, or maybe California. If you wanted American aircraft, those were the obvious destinations. Nor had it occurred to him that the 'team' would consist merely of two men. Inevitably Duclair had set the pace from the start, urbanely announcing that there was no point in going to America, and possibly embarrassing the American government, when the whole affair could be settled in Paris. He had made it clear that, however competent a pilot Mike might be, when it came to arms procurement he was a novice.

'Ah, here we are,' Duclair announced as they neared the Arc de Triomphe end of the avenue. He dived off to the right into a narrow street, continued a few paces, glanced round briefly to check if they were being followed, then hurried up to the front door of an undistinguished building. The door had an iron grille. Beside it a small chromium plate announced the presence of a public relations agency. Duclair pressed the bell and with a buzz the door was released. They entered.

'Third floor,' Duclair observed, moving to the ancient lift. On the way up he held one finger to his lips. 'Remember, my friend, we represent a client. Simply "a client". They know who it is, of course. But the fewer names that are mentioned, the fewer the walls can hear. What was your English saying I recall from the War? "No names, no pack drill".'

Mike nodded.

The lift groaned and halted, swaying slightly. Duclair pulled back the gates and stepped on to the landing, where a sign read 'Pan American World Services'. He pushed open the door. Inside to the right a pretty receptionist looked up from a desk.

'M. Sturgess?' Duclair inquired.

'He is expecting you?'

'Certainly.'

She spoke on an intercom, then rose and escorted them to a further room. Two men faced them. One was a burly fifty-year-old with crewcut hair, a leathery complexion and a loud, red and white tie. Mike guessed this was Sturgess. The other, slimmer and altogether more dapper, as well as younger, introduced himself as Jean Dessenon.

'He's the legal eagle,' explained Sturgess. 'I guess we ought to get the wording right first shot, huh? Sit down, gentlemen, please.'

Mike and Duclair took places on a sofa, the receptionist brought in coffee on a tray, and then Dessenon came forward and handed each of them a manila folder.

'The contract will be in French,' he explained, 'but there is a translation.'

'You already have a contract prepared?' asked Mike, surprised.

'PANWORLD does specialize in technical assistance.' Duclair cut in. 'Within certain parameters many clients requirements are similar.'

'As you say,' remarked Sturgess, 'we know our business. 'Now,' he went on more brusquely, 'if you gentlemen could go just glance through our suggestions. Basics first. Your client requires two things as I see it: aircraft and crew. Paragraph one specifies that you are engaging our assistance in this regard and that we will set up a training school for pilots and mechanics.'

Mike read the document. 'The school,' it said, 'would give the client the ability to operate the aerial transport necessary for the good development of his enterprise.' It was obviously an English translation of a French original.

'Very nicely phrased,' Duclair commented. 'And the transports are?'

'Nine to twelve DC4s and DC3s, plus crews, spares and maintenance personnel. The airplanes become yours once you have their licences.'

'Hmm.' Duclair considered this. 'I'd prefer you to obtain those.'

'If you insist,' Sturgess turned to Dessenon. 'Write that in, will you, Jean?'

'When do we get the aircraft?' Mike asked. He was beginning to feel more and more extraneous to this negotiation. Duclair must have worked most of it out beforehand.

'One month from signature,' said Sturgess. 'Tell you what, though. I'll promise one DC3 and three DC4s within fifteen days. How about that?'

Mike laughed incredulously. For months he had been improvising supply drops with a Cessna while Tshombe's sole DC3 lumbered around the sky on presidential missions, and here was this American offering four aircraft in a fortnight. 'Are you serious?' he asked.

'No less so than the money your client's paying,' said Sturgess abruptly. 'If he wants it and he can pay, sure we can provide.'

'And a lot of airlines are re-equipping with faster aircraft just now.' Duclair smiled sardonically. 'What interests me more are the T6s.' He looked at Mike. 'Aren't those your favourite for support missions?'

'They're solid aircraft.' Mike thought of the Harvard he'd learnt to fly on, its stubby fuselage with the big radial engine up front, the glasshouse canopy for the two seats in tandem, the machine-guns you could fit in the wings and the small bomb-load. 'The RAF found them useful in both Malaya and Kenya.'

'They're in paragraph four,' said Sturgess. 'Six within fifteen days, OK?'

Mike consulted the document and almost laughed again. This was crazy. 'Six single-engine T6', it stated, 'would be for mineral research and aerial photography and would become the property of the client.' He was beginning to appreciate the subtleties of this contract, or '*Protocole d'Accord*' as it was headed. 'Tell me one thing,' he asked, 'how will delivery be made?'

'I guess we have a solution to that problem,' said Sturgess. 'The Douglas transports we can fly in. These birds not. As they're for mineral research, it might just be appropriate if we shipped them as mining equipment.' He chuckled. 'We have a few ideas about that. One snag is, our fifteen-day delivery will be to the ship, not to you. Could be a while before you get them.'

'And the jets our client wants?'

For the first time Duclair appeared flustered. 'We have not requested those,' he said, looking hard at Mike and hastily reverting to questions on the contract.

The remaining paragraphs covered terms of service for the mercenaries PANWORLD would provide. The client could sack an 'employee' without reason and he would be replaced within fifteen days. Employees were entitled to a month's leave in France every six months. Finally, they came to the finance.

'We'll need one million dollars paid into our Swiss bank account within three days of signature,' Sturgess explained. 'That's under paragraph thirteen. Your lucky number! If our own backers weren't sympathetic we'd be asking for a considerably larger down payment.'

'We are delighted at sympathy for our cause,' Duclair said warily. 'None the less, I should have thought a million dollars more than adequate for the T6s and the transports.'

'Sure.' Sturgess was unabashed. 'If we had unlimited time and you required no back-up. Technical assistance costs money. Assistance in a hurry costs more. No, believe me, but for our connections the tab could be one whole lot larger.'

Duclair forbore to inquire about PANWORLD's business links. Instead he turned to Mike. 'Any queries from your side?'

'How about the stores? Ammunition, bombs?'

'Don't worry, my friend.' Duclair was at his most patronizing. 'Those will arrive through the normal channels.' He stood up. 'Thank you,' he said to Sturgess. 'I shall telephone my client tonight as to the terms and if he agrees we shall sign tomorrow. *Au revoir*.'

The Frenchman bowed them out, the receptionist all smiles. Once they were in the lift Duclair remarked airily. 'Really, they had an excellent understanding of our needs. 'He frowned at Mike. 'It was a little tactless of you to mention the jets.'

'Tshombe always told me he wanted them.'

'And they are already ordered. Three Fougas will reach us in February. We hardly need to acquire French aircraft from an American. We shall merely confuse the issue a little by hiring an American charter company to bring them in.'

The lift shuddered and stopped. As he stepped out Duclair added, with a toughness usually absent from his speech, 'I told you being an adviser was competitive. If you don't understand things, keep silent. Now let us make our way to the Rue Faubourg St Honoré and find an appropriate present for your girlfriend.'

'What exactly do you mean?' Mike's temper was rising. Not only had his presence here been unnecessary, there was an innuendo in Duclair's remark which he disliked. 'Why "appropriate"?'

They were in the street now.

'Keep walking,' said Duclar shortly, 'and I'll tell you. It's time you graduated from the nursery. You are an excellent pilot. You have proved yourself. But kindly forget about running our air force for us. Your lovely Chantal imagines things which are most unlikely to happen. Because she has the ear of the President you had to be brought on this trip. We all like and respect her, so we have not objected too much. But you are out of your depth and it's time you acknowledged the fact.'

'Go on.' Mike's voice was taut.

'President Tshombe has several hundred professional military, economic and political advisers from Belgium. You know why?' Duclair did not wait for an answer. 'Very few of us are in Katanga because we share your love of Africa. We are there because the Union Minière has an enormous investment which we intend to safeguard. And fight for.'

As he said this they reached a corner and Duclair paused a moment. 'We turn right,' he said. 'There is a good jeweller a few metres down. As I was saying, we intend to protect Katanga. At a pinch we can leave some of the fighting to amateurs, though that will change. But the overall planning remains in our hands. Is that clear?' Duclair stopped. 'This is the shop,' he announced matter-of-factly.

Mike stood, trembling with anger, looking at the window, seeing nothing. He felt like hitting this bloody Belgian with his unbreakable self-assurance. He felt cheated and sick that they regarded him as a toy of Chantal's. He took a deep breath and turned to Duclair.

'All right. I'll quit, if that's what you want.' His anger began to be released. 'You knew why I went to Katanga. Because I thought I was needed to help create an air force. You may not give a damn what happens to Africa, but I do. I live there. Or can't you understand that?'

'Perfectly well, I am not asking for a resignation.' Again Duclair's voice was unyielding. 'I am not asking anything. I am telling you to keep out of the policy making. No more. Now,' he pointed to a bracelet in the window, 'would she like that? Or a ring? Don't worry about the price. We've just spent a million dollars. A few hundred more is neither here nor there. We have adequate expenses.'

'Go to hell,' said Mike, choking. 'If I buy her a present, I'll pay for it myself.'

Duclair smiled and shook his head sadly. 'My friend, you are obstinate. Accept the advice of an older man. Take opportunities when they are offered. What is the difference between utilizing my expenses or your salary? Both come from the Union Minière.' He took Mike's arm and led him inside.

In the PANWORLD office Sturgess asked for a transatlantic call. When he was put through he aid succinctly. 'The deal's on, no question. Assuming you want it. Your initial contribution will be half a million bucks, OK? It'll be the best investment you made in years.'

In New York the Vice President of Western Mining replaced the telephone and buzzed the President on the intercom. 'May I come along, sir?'

'Well, Bill,' said the company President as Dillon entered. 'What's new?'

'I reckon I have the Katanga programme consolidated, sir.'

'Sit down and tell me.'

'If we fail with the Lumumba contract then in the short term your idea of keeping Katangan copper off the market is in Western's best interest. The simplest way to do that is by promoting civil war. Fortunately fighting comes cheap in Africa.'

Christmas 1960 had a curious air of unreality. This was the season when mist enveloped the town in the early mornings and the airfield sentries were dark ghosts, shivering in blue mackintosh cloaks, until the rapidly ascending sun burnt off the dew and the days became dry and hot, punctuated by occasional tropical downpours. Mauve flowering jacaranda trees were in bloom along the streets and the rains had made the gardens a blaze of colour. Barlow, nurtured on Conrad's novel about the jungle of the 'inner station', his only experience of Africa being his recent stay in the sticky humidity of

Leopoldville, was amazed at the Californian climate of Elisabethville and the sophistication of the city, Belgian even down to the colonial street names that were still in both French and Flemish. Surely there were enough racial divisions in Africa without superimposing the petty enmities of Walloon and Flemish on them! At least, he conceded to himself, Tshombe used only French.

Tshombe's broadly smiling face was everywhere, his presidential portrait prominent in all the bars and shops and hotels. Both Europeans and Africans prepared to celebrate the holiday in the apparent conviction that independent Katanga was a success, even though diplomatically unrecognized. The UN was being outwitted. The arch-fiend Lumumba was securely in jail 100 miles away, put there by Kasavabu after he had escaped from house arrest. If the rest of the Congo was in chaos, here at least there was peace. The shops were well stocked. Many of the Belgians who had fled in July were back.

The manager of the Hotel Leopold Deux shrewdly caught the mood by announcing a special dinner celebrating Tshombe's first Christmas as President, while everywhere in the city banners and flags proclaimed the same idea. One of the posters showed an African boy scout, or maybe it was a paratrooper, Mike Russell never did discover which, sitting under a palm tree in front of a camp fire. The man – or boy – was grinning broadly and looking out of the corner of his eye at a distant civilian squatting, hands extended, before another fire. Above them a star shot through the heavens, leaving a fiery trail, accompanied by the caption, '*Premier Noël du Gouvernment Katangais avec son President Tshombe*'. A more comprehensible placard showed a hand holding out the brightly coloured new banknotes. '*Monnaie Katangaise, monnaie plus forte!*' it screamed. Mike made a mental note to avoid being paid in Katanga francs.

Against this background the UN soldiers, Swedes, Moroccans and Ethiopians, lounged around the city, guarded their offices and the airport, and spent their hefty allowances in the well-filled shops, always in uniform, their blue berets prominent. At the same time the mercenaries came into town on leave, stayed at the unobtrusive Hotel Katanga, and rubbed shoulders as civilians with the UN at the bar in the Leo Deux as they unloaded their danger money on wine and whisky. They were getting double pay for time spent in action now, and they were insured for 1 million Belgian francs each. It was hardly surprising that they swaggered and drank too much.

Among those who came in was Herman the German. On the day before Christmas he turned up at the villa which Mike shared with the two DC3 pilots away from the centre of town, begging a bed because the hotels were full, and demoralized because with only two days off he could not get back to his beloved smallholding in Rhodesia. Mike agreed to have a drink with him in the early evening, unwisely because later on he had to be at his best: Chantal's parents had invited him for the big family occasion of Christmas Eve dinner. Their formal invitation card stood among the spent shell cases and other souvenirs which decorated the villa's living room mantelpiece. He was bidden for 9.00 p.m., late enough for them to see in Christmas Day and exchange presents. The rituals of Europe were the more precious here, out of reach of relatives and normal festivities.

'Man,' Herman said sententiously as they sat at the bar in the Leo Deux, 'it is good to have a proper friend. I have to tell you, Mike, some of these men I am with are from the gutter, no better. I would not have them on my farm, I can tell you that.'

The remark jolted Mike's memory. 'What happened to the village by the bridge?' he demanded.

'You saw that? The major ordered it. We destroy any village sheltering rebels. It is the policy.'

'Do you have to shoot women?'

Herman shook his head, his face reddening. He would not have taken this questioning from anyone else. 'When you let them loose these gendarmes deserve to be called the terrible ones.'

Mike thought of the Mau Mau in Kenya, where the number of their fellow Africans the gangs had murdered had hugely exceeded the white victims. Africa had its own rules.

'You are lucky,' Herman went on. 'As a pilot you are out of that. Tell me, is old Tshombe scared when you fly him?'

'I haven't flown him yet.' Herman had touched an exposed nerve. 'All I've done is ferry supplies and drop a few home-made bombs. Bundles of hand grenades tied together with a fuse! Hell, it's pathetic.'

Herman considered this idea for a full minute. 'It is not what I thought a war would be,' he agreed, 'though those Baluba frighten me, they frighten me a lot, I don't mind who knows it.' He glanced round at the mixed crowd of Belgian officials and businessmen. 'Let's go somewhere more interesting. This is Christmas Eve, man!'

With rapidity they sampled a couple of other bars. But Herman's melancholy increased with every bottle of the local Simba beer he consumed. By eight, as it grew dark, they had descended to a small establishment called the Ruwenzori, away from the main streets. As far as Mike was concerned it had only one merit: it was near his villa. He was keeping a wary eye on the time and wishing he didn't have to match Herman's seemingly inexhaustible capacity for drink. The Ruwenzori bar was not respectable. The barman had a roughly furnished bedroom off the back yard, which he rented out as need arose. A trio of African prostitutes occupied a table in the corner and began making eyes at the two men from the movement they entered, adding provocative remarks as their lack of interest became apparent.

'If things were right I would be home now,' Herman

was saying, 'giving drinks to my friends.' He shook his head sadly. 'Last year I had no money. This year, when I have saved hundreds of pounds already, and could give my friends the best whisky, I am not there.' He sounded close to tears, his elbows on the table, his broad shoulders hunched. 'And where would you be today?'

Mike remembered last Christmas up-country on the farm. The goose his mother had bought some days before, and religiously hung, had gone bad in the heat. She only realized it on Christmas morning and was distraught until he and his father went down by the river and shot two duck. Although they hadn't eaten lunch until teatime, it had been a memorably happy day. He wondered what his parents were having this time, and with whom. Herman's mood was beginning to affect him.

'I'd be at home on the farm,' he replied. 'I wish to God I were back in Kenya now.'

As he spoke two Swedish soldiers entered, both solidly drunk, both in uniform. The taller one stopped to look at Mike inquisitively, swayed across to the bar counter, ordered whisky, then moved across again towards the table next to Mike and Herman. His companion had sat down and was ogling the girls opposite, who began to giggle. But instead of sitting down too, the tall one stood glaring down at Mike.

'Do you say "Kenya"?' he demanded in a heavy accent. 'Are you a colonialist?' He held up one finger and waved it in front of Mike, like a schoolmaster. 'We are here to fight the colonialists!'

Mike stayed still. There was no point in answering. He had learnt in the past weeks that when the Swedes hit the bottle they did so with a determination that took them beyond reason. Apparently alcohol was rationed in Sweden and when abroad they made up for years of lost opportunity. The soldier continued to glower at him.

'Take it easy and sit down,' he said at last.

The Swede wavered, uncertain what to do next, and

looked towards the girls.

'Call themselves mercenaries,' shouted one of the girls, with an instinct for creating trouble. 'They're not even men!'

The only word the Swede understood of her French was *'mercenaires'*. It was enough. He stepped back and fumbled for the gun in a holster on his belt.

Everyone in the bar froze. The bartender stopped in the act of pouring a drink. The girls sat open mouthed. Mike prepared to launch himself forward in a rugby tackle. But Herman was faster. In one movement he straightened up and threw his beer in the Swede's face, with another he picked up his chair, whirled it round above his head almost hitting Mike, and crashed it on the Swede's skull. As the Swede crumpled to the floor the prostitutes began screaming and the bartender ran for the telephone. Herman disregarded them all. He dropped the broken chair back, turned to the other Swede, reached across and lifted him by his collar with one hand. Then he smashed his fist into the side of the man's head. When he let go the soldier sank unconscious on the table, blood trickling from his ear.

'Dirt,' said Herman contemptously, 'the kind who go with black women.'

'Let's get out of here,' Mike said. He could see the barman speaking into the phone and guessed he was calling the police, though the girls' screams obliterated all other sound.

Reluctantly Herman followed. He was suddenly happy again. As Mike accelerated the jeep away, he said contentedly, 'Man, that was better than shooting Baluba. They are betraying the European, those bastards. They should go home.'

'Perhaps we all should,' said Mike, his feelings crystallizing. 'There's no sense in this town.' As he swung into the villa's driveway and stopped, he felt something wet on his cheek, put up a finger to touch it and saw a smear of blood in the light from the verandah. The tip of the chair leg must have scraped him as Herman swung it round. Oh, Christ, he thought, let's hope it doesn't swell. Who would believe he had been an innocent party in a bar brawl prompted by an African tart? Certainly not Chantal's mother! He reversed the jeep round behind the villa, where it would be less conspicuous, warned Herman not to go out again as the police would be sure to be after him, and rushed indoors to clean up. Chantal had warned him to be on time. 'My parents may be a little bourgeois,' she had explained, 'but it's a good fault.' After shaving, sticking a plaster on the cut, and putting on the only suit he had brought with him, he borrowed one of the other pilot's cars and drove cautiously to the Berthouds'. He was only fifteen minutes late.

Chantal greeted him with the same undemonstrative reserve she always displayed, particularly in public. 'How are you? Happy Christmas!' Only her eyes told him anything more. She kissed him lightly on the cheek, then exclaimed, 'Oh, my, what have you been doing to yourself?'

'Nothing. I tripped up.' Mike was aware of Mme Berthoud waiting. He hastily turned to her, wished her the compliments of the season and handed over an elaborately wrapped box of chocolates. She made a show of thanking him, telling her husband she would get disgracefully fat, and guided the family party to the sitting room, pausing to ring a tiny brass bell for the servant. The African must have been waiting behind the kitchen door, his appearance with the champagne glasses was so prompt. Immediately M. Berthoud sprang into a conventional routine with the napkin-swathed bottle in its chromium ice-bucket. Mike felt he was watching a carefully rehearsed play, in which as a member of the audience he had been asked to participate without warning. He watched Mme Berthoud holding her long-stemmed champagne glass delicately between thumb and forefinger, sipping genteelly, and tried to respond to remarks which were largely rhetorical.

'Of course at home we should have Christmas lunch with all our relatives; naturally the family centres on us. Here, with the daytime heat, a proper meal is more acceptable in the evening. The turkey has come specially from South Africa. Christmas would not be the same without one, don't you agree? And of course the evening being cool we can enjoy a fire.' She gracefully indicated the logs burning in the big stone fireplace. 'Yes, in the evenings one can imagine one is back in the old country.'

Mike sat like an amateur actor who had forgotten his lines, bemused partly by the after-effects of the brawl, but more by the further dimension this occasion gave to the unreality of Elisabethville. Up-country the mercenaries were holding off the rebels, who despite Lumumba's now being in jail, having escaped from house arrest and been recaptured were still aided by his supporters. Thousands of UN troops stood idle, spoiling for a fight. A single spark could set the whole place alight. A single battle would reduce the Berthouds to the same panic he had seen when he rescued their cousins in July. Yet here they were playing a charade of civilized living. It was a relief when the meal was announced by the indispensable white-coated servant.

After the five-course dinner came coffee, brandy and liqueurs, M. Berthoud again presiding. Then it was time for the presents.

'I do hope you like yours,' murmured Mme Berthoud. 'It's hard to know what to give a soldier of fortune.'

Mike opened the package. It contained a diary.

'Really, Mama, that isn't very original.' For the first time in the evening Chantal came to his defence. He managed a smile, and then ferreted in his pocket for the gift he had brought her.

In spite of his irritation at Mme Berthoud's airs, he watched Chantal unwrap the gilded paper with pleasure, and was delighted at the excitment in her face as she saw the famous jeweller's name on the box inside.

'Oh, Mike,' she exclaimed as she revealed the bracelet. 'I don't deserve such a beautiful thing.' She took it out gently, slipped it over the hand and admired it, twisting her wrist this way and that, so that it caught the light.

'Isn't it lovely, Maman? From Cartier, too.'

'The customs must have had fun with you over that, Captain,' observed M. Berthoud, in one of his rare jokes.

'Luckily not,' said Mike. 'I was with Duclair.'

He regretted mentioning the Belgian, in the instant of naming him. Mme Berthoud reacted like one of Pavlov's dogs.

'Ah!' Her expression softened. 'Now there is a man of distinction. If only Tshombe had more advisers like him.'

Mike remembered Duclair's sly deal with the customs officer at the airport, surreptitiously passing across brandy and cigarettes, in return for which his two heavy suitcases were not examined. In the car afterwards he had made no secret of their contents. 'For the Christmas trade, my friend,' he had said. 'One should never lose opportunities.'

'We all so admire the wing commander,' gushed Mme Berthoud. 'I am sure he guided your choice.'

Mike's mouth went dry with anger. He saw Chantal's embarrassment but her reaction came too late. His self-control broke.

'Yes, he did guide me,' he blazed at Mme Berthoud. 'He told me precisely where I stood. He told me to keep my nose out of Belgium's business. He told me to forget about forging an air force for Tshombe. He made it bloody clear that I was just one ordinary pilot out of thousands and the only reason I was with him in Paris was that Chantal had influence over Tshombe.' He turned on Chantal, 'If he'd said I was your pet poodle, he couldn't have made things plainer. What did you bring me here for?'

Chantal flushed. 'I told you things had altered, I told you when you arrived. I said you could go back to Kenya if you wanted.'

'I came here with a mission, or at least a sense of one. I'd seen what happened in other parts of the Congo. I wanted to help. I didn't come to defend the Union Minière's private empire and save men like Duclair the trouble of fighting themselves.'

'Please,' M. Berthoud interrupted awkwardly, 'it is Christmas, the time for goodwill, not for quarrels.'

'I'm sorry.' Involuntarily Mike clenched his fists. He stood up. 'I must go anyway. I'm flying tomorrow. The Baluba don't observe Christmas. Thank you, Mme Berthoud.' He couldn't bring himself to say more so he walked towards the hall, Chantal following.

Outside they faced each other. She held out the bracelet, its gold glistening dully. 'I don't think I can accept this,' she said, her voice breaking.

The night air was chill, making him realize he was slightly drunk. He shook his head. 'You keep it. I bought it for you.' He tried a joke. 'Wearing it myself wouldn't do my reputation any good with the others. Good night.' He stepped back and hurried to the car.

Chantal watched him for a moment, then went inside and walked slowly upstairs to her room, where she burst into tears. When her father came up later he found her sitting on the bed, screwing up her handkerchief in her hands, dry-eyed again.

'I'm afraid your mother doesn't like those mercenaries,' he said apologetically. 'Don't take it to heart. Please.'

She looked at him. 'Mike's right,' she said. 'That's the trouble.' She scrumpled the handkerchief into a ball and threw it in the corner. 'What's more, I'm going to do something about it.'

5

Every New Year Chantal's godparent, Father Paul, left his small Mission station in the care of two brother priests and came to Elisabethville. His first call was always on the Archbishop but before that he went to pray in the cathedral, a monumental stone edifice with a campanile reminiscent of an Italian church. The cathedral was deserted, quiet and cool. Father Paul knelt, his white cassock creasing beneath his weight. He prayed for the African children he taught and for their deliverance from war. 'Oh God, our refuge and our strength . . . .' Then he devoted ten minutes to saying his rosary, the five decades of Hail Marys and the doxology, his lips moving soundlessly on the Latin words. After a few further moments of meditation he rose, attached the string of rosary beads with their silver crucifix to his belt, left the dimness of the cathedral for the blinding sunlight outside and strode round to make his official call, an instantly recognizable figure.

Though only of medium height, the priest walked with the erect, resilient bearing of a former soldier. His hair was close cropped, his face and neck tanned from labour in the Mission garden. But his regular features were saved from ordinariness by keen blue eyes, accustomed to sizing up both men and situations. As a girl Chantal used to picture him in the Crusades, leading the assault on Acre.

It was an understandable misconception. Father Paul was a strong character, but no fanatic. He asked questions of his God.

The White Fathers were one of many missionary groups in the Congo, both Catholic and Protestant, who provided education for the entire indigenous population. The Belgian colonial administration had developed no state system. What was different about the White Fathers was that unlike the Jesuits with their vows of poverty, or the Benedictines, they took no solemn vows. Founded in Algiers by the redoubtable Cardinal La Vigerie, as the Society of Missionaries of Africa, they were secular priests bound by one oath only: to spend their whole lives in the service of that continent. Over their white cassock they wore as a cloak the rough-woven, all-enveloping, hooded *burnous* of the Saharan Arabs.

Even among such men Father Paul was unusual. Escaping the Nazis when Belgium fell in 1940 and he was a lieutenant, he had joined the British commandos, fought alongside Tito's partisans in Yugoslavia and finished the war a major. He was a natural choice for the Belgian Para-Commando Regiment founded thereafter and the tough, green-beret-wearing para-commandos were, in turn, a natural choice for garrison service in the Congo. Two years here changed his life. He became aware that the existing pattern of Belgian paternalism was no way to build a nation from the disparate tribes in the Congo, resigned his commission and embarked on the arduous process of becoming a missionary priest. The White Fathers' Belgian branch would allow a man, after four years of theological study, to do a course in tropical diseases in place of the final spiritual year of the novitiate. This appealed to him. He was a very practical man.

As Father Paul entered the simply furnished office the Archbishop acknowledged his salutation and rapidly came to the point.

'How are things at Kiobo?' he asked. 'We have been

concerned for your safety there.'

For half an hour Father Paul told him about the extension he was building to the Mission school and other parochial details. As to security, they had the radio transmitter, and if they were attacked, well, since they were unarmed they would have to talk to the rebels. 'As the British used to say, "give them tea and sympathy".' The phrase had stuck in his mind.

'Sympathy?' The Archbishop felt obliged to question this.

'In my short experience, Your Grace, the African who rages at you will be thanking you an hour later. Often all they ask is for their dignity to be respected.'

'I pray it may continue so. My thoughts go with you.'

'Thank you, Your Grace.'

'I have taken a mild liberty. Your goddaughter Chantal Berthoud is anxious to see you alone. I suggested she come here and wait.' The Archbishop extended his hand. The interview was over.

Father Paul withdrew, wondering what new problem Chantal had. Strictly speaking she was not his goddaughter at all, but that of an old regimental friend who had been in Europe at the time of her confirmation and had asked the then Major Paul to attend the service on his behalf. It had been the start of a relationship made the more dear to him when he became a priest and renounced the possibility of having children himself.

When he came out, Chantal kissed him on each cheek in turn with unaffected emotion. 'Father, would you mind if we went for a walk somewhere? I didn't want to meet at my parents' house.'

'By all means. I have to visit a patient in the hospital. Suppose we go to the little park next to it?'

They set off, Father Paul slowing down from his normal brisk gait, while Chantal told him what was on her mind.

'So you see,' she concluded, as they reached the park,

'my parents don't approve of him. He is not a Catholic. I don't know if he is serious. These English are so casual, they have a terrible reputation, and anyway one can easily become too emotional in this situation. There's a sort of madness here.'

'There is,' Father Paul agreed. He fell silent. He had long wondered when Chantal would marry. Now he was both pleased that she was consulting him and worried by her evident uncertainty. The religious question was, to his mind, not an insuperable obstacle. He said so, then went on.

'Beyond that, I think you are talking about two problems, my dear.' He did not address either the younger generation of Africans as 'my child', although it was common for priests to do so. 'You do not know if you are in love and you do not know if what you have brought this man here to do is right.' He shook his head sadly. 'The troops whom some of these mercenaries lead are not called *"Les Affreux"* without reason. They are burning villages and raping women.' His tone hardened. 'They should be court-martialled and shot.' He looked at her. 'Harsh words for a priest, but true.'

'I promise you he is not like that, Father. Truly not.'

'Then you are talking about a cause. Correct? You work for Tshombe yourself, do you believe in this independent Katanga?'

Chantal stopped and motioned to a bench nearby. 'Let's sit down,' she said, pausing to search for the answer. She saw her godfather too seldom to treat his advice lightly. 'I do believe in racial co-operation. I believe passionately in saving Katanga from the chaos the rest of the Congo is in. I'm not so sure of the way we are going about it. Or of most Belgians' motives.'

Father Paul's penetrating blue eyes were fixed on her face.

'That answers one question. You cannot blame this pilot of yours for being angry with you. Indeed, I should say he has reason. He came here to fight for that cause.' He smiled gently. 'As to the other question, only you can tell if you are in love with him or not. As you rightly say, there is a kind of hysteria about this place. I noticed it immediately I arrived this time, things are too aggressively normal, too tense. There is a smell I recognize of old: the smell of war.'

'Should I wait until it's over? Not see him for a while?' Chantal held out her hand and took his briefly. 'Father, I could so easily be in love with him. I am just frightened to let myself be.'

Father Paul thought of all those precipitate wartime marriages, then dismissed them. Love affairs were sudden by nature. Could he as a celibate really help an attractive, elegant, normally self-possessed woman half his own age?

'If you are in love,' he said at last, 'you must know it. In that case get engaged. Take no notice of your parents, none at all. If you are not sure, then perhaps you should absent yourself from his life for a time. The flying will probably take him away in any case.' He shrugged his shoulders. 'There are some answers you can only look for in your own heart.' He shifted on the bench. 'Shall we go? I should respect the hospital visiting hours even if my cloth does give me dispensations.'

Chantal said goodbye to him outside the long, white hospital building, her eyes damp but her mind made up. She would calm down, see less of Mike, and meanwhile do her utmost to defeat Duclair's intrigue against him. That afternoon her opportunity came when Tshombe called her in. He often sought her advice on minor matters. She reminded him about Mike and for a change, instead of wavering over a decision, he responded dramatically, telephoning Duclair and ordering him to transfer Mike to the organization of the T6 operations as soon as the planes arrived. Chantal returned home that evening if not completely happy, at least feeling more in control of her emotions. She had done her best for the moment. Longer term questions would have to wait.

'May I come in?'

The office door was already ajar. The Swedish colonel pushed it open and entered, blinking in the strong sunlight. Steve Barlow's room in the apartment building which the UN occupied as offices in Elisabethville had no blinds, nor did the door have a name card, merely a printed placard stating, 'Civilian Affairs'.

'What can I do for you, Colonel?' Barlow had spent so much of his three months in the Congo dealing with military colleagues that he had adopted what he thought of as a direct and decisive way of addressing them.

The Swede pulled up a chair and sat down, his expression grim. 'The soldier attacked in the bar died this morning,' he announced.

'Three weeks after the incident?' Barlow knew all about the case, none the less he was caught unawares. It was now 17 January. He had imagined both men had recovered.

'The doctors knew his skull was fractured. Suddenly he had a haemorrhage.' The colonel looked hard at Barlow. 'This is murder. We must insist that Katangan authorities arrest the mercenary responsible.'

Barlow pressed a buzzer and, when his secretary Margaret appeared, he asked her to bring in the file. Not that it was necessary. He could recall the facts. Both versions of them. However, he waited until she returned, then flipped through the papers.

'All the witnesses,' he remarked carefully, 'have made statements to the effect that your soldier was trying to pull a gun. They also say he was drunk.'

'He was trying to extract a handkerchief from his trouser pocket.' The colonel's face was expressionless.

'May I ask if you believe that?' Barlow's manner became perceptibly more akin to an attorney's.

The colonel hesitated. 'No,' he admitted unwillingly.

'But you know the political problem. Our men are volunteers from civilian life, trained during former military service I agree, but now with jobs, girlfriends or wives, families even. In Sweden we regard them as ambassadors of peace. Our people do not like to think of them as drunkards.' The colonel made an abrupt gesture, matching a tougher line in his argument. 'This man's photo will be in our newspapers, there will be an outcry in our parliament. The mercenary responsible must be found.'

'He was only assumed to be a mercenary.' Again Barlow made a show of consulting the file. 'By three African ladies of pleasure.'

'The profession of the witnesses is immaterial,' said the colonel angrily.

For a moment Barlow thought of remarking that technically the Swedes themselves were mercenaries, since they were being paid to quit civil occupations and fight in a country not their own. He thought better of the idea, even though he felt scant sympathy for either side in a bar-room brawl.

'I'm afraid it may be counter-productive to make an issue of this affair,' he said with deliberate pomposity. 'The Secretary General's desire is for conciliation, not confrontation.'

'Is that all you have to say?'

'I will make a formal protest to the Katangan authorities.'

The colonel stood up angrily. 'I shall take this to a higher level,' he said and left the office without the courtesy of a salute.

Barlow remained sitting, reflecting on how internal feuds like this occupied so much of the UN's time, debating whether the colonel's denunciations could harm him. Then he walked across to the window and stared out for a few minutes. The broad avenue below was thronged with Africans, women in print dresses, men in colourful shirts. A group of Europeans strolled past, sun-tanned, muscular. Mining men or mercenaries? How could one tell when they were out of context, out of uniform? Above all, how the hell did one persuade the charming, evasive, impossible Tshombe to dismiss his European advisers and come to terms with the central government? Hammarskjold's words at the briefing meeting in Leopoldville two weeks ago echoed in Barlow's ears. 'You must refrain from unnecessary interference.' Was it possible?

The phone rang. Wearily he returned to his desk and was surprised by a familiar voice on the line.

'Bob Kane here. I heard you were around. I am staying at the Leo Deux. Would you care for a drink?'

'I am pretty busy.' Barlow hesitated. 'Hell, why not? But it will have to be late. We work long hours here.'

'Then join me for dinner.'

Barlow accepted and returned to his paper work. At nine he met Kane at the Leo Deux bar, noticing at once that his former squadron leader looked tired. They both ordered whisky, expensive though it was.

'Well,' Kane said with forced joviality. 'How's business?'

'I might ask the same of you.' The constant intrigues of Congo politics had made Barlow even more wary than he used to be. 'Are you still hoping for that contract with Lumumba?'

'You tell me!' Kane shrugged his shoulders in a vain attempt to laugh off his anxiety. From his point of view things were almost as bad as they could be. On 27 November Lumumba had escaped from his villa in a bid to join his supporters half a continent away in the north eastern city of Stanleyville. Four days later he had been caught by the Congolese army, taken back to Leopoldville and imprisoned to await trial. Despite pleas by the UN he had remained incarcerated since.

'Will they release him? If they do, he'll have the

country behind him.'

'In front might be a more accurate description.' Barlow said sardonically, wondering how far Kane's remark was wishful thinking. 'His supporters invaded north Katanga last week from Stanleyville. They have a hundred Russian trucks and they've captured a mining company fuel depot at Manono. We're trying to make the area a neutral zone.'

'You mean the UN will stop the invasion? I thought you wanted Tshombe defeated?' Kane was amazed.

'Wrong, Bob. We want him at the conference table. We protected Lumumba until he was fool enough to escape. We would do exactly the same for Tshombe. The name of our game right now is conciliation and the prevention of civil war.' Barlow sighed. 'It's a damned hard game to play too.'

During dinner it became evident to Barlow that Kane had a great deal at stake on the Lumumba contract. It was small wonder that he had black shadows beneath his eyes. For the first time since the crash at Frampton he felt sorry for Kane. 'Look,' he said at last, 'we tread a pretty tricky tightrope here. We have to be seen to be impartial. But if I can help in any small way, just say so.'

They had reached the coffee stage when a waiter approached the table and summoned Barlow to the telephone. On his return his face was white.

'What's up?'

'Very serious news.' Barlow was obviously shaken. He sat down, then said quietly, 'This is strictly off the record, OK? The Swedish guard at the airport had seen an aircraft from Leopoldville being unloaded. It brought in three prisoners. They were so badly beaten up, they could hardly walk. All three were Africans and one had a small beard.'

'Lumumba!'

'It could be. If it is, then he's as good as dead. God knows why the central government should have sent him here.' Barlow's perplexity showed itself in his worried expression. 'Maybe to have him killed. The Katangans won't hesitate to revenge themselves on him. I find these people incomprehensible, Bob, one minute the men in Leopoldville treat Tshombe as an enemy, the next they're asking him for collaboration. I guess they're all about equally frightened of Lumumba.' He drank down his coffee, then blew his nose as if trying to clear his head. 'I'm sorry' he said, rising to his feet, 'I have to go find out what's happening. And I thought I had problems earlier today!'

Kane ceased to listen. He had seen this disaster coming, in some form or other, for many weeks. Even so he felt pole-axed. Two years' work and 2 million pounds' commission lost, the chance of a lifetime gone, the chance of 10,000 lifetimes. 'I think I'll have a brandy,' he said. But he spoke to himself. Barlow had gone.

The night which followed was a sleepless one for Kane. In James Skinner's phrase he needed 'a viable alternative' and he needed it soon.

The next day he went for a quiet lunch to the house of one of the Union Minière geologists, a man now close to retirement who had written a dry but technically perfect treatise on the rock structures of the Northern Rhodesian and Katangan copper belts. Kane had mentioned this little book by way of an introduction, had played on its author's vanity and was now reaping his benefits in the form of information.

'Fascinating!' he exclaimed as the old man recounted some of his discoveries. 'From what you say there must be many resources still unexploited.'

'There are, believe me.' He wagged a finger at Kane. 'Take just two places, Tenke Fungurume and Kiobo. The pioneers knew all about Tenke before the turn of the century. The hills there are almost solid malachite in places. But the company have never developed it.'

'Why on earth not?'

'Problems over the treatment of refractory ores. Not insoluble, my friend, in fact we are beginning to evolve a new technique. Soon there will be no excuse for leaving Tenke undeveloped. Nor for neglecting Kiobo.' He glared at Kane through thick glasses. This was a subject he felt deeply about. 'Kiobo has immense possibilities.'

'Where is it?' Kane did not need to feign interest. These were the mineral reserves which company reports never mentioned, the kind successful speculation could be founded on.

'A little further north, near the Lualaba river. I was responsible for planning the whole prospecting programme. In fact I discovered the site.' The geologist sighed regretfully. 'You could take a million tons of copper ore a year from Kiobo for fifty years and I doubt if it would be exhausted. The orebody is on the surface in those hills and we know it goes down to twelve hundred feet.'

'Staggering,' said Kane admiringly. 'How did you prove the reserves?'

'Here, let me show you.' He was warmed by this Englishman's interest. He led the way through to his study, ferreted in a long drawer and laid out a series of plans on a desk. 'Look,' he said, indicating one which showed a section of ground with a contoured wedge shaded within it, descending irregularly. 'There's the down dip of the orebody. There's the oxide zone, close to the surface, and below that the sulphides. We had African labourers digging pits first, and the results from those were so good that we progressed to diamond drilling.' He indicated the long vertical lines of boreholes in the drawing. 'The highest grade we struck was eight point two per cent and the lowest three point seven per cent. The average was five point nine per cent. There they are.'

Kane peered at the figures, neatly written beside each borehole line. He had learnt enough at Delphi Ridge to realize that this had been a very careful and professional piece of prospecting.

'Did you go further?' he asked.

'As far as excavating a trench. We dug out around a thousand tons of ore for the metallurgists to analyze. They recommended a leaching process for the oxides and produced proposals for dealing with the sulphides.' He tapped a thick report.

'And then?'

'Nothing, absolutely nothing.' The geologist shook his head as though the neglect was incomprehensible. 'We had proven reserves of ore, significant uranium and approaching four million tons of cobalt and forty-eight million tons of copper. Those were conservative estimates too, my friend. I am confident that more wide-ranging prospecting would have doubled that figure. Yet the Union Minière did nothing. They claimed they had no requirement to exploit it yet. The trench is still there, I suppose.' He moved around the room. 'Perhaps I am a little over-concerned with Kiobo. They used to joke about it being my baby. To see one's own discovery brought into production is every prospector's dream. I still have specimens of the drill cores.'

Kane badly needed to think for a moment. Eventually he excused himself and in the seclusion of the bathroom made some quick calculations. At an average copper grade of 5.9 per cent the 48 million tons of ore would eventually yield 2,832,000 tons of copper worth, at the current producers price of 240 pounds a ton, 679 million pounds. The annual production would earn close to 14 million pounds, mined conservatively. If, in mining jargon, one picked the eyes out of it, the immediate yield could be more. As for the cobalt, production of that could be an approximate 4720 tons a year at 10,000 pounds a ton; 47 million pounds. This was fantastic. Total world production was only 10,000 tons, of which 8000 came from a very few mines in Katanga. It was both fantastic and possible. He returned to his host in a state of considerable excitement and with a number of questions, the most crucial being why the Uniou Minière had not exploited Kiobo.

'First the technical problems. I concede those existed, as at Tenke. But today they are no longer an obstacle. Then they argued that with mines like the Star of Africa, Kipushi and Leopold in production, they did not need Kiobo. Always the economic climate was wrong for the investment. They were unimaginative fools. Kiobo could be one of the greatest mines in the Congo.' The old man waved a hand impatiently. 'May I remind you of a parallel in Northern Rhodesia? In 1938 the Nchanga mine had reserves of a hundred and forty-three million tons. Today, after twenty-two years of mineral extraction its reserves are a hundred and seventy-eight million tons. Not less. More. Kiobo would be the same.'

By the time he departed Kane was convinced that he had found the 'viable alternative' which IMEX wanted.

The fat-bellied, heavy Globemaster transport taxied in from the main Elisabethville runway. Duclair watched from the terrace, where a group of Irish UN troops were sitting unconcernedly drinking coffee in the warm sun. The polished aluminium plane, its four-piston engines throbbing, manoeuvred into a parking space near the Sabena Boeing 707, due to leave that evening for Brussels. As the airport marshaller waved his batons high up across each other, signalling the pilot to close down, Duclair walked quietly round to the control tower. The Globemaster had arrived as a normal civilian flight. It had to go through normal formalities under the eye of the UN, even though that eye was not especially vigilant today. He doubted if the Irish would wonder why it had an American registration but no airline insignia.

'Everything OK?' he asked when he met the pilot.

'We had a tricky hour or two in Khartoum, otherwise it was just fine. Too damned inquisitive, those guys.'

'Good. I'll arrange the clearance for you to taxi round

to the military side of the field. We'll unload her there.'

An hour later the long, white packing cases containing the fuselage and wings of the first Fouga Magister jet fighter for the Katanga air force were being gently lifted out of the Globemaster.

Duclair glanced at the lined, experienced face of the pilot, an American who had flown many strange cargoes into many strange places. 'We might celebrate tonight, if you wish, Captain. You have brought us something of value.'

'It'll be a pleasure.'

It wasn't often that anyone made him welcome. Normally, once they had the goods in their hands, the guns or mortars or whatever it was, the recipients rapidly lost interest in the crew. The pilot nodded at the cases, now being taken into the military hangar.

'This the first of many?'

'Of enough.' Duclair's smile vanished. He wanted to discover if this airline was one of the fourteen reputedly owned by the CIA, not to give away information to the Americans. 'I will see you at the hotel,' he said and walked away.

A week later the Fouga had been assembled and Tshombe himself came to see it debut. The plane was sleek, low on the ground, slim-winged, swallow-tailed, the jet engine which powered it neatly engineered so that the aircraft looked like a racer, a thoroughbred, too small to be dangerous. In fact it mounted machine-guns and could have bombs slung to attachment points under the wings. Tshombe was exultant. He donned a flying helmet and was photographed in the cockpit, then waved proudly as the Belgian pilot in charge taxied out and made a demonstration flight.

'How fast can it go?' he asked.

'Six hundred and fifty kilometres per hour,' said Duclair. 'It will dominate the skies of Katanga.'

'And the pilots?'

'We have recruited the best qualified from Belgium. Highly experienced men like Delin, up there now.' Duclair chuckled to himself. If that British idiot Russell imagined he was going to lay his hands on the jets, he could think again.

The next day the local newspaper, the *Essor du Katanga*, faithfully carried front-page photographs of Tshombe and the Fouga. Curiously, or so it seemed to Chantal and Duclair alike, the UN took no action. They did nothing to obstruct the jet operating from the airport. When in due course a further two arrived, Duclair was cock-a-hoop with delight. However, he took the precaution of dispersing them to another airfield.

In February Steve Barlow found himself given unexpected additional responsibility. His superior, a level-headed New Zealander who had been under considerable strain, was to go for a much-needed period of leave. Temporarily Barlow would be in charge. He both welcomed the challenge and dreaded its implications. For a career diplomat such opportunities were few and far between. Here he was in his early thirties with the eyes of the world on him in on one of the UN's most nerve-racking and tricky posts. Certainly the Canadian diplomatic service could never offer such a chance, except at the highest level. He saw in it the possibility of making his name with the UN organization in a way hitherto impossible. His fears arose from the knowledge of Lumumba's death which must soon become officially recognized. At the same time troops and rebels loyal to Lumumba had now declared the north of Katanga an independent state, calling it Lualaba. Barlow could see nothing but trouble ahead.

On 13 February the blow fell. The Katanga government announced the death of Lumumba and two companions 'massacred by the inhabitants of a village to which he had fled'.

'We shall be accused of having murdered them,' the Interior Minister remarked brazenly. 'My reply is: prove it!'

Uproar followed in the UN. Reading the official telegrams which flooded into his office, Barlow realized that, if a leader had died, a socialist legend had been born. The world reaction was as violent as it was illogical. Mobs rioted in Cairo and burnt down the Belgian Embassy. In New York the Russian UN delegate accused Hammarskjold of being responsible and demanded his resignation. The General Assembly was split and the whole peace-keeping operation threatened.

In Elisabethville they were besieged by journalistic inquiries. Reporters from all over the world had descended on the town.

A week later, in the early hours of 21 February, the Security Council voted to demand the removal of all foreign military personnel, advisers and mercenaries from the Congo, except of course UN troops. Because Katanga was seven hours ahead of New York time, Barlow found himself forced into giving a press conference without being able to receive any guidance on what he should say.

That afternoon the room used for press conferences in the UN offices, too small and too hot even for the number of journalists who normally came, was crammed with reporters. As Barlow took his seat at the table at one end of the room flash bulbs popped and news cameras whirred. He followed a prepared statement, quoting the exact text of the Security Council resolution, with a brief run-down of the situation as he saw it, and ended with a quote from Hammarskjold's own remarks in an address to the Council a few days before: 'We have again reached a point where a local armed conflict is threatening to lead to a widening of the conflict into the international arena.' 'The only way,' Barlow terminated his brief speech, 'to preserve law and order is for the United Nations to be allowed to carry out its mission without interruption by foreign influences.' He had barely stopped speaking before the first questioner, a British journalist, was on his feet.

'You say the UN is to prevent civil war by the use of force if necessary. Can you explain how you decide the circumstances which justify using force?'

'That has to be a decision of the commander on the spot and depends on the exact circumstances.'

'You realize that Tshombe considers the United Nations has declared war on Katanga?' someone else shouted.

'That is not the case,' Barlow insisted. 'We are trying to preserve law and order.'

'Then why are you not preventing the invasion of Northern Katanga?' demanded the Briton.

'We have troops in that area,' said Barlow.

'And they are turning a blind eye to what is happening,' suggested an American.

'I absolutely deny that. But if they were to take certain actions, these could be counter-productive.' Already Barlow felt he was losing his grip on the press conference. It was one thing to be able to put legal arguments on paper, quite another to convince a basically hostile audience of extremely quick-witted men.

'Surely,' asked a Belgian, 'the gendarmerie and the mercenaries are the ones restoring order in the country?'

'On the contrary, the mercenaries represent outside interference at its worst!' Barlow's temper flared. Since yesterday the mercenary problem had assumed a personal significance for him. He had thought he saw that irresponsible idiot Mike Russell in the street. Checking he had found that Russell was indeed one of Tshombe's 'volunteers.' From that moment the pilot exemplified the undesirable adventurers in Katanga. All foreign advisers should be deported,' he went on angrily.

It was not a wise remark. Shouts of derision came from the Belgian journalists present. After this Barlow did lose control of the conference and fifteen minutes later declared it closed, promising weakly that, when further briefing was possible after communication with New York, he would speak to the press again. The journalists crowded out, muttering their discontent, angry at having so little firm material to send their newspapers. Barlow had no doubt that the reports which would appear next morning in Britain and America would be hostile to the UN and quite possibly to himself.

Later, even worse happened. He decided to go for a drink at the Leo Deux, hoping that in some way he would be able to talk sense to the journalists whom he knew he would find there. It might be easier speaking to them as individuals off the record than in the heated atmosphere of the press conference. But when he ordered a drink at the bar, the Belgian barman refused to serve him. He called the manager and after a long wait was informed by an underling that his presence was not welcome in the hotel. The manager regretted that he must leave at once. Inevitably a small crowd of journalists gathered around as he protested, standing isolated in the foyer, arguing with the staff.

'This is an outrage,' he stormed, beginning to lose his temper.

A few minutes later he was forced to leave – not actually thrown out, but the nearest thing to it. He was trembling at the indignity of a senior UN official being treated in this way. As he stood on the pavement outside, the British journalist who had harassed him came up and said, 'If you think that little performance is going to get you sympathy, you've another think coming.' He walked away leaving Barlow bitterly conscious that his intended rapprochement with the press had ended with his being photographed in the middle of a humiliating eviction.

He returned to the small apartment which he rented shaking with a mixture of anger and apprehension, unable to see how he could face the press again. The only consolation he could find lay in the knowledge that Hammarskjold had been similarly vilified over the past week in the General Assembly. He poured himself a large bourbon and re-read the brief note of encouragement which the Secretary General had sent him on his posting to Elisabethville. There, at least, was a man who understood and to whom one could give complete allegiance. If Hammarskjold felt that the mercenaries should be removed, then removed they must be, although the action would produce international repercussions. If the Secretary General pleased the Russians, as he would now, he would disturb the Americans and evoke outright hostility in Brussels and London. For the first time he felt not only fear for his own reputation, but a greater apprehension that what he knew ought to be done would in fact prove impossible to carry out. When the phone rang he almost didn't answer it; then, remembering that he was the senior official and could never be off-duty, picked up the receiver. To his surprise it was Robert Kane, speaking from London. The pressure of recent events had been such that Kane's interests in Katanga had gone out of his mind.

'I imagine you are pretty pressed at this time,' said Kane, his voice a little distorted. None the less his voice struck the right chord.

'I certainly am. Things are a little hectic here.'

'Well, I won't keep you long. You remember you were kind enough to say you might be able to give me a helping hand?'

'Yes,' He supposed he had said it, but could not remember.

'I hope to be out again in a week or so with an American mining engineer. We would appreciate some small assistance. Nothing much, just in getting around the country without getting into trouble.'

Barlow was relieved. 'That should be no problem,' he said. 'We have a good idea of what's going on even if we can't always do anything about it.'

'That's all I wanted to know. It's very nice of you. Thanks a lot. I'll call when I arrive.' Kane rang off, leaving Barlow with the unexpected feeling that here was a man he could talk to without pressure and without recrimination. When he came to think about it, he had no friends in Katanga, only acquaintances. He poured himself another whisky and went to bed. For the next ten hours Katanga could damn well look after itself.

Kane put down the phone, satisfied at having demonstrated his pull with the United Nations on the spot. He had been lucky to get the call through, too, even though it was the least busy time of day. He turned to James Skinner, whose office at IMEX he was in. 'That's good,' he said. 'With UN facilities I can get up into the Kiobo area without any problem.'

'Can't your politician friend, Sendwe, organize that?' asked Skinner. 'He is supposed to be the Baluba leader, isn't he, and God knows we are paying him enough.' He looked keenly at his employee, sensing a change in him. The straightforward aggressiveness of which he had approved in the past had become overlaid with a veneer of toadying. In the days when Kane commanded 699 Squadron he would never have boasted of his influence with senior officers, as he had a moment ago.

'Sendwe is in Leopoldville most of the time,' said Kane. 'A thousand miles from Katanga, as far as from London to Moscow,'

'Not the most fortunate comparison.' Skinner frowned. The mention of Moscow reminded him of an aspect which troubled Western. 'Before we go any further I'd like to know just how close to the Russians these people are, and I don't mean geographically.'

Kane took a deep breath. The extent to which the tangled skeins of African politics were comprehensible depended on how far you were prepared to throw preconceived ideas overboard. Two and a half years of involvement had compelled him to do this. But Skinner was steeped in the concepts of British parliamentary democracy, while Western Mining thought in terms of a power vacuum which either Russia or the United States must fill when the colonial rulers withdrew. 'If we don't move in there,' Dillon had said repeatedly, 'the Reds will.'

'The basic fact, sir,' Kane began, 'is that Africans are very adept politicians. They lack aptitudes we consider essential, mainly because they never grew up with mechanical toys. However, when they were children they did listen to their fathers arguing local politics all the time. Their village elders didn't hold sway from being elected but from a consensus of support.'

Skinner cut him short. 'What exactly are you trying to tell me?'

'That every African politician I've known has been willing to talk to his opponents if he thought it would give him a slice of power. And secondly, that as far as the Great Powers are concerned, they're convinced they can play the ends against the middle. Take the men I've been dealing with. Lumumba asked the United States for aid, was refused, went to the Russians instead and was being supplied with trucks and aircraft at exactly the time the UN was starting the aid programme he had also asked for. The Russians have made him into a communist martyr because they need one in Africa. In fact he saw everything as open to compromise. So do the others.'

'Do they expect to be murdered, too?' Skinner's cynicism was unconcealed.

'Emphatically not. Lumumba was killed because he had a naturally turbulent personality and went on to create civil war, not consensus. He'd been beaten half dead by central government soldiers before he even reached Katanga in that plane.'

Skinner waved his hand. 'All right, all right. Let's skip the detail. I accept that they're pragmatists. Why does this make your plan workable?'

'In the simplest terms, sir, eventually Katanga's independence must be ended and the Congo reunited. Tshombe will lose power and Sendwe will gain it. The Kiobo mineral deposits adjoin Sendwe's Baluba tribal area. He'll grant us the concession then in exchange for aid now.'

'Aid to the rebels?'

'Whether it reaches them or merely stays in a Swiss bank account I can't tell.'

'So I'm back to my question!' Skinner thumped the desk with his fist. 'How close is he to the communists?'

Kane groaned inwardly. Skinner had not understood. 'As an associate of Lumumba's he's inherited Russian aid. But he'll take it from anyone. He's solely interested in supplanting Tshombe and that must happen, if only because the UN is now demanding the removal of the Belgians and mercenaries on whom Tshombe depends.'

'And suppose Tshombe goes but the Union Minière doesn't, how does our concession look then?'

'Sendwe will simply deprive them of it for failure to develop. They'll have no answer to that.' Kane reached for his briefcase. 'May I show you the locations? It's small beer compared to the Lumumba contract but it still has colossal potential.' He spread his map out on Skinner's wide desk and stabbed a finger at an area some hundred miles north-west of Elisabethville. 'There are two enormous undeveloped mineral deposits, one at a place called Tenke Fungurume, the other at Kiobo.' Kane gained confidence as he explained. 'On my last visit I managed to get access to the geologist's reports. Kiobo's orebody contains a high cobalt content in addition to an average six per cent copper.' He paused, 'as you know, sir, the aircraft industry is going to need a lot of cobalt in the jet age.'

'You're damn right,' said Skinner, his interest aroused at last. Cobalt was the metal which, among many other uses, could be alloyed with steel to give strength and heat resistance to jet engine components. Manufacturing a single turbine blade consumed two kilos of the silvery coloured metal. Furthermore, it was rare. Cobalt did not appear naturally by itself, but only in deposits with other metals. Its market price underlined its importance and now showed every sign of reaching 10,000 pounds a ton, or close on ten pounds a kilo, in the future. If jet aviation boomed, it might even rival silver in value.

'Furthermore,' said Kane, happily conscious of the impression he was making, 'At Kiobo it's in a high proportion, about two parts of cobalt to twenty-five of copper.'

'What are the estimated reserves at this place?' queried Skinner.

'From the boreholes they made, the geologists reckoned on a proven reserve sufficient to produce three million tons of copper and close on one hundred and eighty thousand of cobalt. At current producers' prices, that means Kiobo could earn two and a half thousand million pounds, not counting the further reserves they are certain exist. Fifty years was the life the geologist gave it. What it is, sir, is a damn great hill of copper and cobalt.'

'So it is worth having!' Skinner rose and fetched himself a drink. 'Help yourself,' he added, a sure sign that he was going to agree to a project.

Kane followed his example, still talking. 'Despite Kiobo's value, I'd prefer to be a little cautious this time. Before we sign or give Sendwe more money I think we ought to make our own survey of the site. Would Western allow Rick Croft to come out from Arizona?'

Skinner sat down again, played with his glass for a moment and came to a decision. 'I will recommend that,' he said. 'In fact I'll telephone Western now. They should be back from lunch.' He knew the New York number and dialled it straight away. As it began to ring he looked round at Kane. 'Perhaps it would be better if you left me alone. Come back in ten minutes.'

Kane did as he was told and went down the passage, drink in hand, to the office he used when in London.

Skinner's explanation on the telephone was brief and clear. 'It's not in the same league as the Lumumba contract, of course, but it is a concession we could hope to get even if Union Minière remain important there after Tshombe falls.'

'OK,' replied Dillon, 'I think I can say we will buy that. As a long-term proposition it should be worthwhile. What is the tag likely to be?'

'A royalty to the central government, basically. Of course only an expert like Croft can assess the capital cost involved in the development.'

'You can have Croft, but not for too long. A week at the outside. Now tell me, does Kane know how the fighting is affecting production?'

'Quite seriously, he thinks.'

'Are these, hmm, wild men he's been financing communists?'

'He says not.'

'Our State Department is concerned about communist involvement there, deeply concerned. Listen, James, as you know we have a new President of the United States, John F. Kennedy. He's already pledged his administration to help the under-developed countries. As yet we don't know how, but I'd be surprised if it includes siding with a Soviet-supported rebellion. The concession sounds fine, the way of achieving it may not be. Let's keep this under scrutiny, please.'

'I will.'

'We'll come to a final decision when we have Croft's report, right? How are things otherwise?'

When Skinner put the phone down he swallowed some more whisky and pondered for a few minutes. He suspected Western had deeper commitments in this than they had disclosed to him. Well, he thought, that's their affair. When it came down to brass tacks, everyone at IMEX was only an employee of Western. It did not befit employees to ask too many questions. He went to the door, shouted down the corridor for Kane and told him the good news.

In New York Dillon likewise sat back and took stock of the situation. He disliked the way its edges were becoming blurred. To clear his mind he adjusted his glasses and made some pencilled notes.

1. Congo – wide contract (main aim) lost.
2. Kiobo project long term and fraction of value of (1).
3. In short term probably more profitable to disrupt Katanga copper production so supporting price of our Chilean output.
4. Kennedy policy re Africa power vacuum?

He mulled these over. The company President's instruction had been to pursue the disruption (3) if the major contract collapsed. By equipping the Katanga air force through PANWORLD in Paris, Dillon had established the perfect means of controlling the disruption. So long as no one else had air power in the Congo, the Katanga air force was a regulator in the fighting. It would enable Tshombe to hold out indefinitely against the central government and, if civil war didn't obstruct exports, nothing would. Already several mines were completely closed, according to Kane's reports. The big question mark lay over the Kennedy administration's policy. Both Dillon and the company President were veteran campaigners in the border country where politics and big business met. The President was going down to Washington soon. Maybe he should be asked to add Katanga to the subject on which he would be canvassing views.

Spring in Europe heralded the dry season in Katanga, bringing a new ferocity to the sporadic fighting in the north as the gendarmerie pressed on towards the recapture of the north.

As if to match the mood, a new breed of mercenaries began to arrive: hard, experienced ex-French Foreign Legion soldiers, the embittered veterans of two ruthless wars. In Indo-China they had finally been defeated at Dien Bien Phu by the Vietminh. In Algeria their long campaign against Arab guerillas of the FLN was being made fruitless by President de Gaulle's decision that Algeria could not remain French. Algeria was the home of the Legion. For many the seeming betrayal was too much to bear.

One evening as the light died and the night chorus of insects began, a jeep was driven up to the pilots' villa and disgorged a tall, lean soldier in the camouflage fatigues of the French parachute troops, Katangan badges hastily sewn on the shoulders. He hoisted a set of webbing equipment and a rucksack out of the jeep, dumped them in the verandah, then straightened up and glanced around.

'Not bad,' he commented tersely, walking up to Mike, hand outstretched. 'Jacques. Where do I sleep?'

Mike introduced himself then shouted to the other pilot, who was inside. 'Joe, we have a house guest. Where shall we put him?'

Joe, the Dakota pilot, emerged, a towel round his neck, shaving lather on his face.

'Oh. How do you do? He can bunk in Dave's room.' Dave had been wounded and was in hospital.

'You are a pilot too?' Joe asked the Frenchman.

'I'm here to raise a paratroop company. You fly the Dakota? Good. Is it fitted for static line jumping?'

Both Joe and Mike looked at the newcomer, the same thought in their minds. He was taking over too fast.

'It can be,' answered Joe guardedly. 'I thought you French were all free fallers?'

'Correct. But we are using British parachutes from Rhodesia which require a static line to open them. When proper French ones arrive, we shall see.' His assumption that French equipment was inevitably superior coloured all Jacques' thinking. 'What is the organization here?' he asked.

They explained that there was one predominantly British mercenary force, led by Richard Brown, which was virtually a separate establishment from the Belgian-led gendarmerie and its mercenaries. As he listened, Jacques rummaged in his rucksack and produced a bottle of red wine. He pulled a multi-purpose army knife from his pocket, and had the cork out in seconds. Tactfully, Joe fetched three glasses.

'To saving Africa from the communists!' Jacques raised his glass, drank, muttered, 'Not bad,' and then returned to business. 'Are all the pilots British?'

'There's a New Zealander and an Australian. But we fly for whoever wants us,' said Mike, nettled by this interrogation. 'Tell us about yourself.'

Jacques poured himself some more wine and leant on the verandah rail. Very deliberately he lit a cigarette, blew smoke at a mosquito buzzing near him, then said curtly, 'Twenty years in the Legion. Seventeen operational jumps in Indo-China. Dien Bien Phu. Algeria with the first RPE, fighting in the Bled. We fixed the FLN in the Battle of Algiers. And brought de Gaulle to power, the bastard. When he abandoned Algérie Française we mutinied.' Jacques allowed himself a thin smile. 'Some of us are in jail, some are underground with the OAS. I went to Spain, then I came here. If it's good I shall pass the word back.'

'What's your second name?' asked Joe.

'Jacques. One name is enough. Sergeant Jacques in Indo-China, Captain Jacques here.' He straightened up. 'When's the food?'

'When the cook comes,' said Joe. 'He's gone for a chicken.'

'I prefer steak,' said Jacques, lifting his kit and carrying it inside. A few moments later they heard military music coming from his room. Evidently he had a tape recorder. The tune was resonant on the night air, a marching song with trumpet fanfares and a continuing refrain, *'En avant, en avant, en avant, c'est nous les Africains.'*

The two pilots drank the wine and listened, as the singer's voice rose and fell emotionally.

'He's not mucking about with my bloody Dak without my permission,' said Joe, 'seventeen operational jumps or not.'

'We could use some paratroops.'

'We could use a lot of things. Those fighters you were promised, for a start.'

A week later Jacques strolled in one evening and announced with his habitual abruptness, 'I need air reconnaissance tomorrow. Duclair has agreed.'

'What for?' Mike asked. His initial opposition to the Frenchman had waned as he came to appreciate his ability. Jacques had already recruited thirty volunteers including Herman and was shortly moving with them to a camp at Shinkolobwe.

'Tomorrow,' Jacques said, with an uncharacteristic touch of theatricality, 'I shall equip my men. I cannot wait for supplies. The gendarmerie organization is too erratic.'

'I don't understand. Why do you need air for that?'

'Because it is the UN's equipment.'

'You're joking.'

'No, I am going to hijack their train.' He spread out a map and jabbed a finger at it. 'Here, just after it crosses the Northern Rhodesia frontier.'

The next morning Mike had the blue and white Cessna pushed out of the hangar at eight. Duclair, it transpired, wanted a parcel brought up from Ndola and had concocted a plan for Mike to fly down there, filing a normal civil flight plan, some hours before the train was due to leave Rhodesia. He could collect the package, check the railway timings and fly back overhead as the train puffed its way slowly up the line of rail towards the frontier post at Sakania. Bloody typical of Duclair, Mike thought, dovetailing his private commerce into Jacques's operation.

The weather was perfect. He took off from the strip in the suburbs, formalities at the main airport having been waived, and watched the bush slip away beneath him as he flew south-east into the pedicle, the strip of Congolese territory which jutted into Northern Rhodesia. The trees and scrub stretched uninterrupted as far as the eye could see, clouds laying slow-moving shadows on the landscape. It felt strange observing the normal civil aviation routine for the first time since he had left Kenya, calling the Rhodesian air traffic control as he approached the border, and being passed on to the Ndola approach.

'Roger, November Juliet, you are clear to land, the wind one two zero degrees at ten knots, QNH one zero one two, call when you have the field in sight.' The unhurried voice of the Briton in Ndola tower was in refreshing contrast to the emotional impatience which characterized radio conversations in Katanga. Once again it reminded him that, despite his hopes, all he was doing here was basic bush flying. Barring the occasional risk, he might as well have stayed in Kenya working for Zog. Quite suddenly he decided that, if something more demanding did not materialize soon, he would quit. His initial contract had been for six months. They were up. He could leave with a clear conscience. This in turn reminded him of Chantal. He swore, embarrassed by his memories, and concentrated on the flying. Soon Ndola came in sight, the mine-workings and smelter chimneys rearing up from the surrounding woodlands, which he noticed appeared flat but in fact were higher than the land around the airfield. There was no other traffic and he was allowed to land on a straight-in approach.

After clearing customs, he walked in to the small terminal building and was immediately accosted by a small, wiry man in a tropical suit, carrying a large parcel.

‘Mr Russell?’ The man scanned his features. ‘You are Russell?’

‘Would you like to see my passport?’ Mike was half joking, but the man nodded seriously, examining it carefully before saying more. When he was satisfied, he held out the parcel.

‘These are the documents for Duclair. Don’t lose them. To get duplicates could take months.’

‘I won’t.’ For once it sounded as though Duclair was not black-marketeering.

‘The train is on time. It should reach the frontier at eleven thirty. It has about twenty open wagons and fifteen closed freight cars.’ The man lowered his voice, even though there was no one near them. ‘The Union Minière consignment is in the last five.’

‘Is that important?’

‘Yes. We originally had the vans attached to the UN train to, well, facilitate clearance. Tell Duclair to get them detached again the moment he can.’

‘Right, I’ll pass the message. ‘Mike wondered if this man knew about the attack plan. He certainly seemed to.

‘If that’s clear I’ll be getting back to the office.’ He departed hastily, leaving Mike perplexed. Why was Duclair agreeing to hijack a train which had goods for the Union Minière aboard? It seemed odd, but there was nothing he could do about it, at least until he could talk to Jacques on the radio. He checked the time, went to the tower and filed his flight plan, then killed fifteen minutes over a cup of coffee before going out to the Cessna. He wanted to reach the frontier marginally ahead of the train.

Ten minutes after take-off, deviating from the direct route in order to fly up the railway, he glimpsed the long line of trucks, hauled by two engines but still only creeping along. He wondered how long it had taken them to get from the South African port of Durban to here. A week at least, maybe two. He throttled back a little and looked down. The open wagons were mostly full of packing cases, though some held jeeps. He saw one of the engine drivers wave and waggled his wings in reply, feeling betrayal as he did so. Jacques would make short work of the drivers if they failed to stop.

Five miles ahead lay Sakania, the main road and the line converging on it. He called the Rhodesian air traffic for the last time, then switched to the mercenaries' operating frequency. They had adopted temporary codewords for this operation.

'Hallo, Red, this is Green. Do you read?'

'I read you fives.' For a Frenchman Jacques had a most untypical regard for correct aviation English.

'Red, your target has four miles to run to the border.'

'Roger. Report other activity.'

Mike acknowledged and flew on to search for any signs of the United Nations. Almost immediately he spotted the site of the ambush. A few miles beyond Sakania the railway crossed first the main road and then a side road. Parked a short distance along the lesser road were a veritable fleet of trucks, drawn into the verge beneath the trees. All Jacques had to do was to halt the train and transfer the loads.

As he continued his search, finding no sign of UN troops towards Elisabethville, he called again, warning Jacques not to damage the last five vans. Then he circled and surveyed the bush for several miles either side of the road. No activity. In the distance he could see the train pulling out of Sakania.

'Red, this is Green, all clear,' he called.

'Roger. Keep looking.'

He circled, watching fascinated as one of the lorries moved on to the level crossing, blocking the line, and two men with guns doubled in the direction of the train, presumably to flag it down. He noticed that Jacques had set up machine-gun posts to cover them. A trail of dust revealed another vehicle racing to block the first level crossing once the trucks were past.

The train halted slowly, steam fussing from the engine. Mercenaries ran to both sides of the cab, guns raised. The crew climbed out on to the track. Then Mike saw Jacques appear, recognizable from the red parachutist's beret he wore, and beckon up the convoy. The hijack appeared to have been achieved without a shot being fired. Mike called to ask if they had finished with him. As he expected the reply was immediate.

'Mission complete. Return to base.'

Whoever Jacques had left manning the set evidently had clear orders. For the first time since he arrived in Katanga Mike felt he was working with a totally professional soldier. The operation had been done with marvellous simplicity. Mike chuckled with delight all the way back to Elisabethville. As most of the mercenaries were known to be fighting in the north, the UN had evidently never expected them to become active in the extreme south.

When he landed and taxied in at the small airfield he found Duclair waiting, his grey trousers neatly creased as usual, his blue peaked hat rakishly askew. Mike was never sure whether he was consciously playing a role or not. He walked over to the Cessna as Mike got out, and asked with uncharacteristic seriousness, 'You have the parcel?'

Mike gestured to the back of the plane.

'Good. And what about the train?'

'As far as I could see the hijack went off beautifully. I was asked to pass them a message about the last five trucks containing equipment for the Union Minière. They acknowledged it.'

'Excellent.' Duclair sounded relieved. 'Now all we have to do is shunt those vans down to Kipushi and we're in business.'

'You mean you knew about them?'

'My dear fellow, of course.' His anxiety allayed,

Duclair slipped back into his normal sardonic nonchalance. 'We are not completely stupid. Bring the parcel across to the hangar, will you?'

Mike followed him across and into the office at the side of the hangar which they used as an operations room, its walls lined with maps. Duclair took the parcel, slit it open with a knife, then began removing thick manuals and blueprint diagrams from the wrapping and piling them on a table. 'You may notice something familiar about these,' he remarked.

Mike looked over his shoulder, then moved round closer, astonished. 'Good God,' he exclaimed. 'The T6 maintenance manuals.'

'Also the drawings from which the aircraft can be assembled. We thought it prudent to keep them separate from the consignment.' Duclair laughed, enjoying the moment. 'You have a low opinion of the Union Minière, don't you, Russell? Why deny it, I know. Perhaps you will change your mind when you unload those last five freight cars from the train. They contain an interesting variety of mining equipment from which you and the engineers will shortly construct six T6 aircraft.'

'I will?'

'Precisely. You are going to supervise the assembly in the Union Minière workshops at Kipushi and you are then going to test-fly the planes from the airfield there, all six of them, just to make sure. After that, if both you and they are still intact, you will have earned the job of flight commander.'

Mike was so surprised and taken aback that he stood completely silent. Eventually he managed to say, 'Thank you.'

'Don't thank me. Thank your friends. What is that saying the Americans always quote? "Never underestimate the power of a woman." Not that you'll be seeing much of her down at Kipushi, I'm afraid.' His tone hardened. 'I'd like you to be there tomorrow. The company will find you accommodation.' Duclair picked up his hat. 'Oh yes, the T6 pilots should arrive shortly, too. You had better buy yourself a Spanish dictionary. They're Cubans.' He smiled mockingly. 'From Miami, I understand.'

When he had gone, Mike telephoned Chantal at the President's office. He had not spoken to her since the disastrous Christmas Eve dinner. Now he felt acutely embarrassed, both at having accused her of letting him down and, contrarily, at her having intervened successfully on his behalf.

'Duclair just told me,' he said, when he at last got through, they're sending me to Kipushi to organize the Harvards, the T6s, I mean.' Harvard was the RAF name for the plane, not used much outside Britain.

'I am very glad.' Was there a trembling in Chantal's voice? He wasn't sure. He cursed the impersonality of the telephone, wishing he could see her expression. 'I hope you are pleased, too.' She sounded anxious.

'Yes, of course I am. It's what I wanted. I'm just, well, you shouldn't have done it.'

'Please, what you said that night was perfectly true. We want outside help but at the same time we don't want it. Take no notice of anything Duclair says, he is a rogue, that man, and a poseur. He may have been a good pilot in the war. Now he's just living on the reputation. They say that of him in Belgium too.'

'Listen,' Mike had no desire to talk about Duclair, 'I have to leave tomorrow. Can you have dinner tonight?' He badly wanted to be with her, to celebrate making up their quarrel.

'I am truly sorry, Mike. I cannot. I have to go with the President to Kolwezi. We are leaving in a few minutes. You only just caught me, in fact. When you come back, perhaps. After all, Kipushi is not so far, only just down the road.'

'I'll drive up one evening.' Mike felt more cheerful.

'Telephone me.' In the background a man was calling her. 'Oh, I must go. Wait, though, there is something I must tell you. Yes, you remember once you told me about a former pilot called Kane? He was seen here last month again. No one quite knows why. We suspect he may be sniffing out mining concessions.' The voice behind her became insistent. 'I have to go now. Goodbye. Good luck.' The phone clicked and went dead. Mike walked to his car, his thoughts whirling, and drove home to the villa to pack.

6

The town of Kipushi, dominated by the lift hoists of one of the deepest mines in the Congo, lay smack on the Northern Rhodesian border. Since it was eighteen miles from Elisabethville, it was scarcely necessary for Mike to live there. However, he thought it wiser to comply with Duclair's plan and was duly allotted bachelor quarters suitable for a junior mining engineer. The mechanics recruited by PANWORLD were similarly housed. Led by a Frenchman of former distinction in the aircraft industry who through some misdemeanour had lost his job in metropolitan France, they included air frame, engine and electrical mechanics from South Africa.

On the first day, keen to show himself willing, Mike helped unpack the crates brought in the train. These had been laid out in the huge corrugated-iron-roofed shed which the Union Minière had allocated them, close to the Kipushi air strip. Unpacking caused considerable hilarity. One of the South Africans read out the manifest of contents of the crates, paperwork stamped by customs officials on many borders, beginning with that of the US customs at the port of embarkation, New York.

' "One mine ventilation equipment generator",' he intoned. A T6 engine was duly disinterred and five more followed.

'Ventilation ducting' was the next item. Six hefty

cases revealed the aircraft's fuselages. 'Mine shoring supports' disguised the wings sections. But the item that amused them most was the designation for the aircraft's instrument panels: 'Production control systems'.

'Jesus,' commented one of the South Africans, 'I suppose some ignorant bastard could just think the altimeter was connected with a mine lift going up and down the shaft. But the artificial horizon! How could they explain that one?'

'I am sure they never needed to,' the Frenchman replied. 'The export of mining machinery is big business in the United States. They supply the whole free world. Who would challenge what is accepted as normal?'

The South African admitted that he had a point. The mining companies, whether American, Belgian, British or South African, dealt internationally on such a scale that their power was little less than that of governments.

'They tell me that the Union Minière concessions here cover twenty thousand square kilometres,' observed the Frenchman. 'In Europe that could be a whole country.'

The laughter ceased once the assembly work began. The T6 was far from being a sophisticated aircraft by modern standards. North American had built the first ones twenty years ago. None the less it had its complications. The retractable undercarriage was operated hydraulically, as were the flaps, and Mike recalled from flying training school days that the hydraulics often gave trouble. The machine-gun mounted in the starboard wing was worked by a combination of electrics and compressed air. The bombs were released electrically. The 750-watt generator powered not only these but the instrument panel, the lighting for landing and navigation, the radio and other services. All these involved circuits and pipes which had to be correctly connected up. The one bonus was that, the flaps apart, the flying controls only involved direct linkages. Unless these were inadvertently reversed, an amazingly common cause of accidents after overhauls, the pilot need not fear a failure preventing him from getting the aircraft down on to the ground more or less in one piece, provided he could find an open space. In this and one respect, the T6 was as basic as a Model T Ford. The other was that its engine, although normally started up electrically, had a hand starter crank for emergencies.

Under the Frenchman's directions an assembly line was improvised, using trestles and blocks to support the component parts of the first aircraft. Fortunately the shed had overhead hoists. Gradually, aided by incessant reference to the blueprints and intructions, which Mike often had to translate, the first T6 took shape. The wing centre section, the part which carried the undercarriage and bore the whole weight of the machine both at rest and in flight, fitted to the underside of the fuselage. Next the outer wing sections were bolted on. The tail plane followed, the mechanics methodically joining up the elevators and rudder to the control links which terminated in the cockpit at the stick and the rudder pedals.

Eventually the big radial Pratt and Whitney Wasp engine was secured to the metal struts jutting out in front of the cockpit. The pilot sat immediately behind the engine. Mike remembered asking his instructor what happened if the engine caught fire. 'Don't worry, old chap', the RAF flight lieutenant had siad, 'it will probably fall off before you get burnt.'

Almost the last item was what the RAF called the 'glasshouse', the long cockpit canopy of two sliding sections, one above each of the two seats. The T6 had been designed as a trainer.

Up to this stage there had been little Mike could do beyond give advice. When they reached a series of ground checks, he became the central figure. He was the one who would shortly discover whether these three tons of segmented metal would climb at 1000 feet a minute, cruise at 120 knots and pull out of a dive at 225 without falling apart.

A week after Mike's arrival at Kipushi, the engine run-ups began. The shattering roar of the 550 h.p. Wasp could be heard for miles around. Its sound was distinctive, not least because, when the Hamilton propeller was in fine pitch and the engine had maximum revs, the propeller tips revolved at more than the speed of sound, making an agonizingly high-pitched noise which reputedly could shatter glass. Mike recalled the efforts they used to make in training to change pitch while flying past the control tower in the hope of breaking its windows. They never succeeded. The glass at Kipushi remained disappointingly intact too. Mike wished it had not. He was keyed up with a schoolboyish excitement, as if he had taken on a particularly hazardous dare. Duclair drove down to watch the test flight, bringing with him a small, swarthy-faced man with a black moustache: the first of the Cubans. Three mine officials joined them at the side of the strip near the small control tower. In 1892 the great Jules Cornet had mapped out what was to become the Union Minière empire in a waggon drawn by a team of oxen. Today every mine had its airfield, a facility of unanticipated military significance.

The Wasp engine started, coughing for a second, spewing out grey smoke from the exhaust along the side of the fuselage, then breaking into a healthy roar. Mike taxied the T6 gently towards the end of the strip, giving the engine time to warm up and testing the brakes as he weaved his way. He had to taxi like this because the T6 had a tail wheel, and on the ground the big engine cowling obstructed the view directly ahead. At the end of the strip he swivelled the plane, applied the brakes and began his checks. Oil above forty degrees centigrade. Cylinder head 120 degrees centigrade. He adjusted the cooler shutter. Then he revved the engine up yet again, testing the magnetos and briefly thrusting the throttle up to the gate to give himself plus three pounds of boost and 2200 r.p.m. After easing it back his eyes ran methodically over all the gauges on the instrument panel from left to right and he set about the take-off checks. Trim. Mixture. Fuel, he glanced down at the gauges. Forty gallons in each tank, enough for four and three quarter hours if you flew for range, or less than half of that in any form of combat. But this flight would last an hour at most. Flaps: as there was only a light wind, he gave himself fifteen degrees. Finally he tugged at his harness, tightening the straps, and called the tower for take-off.

'Vous êtes prêt?' The man here made no pretence of speaking English.

'Oui.'

'Allez alors, bonne chance!'

The best of British in other words, thought Mike. He muttered 'here goes' to himself, lined up on the centre of the strip and thrust the throttle forward as smoothly as he could.

Lumbering at first, the T6 gathered speed. After fifty yards he brought the tail up, immediately needing right rudder to correct the yaw. At seventy knots he eased gently back on the stick and she left the ground. The air speed began to rise. Holding her in a climb, he pumped on the lever which cut in the hydraulics system, driven by the engine, switched his hand to the undercarriage handle, lifted it to disengage the safety stud and hauled it back. As the ground lights on the instrument panel flickered out, changing to red and then going off, he felt the clank of the wheels coming up. His right hand on the stick could feel the difference, the plane was liberated. He brought the flap up and began his prepared sequence of tests, starting with a climbing turn to avoid trespassing on Rhodesian air space. Below he could see the group by the tower and it crossed his mind that Duclair might be disappointed. A crash on take-off would have been nicely dramatic.

For half an hour he put the T6 through every normal manoeuvre. Then he climbed higher and tried to stall. No problems. Next the spin. Power off, stick progressively back and then, as the whole plane began to judder, he kicked on hard left rudder. The entry was as sickening as he expected. The plane reared up and flipped over, literally falling out of the air, then whirling round and round, fluttering like a leaf. He did not delay the recovery. Opposite rudder and the stick fully forward. Suddenly it came out, ceased revolving as though stuck on a pin and was in a dive towards the bush below, the speed mounting rapidly. To hell with it, he thought, I've enough height, I'll try a roll off the top. He held her in the dive, the air speed rising fast passed 160 to 180, then at 200 he pulled her back, the G pressing him down into his seat, dragging at his face muscles. He relaxed the tension a little. There was no point in causing a high-speed stall which would flick her back into the dive. Obediently the nose came up, rising above the horizon, up towards the blue sky and the puffy white clouds. He was vertical now and craning his neck back to see the opposite horizon through the rear canopy. When he was completely inverted he stopped the loop, hanging in the straps, dust falling from the floor around him, and firmly pushed the stick sideways, while applying hard rudder. She rolled out. He was the right way up, the speed down to ninety. He took a deep breath. That was enough for today.

A second later the first spot of oil appeared on the wind-screen. After a minute the perspex was coated with it, brown blobs dripping in the slip-stream, obscuring his view.

'Kipushi, I have an oil leak, returning to base.'

'*Parlez Français, s'il vous plâit.*'

'*J'ai une probleme, je retourne.*' He had enough on his hands without further explanations in French. His disregarded the jabber that followed, and yanked back the canopy so that he could see out sideways, his eyes watering in the rush of air. Why had he been so stupid as to fly without goggles? It always used to be an absolute rule to have them.

Nursing the engine, one eye on the oil-pressure gauge, he descended. At 1000 feet he reached for the undercarriage lever, raised it, felt it click into the down position and saw the pair of tiny lights flicker to red. He waited. They stayed at red. He swore. The undercarriage was not coming down, he must have fractured the hydraulic pipe. He tried the hand hydraulic pump, but it made no difference, the lights remained obstinately red. God, he remembered this one. Being unable to see the wheels, he could not tell if they were down or merely partly down. This meant he couldn't use the emergency locking device to secure them. To do so if the wheels were not fully down would damage the locking pins, which in turn could mean that the undercarriage collapsed when one landed.

There was nothing for it but to fly past the tower and ask for Duclair to be brought to the microphone. While he circled slowly around the field, the oil on the windscreen getting thicker all the time although the oil pressure was holding up, he prayed that he would not have to crash-land the plane. He would probably not be hurt physically by a belly landing, but his reputation most certainly would suffer, even if the mechanical fault was not due to him. He saw the men come down from the tower and fetch Duclair and then at last the Belgian's voice came on the radio.

'What's the matter?' He sounded petulant.

'I have an oil leak and my undercarriage lights are not showing the wheels down. Can you tell me if they are down or not.'

'Fly low in front of us,' Duclair ordered.

His forward vision obliterated by the oil on the windscreen, Mike brought the plane down to 100 feet above the ground and did as he was directed. To the left he could see the men in the tower as blurred outlines. He dragged his forearm across his eyes, trying to wipe them clear. The sweat was running off his forehead, adding to the problem of the slipstream.

'Your wheels are only half down.'

'I'll try rocking her.' As he spoke, Mike began waggling the wings violently, heaving the stick from side to side. After half a minute he thought he heard a heavy 'clunk' from beneath him. Perhaps one wheel at least had fallen into place from its own weight.

When he came round the second time Duclair told him both appeared to be down. He forced the undercarriage level fully forward to its emergency position and prayed that the manual locking device would work. The red lights flickered, went off and were replaced by the green. Pouring sweat, he roared round a third time, going through the drills, came in for a low approach and eased her on to the dirt runway, judging his position from the small triangle of ground he could see between the windscreen edge and the wing.

After he had landed safely, he climbed out of the high cockpit, his flying overalls clinging to him like a wetsuit, and jumped to the welcome earth.

'Well,' he said as Duclair approached, 'it flew, even if it has got a bastard of an oil leak.'

'No doubt the mechanics will cure that. By the way,' Duclair went on, 'I have a message from your friend. She wishes you luck on the flight.'

Mike said nothing. It was somewhat typical of Duclair to deliver the message when the event was over. Why was it that he had such animosity against all Anglo-Saxons when he himself had served alongside the RAF? Mike doubted if he would ever discover the reason. Then the mechanics crowded round, congratulating him delightedly, and he dismissed the question from his mind. Enough that he had a success to report to Chantal.

In the evening Mike drove to the city, planning to celebrate with her. They ate at a small restaurant on the Avenue d'Étoile. Yet, despite his good news and the pleasant food and wine, she appeared depressed. Eventually he commented on it.

'We're not achieving enough, that's all,' she said. 'In the north there is what amounts to civil war. Tshombe fears the United Nations will make it the excuse to use force against him. He is very worried because they are bringing Indian troops here soon. And his government is unable to achieve recognition.' She clicked her tongue in exasperation. 'Oh, we have support from Belgium, from Britain, from Sir Roy Welensky in Rhodesia. But still not one single government in the world recognizes Katanga. Not one. We could have such a beautiful, rich, peaceful country here.'

'I know,' Mike temporized, 'but do we have to talk politics? We see each other so little. Can't we do things together? Normal people go swimming, ride, play tennis. Sweetheart, when I'm off duty, can't we do the same occasionally?' It was the first time he had been so forthright with her.

'Please!' Chantal did not respond as he had hoped. 'We Belgians are very reserved, you know. We don't call each other "darling" at first sight like you do. We take a long time getting to know someone.'

'You must fall in love occasionally,' Mike tried to smile, 'surely you must.'

Chantal gave a tiny shake of the head. 'I like you very much. I mean that. But you are fighting a war. Maybe when there is less to worry about, when we have more time ....' She let the sentence slip.

'Is it your parents?'

'No, no. I am very fond of them, but I am a grown woman, for heaven's sake.' She touched his hand fleetingly. 'Don't press me, Mike. We don't want to quarrel again. Tell me about the flying. I am interested, I promise.'

When Mike drove back to Kipushi later all the elation had drained out of him. If he was honest with himself he realized that he had come here as much because of her as because of the opportunity to fly, or his love of Africa. Anyway, he reflected bitterly, this was a different Africa to the one he knew. On the other hand, if Chantal thought it worth fighting for, it probably was.

A single short paragraph of the newspaper story was underlined in ink:

> If under present orders the UN are unable to maintain law and order, the whole future of the United Nations in the Congo will be called into question.

Barlow handed the clipping back across the desk to his superior, Gustavsson, a New Zealander of Scandinavian origin who was the UN representative in Katanga, and for whom he had been deputizing. 'I'm sorry, sir. I did my best to explain about establishing a neutral zone in the north to the reporter.'

Gustavsson sighed. He was still weary despite his leave. One day Africa will have all our bones, he thought. Aloud he said reprovingly, 'If the London *Sunday Times* prints that, is it surprising others say much worse? I don't need to tell you how critical a time this is. The General Assembly still hasn't renewed our appropriation. Here we are in April and technically we've been without finance since 1 January. We need at least a hundred million dollars this year. A bad press doesn't help.' He raised one hand slightly to forestall Barlow's reply. 'We're doing as good a job as we can, somehow we have to get it across.'

'I'll try, sir.' Barlow hesitated. His inclination had always been to stay analytical and aloof from problems until he had come to a reasoned conclusion about them. Journalists, by nature, demanded an immediate and preferably dramatic statement. Nothing less would satisfy their editors. If they didn't get one, they wrote it themselves. His own failure with the journalists could well destroy the reputation he was trying to build here.

'Frankly, Mr Gustavsson, I'm a diplomat and a lawyer, not a press man. Is there no hope of my being relieved from this particular duty?'

'I'm afraid not.' The New Zealander lapsed into his routine phrase. 'I don't need to tell you how short of senior staff we are, from the Secretariat in New York downwards. I'll ask Mr Dayal in Leopoldville again, but don't expect miracles. We have to keep a balance of nationalities and . . . .' Suddenly he let his civil servant's mask slip. 'Look, Steve, let's call a spade a spade for once. If America didn't pay half the cost, this operation would have collapsed already, but the East-West confrontation means they can't provide staff. The British and French and Belgian governments are too partisan for more than a very few of their citizens to be sent. Where the hell are we going to get press officers who can cope with the Western media from? Both our countries are already heavily committed, the Swedish element is dangerously out of proportion. That leaves the Irish and maybe the Dutch. And, as you know, Mr Hammarskjold prefers to appoint people who have impressed him.' Gustavsson leant forward, making an appeal. 'You impressed him, Steve, greatly. He has personal confidence in you. So have I. You just have to soldier on with this double job. Grin and bear it.' He relaxed and smiled. 'Now, how about the civilian affairs side? As the Secretary General is always saying, we should be guided by the interests of the Congolese people. Are there going to be a lot more Baluba refugees coming down?'

Barlow winced. He was still raw from the off-the-record talk with a reporter who had been up north to the neutral zone the UN was trying to create. The reporter had challenged him repeatedly on the facts and ended by remarking caustically that, if he took the trouble to see for himself, he might speak with more authority.

'It's hard to be sure about the refugees,' he admitted. 'We have so much to do here in the office. I feel pretty out of touch with what's going on out of town.'

Gustavsson took the hint willingly. 'Maybe you should make a few trips, go on safari as they say. To be honest, I don't like relying solely on our military for information.'

Two days later a cable arrived from Kane requesting facilities to visit the Kiobo area. Barlow studied the map. When he saw Kiobo's location, on the border of the Baluba territory, he decided to consult the Swedish colonel. He found him sitting reading the *Svenska Dagbladet*.

'Ah.' The colonel put the newspaper down. 'What can I do for you?'

'I need some advice about the Kiobo district.'

The colonel rose and moved across to his wall map, marked with military symbols in various colours.

'Kiobo?' He searched with his index finger. 'Ah, yes. Kiobo. Not such a large place. About a hundred kilometres from Kolwezi. I believe there is good hunting up there. Buffalo, antelope. Quite wild country.'

'I meant how safe militarily?' Barlow stuck to his subject. The colonel's hobby was hunting. Given the mildest encouragement he would start talking about Lapland and white ptarmigan.

'Ah, yes, of course.' The colonel reconsidered the matter. 'There's been no fighting reported since the battle at Bukama. I think our presence is keeping everything quiet. We have the Moroccan battalion at Kolwezi and the Irish at Jadotville, you'll pass them on the way. They'll give you a briefing. I presume you'll take a guard? We can detail the Irish to provide one. Yes, with a couple of jeeps you'll be fine.'

'Would you call this a town at war?' asked Rick Croft, deep-voiced as ever. He was standing outside the Leo Deux, gazing past the palm trees that decorated the wide Avenue de L'Étoile towards the General Post Office. The sun was shining. An African woman in a full, long cotton costume of extravagant gold and brown colouring and a high headdress of the same material smiled at him, teeth flashing. She passed on, clutching her handbag and a newspaper. Opposite a policeman on point duty casually surveyed the traffic, hands on hips, his dark face accentuated by a gleaming white helmet. The flow of cars and people was continuous.

'It's a war of words most of the time,' Kane answered, 'a battle of communiqués. The UN issues one, Tshombe issues his reply, the central government issue theirs, then they all get heated and fire off a few more. They'd be lost without the foreign correspondents.' He laughed. 'So would the management of the hotel. It must be coining money.'

'Maybe this guy Tshombe isn't so stupid,' Croft observed. 'Why fight if you can get away with shouting? Come on, let's find a drink and you can tell me the programme.'

The two men walked back into the hotel, where they had just checked in after the flight from Brussels. Though tired, they had agreed to set about their work straight away.

'The Union Minière management might be less than delighted to learn you're here,' said Kane quietly, after they had ordered two beers, 'however, I did get alongside one of their geologists on my last visit. He could fill in the background if you want. Tomorrow, with luck, we'll leave for Kiobo. It's several hours' drive.'

'Think we should stay overnight?'

'If there is anywhere. Africa is rather short on motels.'

'Well,' the Californian yawned, 'at least this town's more attractive than Tucson. Pardon me. Listen, why don't you go find this geologist while I get a couple of hours' sleep? I'm not in shape for these intercontinental journeys.'

After Croft had gone upstairs Kane telephoned the geologist and arranged to give him lunch, then rang the

UN and asked for Barlow.

'Did you get my cable?' he asked. He didn't want to sound anxious, but a lot hung on having UN sponsorship. Despite his joking remarks about the war of words, Kane knew that up-country the fighting was real and vicious. He didn't want Croft to be exposed to any danger.

'Indeed I did.' Barlow sounded friendly enough. 'In fact you're in luck, Bob. I'd like to visit the Kiobo area myself. I've made provisional arrangements for tomorrow, Tuesday.'

'Magnificent! We're in your hands.' A little flattery would do no harm. 'That couldn't be better. By the way, do we stay overnight anywhere?'

'Kolwezi. There's a UN battalion there. That's about the nearest place with secure accommodation, even though its sixty miles. I believe there *is* a White Fathers' Mission near Kiobo itself.

'Excellent. What time then?'

'I'll pick you up at eight.'

Feeling justifiably elated, Kane went to his room to get his own head down for an hour.

Father Paul was concluding the morning's lessons in the brown brick built school hall at Kiobo when he heard the jeeps drive up. The Mission would never turn away callers. None the less his first duty was to his flock. He did not finish until the large class had answered the last question, put away their books and run helter-skelter out into the big courtyard, laughing and ragging each other. They were mostly ten- and eleven-year-olds, these African children, and he delighted in their keenness to learn. When he did walk out into the wide courtyard his young colleague Father John was already greeting the men in the jeeps. He saw the white UN insignia on them and the blue berets of the four Irish soldiers and wondered what kind of an expedition this was. The UN had never been here before.

'These gentlemen want to visit the mining site,' Barlow explained, introducing himself. 'And I'm on the civil affairs side of ONUC. I hoped maybe you could fill me in on the local problems.' He glanced at both priests in turn. 'We tend to disregard the views of the veterans here. I feel that to be a mistake.'

The implied mistrust of everything colonial, of everyone who had been here before Independence, amused Father Paul. This was precisely how he had imagined the UN would think.

'We're not exactly veterans,' he remarked. Father John was only a year past his novitiate. 'However, we shall be happy to tell you what we can.' He looked at Croft and Kane. 'As for the mine, there's not a great deal to see.'

'Joseph might show them the way,' Father John suggested. 'I'll go and find him.'

'Is the mine far?' asked Kane. 'We imagined it was pretty close.'

'About twelve kilometres. It might be wise to take an escort. It's a lonely place. The only natives who go there are charcoal burners.' Father Paul thought he saw a flicker of concern in the Englishman's eyes, something out of keeping with an otherwise strong face. Thereafter he kept a watch on all Kane said and did.

By the time Father John had returned with Joseph, a pleasant, open-natured African in his early twenties who helped teach in the school, Barlow had decided that two of the Irish soldiers should accompany Croft and Kane. They left immediately, undertaking to be back by five so that the drive onwards to Kolwezi could begin well before dark.

'There is no point in inviting trouble,' remarked Father Paul as the jeep disappeared down the track. 'Now, Mr Barlow. It is lunchtime, would you like some food? We live very simply here, you understand.'

Barlow accepted and as they entered the Mission house began to ask questions about the Baluba people, making notes and seeking elaboration of details.

One of the Irish soldiers drove the jeep, Joseph beside him, while the three other men squeezed into the back. They regained the main road, then bumped and jolted off it again, pursuing a winding track up into an area of low hills. Most of the country was wooded, but there were occasional clearings and some of the humped hilltops were almost devoid of vegetation.

'Just like the geologist said,' Croft remarked. 'Where there's copper near the surface nothing grows well. Are we nearly there?'

Joseph spoke no English so Kane translated. 'Almost. Boreholes were sunk all round here. The actual excavation is further on.'

Grinding in low gear up a steep slope, they suddenly came upon the remains of a small wooden hoist with a dilapidated shed near it.

'Here,' said Joseph.' Stop, please, sir.'

They got out, brushed the dust from their clothes, wiped their faces and stood on the edge of the abandoned mine. The reddish rock had been cut away to form wide terraces, ten feet or more high, though the total depth was only forty feet or so. Effectively all that had been done was to remove a segment of hill-side close to where the original shaft had been sunk. A tunnel hole in the rock face showed where an underground gallery had been begun. A heavily rusted mechanical shovel stood forsaken, lopsided, its tracks broken. There was no sign of human activity, only the calls of birds broke the silence.

'See there, sir,' said Joseph proudly, pointing to where some straight stemmed plants with small blue flowers grew on the lip of the excavation. 'The copper flower!'

'Gee,' Croft exclaimed. 'In all my years I never saw that before.'

'This was a place where in the old days our fathers found ore,' Joseph went on. 'They smelted it in furnaces made of earth and cast the copper in the shape of the Katanga cross. They knew about Kiobo for many hundreds of years. The Belgians began to dig here, then they gave it up. They had too many other mines!' He laughed. 'My father always told me they were stupid. This could be the richest of them all.' He swept the horizon with his hand. 'All these hills have the metal in them.'

'Pretty much what the geologist friend of yours reckoned,' commented Croft. 'Let's go get some rock samples for ourselves.' He began to scramble down a path to the first terrace.

Kane stood still, scanning the horizon, trying to visualize the creation of a Delphi Ridge out here in the bush: roads, housing, offices, canteens and at the heart of it the ever-widening chasm which this would become, the giant yellow trucks revving their engines as they hauled out the rock for the ore crushers, the labourers sweating under the African sun. He saw the name Kiobo featuring in the *Wall Street Journal* and the *Financial Times*. He saw the polished slab of copper from the first smelting of Kiobo ore which he would have placed outside the company headquarters. Above all, he saw himself as not merely rich, but justified in his pursuit of Katangan concessions. The Lumumba fiasco would be long forgotten. 'Kane was right', they would say admiringly, 'got in on the ground floor.'

'Hey, Bob! You dreaming or something? Come on down.' Croft's shout shook him out of the reverie. The Californian was three terraces below, chipping away with a small hammer. Kane hurried to join him.

'Boy,' said Croft excitedly. 'Look at it!' He held out a chunk of greyish rock, striated with thin bands of pale green and brown and a single line of iridescent dark green, glistening against the dull grey. 'There's the malachite,' he pointed out the irregular line. 'Just like the geologist said, the rock's a dolomitic schist, there'll be ore right through it. This stuff is highly mineralized. Jesus Christ, Bob, it's a gold mine! He suddenly realized what he had said and grinned. 'Well, a damn fine grade copper one. I see why they reckoned the proportion of ore would be ten per cent or more and I guess there's plenty of cobalt in there, too. See the blue tinge?' Croft laughed happily. 'Whatever kind of an earth movement thrust these rocks up to the surface a few million years ago, that movement was our friend. Why in hell haven't the Belgians exploited it?'

'Apparently they've been keeping it in reserve. And it is remote, at least from the existing centres of production.'

'That never put a red-blooded mining man off. Here.' Croft handed over one of his samples. 'Souvenir for you.' He carefully wrapped up the rest and put them in his pocket. 'All this place needs is the initial finance. It is away from the basic infrastructure, from power, railways, towns. You're right to consider the area from that aspect. How about driving around some more? Hell, there might be no water. I have to ask that African a lot of questions.'

Three hours later Croft had begun to size up Kiobo's snags. The sun was appreciably lower in the sky. 'We'll just have to come back tomorrow,' he said. 'I could wish we had a better map.'

Kane asked Joseph to guide them back to the Mission and they set off. After twenty minutes of harrowingly slow progress, they rejoined the track they had come by. Then, as they reached the main road, Joseph abruptly demanded that they stop. The Irish driver pulled into the side.

'Turn the engine off, please.'

They all sat in the jeep, Joseph restraining them from speaking. He was staring intently down the road, towards a bend beyond which was the turn off to the Mission several miles away. The others watched, perplexed. The jeep's engine made metallic clicking noises as it began to cool. A bird startled them with a high-pitched, long-drawn-out call. Silently Joseph pointed down the road, his hand trembling slightly. One tree taller than the rest was waving as if in a wind. But there was no wind, everything was still. The tree shook more, then toppled from sight. A few seconds later they heard the crash of its falling.

'What is it, charcoal burners?' asked Kane in a whisper. Joseph's evident fear had communicated itself to all of them.

'The road is blocked now,' said the African quietly, 'They always fell trees to make a barrier. Then they wait in the undergrowth. I saw the signs further back. They began there, then changed their minds and went beyond the bend where the surprise would be greater.'

'What the hell is he talking about?' demanded Croft.

'He thinks there is a rebel ambush further down,' explained Kane, the full irony of the situation suddenly hitting him. IMEX's undercover involvements had not been revealed to Croft.

'These two guys are armed, aren't they?' Croft indicated the Irish soldiers.

'We are that,' said the driver tensely. 'But there'll be maybe twenty of them and we wouldn't stand an earthly chance. We've met the Baluba before, God save us.'

Suddenly Croft became angry, raising his voice. 'All we've seen is a tree fall. This is damn stupid. Let's at least go on to the corner.'

'How fast can you reverse?' Kane asked, recognizing that he was caught. He should have confided in Croft, not assured him there was negligible danger in this trip.

The driver reached down for his rifle, loaded it and turned round. 'Which of you gentlemen can shoot straight?' he asked.

'He's the hunter,' said Kane, nodding at Croft.

The other soldier loaded his weapon and rested it on his knee.

'Please, sir!' Joseph suddenly understood what they

were going to do. 'There is another way to the Mission. We must go back.'

'We'll only abandon this route if we have to,' said Kane. No one was going to have reason to call him a coward. In Barlow's absence he felt entitled to give orders.

'Hold on to your seat, then,' said the driver. 'You won't expect to be playing the sitting duck for them, I fancy.' He restarted the engine and edged the jeep forward in second gear. 'If you must drive into trouble, drive slow,' he explained. 'Otherwise you'll never get a shot in yourself.'

As the jeep approached the corner no one spoke. Croft tightened his grip on the gun. They rounded the bend at a crawl. The view of the road ahead gradually opened up. Fifty yards ahead a mopani tree lay across the surface. Its trunk was not huge but its foliage and branches were enough. They could not hope to crash through. The driver stamped on the brakes. As they all jerked forwards, a bullet cracked over their heads, then another slammed into a mudguard. The driver swung the steering wheel round and reversed hard, throwing up the dirt. Another shot missed them, but still there were no rebels visible, only tall grass and scrub. As they accelerated away, the jeep skidding violently in completing the turn, the soldier in the back twisted round and fired wildly at the first rebel to appear, running gun in hand towards them. Then they were into the bend and racing away.

'My apologies, gentlemen,' said Croft. 'I was wrong.'

Joseph looked at Kane, the fear still in his eyes because he knew what must inevitably follow, either tonight or the next night, or the one after. 'We knew they were coming,' he said. 'They claim all the land near the Lualaba river. You Europeans make fun of what you call our "bush telegraph". Excuse me, sir, but you should not do so. We may not have telephones, but we know our own country.'

For the first time in all his visits to Africa Kane felt justifiably humiliated. It was his first serious encounter with an African who was not either a servant or a politician. He mumbled his excuses and was thankful Croft could not understand French.

When they reached the Mission compound Barlow came out at once. His face was pallid and drawn. He noticed the bullet hole in the jeep at once. 'Did you run into them?' he asked.

'They've blocked the Kolwezi road.' Kane stepped out of the jeep dispiritedly. 'Where else are they?'

'To the north and moving down. As far as the missionaries can tell we're cut off. They've been talking on the radio to another Mission twenty miles away which is in the thick of it.' A spasm of anger distorted his expression for a moment. 'So much for our UN briefing. The Katangan gendarmerie are supposed to be in control of this whole area, they're supposed to have driven the rebels out. We'll have to call for help.' He turned to the driver. 'Can you get through to Kolwezi?'

'It might just be possible, sir, though we're at the limit of range and those Moroccans are the devil to understand. They have neither the language nor the voice procedure.'

Barlow frowned. He was self-critical enough to appreciate that having set out to learn what things were like on the ground as opposed to at headquarters, he was being taught with a vengeance. None the less he was becoming apprehensive.

'Can't you raise your own battalion?'

'At Jadotville, sir? That would be a miracle at the distance.' He pondered the problem. 'Have we the aerial extension with us, Mick?' he asked his companion and began tuning the set.

Barlow, Kane and Croft left them and went inside, followed by Joseph. They found Father Paul preparing for the evening Mass as though everything was normal.

'Do you want to be evacuated from here?' he asked casually. 'If you do we can pass a message to Elisabethville. We use long range HF sets. Our missionary network is quite effective, almost too much so.' He smiled. 'We were accused of passing military information recently.'

'Are we in serious danger?' It was hardly necessary to ask, the sick feeling in Barlow's stomach told him, but he wanted someone else to say it.

'I think so. Word pases quickly in the bush and the rebels are not good at distinguishing between one army and another. As far as they are concerned a jeep and white soldiers spell enemy.' Father Paul gathered up the sacraments, placed a cloth over them, and excused himself. 'Father John is on the radio now. In the dining room.'

Only after he had gone did it occur to Barlow that the priest had made no mention of his own safety.

Duclair was in a hurry, disregarding traffic lights, speeding through the dusk to reach the gendarmerie headquarters, the car lurching and shuddering across occasional potholes. When he got there the major on duty was waiting.

'If I lay on the aircraft, can you provide a Dakota's worth of paratroops?' Duclair demanded. 'For dawn tomorrow.'

'If Captain Jacques is available.' The major sounded doubtful. 'He could be out.'

'In Shinkolobwe? The guard could find him in half an hour! Tell him we must have his twenty six best men ready to emplane at six thirty. They'll need plenty of ammunition grenades and light mortars if possible. I'll arrive later this evening to brief him.'

Duclair ran down the stairs, leapt into his car and drove to the pilots' villa. Mike was back in residence now that the T6s were flying, and he and Joe were about to have dinner. Duclair stifled his impatience long enough to accept a whisky, then, glass in hand, explained his plan, pinpointing Kiobo on a map.

'The strip is too short for the DC3,' said Duclair. 'We've been trying to get the missionaries to lengthen it. You'll have to take the Cessna, Russell, with a T6 as back up.'

'Is the Mission under attack?' Joe asked.

'Not yet, but it could be.'

'Why the panic, then?' He had never seen Duclair display such energy before.

Duclair relaxed a little, conscious that he had been over-dramatic. 'There is very real danger for the Mission at Kiobo and for the one at Upemba, but, since the priests will only consent to leave when their house is burning around them, that is not the whole point. In fact they have not demanded help for themselves. It is for their visitors. Their visitors,' Duclair played with his glass, 'are a senior UN official and two others, plus four soldiers. They have been unable to make contact on their own radio. Perforce their request for evacuation has come to us.' Duclair could barely contain his pleasure at the thought. 'Naturally we shall pass it on to the UN – later tonight. As they have no aircraft, they will have to fight their way up the road. Meanwhile we shall have beaten off the rebels and rescued the official. The operation will prove conclusively that the only force capable of maintaining law and order in Katanga is our own. And that the UN itself is amazingly incompetent.'

'Who's the official?' asked Mike.

'A man called Barlow, he was in charge briefly while you were down at Kipushi. Managed to get himself thrown out of the Leo Deux one night. He'll be getting quite a reputation by the time we've finished with him.' Duclair turned to Joe. 'You will take the Associated Press correspondent with you in the Dakota. I intend this to hit the headlines.' He gulped down the whisky and stood up.

'So for God's sake drop Jacques' boys in the right place. I don't want them strung up in the trees with the Baluba taking pot shots at them, and the world laughing.' Duclair trotted out through the verandah and was gone.

Seven of them assembled for dinner at the Mission, Father Paul saying grace beforehand, a minor ritual which caught both Kane and Croft unawares.

'Does Joseph live with you?' Barlow inquired after they had sat down and Father John was spooning out the vegetable soup.

'He does,' answered Father Paul. 'But this evening he has gone to find out what's happening.'

'Where the rebels are, you mean? Isn't that a pretty hazardous undertaking?' The afternoon had taught him just how fluid and unpredictable the rebels' operations were.

'Very. Particularly since Joseph is a Lunda, one of Tshombe's tribe. He is a brave man, no more than a boy really. We are trying to find him a place at a university.' Father Paul sighed. 'The tragedy is that we Belgians gave the Congo a primary education system only. We taught them as children, not future leaders.'

With a sharp crackle of static, the radio in the corner, which had been left switched on, came to life. Father John quickly left the table and took up the microphone. They could all hear the loudspeaker, but the interference was so severe that even the priests could barely piece together the words. Father John turned down the volume in the hope of being able to follow the sense more easily. Gradually his expression became more and more worried. Eventually, when there was a lull, he turned to Father Paul.

'The rebels have surrounded the Upemba Mission. What can we do?'

'Inform Elisabethville. Beyond that we can only pray.' Father Paul sank his face into his hands, his lips moving silently.

Respectful of his privacy, Barlow left the table, followed by the others. For half an hour there was no general conversation. The soldiers absented themselves to make further attempts at contacting Kolwezi. Kane and Croft talked in low voices in a corner, discussing the feasibility of making a dash for safety. Barlow sat by himself, a prey to conflicting thoughts, dominant among which was one born of Father Paul's remark about the rebels regarding all soldiers as enemies. If they left in the jeeps they would stand an excellent chance of becoming lost in the dark and, if caught, must expect to be killed. On the other hand, remaining here put everyone else in the Mission at greater risk than normal. As priests alone they might be spared; harbouring military men they might not be. Apart from this moral consideration, his instinct was to stay here until help arrived.

The radio became active again and this time the transmission from Upemba was unmistakable. The words were those of the Lord's prayer, spoken with barely controlled emotion and great sincerity.

'Our Father who art in heaven, hallowed be thy name. Thy Kingdom come, thy will be done, in earth . . . .'

A thunderous blast of noise cut off the voice and the static on the frequency ceased. Kane looked at Croft, both knowing the set had been destroyed. Father Paul waited a full minute and then in firm tones completed the remaining words of the prayer and made the sign of the cross.

'Listen here.' Croft could hold back no longer. 'Can't we organize some defence? We have four soldiers. I'm pretty handy with a gun. Didn't I hear you were a commando once, Father? Damnation take it, we're nine able-bodied men. We can hold off five times our number if we set about it right.'

'I am sorry.' It was no euphemism, Father Paul felt deeply for these strangers in their predicament. 'We are here to serve Africa, not to fight wars. We carry bibles, not guns. Indeed we have no weapons of any kind. The day a mission station becomes a fort will be the day our power for good here dies. I would rather die myself.'

'There must be something positive we can do!' Kane had to see Croft safely out of here even if he stayed himself. If Croft was harmed he knew his career would be over. Assuming he survived. He desperately wanted to take some action, any action. He turned on Barlow. Damn it, Barlow had agreed to be used, he had brought them to Kiobo. 'You're responsible for our transport, have you no plan?'

'What is Father Paul's opinion?' Barlow asked, hoping the answer would ease his conscience.

The lighting from the Mission generator was not bright. However, the bulb above the table illuminated Father Paul well enough, glowing on his white cassock, deepening the lines of experience in his face. 'For myself, I shall do two things,' he said. They had been hardest for an ex-commando to reconcile himself to. 'I shall pray and wait. When the rebels come, I shall talk to them. If they once start to talk, we shall have a chance.'

'I reckon we should make a run for it,' said Kane.

'Not necessarily.' Barlow cut him short. 'Let's make a logical appraisal. As a UN official I am neutral, we are here simply to keep the peace. Is there no chance of the rebels respecting that?'

'There are neutral countries but no neutral men, especially not here,' Father Paul observed. 'That is your organization's main problem.'

'I take issue with that,' said Barlow hotly. 'We go to absurd lengths to be impartial.'

'It will never be appreciated. My friend, Africans are not cerebral like us, they are sentimental. The rebels may rage at me for an hour, then thank me for running the school. Or they may burn the place down. Either reaction could be because the only education they have had was from the Church. It is impossible to forecast.' His manner became more brisk. 'Let us at least summarize our information. Father John, will you talk to Elisabethville again while I find out what has happened to Joseph?' He rose and walked out to the courtyard, aching to take some action himself.

An hour later, at eleven, Barlow could no longer hold off the obligations of leadership. He gathered his group together and spoke to them. 'We might as well face up to being in a pretty tricky situation. Joseph reports that most of the villagers have gone into hiding in the bush. The only ones he met were too scared to tell him anything. He thinks the rebels will wait until daylight to attack us. We've failed to raise our own troops at Kolwezi on the radio. On the other hand, there is a promise from Elisabethville that some kind of a plane will be here as early as possible tomorrow. I imagine our people there have chartered one. On balance my feeling is for sticking it out here. OK? It'll be a pretty uncomfortable night but it may be a better bet than risking an ambush in the dark.'

Sullenly Kane agreed.

'I guess, you're the boss.' Croft didn't sound happy either.

Watching them, Father Paul noted the reluctance with which Barlow had come to the decision, the way the American regretted not making a straightforward last stand and, finally, Kane's evident fear of something beyond the simple physical danger. They were an odd trio, he thought. Then, since he intended to stay up all night, he asked if any of them played chess. He was not surprised when the one who took him up on it was Barlow. He had expected the Canadian to welcome an intellectual distraction. He did himself.

Although the others tried to sleep, they did so in their clothes sprawled in chairs. From time to time Father Paul would quietly go outside and listen. There was a full moon and every shape seemed to move. However, nothing happened until dawn, when Joseph entered the Mission house unashamedly frightened.

'Father, they are leaving the village and coming down the road. Thirty at least. I have been out in the *shamba* keeping watch.'

'Are they coming fast?'

'No, Father. They are stopping to burn the huts.'

Father Paul considered this. The village was two miles north of the Mission and the airstrip was in that direction. They had perhaps half an hour's grace. 'Make us all some coffee, will you, Joseph?' he said and went to shake the four soldiers awake. Then he spoke quietly to Barlow. 'Now that it is light you stand a chance. Be ready to drive south. I would like you to take Joseph with you. He is certain to be killed otherwise and he knows the road.'

'You don't think the plane will come?'

'Regrettably I am a priest, not a clairvoyant.'

Humbled, Barlow retreated and began chivvying the soldiers.

Mike had taken off in the dark heading north-west. He had 150 miles to fly and the Cessna was slow. He wanted to be overhead Kiobo at seven. Once there he would orbit and talk in the Dakota and T6s. He had done this once on an RAF training exercise. Inevitably the memory of 699 Squadron reminded him of Barlow. Steve Barlow had been at the back of his mind for weeks. He had known he was around ever since the *Essor* published his photograph, while the incident in the hotel had made him a regular butt of the mercenaries' humour. Initially Mike had thought their paths unlikely to cross. Reflecting on it now, such optimism was unrealistic. The UN was demanding removal of the mercenaries and he was one. Personally, he had nothing particularly against Barlow. The Canadian's evidence had made no difference to the court-martial sentence. At the same time, he had seemed unpleasantly aloof from other people. Well, Mike thought, listening to the steady drone of the Cessna's engine, it will be interesting to see how he reacts this time.

Behind him the dawn crept up, a band of orange encircling half the horizon. The rapidly strengthening light flowed into the Cessna's cabin while the country below was still in darkness, then gradually revealed the landscape. Wisps of smoke curling up from the bush showed where Africans had lit early fires to cook maize porridge. Finally he could distinguish the shapes of thatched huts and irregular patches of cultivation. But the valleys were troughs of most. He hoped Kiobo was not in one. He checked the time, 6.30 a.m., and climbed to a safe 5000 feet above ground. Commandant Van Damme had been killed recently, hit by a bullet which came up through his plane's belly at 1500 feet. Levelling out, Mike began scanning the bush for the Kolwezi road and, beyond that, the straggling course of the Lualaba river. These plus the Kiobo hills were the only landmarks shown on the map. He called the other aircraft and asked where they were.

'My position at rail junction heading north.' Joe's unhurried response told him the Dakota was on track. They had agreed it should follow the Kolwezi road north. Next the Cubans' Spanish American accents confirmed that they were both formating on the Dakota. The three of them should be easy enough to spot. The problem was communicating with the Mission. Because the Cessna had no HF set, he would have to relay through the Dakota.

'Joe,' he called, 'will you advise Kiobo we expect to be overhead in twenty minutes?'

This time Father Paul took the microphone. He wanted there to be no misconceptions. 'The rebels are advancing from the village to our north. The end of the airstrip may already be in their hands. The United Nations party is preparing to escape. Father John and I shall remain here. Do not, repeat not, attempt landing on our account.'

'Message understood.' Joe relaxed his normal strict phraseology. 'Don't worry, Father. We'll see you safe. Chantal will skin us if we don't. Just stay inside, all of you.'

Barlow, Croft and the others had crowded around the set. 'Who is Chantal?' asked Barlow puzzled.

'My goddaughter.' Father Paul guessed who the pilots were, knew they would bring air support, and reluctantly admitted to himself that it was now beyond his power to prevent the battle. He put down the microphone and rubbed his unshaven chin. 'Since we have to remain indoors, I shall go and wash.'

'Sounds like a tight schedule,' Croft commented apprehensively. 'Maybe we ought to try holding off these savages after all.'

'No.' Father Paul stopped on his way to the bathroom. 'Just stay under cover when the shooting starts.'

'I don't understand,' Barlow pursued him. 'Is this a UN aircraft?'

Father Paul paused in the doorway. 'My son,' he said, allowing himself the luxury of the phrase he normally eschewed. 'The ways of the Lord are sometimes strange. If I were you I would not question where your salvation comes from, only pray that it comes in time.'

As he had feared, the Kiobo hills were swathed in mist. Mike gazed at them searching for the line of the road until his eye was caught by smoke to the east. He caught his breath sharply as he realized it came from blazing huts. A moment later he recognized the Mission to the south with its group of buildings round a courtyard near the end of a short airstrip, a rough swathe cut out of the bush. Circling above he saw a group of rebels half-way down the airstrip and more on the road. There was not time to prepare orders.

Clutching the map, he called the T6s.

'Target rebels on Mission strip. Attack heading zero zero five to right of Kolwezi road. Target is one mile six o'clock from smoke.'

The Cubans acknowledged and, as he watched the horizon for them, he warned Joe to prepare for action.

In the Dakota Jacques shouted out 'action stations' and began hustling his men into readiness. Standing up, lurching with the plane's motion, Herman hooked up the strap from his parachute to the wire which ran the length of the plane's side, then methodically checked the parachute of the man doing the same in front of him. On both sides of the aircraft the line of men was doing the same.

'Port stick number!' Jacques roared at them. Starting from the back they obeyed, each man slapping the shoulder of the man in front to denote that his equipment was in order. 'thirteen, twelve, eleven ....' Herman was number eight. Finally Jacques himself yelled out 'one' and took his own place at the front. A sergeant, the man who would despatch them, hauled open the door. The slipstream surged in, bringing with it a crescendo of engine noise. Herman clutched for support as the plane swayed into a turn. They must be lining up for the drop.

In the Mission they heard the Cessna high overhead. Barlow ran to look out of a window, craning his head upwards.

'Get back, you idiot,' yelled Kane.

Father Paul appeared, a towel round his shoulders. 'It is essential to keep calm.' he said reprovingly. 'Please sit on the floor.'

White-faced, Barlow obeyed him. They could hear distant shouting outside. With a splintering crack, the first bullet hit the building. The tension was unendurable. They all watched the windows, expecting them to shatter at any moment.

Suddenly they were deafened by the swelling roar of two aircraft passing low overhead, accompanied by the unmistakable rattle of machine-guns. A few seconds later a heavy explosion shook the house, followed by another. As abruptly as it came, the aircraft noise died.

'What the hell's going on?' asked Croft.

'It sounded exactly like a pair of Harvards, didn't it?' Kane looked at Barlow. 'What kind of air force does the UN have?'

'We haven't got one,' Barlow replied perplexedly, 'only chartered transports.'

The walls shook again as the T6s returned. Then they heard the quite different note of the Dakota's engines.

Herman's eyes were fixed on the door, or as much of it as he could see past the men in front of him. Above its void a red light flickered on. He saw Jacques brace himself in the opening. The red changed to green, Jacques' equipment-encumbered figure vanished, the men behind him tramping forward like a chain gang. Seven seconds later Herman was in the doorway himself, the sergeant's hand thumping his shoulder, the voice yelling 'Go'. Without thinking he launched himself out. The slipstream hit him, carrying his body away, he felt a tugging, looked up and saw the chute open. He released the weapon container strapped to his leg so that it fell and hung suspended on a rope clear out of his way. Then he looked down. He was going to land on the grass by the runway. Twenty yards off a Baluba rebel was standing, staring up, not attempting to fire. Herman felt like a puppet suspended in mid-air. But the ground was coming up at him fast. Legs together, knees slightly bent, he hit, rolled over and was on his back, struggling to unclip the parachute harness. As it fell away he got his hands on his sub-machine-gun, rolled back on his stomach, hoisted himself up and looked round for the Baluba. The man was thirty yards away and sprinting. Herman loosed off at him but missed. The T6s roared overhead again. There were spasmodic bursts of machine-gun fire. He heard the shrilling of a whistle. Jacques was at the end of the landing strip, giving the sign to close in on him. As Herman picked up his container and doubled down there, the Dakota came round again, dropping the second stick of thirteen men. He glanced up at it exhilarated and happy. It was his first operational jump and the rebels had run.

Fifteen minutes later Mike saw a green flare below. He cut the Cessna's engine and let down with a precipitateness which would have scared the wits out of any safari client. When he taxied into the parking space near the Mission buildings Jacques was already there, grinning and making an ebullient thumbs up sign. As Mike climbed out he said, 'Now all you have to do is collect the passengers!'

Father Paul came out of the house and Jacques saluted.

'Ça va, mon père?' he asked. 'I apologize for the noise.'

'You forced me to postpone the seven o'clock mass. It is unforgivable.' Father Paul smiled, then shook hands warmly, almost laughing with relief. He shook hands with Mike. 'You must be Chantal's friend.'

Mike was about to reply when the others came out. Barlow he had expected to see, but Kane! He stared amazed at the unshaven men in their creased clothes, and they stared back at his khaki uniform and the red badges on his shoulders.

'Can you take three?' Father Paul asked, aware of the embarrassment.

'That is the number I came to fetch.'

It was Kane who broke the ice. He stepped forward and said, 'Good to see you, Mike. You arrived in the nick of time.' Then he turned to Barlow. 'However you look at it, Steve, this is one for the book.' But the bonhomie in his voice was forced.

'What the hell are you doing here, Russell?' Barlow was

trembling. He had known the paratroops could not be his own men, but had shrunk from admitting the corollary to himself. Now he could evade it no longer. 'We requested UN assistance,' he protested, white faced. 'Yours is completely unacceptable.'

'I can't answer for the UN.' Although Mike was slightly ashamed of Duclair's manoeuvre, it did not alter the facts. The Mission had been saved and Barlow with it. The bloody man hasn't changed, Mike thought, he is still standing on legal niceties. 'We were asked to rescue you,' he said shortly. 'We have succeeded so let's go!'

'I am sorry. I can't.' Barlow cast around in his mind for reasons more immediately convincing than his own susceptibilities. 'I am obligated to the Irish soldiers. What happens to them? No, I must remain until a UN force arrives.'

Jacques missed a few words of this, but he caught the gist. His expression froze. 'You have my word they will be returned safely to their unit. I, Jacques, vouch for it.'

Barlow shook his head. 'I regret it is impossible. There has been an appalling misunderstanding. I cannot accept transportation from the gendarmerie.'

Up to this moment Croft had said nothing. Now his temper boiled over. He stepped up to Barlow. 'These guys just risked their lives for us,' he said tautly. 'Get in that plane before I bust your face.'

Barlow hesitated. Jacques, his hand on his gun, was on one side of him, Croft on the other. 'I do so under protest,' he said stiffly, then turned and thanked Father Paul, adding, 'I am sure this situation is not of your making.'

Father Paul could exercise great self-control. This demanded his full reserve of it. 'My son,' he said, 'we are none of us perfect. Try to thank God that you are still alive.' He walked back into the Mission.

The conversation on the flight back was limited to Mike's routine radio calls. In accordance with Duclair's instructions he landed at the Elisabeth International airport. As he taxied in Barlow said huskily, 'I guess we were all under a lot of stress out there. Whatever I said I am deeply grateful to you, Mike.'

'Forget about it. We will probably never meet again.'

'May I give you some advice just the same? Quit before it's too late.'

Mike glanced quickly at him. 'I am not the quitting sort, thank you.'

As he parked the Cessna, the photographers and reporters descended on them. Kane and Barlow hurried away, Croft following at a more leisurely pace. Watching them go, Mike realized he had never even asked Kane what his business in Katanga was.

7

'I am sending you on immediate sick leave,' Gustavsson frowned. 'Who are your nearest relatives?'

'My mother and father.' Barlow felt too exhausted to argue. He had reported to the UN representative immediately he arrived back from the airport. He had explained the last twenty four hours' events and the impossible dilemma in which he had been placed. Now his superior was delivering judgement.

'We shall announce that you are suffering from serious overstrain and are flying home. It is Toronto, isn't it? Take ten days' rest, then come back via New York. If you can, bring an up to date idea of the Secretary General's thinking. His staff ought to be glad of the chance to pick your brains, too. As I see it, our first priority is to get rid of the mercenaries. As long as he has them Tshombe can defy our anyway limited authority.' Gustavsson forced a smile. 'So the trip will have its uses.'

'Do I have to go, sir?'

'Yes. No blame attaches to you. I shall make that absolutely clear to New York. I sanctioned your expedition. The military briefed you wrongly. Finally, your plight was very cleverly exploited, very quickly and very cleverly.' The representative emphasized his point. 'I mean this, Steve. I do not regard you as at fault. But the Katangan propaganda machine is just too slick and too well tuned for there to be any alternative. We have to remove you from the scene until the publicity dies down. Here in town you're a walking advertisement, not simply for the mercenaries' efficiency, but for their willingness to help us out of a jam. In a couple of weeks the affair will have been eclipsed by other news. In any case, you look as though you could do with a rest. This place is enough of a madhouse without the sort of experience you've been through.'

As Barlow boarded the Sabena 707 that evening, his eyes dark with fatigue, the photographers crowded round and he was forced to admit the correctness of Gustavsson's analysis. The press were not normally allowed on the tarmac. Now they were deliberately encouraged to hound him and the felt the loss of face acutely. Even if he was not being officially reprimanded, the incident would inevitably be recorded on the personnel department's files. His career was being endangered.

A few days later Croft departed, having drafted his report in Elisabethville, employing Kane to research additional information which he needed. At their final meal together in the Leo Deux he bluntly offered to satisfy the Englishman's curiosity.

'I guess what I recommend could be important to you, right?'

'Very.'

'Well, it's supposed to be strictly for the company President, but I could let you in on the general outline. There's no disputing Kiobo could be a damn valuable mine. If you could obtain a concession on Tenke, too, what with their not being so far apart, then it could become a very major operation indeed. I'm recommending you try, OK? Even so, Kiobo alone is worth having. As to costs, I don't see the tab coming out at much under a hundred million dollars, but we already agreed the potential mineral sales could top sixty million pounds a year, which is near enough a hundred and fifty million bucks. So, even allowing for running costs, it's a proposition. One problem is we would want to use the Union Minière smelters.' Croft grinned. 'You already figured that snag out, huh?'

Kane nodded. 'And for that Union Minière would have to be taking orders from the central government?'

'Or from someone who was not in the pockets of the Belgians. You know something? Although the English were the first to discover copper here, they've very few interests left, apart from a fourteen per cent share holding in Union Minière itself. The other businesses were eased out thirty years ago. What's more, if there's one thing the local Europeans reckon is worse news than you limeys, it's us. They are plain scared of United States companies getting any kind of toehold. So long as this Belgian backed regime is in power, we don't stand a chance.' Croft put his elbows on the table, shoulders hunched, speaking confidentially. 'Now I'm no politician, I'm just considering what factors make a project viable. And we sure as hell know another one that doesn't. Those damn rebels! That little expedition of ours was not an experience I would wish on my worst enemy. So long as the area is lawless, I'm advising against investing a single dime there.'

'But the situation won't last,' Kane countered. Yet again he saw his own plans being thwarted by the appalling complexity of Congo politics. Anyway, what the hell were IMEX doing agreeing to fund the rebels if Western Mining hadn't reckoned on them as being part of the overall plan to overthrow Tshombe? Western must know. They merely wanted someone else to carry the can if the manoeuvre was exposed. Yet he dare not hint at this to Croft. 'Once Katanga is re-united with the rest of the Congo,' he insisted, 'there won't be any rebels.'

'I told you, politics are not my game. But until there's genuine peace here, Western should stay away. Given a state of law and order, we could go ahead. Kiobo's a long term project, Bob.'

Kane reflected. The corollary was inescapable. 'We have to hope the United Nations succeeds in its peace-keeping,' he said.

'With guys like your friend Barlow running it?' Croft's scorn was undisguised. 'Thank God all Canadians aren't all like him. What do you see in the man?'

'Nothing. I mean it. He's an intellectually arrogant fence sitter. His only virtue is that we can use him occasionally.'

'The one occasion was enough for me.'

'He also has access to information which I need.'

'Even so.' Croft swore. 'Didn't you say he used to fly in your squadron? Didn't you find him out then?'

'I did. Too late. He gave the evidence which forced me to resign my commission. I never told you that.' Kane related the story of the Frampton crash.

'Jesus,' Croft exclaimed when he had finished. 'If I were you I'd loathe the guy's guts.'

'I do. I also need every card I've got in setting up this deal. I admit I've wondered why he's prepared to be helpful. At first I thought he felt some vague sense of guilt, but I don't any more. He's too intellectually aloof for that. I've come to the conclusion that inside himself he's a lonely person.'

'So you'll reckon to exploit that?' Croft looked levelly at him across the table. 'You've become a pretty ruthless guy, haven't you, Bob?'

'Perhaps,' said Kane noncommittally. His qualities did not include letting his scruples obstruct his career. 'But we have a lot at stake and, as you say, I have no cause to love Barlow.'

'When do you go back to London?' Croft asked, deliberately changing the subject.

'In a week or so. I've a few more arrangements to make out here.' As they concerned Sendwe and the rebels he did not enlarge on their nature. Indeed he was now in some doubt whether he should continue with them. After Croft had left he telephoned IMEX and asked in guarded terms for advice.

'Are your friends winning?' Skinner demanded.

'I can't say they are,' he admitted.

'Speak up, will you? The line's terrible.'

'No, they are not. The opposition has a lot of new equipment.'

'So we heard. You'd better return for discussions, understood?'

When Kane reached London three days later, having decided after all to call on Sendwe in Leopoldville en route, one of the first things he saw was a newspaper headline: 'Tshombe arrested in Congo Drama'. Hastily he bought a copy and read it on the way in from the airport with a sense of disbelief. The Katangan President had left his province to attend a meeting of Congolese leaders, become angered at President Kasavubu's agreeing with the UN that all foreign advisers should be withdrawn, walked out in a fury and been held as he was about to board a plane for Elisabethville. Now he was under house arrest, accused of massacring the Baluba, inciting rebellion and a host of other offences.

By the time he reached the IMEX offices Kane was jubilant. The all-enveloping lassitude and sense of frustration which had gripped him since his last conversation with Croft had disappeared. At long last events were going his way. He had a rapid wash and shave, then went straight to see Skinner.

'Well, sir,' he announced, 'Tshombe's arrest is the kind of improvement money couldn't buy. He must be finished.'

Skinner nodded. He anticipated having a showdown with Kane this morning, but he wanted to let the man say his piece first. 'It would appear so. On the other hand it's not so long since you sat in that same chair telling me how often African politicians come to terms with their opponents.'

'Unpredictable as the Congolese are, sir, this must be the end of the road for Tshombe. They killed Lumumba for less than Tshombe's being held for. All we have to do is keep our contracts warm and the Kiobo concession will be ours.'

'I suppose you know Croft has argued strongly for biding our time?' Skinner had plenty to say on this subject.

'He did tell me,' Kane conceded. 'However, the situation is altering now. Order will be restored. Even if we postponed major investment in Kiobo for a while, I feel we should take the concession.'

'And pay for it?' Suddenly Skinner thumped the desk with his fist. 'Listen, Kane,' he said, deliberately dropping the use of Christian names. 'You are on the wrong track. I suspect your anxieties are more for your commission than for our company's success. Even Croft thought you were blinded by visions of a colossal profit. What the hell do you think you were doing, leading him into a rebel ambush? Western are furious and I don't blame them! Apart from that, will you kindly come to your senses over what is involved? Kiobo may be the richest mine on earth, but no businessman in his right mind is going to commit himself to financing it until the area is completely and lastingly peaceful. It's a five-year project getting even an opencast mine into production when the area is as totally devoid of facilities as this one.'

Kane was not the sort of man who sat and stared open-mouthed when attacked. His expression tightened. 'You asked me for a viable alternative to the original contract, sir. This is one. I admit it's a considerable step down from replacing Union Minière in the Congo, but this is potentailly one of the world's greatest copper and cobalt mines. As for taking risks, a guard of four UN soldiers ought to have been adequate protection.'

'May I remind you,' Skinner allowed his anger to show, 'that you have been funding the very rebels against whom you needed protection?'

'But you agreed to our supporting Sendwe.'

'We relied on your judgement.' Skinner was not prepared to admit liability. 'To put it in the crudest terms, neither here nor in New York did we appreciate who were the bad guys and who were the good guys. You spun me a long tale about the complicated way African politics works and I fell for it. We've ended up supporting the same rebels to whom the Russians are supplying arms. God knows whether Tshombe is good or bad.' Skinner shook his head vexedly. 'To be fair, he's probably neither. But I am in no doubt that Sendwe and the rebels are bad. If what you have been doing ever became public knowledge ... Christ alive, I don't even like to think about it.'

'You're not going to drop the Kiobo project?' For the second time in two hours Kane felt completely disoriented. The fatigue of the journey seeped back into his joints. He concentrated all his energy on thinking clearly and on keeping his temper. There was a flaw in Skinner's logic which he could not pin down, and he sensed he was in some way being made a scapegoat although he had done nothing of which IMEX had not been aware.

'Let's say we're putting Kiobo on ice. We are emphatically not committing ourselves to any of the costs which a concession would entail.' Skinner was cooler now that he had let off steam. 'I've never been at the sharp end of the business, but I know that the days are gone when a prospector obtained a licence, pegged out a claim and then hung on until he could either develop it or sell it. Your Kiobo concession is going to involve guaranteed commitments to development, time limits, the lot. Not to mention the kickbacks. No, Kane, we're waiting until we can negotiate a relatively above-board deal with the

Congo government, which, if you remember, was our original aim.' He drew in his breath. 'Meanwhile Sir John and I would like you here in London for a spell. We're very short-staffed at the moment.'

Slowly Kane grasped what this meant. He had heard the phrase about being short-staffed doled out to others when they had failed and were being relegated to less responsible duties. It was better than dismissal, but only just.

'A little routine broking will do you no harm,' Skinner went on. 'Is your flat still let? Well, try to get it back. We'll pay your hotel bills until you do. Reasonable bills, right?'

At last Kane found his voice. 'How long will this be for, sir?'

'I can't say. We feel you've spent enough time hanging around Africa. And enough money. Possibly, when the time is ripe, we'll send you back.'

When Kane had gone, Skinner scribbled his customary post-interview notes for the confidential files. He felt considerable relief. The negotiations Kane had been conducting had gone against his instinct from the start. It was one thing to deal with a Prime Minister like Lumumba, however erratic, quite another to be linked with a communist-inspired revolt. He was also beginning to feel a sneaking regard for Katanga's curious independence struggle, an enthusiasm which he noticed several influential friends of his shared. It was obvious from reading the *Telegraph* and the *Sunday Times* that Tshombe was a man the West should support. He concluded his summary of the conversation with the comment, 'Have over-estimated this employee's sense of judgement and loyalty to the company.' Then he telephoned Dillon at Western Mining.

Dillon listened to the brief exposition. 'Good,' he commented. 'This could have become an embarrassing involvement. We're well out of it. The White House is deeply concerned at communist penetration of the area. In fact, I would say that should we ever decide to proceed with the concession it should be negotiated by another intermediary.'

'You may be right,' Skinner temporized. He had a keen sense of justice and this seemed unduly hard on Kane.

'I am right.' Dillon discussed a few other points, then returned to the subject. 'Say, Jim, Senator Dodd is creating a lobby in the Senate in favour of Tshombe which is gaining a lot of ground. How does it look from your side?'

'The feeling here is that Katanga has a case.'

'Thanks, Jim, we'll be in touch.' After he rang off Dillon likewise made some notes. The essential point was that the fighting was definitely impeding Katangan copper exports. Western's support of the air force was proving an effective regulator. Futhermore, in the unlikely event of this connection becoming public knowledge, the company would have strong supporters in the Congress. He glanced at Croft's report again. Kiobo was a damned interesting looking project. Maybe Western should go after it direct one day.

That evening Kane stayed at the RAF Club on Piccadilly, where he ate a desultory meal, plagued by inability to discern precisely where his plans had first gone wrong. The frustration at having the coup which would make his fortune snatched from his grasp was unbearable. After dinner he strayed round the corner to the narrow streets of Shepherd Market. The ensuing pick-up by an extravagantly blonde prostitute in a coffee house was as unsatisfying as it was inevitable. He had arrived too late for his one girlfriend of old to break her date for the evening and he desperately needed someone to talk to. The blonde wasted the minimum of time on her warming-up conversation and then allowed him a scant fifteen minutes in her second-floor room. He emerged disgusted with himself. Yet, as he walked back to the club, her cheap scent still in his nostrils and the memory of a soiled green crêpe-de-chine bedspread before his eyes, he felt a new determination to succeed. He would sink no lower than tonight's mood. If IMEX did not back him, he would find a firm which would. 'A viable alternative', in Skinner's phrase.

Coming home to the house outside Toronto was a tonic to Steve Barlow. April had seen the last of the snow melt, revealing the sidewalks' unsightly burden of winter's litter and cigarette butts, but now that was all cleaned up and the first days of May gave the lake shore a beauty only rivalled by the autumn. His father took time off from the *Globe* and they went for long walks and fishing trips. Africa seemed to belong to another planet. Nevertheless it was seldom far from their thoughts.

Towards the end of the short holiday Jake Barlow tackled the question directly. 'Steve,' he said, 'this Congo business is generating a lot of emotion. It's so damned complicated no one outside of a racial studies group is going to understand it properly. So we have to ask ourselves in simple terms, why all the fuss?' They were close to a wooden bench and he sat down, drew on his pipe and contemplated the lake briefly. 'I'll tell you why I think there is. We see a huge, rich country in chaos because of interference by the communists.'

'That's an oversimplication,' his son protested. 'The French and British and Belgians are intriguing, too, especially the Belgians.'

'Let me finish, Steve. I'm in the business of simplification, remember? I try to think of this as readers of the *Globe* may do. They see one pro-Western part called Katanga where Europeans and Africans work together. There's no way we can disapprove of that. Then we see the United Nations committed to destroying that Katanga regime, yet doing nothing about other parts of the country which are completely under communist control.'

A week ago Steve Barlow would have exploded at this. Today, rested and talking to his own father, a man against whom he had never consciously been in revolt, he restrained himself. 'Forgive my saying so, Dad, but that is a gross distortion.'

'OK.' Jake Barlow recommenced his favourite sport of wheeling around a controversial subject. 'We're liberal-minded guys on the *Globe*. We show both sides of the coin. The last paragraphs of a leader I wrote recently admit that the mercenaries sound pretty rough diamonds and the West has a lot of copper at stake, while the UN has a tough job.' He shook his head. 'That does not alter the conclusion, which is: if the UN is going hand in hand with the communists, we should reconsider our support for the whole operation.' Jake Barlow swung round to face his son. 'Let's strip away the fancy notions. You're ambitious in a way I never was. I know that. Come to think of it, I admire you for it. So I'm concerned. Didn't you have a college expression about scoring? Well, this UN operation looks more likely to fail than to score, which does not spell promotion for men attached to it. Why don't you transfer out again?'

They strolled back along the lake shore, the breeze in their faces, the white-painted houses pretty in the spring sun. As they reached their own house, Steve stopped. 'I'll sleep on it,' he said, 'but I think the answer's no. I'll never have a chance like this again, it's the equivalent to a soldier's active service. The Congo is where the East-West conflict is taking place on the ground. As I see it, the great powers are pre-empting the Third World War by fighting in the Third World. We have to stop them.'

Jake Barlow laughed. 'That's a nice aphorism. Mind if I pirate it some time?' He paused in the big old-fashioned porchway. 'I'm glad you feel a sense of moral duty too. I don't like ambition by itself, naked.'

'You know something?' said Steve. 'At the worst moment of that night in the Mission I had a long talk about the morals of intervention with the priest. He maintained that countries could be neutral, but men could not.'

'Did he now?' Jake Barlow chuckled. 'And did he mention who made that remark originally? Nikita Kruschev, Premier of the Soviet Union, that's who. Kruschev said it to Walter Lippmann.'

'It's hardly likely that a White Father out in the bush would have known so.'

'Maybe,' Jake conceded. 'But watch out, son. When communists and Catholics agree there has to be trouble in store for someone.'

When he arrived in New York Steve Barlow found the UN Secretariat even busier than before. He was given a long briefing by one of Hammarskjold's aides. The new financial appropriation had at last been approved by the General Assembly: 100 million dollars for the period to 31 October.

'So that gives us another deadline?' Barlow queried.

'Unfortunately, yes. It should not. But it must do, since the refusal of Russia and France to contribute casts doubt on the whole operation.'

'We had a strong feeling in Elisabethville that, so long as his foreign advisers remained, Tshombe would never relinquish Katanga's independence.' Dutifully Barlow conveyed Gustavsson's ideas, then asked, 'Is Tshombe still under arrest?'

'Very much so. Naturally the Secretary General is appealing for him to be given fair treatment under the due process of law.'

'Can't we set a date by which they must leave?' Quite perceptibly, Barlow began to feel the frustrations of the UN task bearing down on him again.

'The General Assembly recently voted down a proposal for a time limit.' The aide clicked his tongue aggravatedly. 'It is infuriating, but one can see why. The north of the Congo is still communist controlled and almost as independent as Katanga. Futhermore, the Katanga public relations machine is superb. There is a lot of support for Tshombe in the United States Congress, which matters to us since they foot half the bill. I'm afraid this continues to be one of the most politically involved tasks the UN has undertaken.' He glanced at his watch. 'Can you come back after lunch? Mr Hammarskjold would like to see you, though he can only spare a few minutes. We could catch him before he goes into the afternoon meeting.'

Barlow ate alone in the delegates' dining room, his mind fully taken up with the dilemma which would again confront him on his return: attempting to cajole Katanga into agreement with the central government when its leaders respected only force. Was Father Paul right? Could one avoid taking sides?

Shortly before three he was ushered into the Secretary General's office, a unique room which had held him momentarily spellbound when he had first entered it and which did so again. Dag Hammarskjold was a man of considerable aesthetic refinement. The Museum of Modern Art in New York had lent him a group of pictures for this room, to which he had added acquisitions of his own. Paintings by Braque, Matisse and Leger were among those which confronted the visitor, while a statue by the English sculptress Barbara Hepworth, a close friend of his, stood there too. Typically, his taste had extended to the decoration of the whole building. He had written to Braque, 'For the home of the United Nations only the perfect is good enough.' But his office was where one felt this most strongly. Yet Hammarskjold was not dwarfed by it. He was always in control of his surroundings. He rose to greet Barlow, his lined face crinkling into a smile.

'I hear you've been having some adventures out there,' he said genially. 'Tell me about them.'

Knowing that this invitation was not intended to

provoke a lengthy discourse, Barlow kept his reply brief.

As he finished the Secretary General's expression became grave and he leaned forward a little, looking at Barlow quizzically. 'I appreciate the stress of the occasion,' he said. 'It would still have been better to have refused assistance from the mercenaries.' He did not speak as if this were a rebuke, however, more a mature reflection. 'You see, it is for the Congolese to decide what they want, not outsiders, and the greater discretion we show, the better I believe it is.'

'That is not so easily done, sir. We suffer from constant provocation.' Barlow had not forgotten being expelled from the Leo Deux, it rankled more than any of the more important incidents like the hijacking of the supply train.

'The Belgian factor. True.' Hammarskjold knitted his fingers together. 'As it happens I've been giving a great deal of thought to our role lately. At the end of the month I am to speak on the role of the international civil servant. We in the United Nations are bound to be exposed to controversy and to accusations of a lack of neutrality. But this does not mean one should not make a stand when it is one's duty.'

'I agree, sir.'

'The problem is one gets into an area where one's own personal judgement must come into play, as I fear it constantly must in Katanga.' His deep-set blue eyes searched Barlow's face intently. 'In that last resort, I think how you act can only depend upon your personal integrity and moral conscience.' He straightened up. 'That is the best guidance I can give. Good luck and I wish you a safe journey.'

Descending in the lift from the forty-fourth floor, Barlow experienced a new misgiving. It had not before occurred to him, with his brilliant academic record, that his own intellectual grasp and stamina were ever likely to be markedly less than that of those he worked for. This time he knew they were. When Hammarskjold explained a principle, it shone like a guiding star. Alone, without guidance, would he himself be strong enough to enshrine the Secretary General's ideal in action? For the first time he was uncertain. His father's jocular warning rang in his ears, 'There has to be trouble in store.'

The Fouga was returning from a training mission. It was being flown by a newly recruited Dutchman and Duclair stood by the control tower waiting for it. He had enjoyed less success than he had hoped for in attracting first-class jet pilots. Three of the sleek Fouga Magisters were operational, and more were awaiting assembly, so he needed more crews. Duclair expected the Dutchman to go through the routine joining procedure, but to his annoyance he saw the plane bank steeply in the distance and disappear. He had a sudden fear that the pilot was trying to show off by overflying the city centre. He scanned the horizon anxiously, then ran up the control tower steps to improve his view.

A dark speck over the city was rapidly becoming distinguishable as the Fouga. Too low, Duclair muttered to himself, and was stepping into the tower itself to give orders to the controller when to his horror he saw a pair of police jeeps bucking out over the grass to the runway. The vehicles' tops were down and the white-helmeted African drivers were gesticulating excitedly at each other. They were obviously having a race.

'Stop them!' he shouted. 'Get them off.'

'No radio,' snapped the controller and began calling the Fouga to abandon its approach. But the Fouga was now less than a kilometre from the runway and dangerously low. Duclair seized a signal pistol, slammed a red cartridge into it and ran out to fire a warning. As he did so he heard the howl of the jet engine. The pilot, appreciating his altitude, was putting on power. He was too late. As the red stars arched out into the sky, there was a far brighter flash in the distance. The Fouga's wheels had caught the low slung electric wires outside the perimeter, which were the airfield's major hazard. Miracuously the plane continued flying, but with its nose pitched up too high. Duclair held his breath. Ten seconds later it stalled, pancaking down on to the runway in a shower of sparks, skidding straight in the path of the jeeps and immediately catching fire. Duclair pounded down the steps, but when he reached the wreckage he was held back by the intense heat.

An hour later, sombre faced, he walked to his office, swearing under his breath. One policeman had been decapitated by the wing, another was crushed, the pilot had been burnt to death. Above all, one third of Katanga's operational striking force had been lost in the most bizarre and unnecessary accident he had ever witnessed. Even though Duclair was not given to self-catechism he knew who was at fault. The Dutchman had no flying discipline. The airfield police had no ground discipline. He was responsible for both. As he entered his office he pulled off his peaked hat and mechanically tossed it across to the peg on the wall. It missed, fell, and rolled on the floor. He stared at it, remembering his habitual joke about a bad omen, then exploded in a volley of curses. Things had begun to go wrong.

London was pleasantly warm in late June and Sir John was in excellent humour. The social season had been active and enjoyable as far as he was concerned. He had backed winners at Ascot, where he was a familiar figure in the royal enclosure. His yacht was proving well and soon he would be superintending a series of trials for forthcoming races. Accordingly, when he chanced on Kane walking down Pall Mall one lunchtime he greeted him with a cordiality which he might not have shown in IMEX's offices. Kane, he recalled, was a potential crew member.

'You busy this weekend?' he asked. 'We're limbering

up for the Fastnet and I'm a man short.' He glanced quickly at Kane's appearance. 'You look fit enough.'

Kane bit back a desire to tell his employer to go to hell. He was not enjoying the firmness with which Skinner had pinned him down into routine broking. But he knew that when Sir John went sailing he invariably organized some kind of party which like-minded city magnates attended. In its top strata the yachting world was rich and influential. 'In fact I am pretty well at a loose end,' he conceded.

'Meet me at the Royal Yacht Squadron for dinner on Friday evening then. We'll find you a bed somewhere!' As they continued walking down the street, Sir John touched on the subject of business. 'What's happening down in the Congo now?' he asked. 'Didn't I see something about your friend Tshombe in the *Financial Times* the other day? Is he back in business?'

'He managed to talk the central government into releasing him and now he's re-affirming Katanga's independence.'

There was a sourness in Kane's voice which Sir John could not fail to notice. 'No use being disgruntled,' he said with slight asperity. 'Those Congolese are totally unpredictable. It's a damn good thing we're out of that entanglement.'

Kane made no comment. IMEX might have dropped the Kiobo project, but he had not.

The weekend at Cowes followed a traditional pattern, except for the night out Sir John gave his crew in between the two hard days of sailing on the Solent. He took them a few miles along the coast of the Isle of Wight to the little harbour of Bembridge, where the sailing club was holding a black tie dinner dance. If Sir John had devoted half the organizational ability he possessed to IMEX, Kane reflected as they arrived, the firm would never have been swallowed up by Western. What had sounded like a purely local affair was a meticulously put together occasion. Spare girls had been found to partner the crew, while the other guests included a well-known general and a Member of Parliament with extensive city interests. It was the latter, a balding, rotund, ruddy-complexioned man in his mid-fifties called Eric Ironstone, who interested Kane. To his surprise the interest was mutual.

Later in the evening, when the dance was at its height, but both of them were sitting at the tables, temporarily without partners, Ironside said, 'It's too hot and noisy in here. Let's take our drinks outside.'

Kane followed him out to the wooden-railed balcony overlooking Bembridge Harbour, where the moon was shining on the water and the lines of moored boats. 'A very attractive place, this,' he ventured.

Ironside replied with a few generalities, then came to the point. 'I understand you're something of an African expert.'

'I've spent the better part of three years bashing the bundu, as they say.'

Ironside leant on the railing, his cigar glowing. From indoors the beat of the music swelled as a tune reached its end. 'Some friend of mine could be interested in your contacts,' he said quietly. 'Do you know of any particular investment opportunities out there?'

'There's a copper and cobalt project.'

'How much does it require?'

'About a hundred million dollars.'

Ironside slipped his free hand into his pocket, produced a visiting card and handed it to Kane. Inside the music had ceased. Couples were crowding back to their tables. 'Give me a call,' he said. 'Now I suppose we'd better rejoin the ladies.'

Father Paul waited patiently in the reception hall of the presidential palace. He had come to make a personal appeal to Tshombe and Chantal had promised to secure him an audience. It was August and nearing the end of the dry season. The fighting had disrupted food distribution at a time when it was always short and to make it worse Baluba refugees were flooding down from the north. The Kiobo district needed help. As he sat on the prim gilt chair which was part of the furniture Tshombe had inherited from the former Belgian governor, Father Paul saw Steve Barlow emerge from a corridor. He was not surprised. Chantal had warned him who the earlier visitor was. What did catch his attention was the pallor of the Canadian's face and the strain in his expression.

Barlow, caught unawares, stopped and half smiled. 'Say, Father Paul! It's been a long time. The three months felt like a century.'

The priest rose and shook hands, again remarking to himself on Barlow's tenseness. 'You are having difficulties?' he suggested sympathetically.

'We are indeed!'

There was no one in earshot. Outside the guards stood more or less at attention, trying to keep awake in the midday heat. Even so he lowered his voice. 'Tshombe is just not prepared to commit himself. In no way. He claims the agreements which were the condition of his release a month back were made under duress and he continues to denounce them.' He moved closer to Father Paul, glad of a confidant whom he felt he could trust. Steve Barlow was not a Catholic, but at this moment he felt sorely in need of a confessor. 'It isn't often I reckon a man is impossible, but Tshombe is. We are doing our damnedest to talk him round. We've tried to persuade him that the Congo is a whole new ball game since 2 August. Now that all the other provincial leaders have come together in a new central government, with even the Soviet-backed ones included, Tshombe is the only odd man out. And he is going to be their number one enemy. The Belgian government has agreed to recall its advisers. Spaak has said so. Who's going to command the gendarmerie?' Barlow glanced in the direction of the soldiers outside. 'They'll fall in the hands of the mercenaries, the ex-OAS types, the ultras. Father Paul, maybe you can persuade him they're more of a danger than a protection. The mercenaries have got to go.'

'He may feel himself threatened,' observed Father Paul wryly. 'You have thousands of United Nations troops here, after all. Indians, Irish, Moroccans, Swedes. The place is alive with blue berets.'

'We can only use force to prevent civil war.'

There was a precision about this statement which aroused the priest's scepticism. It was too exact, too legal. Although he looked impassive as he stood there, the long white soutane giving his spare figure the solidity of marble, Father Paul summed up what Barlow had said with an almost irreverent objectivity.

'Would it be civil war if this new central government tried to force Tshombe to keep his undertakings?' He watched Barlow's face keenly, wondering if the Canadian would be honest enough to give the obvious answer. 'Six months ago you would have said it was,' he prompted.

Barlow flinched. 'There is a rather closer identity of views between Mr Hammarskjold and the central government than there was before,' he admitted uncomfortably, then took refuge in a further official response. 'As of the UN's 3 August statement in Leopoldville we could not regard that eventuality as constituting civil war.'

'I see.' Father Paul instinctively rejected this as pompous nonsense. 'And does the UN think that when the army of the North clashed with the troops of the Confederacy in 1860 it was a peaceful affair of which everyone could approve and to call it the American Civil War is a travesty of the facts?' Suddenly his latent anger burst out. 'Do you not realize that if you stand by and permit war it is ordinary Africans who will suffer?' He looked Barlow straight in the eyes. 'I told you no man can remain neutral. You were bound to take sides. But for your organization to do so is wrong.'

‘It has not.’ There was an agony of protest in the reaction. ‘Mr Hammarskjold is determined to work for conciliation.’

‘Then the organization is not speaking with his voice.’

The logic was undeniable. Conciliation was incompatible with standing by as two sides fought. Barlow flushed. ‘We are a long way from New York,’ he said wearily, in effect making his confession. ‘It’s not always so easy to follow the Secretary General’s wishes. The pressures here . . . .’ He felt that prickling behind the eyes almost forgotten since childhood, when exasperation made one cry. ‘But damn it, Father,’ he almost shouted, ‘I do try!’

‘The President is free now.’ Chantal interrupted them and Barlow said goodbye abruptly, hurrying out and not looking back.

As Father Paul had feared, Tshombe was too preoccupied with the UN’s demands to pay more than lip service to the plight of refugees.

‘They insist that all the advisers leave at once.’ His broad face was without its usual smile, his forehead creased with worry. ‘How can I agree? How can I replace one hundred and fourteen Belgian officers overnight, or the four hundred and fifty volunteers? We must defend our independent Katanga. The UN demands are not acceptable.’

‘Could it be done in stages, your Excellency?’

‘Ah, the Norwegian colonel has suggested that. But they want all or nothing. If they were reasonable I could co-operate.’

When Father Paul left he was convinced that it would be touch and go whether Tshombe surrendered or fought if the UN sided with the central government.

‘There seems to be no middle ground,’ he told Chantal sadly as she gave him a quick cup of coffee in her office. Then he asked her about Mike.

She flushed slightly. ‘I’ve hardly seen him. He is flying so much now. I wish there was a chance to talk to him properly, but he is always on the move. Anyway, if the UN has its way, he will have to leave along with the rest.' She played with her cup restlessly. 'Maybe that would be better. I could visit him in Kenya some time and we would have peace and quiet.'

'So you are still fond of him?'

'Yes, Father,' she admitted. 'Very fond.'

The hammering on the door and shouts outside woke Duclair from a heavy sleep. He rolled over, switched on the bedside light and saw it was 5.20 a.m. Although a bachelor, he was provided with a large villa. The bedroom was some way from the front door. He sat up, wondering what the devil was going on. Then, unmistakably, he heard the splintering of wood. The house was being broken into. He scrambled out of bed, pulled his revolver from under the pillow, and flung open the bedroom door. As he did so the front door crashed open. Duclair hastily stepped sideways into shadow, out of the illuminated frame of the doorway behind him.

'Hands up,' shouted a voice in English, but with a curious accent.

'Who the hell are you?'

'United Nations.' The band of light from the bedroom fell on a young Indian officer advancing across the hall. 'Drop your gun,' he ordered.

Slowly Duclair lowered his hand so that the revolver was aimed at the floor. He could see them clearly now. Three soldiers behind the officer. 'If I drop the gun,' he said, 'it may go off.' There was a trace of contempt in his tone.

'Then you will give it to me. No fancy tricks, please.' Carefully Duclair held out the gun and the Indian took it. 'You are under arrest by order of Brigadier Raja,' he said.

'In that case, why not put on the lights?'

The Indian looked at him suspiciously, then retreated to the front door and flipped the switch by it. Standing fully revealed in his pyjamas, Duclair suddenly felt both awkward and angry. But he also noticed how young the officer was and a plan began to form in his mind.

'May I get dressed?' he asked.

'You must be quick.'

In ten minutes Duclair was shaved and arrayed in his service dress uniform, air force wings and medal ribbons prominent on his chest. When he walked out of the bedroom his appearance created the effect he had anticipated. The Indian officer, who was very young, seemed embarrassed.

'I am a wing commander in the Belgian air force,' said Duclair without emotion. 'I would like an explanation.' He knew what was happening, of course. The new UN representative O'Brien had been threatening this for several days. Because of it he had transferred most of the aircraft away from Elisabethville.

'We have orders to arrest all mercenaries.'

Duclair studied the Indian's face. Regular features, properly shaved, neat moustache. He might well have been to the Military Academy at Sandhurst in England. He had that look about him. Duclair decided he was right to play on it.

'You cannot seriously think a mercenary would wear either this uniform or British wartime decorations,' he said. 'I quite understand you are doing your duty, but there must be a mistake.'

'I am sorry, sir. I have to take you to UN headquarters.'

Well, thought Duclair, that's better. At least he is calling me 'sir'. Aloud he said, 'Then I suppose you must. But I would like to telephone my daughter. She is staying with friends. If she comes back and finds this,' he indicated the smashed door, 'she will be terribly worried.'

The trick worked. The officer reluctantly agreed. 'But be quick. My orders are to bring you at once.'

Duclair rang the Berthouds. After two minutes, which

seemed like ten, Mme Berthoud answered.

'Can I speak to Chantal?' said Duclair in French. 'It is urgent.'

'Eventually, after asking several unnecessary questions, Mme Berthoud complied.

'Listen,' he said when Chantal came on the line. 'I have been arrested by the UN. You must get hold of your boyfriend at Kipushi and tell him.' Duclair hesitated, worried in case the Indian understood French. 'Tell him to take everything to the country. No, I can't say where. A safe place. Tell him to use his imagination. And Chantal, get round here if you can. The bastards broke down the door and anyone could walk in.'

He put down the phone. 'Thank you,' he said to the Indian. 'She will come home at once. Now, I am at your disposal.'

'If it had been anyone except Duclair,' Mme Berthoud protested, 'I should have given him a piece of my mind. Telephoning at dawn, indeed!' She stood in her dressing-gown, watching Chantal hurriedly putting on her clothes.

'Please, Mama. There is an emergency. We were half expecting it. If I am not back in three hours telephone the President's office. Say I went to Kipushi.' She was surprised to learn that Mike was there, but presumably Duclair knew what he was talking about.

As she hurried out the sky was lightening with the sunrise. There would be full daylight in minutes and the UN's round-up would be easier. To reach the main road south she had to drive through the city centre. Approaching the Avenue de l'Etoile, opposite the prominent white General Post Office building, she was stopped by a group of Swedish UN soldiers at a roadblock.

'You must go back,' the NCO told her politely, leaning down to talk through the window of the little Citröen. 'The Post Office and the telephone exchange are prohibited areas.'

'What is going on?' Chantal could guess, but she wanted confirmation.

'All foreign officers and mercenaries are being caught.' The Swede sounded pleased. 'Do not be frightened. It is all peaceful. But you may not use this street.'

Beyond him, she could see that the open space in front of the GPO was patrolled by troops in blue berets. She turned the car and made her way by other roads to the outskirts of the town. Elisabethville was built on a simple gridiron pattern and it did not take her long. Half an hour later she was at the Kipushi airfield and searching for Mike. She found him in flying overalls outside the hangar checking one of the Harvards and ran up to him, breathless.

'Hallo, what brings you here so early?' Mike greeted her cheerfully. It was going to be a beautiful day and he was due to fly in half an hour. Then he realized something was amiss.

'The UN are arresting everyone. Duclair sent me.' She could hardly get the words out. 'Mike, I think he wants you to take all the planes out to one of the bush strips. "A safe place", he said.' She quickly related what she had seen in the city. 'If Duclair is under arrest, then so will all the Belgian advisers be.' She looked at him, half fearful and half excited. 'Mike, the message can only mean you are in charge now.'

'So that's why he sent me here! He must have been expecting the worst.' Mike grinned, then glanced round the field. Three of the T6s were lined up on the grass, the cowlings of their big radial engines glinting silvery in the sun. Another was under repair in the workshop. Two more were up in the north. He bit his lip. 'I can account for these and their crews,' he said. 'But God knows about the two remaining Fougas and the helicopters. They're probably on the military airfield in Elisabethville.' He pulled a map out of the long pocket in the side of his trouser leg and spread it out on the Harvard's wing.

'What do you think, Chantal? Kolwezi perhaps?'

She moved round and stood beside him, bending down over the map. 'Why not take them to Shinkolobwe?' she suggested. 'Jacques and his paratroops are there and no UN.'

'That's not a bad idea. We can take one mechanic in the back seat of each plane. The rest can melt across the border into Rhodesia if necessary.'

'Don't worry about them.' Chantal knew where most of the mercenaries would go, if they escaped arrest. 'The Union Minière had a very elastic payroll.' She straightened up, instinctively smoothing back her hair, which was blowing in the light breeze, and faced him. 'Listen,' she said. 'We can't use the ordinary telephone. The Swede told me they've seized the exchange. But there is an alternative. The mining companies have their own link which runs in the power lines from the Le Marinel hydro-electric station right down the Copperbelt. Don't ask me how it works. I never did understand. All I know is you can talk through it to any mine which is on the power grid. So from the Shinkolobwe mine you can contact the Union Minière in Elisabethville. Send me a message when you're safe.'

'Are you going back? Isn't it dangerous for you?'

She tossed her head impatiently. 'Of course I shall be all right. There was no shooting. Anyway Tshombe will be in a terrible panic. He'll need me.' She took his hand for a second. 'Don't worry, Mike. Just get those planes out of reach.' She looked at him affectionately. 'It's funny, a few weeks ago I thought if you were all forced to leave, it might be the best thing. Now I've seen those UN taking over my home town, I've changed my mind. What right have they to interfere, damn them? It's that Irishman O'Brien, I'm sure.' She leant forward and kissed Mike on the cheek fleetingly. 'Look after yourself,' she said. 'Now I must go.'

Two hours later Mike led the three Harvards in loose

formation across the wide horizon of the bush towards Shinkolobwe. They landed one after the other, raising the dust as they swung off the dirt strip and taxied in. This time he did not park them in a line but dispersed them out of sight around the field. Following, taking minor roads and tracks across the bush, avoiding main roads, came trucks with the ammunition and bombs, jerricans of fuel, and a basic supply of spare parts. One of Mike's last actions before he left Kipushi was to send an English pilot across into Rhodesia to make arrangements for more ammunition to be stockpiled. He could not be sure how long the existing system of supply from South Africa would continue.

Shortly after five in the evening of that day, 28 August, Barlow attended a briefing of the senior UN staff. It was presided over by O'Brien, who had been the Secretary General's representative since June. Backing him was Brigadier Raja, the Indian commanding the UN troops. Between them they summarized the day's events. 'Operation Rumpunch', as they called it, had been a spectacular success and a bloodless one. There had been no fighting. The round-up had netted 338 men in various parts of Katanga, including eighty-one Belgian officers. Of the mercenaries known by name to UN Intelligence, only 104 were still at large. Better still, Tshombe had agreed to announce on the radio that he would co-operate in the dismissal of all mercenaries. In return O'Brien had withdrawn the UN guards from the Post Office and radio station.

As the meeting ended Barlow was told by O'Brien's assistant, a Frenchman called Tombelaine, to escort Wing Commander Duclair to the Belgian consul to discuss the repatriation of Belgian servicemen.

'Are we really leaving it to the diplomats?' he asked. 'Shouldn't we put them across the frontier ourselves?'

Tombelaine shrugged his shoulders. 'That is what has

been agreed. We've had the British, French and Belgian representatives arguing all day.' He gave Barlow a curious look. 'Aren't you in favour of conciliation any longer?'

Duclair made only one remark as they drove in the jeep to the consul's residence.

'You realize you are acting far beyond your powers?' he said coldly.

'On the contrary, I am sure we are within them.' Barlow yet again considered the actions leading up to Rumpunch, culminating in a central government ordinance requesting UN help in expelling the mercenaries. Hammarskjold himself had suggested its wording. If the Secretary General authorized an action, Barlow felt totally confident in its legality. He derived considerable relief from this conclusion, since Father Paul's condemnation still lay on his conscience. 'No,' he repeated. 'We are acting correctly.'

None the less the scene at the Belgian consul's house was so unexpected as to give Barlow an immediate twitch of disquiet. He had envisaged handing Duclair over, if not like a criminal, at least in the manner of an officer facing proceedings. Instead the wing commander received an unabashed welcome.

'Ah,' said the consul. 'So you've come at last. Join the party.' Inside a group of arrested advisers were having drinks and talking vociferously. He turned to Barlow and smiled frostily. 'You people were very sensible to let us make the arrangements for repatriation. Public opinion in our country would have been outraged if Belgian officers were not released to my protection.'

'They've had since the 21 February resolution to leave. Six whole months.'

'Let us not argue. They are now under my orders.'

'There are still over a hundred mercenaries at large,' said Barlow, resolutely following his brief. 'A proportion are Belgian. We want them out too.'

'Mercenaries?' The consul's expression was a masterpiece of powerless concern. 'Naturally we shall do what we can. However, they are private citizens, not servicemen.'

'As I understand things,' said Barlow firmly, 'you are obligated to Mr O'Brien to make arrangements for them as well. What's more, President Tshombe promised to co-operate in their dismissal.'

The consul and Duclair exchanged glances. 'In that case,' said the consul silkily. 'I am sure there will be no problems.' He paused, as though searching his mind for forgotten items. 'Oh, yes,' he added. 'A small point of protocol. Would you remind Mr O'Brien that it will be appropriate for the UN to mount a guard of honour when these officers leave?' He gestured with one hand. 'Nothing elaborate. Mere reciprocity for the respects Belgium always pays to UN officials.' He said goodnight, bowing fractionally, and ushered Duclair inside.

Back in his office Barlow felt both triumphant and bemused. To have negatived what Hammarskjold called 'the Belgian factor' in a mere twelve hours when it had plagued the UN for twelve months was magnificent. Yet what kind of an Alice in Wonderland situation was it where the Belgians being expelled wanted an honour guard and instead of being in custody were throwing a party? He mentioned these thoughts to a colleague in the Civil Affairs section.

'Does it matter? The important thing is that Tshombe is collaborating and his regime cannot survive without the Belgians. We have made the breakthrough the Secretary General wanted.'

Later on, Barlow suddenly recalled the near-forgotten incident of the Swedish soldier attacked in the bar. Technically it remained his responsibility. He decided to check through the list of captured mercenaries, but soon realized the impossibility of interrogating them all. As he put away the list it occurred to him that a name he was particularly interested in was missing. How the hell had Mike Russell got away?

Captain Jacques sat hunched by the radio in the hut at Shinkolobwe, a bottle or red wine on the table. As the broadcast ended he swore, switched off the set with such violence that Mike feared he would break it and said bitterly. 'No moral fibre, that's the trouble with these blacks.' He reached for the bottle. 'Here, have another swig.' He sniffed his own glass. 'Not bad. They live well, these Belgians.'

But Mike's mind was on the broadcast. 'You think Tshombe intends us to give ourselves up?' He wished he could speak to Chantal again.

Jacques shifted round in his low chair, his expression cast in sharp relief by the solitary, unshaded light bulb hanging above. 'Like hell we surrender.' He uncoiled his tall frame from the chair, fetched the tape recorder and set it in motion. The tune blared out with trumpet fanfares and the exultant matching beat of its refrain. *En avant, en avant, en avant. C'est nous les Africans*.'

'We surrendered after Dien Bien Phu,' he said roughly, as the tune ended. 'We're abandoning Algeria. We're not quitting here. You keep those planes flying, my friend. The UN may think this is the end. It is not. It's the beginning.'

From the shadows, Herman's slow voice interrupted. Hitherto he had been listening in bewildered silence.

'I am glad to hear that, man, I can tell you. I do not like to give up without a fight and I am saving very useful money.'

Jacques picked up the bottle, refilled his glass and stood upright, a gaunt, hard figure in his camouflage uniform. 'To hell with the communists. And the UN.'

8

One of the soldiers slouched up to the line of baggage in the airport customs hall. He was a big, muscular African and his uniform was cut absurdly tight, so that the drab olive-green trousers clung to his broad buttocks. He jabbed at Kane's suitcase with his rifle.

'Ouvrez!'

Kane flipped the locks. The soldier reached down and foraged among the clothing, felt something hard and pulled. Shirts and socks tumbled on to the floor. He inspected his find, a suede ankle boot, and flourished it in Kane's face.

'What is it?'

'A shoe.' He mimed putting it on his foot.

'Wait.' The soldier disappeared bearing the boot. Kane made a great effort to control himself. It was eight in the morning, but the interior of Leopoldville airport was as sticky as a swamp. He repacked his case, mopped his forehead and waited. Ten minutes later the soldier re-appeared with an officer.

'Why do you have this?' demanded the officer and, before Kane could answer, upturned the case. This time the entire contents spewed out on the floor. The officer stirred through the heap with his cane and picked out the other boot. 'Why do you have this military equipment?'

'In Britain people wear these all the time.'

'You are a mercenary.' The officer gave him a crafty look. 'Don't deny it. These are military boots. We are not such fools as you white men think.'

'Please.' Kane suddenly realized that he was in danger. 'I have come to see the Vice Prime Minister, Mr Jason Sendwe. Let me show you.' He reached for his briefcase and the next moment felt an agonizing pain as the soldier slammed the rifle butt down on the back of his hand.

'Not so fast,' said the officer. 'We will look.'

Kane clutched his wrist and watched in fury as the officer shuffled through his papers.

'Inside,' he said, 'there is a telegram from Sendwe.'

The pantomime lasted another twnety minutes. In spite of the telegram, Kane lost his boots and 100 pounds in travellers' cheques. His hand was completely numbed and he was worried that Suzy would have assumed he was not on the plane and left. To his relief she was waiting when he emerged.

'Where have you been?' She kissed him. 'My God, you look terrible.'

It occurred to him that this was becoming a refrain among his friends. He contrived a smile, embraced her with his left arm, and thanked her for coming. Then he told her what had happened. 'The bastards even took half my money.'

'This place is a snake pit,' she said as they walked to her car. 'It gets worse and worse. They imprison people on rumour, the army is a rabble.' She guided him by the elbow. 'Never mind, you're here. Where are you staying?'

'Could I stay with you?'

She swung round. 'Robert, you are impossible. You don't write for months. Suddenly a cable. How do you know I haven't another boyfriend? Do you always take women for granted?'

'I'm sorry. This is a private trip and I never expected to be robbed.' His hand was beginning to hurt now the numbness was wearing off and he felt foul. 'Seriously, Suzy, I didn't plan to ask you.'

'It would be nice if you said something about missing me, wouldn't it? Or am I simply a substitute hotel room?' She pouted angrily, then, seeing how crestfallen he had become, relented. 'All right then, I forgive you. This once, but I will have to drop you off, I'm late for work already.'

Outside the entrance to the Residence Mayumbe she stopped the car, gave him the keys to her apartment and examined his damaged hand. The skin was a blotchy purple and the finger joints were swelling. Even her gentle touch made him wince. 'You ought to see a doctor,' she said. 'Meet me for lunch at the Greek restaurant. I'll have an appointment arranged by then.'

As Kane lugged his case through the hall to the lift, he cursed the bad luck of its being his right hand which had suffered. This trip was so crucial that the slightest disability seemed a threat to it. He couldn't afford to spend time in surgeries, when he was paying his own expenses.

After a tussle with the front door lock, he gained entry to the apartment and heaved his case through the living room to Suzy's bedroom, dumping it on the wide bed. He went next door and turned on the bath, then began to sort out the jumbled contents of his case. While he was doing this he noticed the waste basket by the frilly covered dressing table. Protruding from the basket was one of those rectangular pieces of cardboard which laundries insert in men's shirts. He gazed at it and saw deeper in the basket the thin strip which had stiffened the collar together with some scrumpled tissue.

The bloody bitch, he thought, she must have had a man here last night, otherwise the maid would have emptied the basket before now. He sat down heavily on the side of the bed. No wonder she had been annoyed at his wanting to sleep here. His instinct was to confront her with the evidence, create a scene. Then he remembered that he no longer had adequate money for a decent hotel room. The only decision he came to, as he soaked the weariness out of himself in the bath, was that if the maid failed to clear the basket, he would do it himself.

Shaved and clean, he made several unsuccessful attempts to telephone Sendwe's office, then decided to rest for an hour. Banishing previous occupants of the bed from his mind, he stretched out in his underclothes and fell asleep, to be wakened by a shrill giggling. The African maid, a young girl in a print dress, was standing in the doorway, one hand over her mouth, struggling to control herself.

'Oh, *pardon M'sieur,*' she stuttered, her eyes wild with amusement, and retreated in disorder to the kitchen, from whence a gale of laughter echoed round the apartment.

Kane realized to his horror that it was after midday and rolled over sideways, sitting up and instinctively pushing down with his hands to raise himself. Normally he jumped out of bed in a single continuous movement. Now an excruciating pain shot through his right wrist, he stumbled and when he was upright had to stand completely still for half a minute until the worst of the throbbing ebbed away. His hand was severely swollen and a livid bruise was staining the flesh where the rifle butt had struck. He dressed with difficulty, and bade *au revoir* to the maid, who responded with a grin of the purest wickedness when he asked her to tidy the bedroom. As he emerged into the street from the air-conditioned building the humid heat seemed to scorch the back of his legs. In seconds he was sweating. I'm not on form, he thought, not on form at all.

Suzy was sitting at a table in the Greek restaurant on the ground floor of the UN building, desultorily studying the menu, her chestnut hair neatly framing her face, smiling refusal at a man wanting to join her in a way which said quite clearly 'any other time you'd be welcome'. The stranger drifted on reluctantly as Kane walked up. To underline his rights, however temporary, Kane kissed her on the cheek.

'You look a bit better. Let's see that hand of yours.' She made a brief inspection. 'Not so beautiful. Does it hurt?'

'Like hell.'

'I've made an appointment for three.' She waved the menu at a passing waiter. 'Now let's order and you can tell me what this visit of yours is all about.'

Whether it was due to the pain or his fury at being robbed, Kanc allowed her to wheedle far more out of him than he had intended.

'I thought you were only interested in clothes and chattering!' he exclaimed at one point, tactfully omitting her primary preoccupation.

'Oh, no.' She made a face. 'This place is such a circus you can't help being fascinated by the intrigues. 'So you've taken a week's holiday and are trying to get the Kiobo concession for yourself? Won't your company find out?'

'Not until it's too late. Don't forget, Suzy, I worked damn hard for them. It was their decision to drop the project.' He wanted to impress her. 'If I can get the concession, this financier Eric Ironstone will stitch together a consortium to raise the hundred million dollars we need.'

'It sounds an awful lot of money.'

'It's an awfully valuable mine.' Kane laughed. He knew high finance held an almost sexual attraction for her. 'With three per cent of the shares in the company we form, I shall be an extremely rich man.'

'Straight away?' Like most Swiss, she preferred money on the table.

'When the mine is in production. That's the difference.' He tried to display the deal as the triumph it was. 'IMEX would have allowed me point two of one per cent of the contract value. Cash, I admit, but once for all. Ironstone is giving me a full three per cent of the profits for ever. I don't have to contribute capital: simply the concession Sendwe had already promised.'

Suzy wrinkled her nose. 'Promises are the only commodity this wretched country has enough of.' She noticed the disquiet in his eyes. He didn't like being ridiculed. 'All right,' she admitted, 'Steve Barlow said that originally. But it's true. When are you seeing Sendwe?'

'Tomorrow, I hope.'

'Well, you might be able to tonight.' She enjoyed the questioning look this statement evoked, remembering that it always was fun teasing him. It made him more determined to prove himself in bed later. She enjoyed manipulating his emotions. Their sporadic relationship was not as one-sided as he imagined. She tilted her head slightly to one side, regarding him quizzically. 'I'm not sure you deserve to be helped, though. Perhaps for a price.'

'For heaven's sake, Suzy. What are you trying to say? In words of one syllable.'

She smiled. He was becoming satisfactorily exasperated. 'You chose the right girl to cultivate, you know. I still work for the Officer in Charge of the whole UN operation, though it's a Swede now. He's throwing a party for Ministers tonight. You can come: if you buy me a really good dinner. None of that "*à la carte* in the Memling and put it on my room bill, waiter". There's a new restaurant I haven't tried. I warn you, it's expensive.' She studied his expression.

'Name the place.' Kane put a good face on it. 'Can we take Sendwe, too?'

'Not to the night-club afterwards.'

'Done.'

Suzy's hazel eyes glinted with pleasure. 'You're learning, Bob, darling. May I let you in on a secret? It's very sexy to spend money.'

By Suzy's standards, Kane had cause to reflect later

that afternoon, the session in the surgery was an orgy. An X-ray revealed two metacarpal bones fractured and also the fragile scaphoid in the wrist. As the doctor encased the lower arm in plaster he commented, 'You were lucky not to have been beaten up and jailed. They have mercenary phobia, the army. I heard of a man killed because they believed his gold tooth contained a radio transmitter. Don't laugh. Such things happen. This Congo of ours is a madhouse now. I shall go back to Belgium as soon as my contract expires. There,' he straightened up. 'Now all you need is a sling. That will be five thousand francs.'

In the evening Suzy drove him out in her white Volkswagen to the UN chief's spacious villa, set in a luxuriant tropical garden. After introducing him to the host, Suzy bear-led Kane around. United Nations receptions were always colourful affairs. Every African diplomat sported a different national dress, vividly outshining the Europeans' subdued tropical suits. The first group they joined included a Ghanaian in a magnificently woven kente cloth of gold and other colours, swathed around him like a Roman toga. A Tunisian, apparently a UN official, was speaking vehemently.

'All the mercenaries must go and Tshombe with them.' He struck his palm with a clenched fist. 'All of them. This time there must be no half measures. If the central government is powerless, then we must act.'

While they all listened, Suzy slipped away. To Kane's pleasure, she re-appeared with Jason Sendwe. But he was immediately monopolized by the Tunisian. 'Those arrest warrants are in O'Brien's hands, Minister. This time we'll end the secession.'

So, Kane commented to himself, the UN has taken sides at last. Suzy told him how the effectiveness of Operation Rumpunch had been circumvented and many mercenaries had escaped to hiding in the bush.

When the Tunisian had concluded what had become a

tirade, Suzy touched Sendwe's arm and suggested that they stroll in the garden before it became dark.

'Events are moving our way at last,' said Sendwe as they wandered out through the French windows, down some steps and on to a lawn. A soldier stirred among the bushes and Kane realized there were sentries all round. Otherwise they were alone.

'Minister,' he said without preamble, 'I would like you to sign an agreement for the Kiobo concession on the lines we discussed.'

Sendwe's eyes were sleepy and inscrutable, their whites a cloudy brown. 'I have appreciated your help in the past, Mr Kane,' he said slowly. 'Now all we need is Tshombe's fall.'

'Do we have to wait for that?'

'We do, my friend. But it will not be long. On the 9th we issued the warrants for the arrest of the leaders in Katanga.' He accented the word 'leaders' heavily, as though it had special significance. 'Today, as you heard, the warrants reached O'Brien. In another three days it will be over. At the end of this week, if my colleagues agree, the concession can be yours. Until then, we have other priorities.'

Try as he might, Kane could not budge Sendwe further. When the dusk forced them back indoors, all he had achieved was an appointment for the following Monday, which he accepted with apprehension. It would mean cabling IMEX to plead medical reasons for a late return from holiday. Damnation, he thought, I can't send that from here. And I shall run out of money.

The remainder of the evening underscored his problem. The dinner was indeed expensive. He had come with 200 pounds, reckoning twenty a day a generous allowance. The theft had taken 100, the doctor thirty-five, now this meal would absorb ten. Three quarters of his funds were gone. There was only one answer. He had an airline credit card and a bank account in Johannesburg. The living was cheap in South Africa.

'Suzy, my sweet,' he said, holding her hand across the table. 'The doctor ordered me to rest. How would you like a beach holiday in the Cape this week?'

For a moment she was taken aback. 'Are you serious? I'd adore it.' She giggled. 'Do you really think it would be a rest?' Later, over brandy, she said affectionately, 'I misjudged you, Bob. I thought you could only be generous with company funds. Your hand must hurt. Let's forget the night-club and go straight home.'

Without complaint she made the running that night, undressing him, then letting him lie recumbent with his injured hand comfortable while she manoeuvred herself to satisfy them both. As she lay in the crook of his good arm afterwards she whispered, 'Bob, darling, that was a very sexy idea to go to the Cape. Thank you.'

The next morning her boss categorically refused her leave at such short notice. The Secretary General himself was now coming out from New York. All the staff were to be on call. When Kane boarded the plane in the afternoon he did so in the comfortable assurance of a free bed on his return. He had never expected Suzy to be able to disentangle herself from work and reckoned he had played a poor hand pretty well. Now all he needed was a blonde to be photographed with on the beach, just to show IMEX that the holiday was genuine. He would send Skinner a postcard too; followed by a cable announcing his injury.

When he heard the new operational codename Barlow rebelled. His conscience gave him no option.

'*Morthor*,' the Indian staff major had explained, 'is our Hindi word for "smash". Very appropriate. We shall smash both the mercenaries and their masters. You will see.'

'Does New York know this?'

The major had winked. 'Why trouble New York with

details? You have heard the instructions from Leo. "No half measures this time." Wait until our Gurkhas are going in.' He smiled happily. 'Those mercenaries will be running.'

'This is far beyond our mandate,' Barlow had snapped and left the major to seek a higher authority. When he found it, in the shape of a senior UN official visiting from Leopoldville, he received an assurance which only worried him more.

'My friend, you are concerned unnecessarily.' The official was an Arab and Barlow was struck by the watchful impassiveness of his hawklike face. 'The Secretariat far away in New York cannot fully appreciate the situation here. We must exercise our own initiative.'

'But the Secretary General sent us a summary of nine legal principles only last week! They specifically exclude any military action beyond preventing civil war and self-defence.'

'You expect a Gurkha or an Ethiopian to consult nine complicated principles before deciding whether to open fire? Sometimes, my friend, you lawyers have to step aside. The brigadier assures me Morthor will be quick and effective. When we present a *fait accompli* the General Assembly will not dispute the provocation. It will be enough that there were mercenaries still at large.'

The cynicism of these remarks hit Barlow like a hammer. What had an admirer said of Hammarskjold? 'He has a very exact and pure perception of principles.' The crudeness of the Morthor planning made a mockery of all Hammarskjold was striving for.

'You mean we are brazenly acting on behalf of the central government?' he protested. 'Hammarskjold specifically enjoins us to seek conciliation and bring the two sides to the conference table.'

'By the time he arrives in Leopoldville tomorrow it will all be over.' The Arab was losing patience and his voice became taut. 'Tshombe and his cabinet will be under arrest. Then perhaps they will talk sense.' He looked at Barlow sharply. 'That man is impossible. He will not listen to O'Brien. His broadcasts vilify us.'

'I've met him often enough,' said Barlow hotly, 'I admit he's difficult. But surely we must follow the Secretary General's instructions.'

'If you think you may succeed where we failed, you are welcome to try a final time.' Again the impassive, almost disdainful intonation. 'In the end you will know we are right.'

After leaving the Arab, Barlow telephoned Chantal, whom he now knew quite well, and asked her to arrange an urgent interview with Tshombe. An hour later, in the early evening of Tuesday 12 September, he drove up to the gates of the presidential palace and was admitted. The guard, he noted, had been doubled. When Chantal met him she was tense, her elegant features drawn with worry.

'Permit my asking you,' she said, before taking him through, 'have you come with a sincere desire for peace? If not, it is pointless seeing him.'

'I emphatically have.' Though he gave the assurance readily, Barlow was taken aback. He had not encountered such directness from Tshombe's staff before. Nor had it occurred to him that they might be as emotionally concerned as Chantal clearly was.

'I am glad,' she said. 'Too many attempts are being made to double-cross him. Be patient. He has reason to distrust the UN.'

With this blunt warning, she opened the wide doors of the study and announced him.

Tshombe had evidently been pacing the room. His well-cut suit was rumpled and Barlow saw to his amazement that the blackness of his skin had a slight purple-blue tinge, a flush of either fear or agitation. He shook hands rather peremptorily, then turned to Chantal. 'Please stay. I would like a record kept of what is said.'

While she perched on an upright chair, her shorthand pad ready, he motioned Barlow to the sofa, but remained standing himself.

'You realize we have known what you are planning since last Friday? You intend to seize the radio, disarm my gendarmerie and arrest myself and my Ministers.' He faced Barlow, his tall, broad-shouldered figure dominating the room.

'I cannot deny it, sir.'

'Your colleagues have attempted to.'

Seated low down, the African towering over him, Barlow felt at an impossible disadvantage. He had only one card to play and he did not want its effectiveness diminished. He stood up awkwardly. 'I happen to believe, sir,' he said with all the dignity he could muster, 'that it is counter-productive to lie in a situation as serious as this one. I also believe us obligated to follow Mr Hammarskjold's directions more faithfully than we are.'

Tshombe appeared to query this sentiment, then accept it as genuine. He nodded. 'I appreciate your honesty. I wish I could find it elsewhere. Is the Secretary General still coming to the Congo?'

It was the perfect cue. 'He is, sir. Tomorrow. I believe he would welcome the opportunity to speak with you and avert what I think is a potential disaster.' He looked quickly at Chantal. 'Can this be off the record?'

She sought confirmation from Tshombe and when he nodded assent, put down her pad.

'Thank you. What I have to say, sir, is simply that I personally do not agree with what is being done and I am convinced that the Secretary General would be most alarmed if he knew. An agreement to meet him, under UN protection, could defuse the present explosive situation.'

'To meet him in Leopoldville?' Tshombe suddenly flared up. 'I have already told O'Brien I will not go there. Discussion of reconciliation with the central government, yes. Surrounded by their army, and under duress, no. Look what happened in April! Two months' house arrest. Did the UN come to my aid? Not at all. How can you speak of UN protection?' For five minutes he unburdened himself of a violent diatribe against the UN in general and O'Brien in particular.

'I am sure the Secretary General would agree to meet with you anywhere convenient,' Barlow suggested, when the storm had abated.

'Can you guarantee that?'

'No, sir. I can only do my utmost to bring it about.' He had no authority to commit Hammarskjold, who must by now be preparing to leave New York and who would be incommunicado on the aircraft right through the period of the Morthor operation. Given Tshombe's immediate agreement, he might be able to pass a message before the plane took off. But officials in Leopoldville would have to sanction it and they were beset by intrigue.

'Without guarantees it is extremely difficult.' Tshombe was hesitant, attracted by the idea, yet apprehensive.

'It requires a great deal of goodwill, sir, I admit. Maybe more than we merit.' He didn't mind denigrating his own organization if it would sway Tshombe. However, there was one condition the UN would rightly insist on. 'I must be honest, sir. We would have to ask you to broadcast to the gendarmerie again, ordering them to co-operate with us.'

Listening, Chantal bit her lip. She knew that the ultras, the ex-French Foreign Legion mercenaries who had escaped the last round-up, were not going to be caught out again. The Katangan information about the UN plans was exact. The so-called preventive action was due before dawn tomorrow. In consequence the gendarmerie was moving into position tonight. Tshombe would need to appear in person to stop them.

A long silence followed, during which Tshombe strode up and down the room, his perplexity disturbing to watch. Finally he sat down behind the desk and Chantal knew Barlow's mission had failed.

'Convey my good wishes to the Secretary General,' he said, choosing his words with care. 'Kindly tell him I shall be amenable to a meeting on neutral ground, the modalities to be discussed at the time. I suggest Bancroft in Northern Rhodesia. As to the broadcast, that must depend on his reply.' Tshombe turned to Chantal. 'You have taken that down?' When Chantal said she had, he relaxed slightly and added. 'On a personal note, Mr Barlow, I appreciate your having come.' He sighed. 'Alas, we are all prisoners of circumstance.'

Later, when he returned to admit his inability to contact the Secretary General, Barlow found many more gendarmerie around the presidential palace. Tshombe's big Dodge automobile was in the driveway, being loaded with gear. He knew all about the car. The boot was crammed with radio equipment. It was Tshombe's mobile command post. When he bade goodbye to Chantal she did not smile. 'O'Brien will find he is making a mistake,' was all she said.

The Belgian major who had led the gendarmerie column in the north six months before was in civilian clothes. He parked the car in which he had driven from Elisabethville, heavy with dust, beside the hut and entered without knocking. Inside Jacques and Mike were poring over maps laid out on a trestle table. They straightened up, then shook hands.

'Legrand,' the major introduced himself bluffly. 'Remember you flew reconnaissance for me?'

'That's right.' Mike also recalled the burnt village. 'What can we do for you?'

'Tonight we return to operations. Our time in the bush is over.' His speech was as brusque as ever. 'Orders from the President's military adviser. We expect the United

Nations action at dawn. Unbelievable, but they are trying exactly the same as before: the radio station, the GPO, the government offices. This time we'll be ready. Minimum white leadership in Elisabethville. We want the UN fighting Africans where the press can see it. Outside the city, mercenaries lead attacks at many points.' He strode across to the map table. 'You, Jacques, are to take your para-commandos to strengthen a gendarmerie encirclement of the Irish at Jadotville. Other units will be attacking the Kamina base.' He turned to Mike. 'Captain Russell, we want air support for both operations.'

'Where are the Fougas?'

'Good question. Since Duclair was forced to leave, the air side has lacked co-ordination. Delin's still around. He's kept one Fouga in safety. The other one's unserviceable.' The major eyed Mike in a not unfriendly way. 'I suppose you're aching to lay your hands on a jet? If Delin will check you out, OK. But for the next couple of days we want you organizing the T6s.'

'If you say so. May I ask a couple of questions?'

Legrand nodded agreement.

'What's our strength now?'

'The gendarmerie: as before. Ten thousand, plus. Two-thirds the size of the UN Congo force. So we must strike first. The mercenaries: maybe one hundred. Quite a few have come back.' He permitted himself a smile, 'Including myself. My own repatriation to Belgium did an about turn in Rhodesia. What else do you want to know?'

Mike looked at him very straight, creasing his eyes as though gazing into the light. 'Did you order the destruction of that village?'

'The one by the river? I did. We were fired at from it.' There was an unrepentant toughness in the reply which silenced Mike. 'We are not in this business to make friends and influence people. We are here to survive and win. The Baluba would have done far worse to us. If you don't like the heat, my friend, don't come into the kitchen.' He swung round to Jacques. 'Ready to move in two hours, right? You'll have five hundred gendarmes to surround one hundred and fifty Irish. Any problems?'

Jacques grinned. 'Only one. We haven't drunk to success.' He crossed to the cupboard, took out the ever open bottle of *vin rouge*, and filled the glasses. 'To hell with the UN. And the communists.' He tossed down his wine. 'Now, let's get cracking.' He walked to the door and bellowed out, 'Herman!'

After a few seconds there was an answering shout.

'Parade the company.' He came back inside. 'Could we agree the rendezvous point and some other details?'

Mike listened, recovering his self-possession after Legrand's rebuke and planning the air support in his mind. Without night navigation aids there was little he could do until daylight anyway.

The night was surprisingly cool. Between three and four in the morning, Barlow seemed to remember, was when the body's temperature was at its lowest, the human frame at its least efficient. It was 3.50 a.m. He shivered. Ahead of him stood the dim, grey shape of the Elisabethville radio station, its flat roof a dark edge against the night sky, the aerials barely discernible. Lights were on inside, throwing random patterns of illumination on the waste ground in front of the building. Strung out across that ground were perhaps thirty Katangan guards, some silhouetted against the lights, others only vague shapes. Facing them stood at least four times the number of Gurkhas, small men, their curved kukris slung from their belts, their rifles and machine guns trained on the Katangans. Barlow was with the Indian major.

'Lay down your arms! You have five minutes to surrender.' The major spoke in laboured French through a primitive loud hailer. In the same instant the headlights of several vehicles blazed into life. The Katangans wavered, blinking, trapped in the glare. Barlow could see several were civilians and unarmed. The rest appeared to be police, not gendarmerie. He scanned the irresolute line. There was not a white face there, not a single mercenary.

'*Hapana!*' One of the police shouted the refusal defiantly.

With sudden knowledge of what must happen, Barlow realized that none of the UN present spoke Swahili and it was ninety to one that the Africans did not understand the Indian's French.

'You have one minute!' The Indian abandoned the unfamiliar tongue altogether, reckoning his meaning must be clear.

In answer the Katangan who had shouted raised his rifle.

'Fire!' The officer did not hesitate.

The fusillade was accurate, sustained, merciless. Most of the Africans fell immediately, some spinning round, others pitching forward throwing up their arms, screaming, crawling on hands and knees to escape until more bullets thudded into them. In less than a minute it was over. A few survivors were pinioned by soldiers. Most lay between the Gurkhas and the building.

The order to cease firing rang out. Another officer walked forward, counted the bodies, shot one man, who was still squirming, in the head. From the doors of the building a small group of others emerged and the officer came back to the major and saluted.

'Operation complete, sir. Casualties: enemy twenty-six dead, own troops nil.'

Appalled, stunned by the savagery of the massacre, Barlow turned on the major. 'You told me it would be bloodless! That wasn't self-defence. It was murder.'

'We all saw the Katangan threaten to shoot. Our ultimatum was clearly given and defied. Our troops merely obeyed orders.' If the major was shocked, he did not show it. 'The radio station is now ours. A few casualties are a small price to pay.'

In disgust Barlow stumbled away to his car. The radio station was supposedly a key point from the civilian affairs side. He could not bring himself to enter it at this moment. He must find the brigadier and prevent any further slaughter.

As he reached his car, parked two streets away, the unmistakable sound of firing came from the direction of the town centre; sharp, unrhythmical cracks of noise. A few rounds of track arched above the rooftops, glowing pale red in the darkness, followed immediately by the staccato chatter of a machine-gun. He stood and listened, guessing things had gone wrong at the Post Office, too.

'It will all be over in two hours,' the brigadier had assured them last night. As he drove towards the UN offices Barlow knew it would not be. The city was in confusion. There were UN roadblocks in many places. Frightened civilians were trying to leave the city, both Africans and whites. But as the sun rose and the day began, the firing slackened. Maybe the brigadier had been correct after all.

At nine, going out to find himself some breakfast if possible, Barlow was stopped by a British journalist.

'Hey,' he caught at Barlow's sleeve in his excitement, 'I missed O'Brien's press conference. Is it correct that he said Katanga's secession is over?'

'I understand so.' The offices had been crowded with reporters and other things were dominating his mind, mainly the need to locate Tshombe, who had telephoned O'Brien at 4.45 a.m. asking for a ceasefire, but who now had vanished, the UN troops having inexplicably neglected instructions to surround the presidential palace.

'In fact you're ending secession by force?' The reporter was still holding his coat.

Barlow jerked himself free. 'I did not say that.'

'Are you denying there were five hundred troops besieging the Post Office just now? Isn't that using force?' The journalist was young and impatient. 'For Christ's sake, who do you think you're kidding?'

'We believe secession may have ended because Tshombe has requested a ceasefire.'

'He has? Jesus, thanks. Thanks a lot.' The young man dashed off again, back to the Leo Deux to find a telephone and file a story which would surely lead the front page of his paper tomorrow.

Unable to find a café open, Barlow wearily returned to the office and asked his secretary to brew coffee.

'Mr O'Brien's been asking for you,' she said. 'He wants you to go and find Tshombe personally. He's seriously worried.' A few minutes later she brought the drink and Barlow gulped it down gratefully. He had been up nearly five hours without anything. 'Thank you, Margaret,' he said. 'That was great. Now tell me, what the hell do you think's happening?' He could ask her that kind of question. She was a fellow Canadian, discreet and loyal, which was more than one could say of most of the men in the headquarters.

'If you really want to know,' she said, removing the empty cup, 'I guess Operation Morthor's blown a fuse.'

Jadotville was a company town. Agreeably set among low wooded hills, its residential quarters were laid out with the spaciousness Union Minière could well afford. Comfortable villas in large gardens, tree-lined streets, pleasant walks. The area reminded Belgians of their native Ardennes. For Mike, surveying it from 2000 feet, this generous use of land offered a different advantage: the positions taken up by the Irish infantrymen were easy to spot. With only 150 men to protect a town of 75,000 inhabitants, they had concentrated in one place, sending out patrols as necessary. Squinting down ahead of the Harvard's wing, he observed that they were now well and truly encircled by the gendarmerie. Calling a warning to the pilot in the T6 astern of him, he pulled into a tight turn and took stock of the opportunities.

The snag about these planes was one for which Mike still cursed Duclair. They had no air to ground radio link such as had been fixed up in the Cessna. His task was to strafe the Irish, but Jacques was unable to direct him on to particular targets. He held into the turn, gazing down, then recognized what must be the vehicle park. A truck and several jeeps were dispersed beneath trees. Though camouflaged, their angular shapes gave them away and sunlight glinted on a windscreen. This was the kind of target he was seeking. To knock out their transport would be a step towards forcing their surrender.

He called the Cuban in the other plane. 'You see the villa? Fifty yards away, in trees, are trucks. We'll go for those. Follow me down.'

'OK, I follow.' The Cuban's command of English was still far from perfect.

Mike straightened out and checked the gyro-gun sight mounted straight in front of him and the short row of bomb selector switches on the instrument panel. He headed away from the town, then called that he was turning, doubled back on his track, flipped the bomb master switch on and dived down in a crescendo of noise towards the villa, releasing the bomb and immediately pulling up into a climbing turn to observe the effect. A pall of smoke hung over the trees as he watched the Cuban's bomb exploded close to it. That should have given the bastards a puncture or two, he thought.

The Irish were running around below, taking cover, while he could see a pair with a heavy machine-gun preparing to fire back. He watched them with the detachment of an observer from another world. The tiny figures scrambling about below could be considered with the same objectivity as fish in a pool. Until you had one hooked and it lay gasping its life away on the bank, the fish's existence was totally unrelated to one's own. Looking down from the sky he felt similarly detached. He had nothing particularly against the Irish. They had simply changed from being neutral to being the enemy. He would never be incensed over what happened to them in the way he had over the burnt village, because they were professionals, not innocents.

'We'll go in on the deck this time and shoot them up,' he ordered, Legrand's criticism hard in his memory.

The second time they came in at tree-top height, strafing the vicinity of the vehicles with gun fire. Then, keeping low, the engine at close to full boost, he roared over the town and the gendarmerie positions before flying back to the airstrip. At midday he received a call through the mining company to say that the raid had been effective. Although Jacques had no direct observation of the villa, the column of smoke that rose afterwards suggested one or more vehicles had caught fire. An hour later he was told to transfer all three aircraft and crews to Kolwezi, where the jets were now operating. It was to be the air support centre. After a hurried lunch, they cleared up and prepared to move.

Kane's hand had given him such pain that he forsook ideas of a beach holiday. Angry at the unnecessary injury, he decided to compensate by indulging himself. From Johannesburg he flew straight on to Capetown and there hired a car and driver to take him out to a vineyard among the hills. Lawson's hotel at Lanzerac was all but unique, a Cape Dutch homestead with white walls, high gables and fine old rooms, modernized and converted in immaculate taste. There he could relax, eating well, enjoying the delicately flavoured local wines, lazing in the sun, until he felt better and it was time to fly back to the Congo. It was there that he heard about the Katanga war.

The South African newspapers were not slow to gloat over the United Nations' embarrassment. Kane read them exhaustively and with amazement. It was now 15 September, two days since Operation Morthor had been launched, although of course the reports covered only to the 14th. How the devil, he wondered, had the UN managed to make such a colossal nonsense. They were under air attack throughout Katanga. The Irish surrounded at Jadotville were having to be supplied by helicopter. 5000 tribesmen were besieging the Kamina base. Tshombe was not to be found. Above all, the governments of the western world had responded with a storm of protest. Both President Kennedy and Dean Rusk were reported 'very upset' and threatening withdrawal of US financial support for the UN operation if the communist line was to become dominant in the Congo. Britain was sending out a Minister of State, Lord Lansdowne. Belgium was accusing the UN of 'a premeditated crime'. Although Hammarskjold had accepted full responsibility, it seemed to Kane that the villain of the piece was O'Brien. All the papers reported him as saying that the UN action had been taken at the request of the central government in order to end the secession of Katanga, an action demonstrably exceeding the UN's mandate. The organization was on the defensive both militarily and morally.

One thing is for sure, Kane observed to himself, Steve Barlow must be hating every moment of it. But the sardonic amusement he derived from this was short-lived. What mattered was the concession. With Tshombe at large and apparently inflicting a humiliating defeat on the United Nations, the prospects for Kiobo looked bad indeed. Today was Friday. On Monday he was due in Leopoldville again. Was it any use going?

In the afternoon, as he was half asleep in a deckchair, an African servant approached him, bearing a cablegram. He tipped the man and tore open the envelope. It was from IMEX.

REGRET HEAR ACCIDENT STOP IT FIT ENOUGH RETURN VIA CONGO STOP REQUIRE EVALUATION EVENTS PROWESTERN

STOP CABLING FUNDS BARCLAYS DCO CAPETOWN SKINNER.

Kane read the message twice. He knew what Western Mining wanted: an estimate of how the Union Miniére's production was faring. The only question was a moral one. Could he pursue his own interests with Sendwe if IMEX were footing the bill? It took him less than a minute to decide that he could. Only men like Barlow, civil servants on assured salaries, could afford the luxury of a conscience.

Herman peered through the curtain of grass which concealed him. He lay prone, having crawled snakelike through the last few yards of undergrowth until he was on the river bank. The muddy water was low and flowed turgidly in the channel as if reluctant to move at all. Flies buzzed around him. Very carefully he lifted the binoculars slung round his neck, freed some strands of grass from them, and began surveying the opposite side. He didn't want the lenses to catch the sun, and he shaded them with one hand. He was a long way from the others and completely alone. An insect crawled over his wrist and he flicked it off. His eyes swept the river further and further downstream. At last he saw the enemy, a group of soldiers heaving something along. He played with the focus, trying to improve his vision, until he recognized what they had with them. Boats. Man, he said to himself, pleased at the success of his reconnaissance, it's obvious once you think about it. We are holding them at the bridge, therefore they must try to cross further down and take us from behind. He edged backwards, sliding on his belly, until he was screened by the bush, then stood up and doubled heavily back along the track to the company headquarters. Jaques had promoted him to sergeant major recently and at present he was in charge of the 100 para-commandos. He was acutely conscious of his responsibility.

The junior NCOs crowded round as he gave new orders, grinning excitedly, black faces gleaming under their red berets. Jacques had instilled a spirit into them which the rest of the gendarmerie lacked. They had kept the UN re-inforcements from relieving the Irish at Jadotville for three days now and with minimal losses.

'You have done well,' Herman told them in Swahili. '*Mzuri sana*. The Irish must surrender soon.' Then he handed over to a South African sergeant, took the jeep and drove the few kilometres to the nearest house with a telephone. He wanted air support.

There was a long blackboard in the operations centre at the Kolwezi airfield. Mike had 'borrowed' it from a local school. The various aircrafts identification numbers were written down the side while the hours of the day ran along the top. As missions were allotted they were chalked into the appropriate space. The date was prominent: Saturday 16 September.

When the telephone rang Mike picked it up and immediately ran his eyes over the aircraft availability.

'Good to hear you, Herman. How's tricks?' They were all ebullient at Kolwezi. 'Downstream, you say? North, in other words? The Fougas are busy, we'll give you a T6 at eleven hundred. OK. Have fun.' He put the instrument down, crossed to the board and filled in the mission detail. Then he went to the crewroom and called in one of the waiting pilots for a briefing, marking up the man's map to be certain there was no error.

'Don't forget the UN are on the east of the river and our boys on the west. I wouldn't want you dusting up my friend Jacques' paras. He'd kill us.'

'Where is the Fouga?' the pilot asked. The board showed only one serviceable.

'Everywhere.' Mike grinned. 'Should be attacking Kamina in ten minutes. Back to refuel, then Elisabethville. Delin's having the time of his life.' The only fly in the ointment was that the jet had been too busy for him to check out on it himself, so his own flying was still confined to the piston-engined T6s. But he was not resentful. The Fouga was dominating the skies of south Katanga, and the UN, possessing only helicopters and transports, was powerless to stop it.

The shrill whine of the jet engine overhead was audible to everyone in the building. Barlow tensed, listening. The sound died away. He resumed dictating a telex message to Margaret. He had hardly spoken two sentences when with a rending crash the window shattered, bullets slammed into the wall and the jet screamed past a few feet above. They both dived for the floor and lay among the broken glass and chunks of plaster, hands clasped over heads. Again the Fouga's wail died away and again, just as they were raising themselves, the buffeting, deafening noise returned. This time they heard the rattle of its guns. Barlow guessed it was shooting up the Post Office, which remained firmly in UN hands despite sporadic fighting in the city. The jet did not come back a fourth time.

'Phew,' said Margaret, dusting herself down, 'that was close.' Outside in the corridors there was sudden commotion as others of the staff realized the attack had finished. The door was flung open and the Indian major entered.

'We must have our own air force! I demand to know what is happening to our Indian Canberras and the Ethiopian jets. Why are they not coming? What is Leopoldville saying?'

'Calm down, please!' Barlow was only just recovering himself. 'You know the British are refusing to allow them to overfly Uganda.' Barlow corrected himself. 'Well, insisting that there are problems.'

'We must have more troops!'

'Major, a day ago you were telling us the military situation was under control.'

The Indian gestured to the holes in the wall and the debris. 'Are you saying this can be tolerated?'

'I should be asking you that question!' Barlow's patience broke. 'We are not going to get more troops. Even the United States has recalled the transport planes sent to bring in more.' His voice rose in anger. 'Your damned Operation Smash has done the organization more harm than anything in the past ten years. What we need is a ceasefire.' He almost spat at the officer. 'And the only man likely to get us that is the Secretary General himself.'

The Indian eyed him balefully and retreated, muttering under his breath.

'This place is a hornets' nest,' Barlow exclaimed. 'Now things have gone wrong, no one wants to be responsible.'

Margaret shook her head in puzzlement. 'What does he think you can do? Gee, I never knew how quick people could be to blame others.' The spattering of glass on the desk caught her eye. 'Here, let me go fetch a brush.'

Barlow dusted off his chair with his handkerchief and sat down, his thoughts in disorder. To help marshal them, he began making notes. Last night Tshombe had failed to show up for a meeting with O'Brien at the British consul's house. Today they were trying to pass across a message from Hammarskjold proposing an unconditional ceasefire and, if necessary, a meeting outside the Congo with the Secretary General in person. It was virtually the formula Barlow had unauthorizedly put forward himself before the fighting. But how could Tshombe be contacted direct? No one in the UN knew where he was, yet Radio Katanga was active, pouring out non-stop vituperation at the UN and threatening 'total war'. There must be a link to Tshombe somewhere.

It was as Margaret began tidying his papers and sweeping the floor that the idea came to him.

'Chantal Berthoud will be with him,' he exclaimed half to himself. 'And if she is she'll have been worried about her parents.'

'What are you saying?' asked Margaret, still busy.

'I think I have a way to him. He listens to Chantal and I believe she'll listen to me. If her family will co-operate.'

Outside the streets were nearly deserted, shops closed and shuttered. As he drove to the Berthouds' in a jeep with an armed escort, Barlow passed burnt-out trucks and cars. Prosperous Elisabethville had become a ghost town, its population hiding behind barred doors. The crackle of gunfire still came from the suburbs, where groups of mercenaries continued to harass UN positions. Occasionally the distant banshee whistle of a mortar bomb split the air, followed by the crump of its explosion.

When they stopped at the villa there was a flickering movement of the drawn curtains. Their arrival had been noted. Telling the guard to conceal their weapons, Barlow walked alone to the front door and knocked. After a long pause a man's voice shouted, 'Who is there?'

'I have an important message for Chantal.'

The door inched open, still held by a security chain inside. M. Berthoud's balding head appeared in the narrow aperture.

'I have not come to make arrests,' Barlow assured him. 'If you want to end the fighting you must help me reach your daughter.'

Reluctantly he was admitted. Mme Berthoud stood in the hall, arms folded, her face grim and defiant.

'Have you done enough to our city then?' she asked acidly. 'Or are you frightened and want to stop?'

Keeping himself rigidly under control, Barlow explained that, if they knew of a way to speak to their daughter, they must let him use it.

'In everyone's interest. For the record, I opposed this military action from its inception.'

Eventually they agreed to telephone her, provided he stayed out of earshot. They had a contact number for emergencies. It was the Kipushi mine office, but they had no intention of revealing the location.

After a long wait M. Berthoud called him through and handed him the telephone.

'We are urgently trying to arrange a meeting with the President,' he said. 'Without escort.'

'He will not deal with O'Brien.' At her end of the line Chantal was sitting in the Kipushi mine manager's office, which also had the vital telephone link along the electric cables to Rhodesia. Tshombe was not there. He was in conference with other Katanga politicians in a villa. She could only act as a go-between.

'Listen, Mlle Berthoud, this is of crucial importance. For everyone's sake we have to fix a ceasefire. I have here a personal message from Hammarskjold. If talks with O'Brien cannot be arranged, he will meet with Tshombe himself. It's like I was saying six days ago. The Secretary General can sort this mess out as no other man could.'

'What does he say exactly, please?' She reached for a pad. 'I will take it down.'

Barlow read, holding the telex paper up to the light. With all the curtains drawn it was dim in the room. 'I quote,' he said, reading the French of the special additional instructions Hammarskjold had sent to meet this eventuality. ' " I suggest that I should meet you personally, so that together we can find peaceful methods of resolving the present conflict .... As I shall have to go to the meeting place by air, I suggest that the meeting should be at Ndola ...." '

The text was long and Chantal needed several minutes to get it all down. 'I shall pass it to the President immediately he is free,' she promised.

'Please don't delay. How will you reply?'

'Through the British consul. Mr Tshombe is not prepared to communicate directly with your office.' She tried to soften this refusal. 'It's nothing personal, Mr Barlow, but you must understand his feelings. He trusts no one there.'

'I swear he can talk to me with confidence.'

'I am truly sorry, but those are his instructions.'

For all Chantal's tact, Barlow did feel offended. If anyone had consistently striven for conciliation, it was he. Those efforts deserved better recognition. As he left the Berthouds' house, Madame still hovering sour-faced by the door as if seeing a criminal off the premises, he consoled himself with his faith in the Secretary General's ability to end the crisis, in spite of Tshombe's intransigence, if once the two men could be brought together.

Chantal's call to Mike come late in the evening. He had to be brought from the mining executive's villa he had been lent, excited when he was told who wanted him and at the same time anxious. It was not her style to make dramatic middle of the night requests.

'How are you? Good,' she sounded pleased to hear him. 'Listen, I won't waste time. The President wants a plane to take him to Rhodesia. Where can we find one?'

'The Cessna's here. I could fly it down in the morning. No problem.' His enthusiasm was bolstered by the prospect of seeing her.

'I'm not sure it's large enough.' She had precisely the same thought and was keenly disappointed. 'He wants to bring three of his Ministers as well.'

'Oh, damn. What a bloody nuisance.' Mike swore beneath his breath. 'He'll have to charter something bigger, a Comanche or an Aztec. There's a firm in Kitwe, I think the pilot's name is Kearns.' He spelt it out for her, then asked, 'What's up?'

'He's meeting Hammarskjold. The UN might have sent a plane but he's afraid they would kidnap him.'

'Well, he can trust the Kitwe people. Look, there's something much more important. When am I going to see you?'

'Mike, I wish I knew. As soon as this is over, I

promise.'

'I'll hold you to that.' He rang off feeling decidedly happier. Altogether this had been a magnificent week.

In the UN offices the telex machines clacked out message after message through the early hours of 17 September. When Steve Barlow came in he learnt to his undisguised pleasure that the Ndola meeting was to take place. Tshombe had agreed. O'Brien himself was not going to attend the negotiation. Instead Barlow would drive down there to be available should Hammarskjold require any local briefing. He left Elisabethville, jubilant, after lunch, recalling his father's fear as they strolled around the lake shore in the spring. His father had been shown wrong. To use college jargon, he had scored. Even the news that the Irish at Jadotville had surrendered did not disturb him. The solution of the Katanga problem was in sight, thanks to the success of his own diplomacy.

The Albertina was a four-engined Douglas DC6B airliner, roomy, not a jet but relatively fast. Normally used by the UN Force Commander, on this occasion it was allocated for the Secretary General's special flight. It was Swedish registered with the letters SE-BDY and carried a Swedish crew. Because of the activities of the Katangan air force, the captain filed his flight plan for the Congo town of Luluabourg to preserve secrecy. He would not land there, but proceed the rest of the 1100 miles to Ndola by a complicated and much longer route, completely avoiding the dangerous Katangan airspace, whilst also maintaining absolute radio silence.

The 17th was a Sunday. Leopoldville was quiet, the weather sultry and overcast. At 4.30 p.m. Hammarskjold and his nine staff arrived at the airfield. The two security men among the nine searched the plane, finding nothing suspicious. At 4.51 local time the Albertina lifted off the long runway and headed east.

Steve Barlow, aware that Tshombe had already arrived and was being cared for by the Rhodesian authorities at a private house, waited at Ndola airfield. It was not an attractive place to be idle in for a long period. The passenger terminal was a large, green-painted, corrugated-iron construction, like an oversize Nissen hut, a great arch of ribbed metal into the curve of which windows and doors had been cut. 100 yards away stood the white control tower with a big yellow C on the wall to indicate its function. From time to time he went across there, religiously proving his identity, but the answer was always the same. No flight plan had been received for the Albertina, only for a smaller DC4 carrying the British Minister, Lord Lansdowne.

Yet the word was out that Hammarskjold was coming. The resources of the airport's rudimentary snack bar restaurant were strained by journalists, police and officials. Darkness fell with still no time schedule. Barlow had brought a book with him, *Politics and Morals* by a distinguished Italian philosopher, Benedetto Croce. He had been meaning to get down to it for months, since buying the translation in New York. But now that he had time on his hands and the quiet of a VIP waiting room, he was unable to concentrate. 'In political action', he read, 'in attempts to reach a definite goal, everything becomes a political means . . . the men with whom we have to deal are always what they are.' A self-evident truth, he thought, until it occurred to him how closely the dictum applied to his present mission. Would anything change Tshombe's character?

These musings were interrupted by the appearance of a police inspector in immaculately pressed, shorts and shirt, a revolver handle protruding from a holster on his leather belt.

'Mr Barlow? We've had a radio report at last, sir. The aircraft's ETA here is 12.35 a.m. local. Lord Lansdowne's plane is due any minute.'

Barlow thanked him and checked the time, 10.20 p.m. Two and a bit hours to go. For God's sake, how could the flight be taking so long?

'What is Lansdowne doing?' he asked.

The policeman gave him a suspicious glance. 'Paying his respects to Tshombe. He'll fly on to Salisbury before your man gets here.' He indicated a tray of drinks. 'Help yourself, sir, compliments of the federal government.'

Barlow poured himself a whisky, reflecting bitterly on Tshombe's willingness to talk to the British at any time. He forced himself to attempt a further chapter of *Politics and Morals*.

Two hours later the drone of engines made him spring to his feet and dash outside. The green, red and white navigation lights of a large aircraft were passing overhead. A flashing red light showed behind the others: the anti-collision beacon. The lights continued their path steadily north-west, their pattern slowly altering until only the flashing red beacon and another white light beneath it could be seen. Then they too disappeared. Barlow hurried to the control tower.

Upstairs the controllers were gazing into the night, the lighting deliberately dim.

'Its BDY,' one told him. 'He's two thousand feet above ground, has the field in sight and is descending. Earlier on he said he would be taking off again almost immediately but would not give any destination.'

'Mind if I stay up here? I'm a pilot myself.'

'Oh.' The controller became more friendly. 'OK. You understand we're busy, though? We're holding the DC4 until the DC6 is down.'

Barlow stood by the wide windows, straining his eyes for a sight of the aircraft. Presumably it was turning to make its approach, but the controllers were unable to get an answer from it. The minutes passed. Loud over the radio came the pilot of Lansdowne's DC4 asking how much longer he had to wait. The controller called BDY yet again, with no reply.

'If the BDY were landing she'd have done so fifteen minutes ago,' commented one controller. 'We'd better let the other go.'

At 12.35 the DC4 was authorized to taxi out and take off. As it disappeared south-east towards Salisbury Barlow felt his first serious twinge of concern. The captain was also radioing BDY and obtaining no response.

'I can't understand it,' he insisted. 'Hammarskjold was definitely coming here.'

'We've still had no flight plan. They warned us they'd be taking off again immediately.' The controller was puzzled but not alarmed. 'They took a curious route, too. At 8.30 GMT they reported over the southern end of Lake Tanganyika. That means they flew two sides of a triangle from Leo, east then south. Maybe your boss changed his mind again.'

'I don't believe that,' said Barlow hotly.

'Listen!' The controller disliked emotional outbursts. 'If you're a pilot, you know the importance of filing proper flight plans, OK? We have no details; no alternate airfield for landing; no take off time; no ETA; no endurance figure. We don't even know the pilot's name or the number of persons on board.'

'It must be for security reasons.'

'Well, one thing I do not believe is that if the pilot was in trouble security would prevent him putting out a distress call. If you're worried, why not go down and see the police? Maybe there's a governmental message floating around which nobody's bothered to tell us about.'

At the foot of the stairs Barlow met one of the staff of the Rhodesian High Commissioner, who was waiting to receive Hammarskjold. The aide shook his head. 'No news. We can only assume the Secretary General received a message in flight and changed his plans. We're authorizing the airfield's closure until morning.' He left

Barlow and went up to tell the controllers. When he came down again, he offered Barlow a lift into the town and found him a hotel room, apologizing that official accommodation had only been arranged for the Secretary General and his nine staff: they had not been warned of Barlow's presence. However, he promised to come round in the morning.

During the night, Barlow barely slept. The whole business seemed inexplicable. When, at breakfast time, he heard the steady sound of aircraft patrolling to and fro, he knew the worst was feared and a search had been started. He rang the aide and demanded information. There was none. He was fetched and taken to the police headquarters, where he found himself as powerless as at the hotel. All he could do was wait.

Slowly the evidence of disaster accumulated. A police report of a flash in the sky shortly after midnight acquired a new significance. Then an African charcoal burner was arrested, trying to sell what he imagined to be a typewriter. It was identified as a coding machine and the African admitted looting it from a place in the woods where there had been an explosion and a fire. In mid-afternoon the search aircraft located the wreckage of the Albertina, nine and a half miles north-west of the town.

The police Land-Rover taking Barlow to the scene raced along the tarmaced Kitwe road until, a few miles out, the driver braked and swung right on to a track through a forestry plantation. It wasn't difficult to find the route, already scarred by the first emergency vehicles. Beyond the pine plantations they came into virgin bush. Giant ant-hills reared up in twenty-foot-high mounds, often with thorn trees growing from them. The grass was high and yellow brown, everything as dry as tinder. The Albertina had come down among trees and low thorn bushes, and the area was still hazy with smoke from the fire that had broken out after the port wingtip hit an ant-hill and the aircraft cartwheeled to complete destruction.

Barlow jumped out of the vehicle and ran forward in bewilderment, searching without hope for signs of a survivor. Already ambulance crews were covering bodies in blankets and carrying them to trucks. All that was identifiable of the Albertina were two engines and part of the tailplane. One of the engines lay crushed against a tree with its propeller blades bent back like tinfoil. Shards of metal were scattered in the smouldering rubble. Beyond, the tops of the trees had been sliced off as the descending airliner cut a swathe through the bush. He caught a rescue worker by the arm.

'Have you found Hammarskjold, is anyone alive?'

'One man is. Just. Very badly hurt.'

'I am from the UN. I must see him.'

The worker led him to a doctor kneeling beside a body on a stretcher. Barlow's stomach turned over as he saw the terrible burns. But it was not the Secretary General.

The doctor looked up. 'Its a miracle he's alive. Most of the day exposed to the sun on top of the fire.'

A police officer came up to Barlow. 'Would you be able to identify any of the dead?'

'Possibly.'

'There's one not touched by the fire.'

Barlow followed, picking his way through lumps of jagged metal and ash. On the perimeter of the burnt area, by a small bush, lay the corpse of a slightly built man in a lounge suit. He was on his back, the body crumpled, one hand stretched out clutching a tuft of grass. The face, staring sightless at the blue sky, seemed at peace, its familiar features calm.

'It's him,' said Barlow, the words catching in his throat, his voice cracking. 'It's Hammarskjold.' He turned away, disregarding the police officer, and stumbled back to the Land-Rover, where he sat until his emotions became uncontrollable and he leant his forearms on the dashboard and sobbed.

The UN spokesman who flew into Ndola with other officials from Leopoldville told newspaper correspondents how efforts by the Ndola controllers to contact an unidentified circling plane around the time of the crash had failed. 'There is something very strange about it,' he commented, observing that Ndola was within range of the Katangan Fouga jet based at Kolwezi some 150 miles distant. The UN Intelligence Chief announced immediate investigations into whether the Albertina had been sabotaged or shot down.

Barlow made no statement. Tight-lipped, he rebuffed reporters' questions regarding the storm of accusations now being made against Tshombe, the Rhodesians and the British. He was totally preoccupied with a far more awful fear: had he, by so enthusiastically promoting the meeting, been the unwitting cause of the Secretary General's death? Had his hopes of conciliation killed the man he most admired? The idea was almost too painful to bear and he became obsessed with it. He stayed on in Ndola until Hammarskjold's body was placed in the church of St Andrew's, the mahogany casket draped with the Swedish flag and four sentries, two European and two African, guarding it with arms reversed. Then he joined other mourners to pay his last respects, filing past, sombre faced, his hands clasped behing his back. Tshombe, too, came there and laid a wreath of white lilies, murmuring in shaken tones as he left, 'It is very sad.' Barlow made no attempt to approach him. He could not have done so. His heart was frozen with grief and remorse. On the 20th a ceasefire was signed and he returned to Elisabethville at last.

For three days Kane hung about in Suzy's apartment, reading every newspaper he could obtain, listening to the radio, pumping her for every item of UN gossip she could procure. On the fourth the long-promised summons came from Sendwe. He made a final check of the Letter of Intent he would persuade the Vice Prime Minister to sign and took a taxi to the government offices, prepared to join enthusiastically in a condemnation of all that Tshombe represented. The morning's headlines reported his return to a hero's welcome in Elisabethville. 'Tshombe the Magnanimous permits defeated UN to remain' was apparently a fair specimen of local Katangan reaction to the ceasefire.

In the circumstances Kane did not expect to find Sendwe in good humour. Even so he was not prepared for the reaction he got. The African read the Letter of Intent with care, picked up a pen, added a sentence below the last paragraph and signed. Amazed and gratified Kane thanked him profusely and took it back. The handwritten words read: 'This contract conditional upon the delivery of Moise Tshombe to representatives of the Congolese central government, whether alive or dead.' Kane stared at it, forcing a smile but completely taken aback.

'That's rather a tall order, Minister. I'm a mining man, not a kidnapper.'

'On the other hand,' said Sendwe with a toughness usually absent from his speech, 'that is all that now interests me. Tshombe is the murderer of Hammarskjold and our enemy. The time for negotiation is past. If you want the Kiobo concession, Tshombe is the price. How you achieve it is your affair.'

9

The town was *en fete*, celebrating a triumph. Flags fluttered along the streets, hastily cleared up after the fighting. Portraits of Tshombe hung everywhere, the Avenue de l'Étoile was to be re-named after him, the broadcasts from Radio Katanga likened him to Jesus Christ, crucified but now risen again. Steve Barlow read the transcripts with disgust and stoically bent himself to drafting conditions for the exchange of prisoners. The ceasefire had yet to be enshrined in a diplomatic protocol. He found some relief in refining the legal niceties of the agreement, the familiar words and phrases known since his law school days acting as a balm to his mind, which was otherwise dominated by the failure of his attempts at that conciliation. One of the world's few great and good men was lost, killed in pursuit of it, and immediately the Katangans behaved as if they were victors. The UN's flag alone flew at half mast for the Secretary General. At Ndola he had felt personally responsible for Hammarskjold's flight to death. Now back in Elisabethville the outrageous hero-worship of Tshombe, and the open boasting of mercenaries in the hotels and bars, revolted him. The others in the headquarters had been right. Force was the only answer.

The pilots were given leave, and cash bonuses. Mike

Russell, longing to see Chantal, flew in one of the Dakotas back from Kolwezi. Because it nominally belonged to Air Katanga and would resume civil flying, they brought it into the main Elisabethville airport, still under UN guard. As they taxied in a new and ominous sight caught his eye.

'So they arrived at last,' he remarked grimly to the other pilot, Joe.

'I heard the British let them through Uganda within twenty-four hours of the Ndola crash. Does depend how good the Ethiops are, though.' He slowed down to a crawl so that they could get a good look.

On the UN side of the airfield three F86 Sabre jet fighters were parked neatly in line, as aggressive as sharks, their high tailfins emblazoned with Ethiopian air force colours, their jet intakes like gaping mouths.

'The Yanks in Korea used to paint teeth around those intakes,' Joe commented. 'Seemed appropriate. In the right hands the F86 is a killer.'

As they left the airfield Mike made a mental note to start stock-piling ammunition and spares for his own aircraft, though only the Fougas could begin to be a match for these UN jets. Despite such depressing considerations it was nice to be back. Once at the villa, he began checking the few possessions he had left there. His car was untouched and surprised him by its willingness to start. He telephoned Chantal and confirmed their dinner date at the hotel, bathed and drove to the Leo Deux rather earlier than necessary.

The Hotel Leopold II seemed relatively unscathed by the week's battles. It occupied a corner site on the Avenue de l'Étoile, not far from the much-fought-over Post Office, however the gracious white painted balconies encompassing its three storeys were pocked by bullets in only a few places. Mike strode briskly in through the main entrance, heading for the bar and wondering if he would run into anyone he knew. To his embarrassment the first person he encountered was Steve Barlow, unobtrusively dressed in a grey tropical suit.

For a split second Mike thought of merely nodding acquaintanceship and passing on. Indeed, he got as far as saying, 'Hallo, Steve,' in a casual way when Barlow blocked his path.

'I've been wanting a word with you, Russell.'

Mike stopped and decided to disregard the apparent hostility of the remark. 'Let's go to the bar,' he suggested. 'I can spare a few minutes if it's important.'

'Under no circumstances will I drink with you!'

'In that case come outside.' A year ago he might have stood for the insult. But life among men like Jacques had toughened him.

'I am not proposing a pavement brawl, thank you.'

The intensity of Barlow's voice was attracting attention. At the reception desk the clerk reached down and pressed a bell to summon the manager. The two men facing each other spelt trouble; the one tanned, his seldom-worn suit looking out of place on him, no kind of a bruiser but obviously a mercenary; the other the same ascetic UN official who had caused an incident in March. The clerk watched apprehensively, waiting for the fight.

'For Christ's sake, let's sit down somewhere.' Mike held back his temper. 'I'm spending the evening here and I don't want it ruined.' He led the way to a group of unoccupied armchairs set around a small table. 'Whether you drink or not, I'm having one.'

At this point the manager appeared, asking with transparently false solicitude, 'Is everything all right, gentlemen?'

'I'd like a beer,' said Mike. 'A Simba. Otherwise everything's fine.'

The manager retreated mistrustfully and Mike sat down, but he was having to control himself. 'If you have something on your mind, you'd better spit it out,' he said. 'Chantal will be here soon.'

The mention of her name only aggravated Barlow more. 'I imagine she is as aware of this as anyone,' he said tautly. 'I want to know who shot down the Albertina.'

'Are you crazy? No one did.' Mike was shocked. 'If that's what you imagine, you're dead wrong. We knew about the meeting. Do you seriously think we would have attacked Hammarskjold's plane?'

'You can hardly boast of a sense of responsibility. Your record at Frampton speaks for itself, doesn't it?' There was an ugly, irrational venom in Barlow's words. 'Now you're mixed up with the ultras, not men noted for prudence or honour.' He leant forward. 'Bullet holes have been found in the Albertina's hull, Russell. An African saw another light above her immediately before the crash.'

Mike's temper broke. 'Since when have fighters made night interceptions with their navigation lights on, Flying Officer Barlow?' he demanded scathingly. 'You of all pilots should know they don't. You're the one who always flew by the book.'

The contemptuous use of his low air force rank stung Barlow, who flushed. 'We have to investigate every possibility,' he said defensively. 'Your Fouga has the range.'

'And your public statements stink! The Fouga's operational range is a hundred and fifty miles. Maximum. If it flew from Kolwezi to Ndola it would have to turn back before it could make a night interception: even if it was capable of one. Would you tell me how to do that with no knowledge of a target's position and no radar? You're talking unadulterated nonsense and you know it.'

'The court of inquiry may think differently.'

Mike had heard enough. He would have liked to throw his beer in Barlow's face. Instead he left it unfinished on the table and stood up. 'If you want to trade insults, come outside. If not, leave me alone.'

Across by the reception the manager hovered anxiously. Barlow noticed him and rose to his feet too. He did not wish to be humiliated again. Trembling, he faced Mike. 'I hold you responsible for the Secretary General's death, if only by your illegal attacks on our troops. You forced the Albertina to fly a circuitous route which may well have contributed to the disaster.'

'Attacking!' Mike lost his temper completely. 'Who, for Christ's sake, planned the first attack, you or us? You make me sick, Steve. You always did. You were a po-faced bastard in 699 Squadron, and you're worse now.'

Barlow was gripping the back of his chair, his knuckles white, his fury uncontrollable. 'We're getting the planes, Russell,' he said. 'Give us the smallest reason and we'll knock you out of the sky. That's a promise.' He released the chair and walked to the door, visibly shaking. The manager immediately moved to see him out, then came across to Mike.

'Pigs,' he said bitterly. 'No better than the communists. I should not allow them on the premises.' He gave Mike a friendly glance. 'You are Captain Russell? I thought so. Mlle Berthoud is waiting for you in the bar.'

Conscious of his need to calm down, Mike went quickly to the men's room and splashed cold water on his face, dried himself briskly and combed his hair before going through to find Chantal. She was seated at a corner table, a waiter fussing around her, and she smiled as he hurried across.

'You're just in time to order me a *vin blanc cassis*.'

'I thought we might have champagne.' He had special plans for this evening. 'After all, we can afford to celebrate. Come on, you're looking stunning, you deserve a treat.' He gazed at her fondly. She must have had an instinct for the occasion. Her long brown hair was brushed back in a style he hadn't seen before and she wore a faintly provocative crimson silk evening dress, with the bracelet he had given her gleaming on her wrist.

'Thank you, Mike. Yes, let's choose champagne. Why not?'

The waiter bustled off to bring a wine list. When the marque was chosen, their glasses full and the bottle resplendent in a chromium ice bucket with a white napkin around its neck, they toasted each other.

'This is an improvement on Jacques's *vin rouge*,' he commented. 'I've been looking forward to this evening, even though I didn't know when it would be. I haven't seen you for ages.'

'We've all been rather busy.' She paused, deciding to dispose of the thing that was worrying her straight away. 'I saw you with Barlow. What was the matter?'

'He intends to avenge Hammarskjold's death on us.' Mike explained their clash.

'But he was the one UN man here who argued all the time for conciliation.' Chantal was mystified, though having seen Barlow's expression she did not doubt Mike's account.

'In that case he's changed his mind. There's one thing to be said for Steve Barlow,' he remarked with unwonted sarcasm. 'When he does decide on a course of action he always gets it wrong.'

'Are you sure that's fair? He really made extreme efforts to follow through Hammarskjold's policy.'

Mike bit his lip. The last thing he wanted to do was talk about Barlow. Yet he now felt obliged to. 'There's a difference,' he explained. 'Steve would obey orders to the letter. But he was always paralysed by decision-making. I told you about the crash at Frampton. I'm sure that, when he overheard Jake and I planning to fly under the bridge, he just couldn't make up his mind whether to tell Kane or not and finally only gave evidnece at the court-martial on the spur of the moment. By then all he could do was make matters worse. He damned Kane and he muddied the squadron's reputation. He's a very dangerous man to give responsibility to, especially in a crisis. You saw him just now. He was literally shaking with rage.'

'He did seem very emotional,' Chantal admitted.

'But he's been a fighter pilot himself. If he could calm down for ten seconds he'd have to accept that it was a technical impossibility for us to have shot down Hammarskjold's plane. Especially if it made some huge detour to avoid Katanga. Yet he holds us responsible. If he hadn't been academically brilliant I'd say he was off his head.'

'The UN has been deeply humiliated, Mike. No one likes that. Myself, I wish Tshombe wasn't being made such a hero. It is not a good situation.'

'Let's try to forget it all for an evening, shall we?' He raised his glass and clinked it against hers. 'Here's to us.'

An hour and a half later, when the coffee had been served and the restaurant waiters were out of earshot, he made his proposal. 'Chantal, darling. I've been in love with you since we first met. Will you marry me?' When he had said it, the words sounded too abrupt and he added, 'Kenya's not a bad place to live. You'd like it.'

'I would like any place if you were there. Tremendously. But Mike ....' She had been expecting this and even so wasn't certain how to reply. The actual moment threw her mind into a whirl. She reached out and touched his hand. 'Becoming engaged is a big commitment. Even here in the Congo my family would insist on four or five months before we married. Where will we be then?'

'Does it matter? If this place falls apart, we can be together in Kenya. I want to marry you. There's nothing dishonourable about that.'

'It is hard for a foreigner to understand, Mike. I know we are not in Belgium. I know the behaviour of many people out here is not so good, they lose their heads in Africa. But I don't want to be like that. Remember this is a small community. If one has a short engagement everyone assumes the worst. When I marry it must be done properly for my parents' sake.' She paused, smiling at him affectionately. 'And I myself have to be quite absolutely certain I am doing the right thing.'

'Chantal, darling, I love you. I don't care about anything else and I see you so seldom now. Can't you love me too?'

'Yes, I think so .... Oh Mike, we shall have to wait a little.'

'Couldn't we be unofficially engaged? Then you wouldn't have such a commitment.'

She shook her head regretfully. 'Maybe I am too bourgeois. For us it's either official or nothing.'

'You mean nothing?'

She felt for his hand again, lifted it gently, kissed his fingertips and then released them. 'I mean neither yes or no. Let me think about it more. Give me a little time.'

He was about to protest that they had already known each other more than a year when he saw in her face that it was no good. She would not be rushed. But when they eventually left the Leo Deux she kissed him goodbye with an affection she had never displayed before.

The letter was scrawled in Suzy's untidy writing on official paper.

Operation Nations Unies Congo
ONUC
BP 7248 Leopoldville

le 20 octobre 61

Chéri,

It was a lovely surprise to hear your voice – however did you manage to get through? Yes, I found out I have leave at Christmas and should adore to meet you somewhere. Dakar, perhaps? I heard the beaches are wonderful. You never mentioned your hand. Is is healed now?

What else are you doing in your cold, Sunday-dull country? Business, business, always business I suppose. You men are so boring sometimes. Anyway, you'll be pleased that everyone here feels the same about what you asked. The ceasefire protocol was signed last week, but it can't last. The most recent report said many more mercenaries have returned to Katanga and there are now 237. (It doesn't sound many to me, we have 6000 troops there.) The main thing is, the UN is frightened the central government will break up if Tshombe isn't brought to heel. So sooner or later he will be, and it has to be sooner because ONUC is again having to ask the General Assembly for more money.

I hope this helps and wish you were here. Don't forget about Dakar, will you? Or maybe the Ivory Coast. I don't expect the UN would actually stop me going to South Africa, but they'd make it very obvious the organization doesn't approve.

Love and kisses,
Suzy

P.S. You left a shirt here. Why not come and fetch it?

Little bitch, Kane muttered as he put the letter down on the kitchen table. Senegal and the Ivory Coast were about the two most expensive countries in Africa and as for the shirt! He had left nothing behind on the last trip. However, she had provided the basic information he wanted. He swallowed the last of his coffee and prepared to leave the flat for work, resignedly going through the process of edging the cast on his wrist down through one coat sleeve, then awkwardly wriggling his left arm into the other, pulling the coat straight round his shoulders and putting on the sling. If that blow from the rifle hadn't bent his wrist so sharply as well as crushing the back of his hand, he would be out of plaster by now. As it was, he would be incapacitated a further two months.

As the underground train rattled its way from Kensington to the City, Kane puzzled over his next step. Should he risk quitting IMEX if the ingeniously simple plot he had devised was acceptable to Eric Ironstone? Or rather, if the part he intended to reveal was. It all hung on the Member of Parliament's reaction. At least Parliament was in session again and Ironstone would be easily available, instead of on holiday in the Mediterranean, as he had been in September.

Three days later Kane was strolling along the riverside terrace of the House of Commons beside the portly figure of the MP, a sharp autumn breeze rumpling his hair. They stopped by one of the ornate Victorian lamp standards and gazed over the stone parapet at the skyline of the South Bank.

'So,' Ironstone observed urbanely, 'you intend to ask Tshombe to this place Kiobo in order to meet potential backers, having offered him armaments in exchange for the concession. I am possibly rather simple-minded.' The expression on his heavily jowled face made it clear that he meant the reverse. 'But as I understood it before, you were obtaining the concession from Tshombe's opponent.'

'In view of the way Tshombe turned the tables on the United Nations last month, we ought to back both horses.' Kane studiously avoided his host's eyes, instead watching a barge churning its way through the murky water of the Thames. His plot had two dimensions, but he was uncertain how far he could deceive this shrewd-eyed and reputedly avaricious politician. Their two business meetings since the initial encounter at the Bembridge Sailing Club had displayed Ironstone as a far more intricate personality than his original bluff manner suggested.

'It's chilly out here.' The MP shivered. 'And your idea begs a lot of questions. Let's eat.' He led the way back across the flagstones and down a short flight of steps into the Strangers' Bar. The small room was full of cigarette smoke and chatter. 'We might forgo the pre-lunch ritual.' Nodding to various acquaintances, Ironstone ushered Kane out again, through dark corridors and up more stairs to the Members' Dining Room overlooking the river from a higher level.

Kane recognized several occupants of neighbouring

tables in the spacious panelled room and Ironstone briefly indicated a Cabinet Minister's presence before ordering aperitifs, settling his heavy frame into his chair and tackling the main subject. He had a remarkable capacity for speaking perfectly distinctly, yet in so low timbre that he was inaudible to outsiders.

'Under precisely what circumstances do you envisage Tshombe agreeing?' he asked.

'When his back is to the wall. Given your agreement, I shall fly out there shortly and make the offer, anticipating a refusal, but leaving it open. When the UN make a further attempt to end Katanga's secession by force, as they seem certain to do, I will arrive again and renew the proposal. I believe he will then accept.'

'You're very confident in your timing.' Ironstone sipped at his schooner of pale sherry.

'It will be delicate,' Kane admitted. 'I need the moment when he realizes defeat is imminent, but has not given up.'

'You do appreciate the degree of support Tshombe enjoys here in Britain? It has increased hugely since the UN's recent action.' Ironstone put his glass down on the white tablecloth. His small eyes were fixed on Kane's face. 'Arms we can obtain and send in through Rhodesia. Providing nothing is forced upon the government's attention, through a General Assembly debate for example, I think we could honour that bargain. Indeed, we can give you introductions to Tshombe which will smooth your path very considerably.' He pursed his lips. 'What of the alternative, the original scheme? If Tshombe's regime is destroyed, do you then revert to the contract with Sendwe? And did that not have a somewhat unusual condition attached?'

'Sendwe never specified who must deliver Tshombe to the central government. In practice the United Nations will do it.'

'Are you sure? They have shown themselves outstandingly incompetent hitherto.' Ironstone leant forward as much as his bulk comfortably permitted. 'You are not by any chance going to take matters into your own hands, are you, Robert? Give the situation a little push, as it were.' He motioned with his palms as if propelling something away to one side.

Kane flushed. This was exactly what he was planning. He lifted his injured arm. 'I can hardly attempt anything physical with this encumbrance, or did you mean metaphorically?'

Ironstone's cold, pig-like eyes remained unblinkingly fixed on his guest. He had served as an interrogator during the war and his instinct for what was false remained strong. He knew this young man opposite was lying, but could only guess at the reason. 'If you were able to trace Tshombe when the United Nations could not, you would have an exploitable advantage,' he remarked softly. 'A most exploitable one.'

'I would indeed. I should use it to obtain the Kiobo concession.' The statement was both true and gave little away.

'I hope you will use discretion, too, even though you have a great deal at stake, because there are also political considerations. If Tshombe were to fall, the opprobrium *must* rest on the United Nations. Do I make myself clear? I do? Excellent.' He relaxed a little. 'Talking of what is at stake reminds me. I have never understood why that Belgian geologist confided in you. To do so was a downright betrayal of his employers.'

'For emotional reasons.' Kane was relieved at the change of subject. 'Very few geologists are ever lucky enough to exploit their own discoveries. He had both found and proved Kiobo. It was more than he could bear not to see it developed.'

'Dreams and avarice,' Ironstone murmured. 'Those are what make the world go round. Some fools suppose it's sex, but we know better, eh?' The waiter appeared with the first course and he pulled his chair up to the table. 'Well,' he said, squeezing a slice of lemon over his smoked salmon, satisfied that Kane would serve his consortium's purposes, 'my colleagues have agreed in principle to financing the necessary travel. No salary, of course, at least until we have the concession. Then I've no doubt we shall create an executive role for you. Meanwhile we're joint speculators, our contribution being money and yours time.'

'We draw up an agreement?'

'Naturally. You should be able to bid farewell to my old friend Sir John in about a fortnight.' He cut into the thin slice of fish, forked it up, swallowed appreciatively and smiled. 'Better give me the name of your lawyer before we leave. We won't want any loose ends or misunderstandings, will we?'

'So there's been a policy shift? That's the message, is it, George?'

Andy Dillon was closeted with a State Department official at the Army and Navy Club in Washington. The two men had served together in the war, but it was not camaraderie which kept them in touch. It was inter action between government and business.

'There's a UN debate on the Congo due in a few days and JFK has agreed with Mr Rusk on taking a very much firmer line,' the diplomat explained. 'Between ourselves, the United States will urge that the UN be given authority to destroy hostile aircraft and war materials wherever necessary to prevent their use against either civilians or the UN itself.'

Dillon took off his steel-rimmed glasses and polished them gently with the corner of a silk handkerchief. He felt no obligation to disclose the half-million dollars Western Mining had contributed towards those 'hostile aircraft'.

'How about the Katangan lobby in Congress?' he asked. 'They won't like seeing Tshombe lose his air force.'

'The President hopes to persuade them that Tshombe's independent regime is no kind of an instrument for stability in central Africa. It threatens civil war, anarchy and a real danger of communist penetration. We have to keep the whole Congo in the Western camp.' The official glanced sharply across the table. 'Not that stability in the area benefits your industry, Andy. The disruption must be pretty helpful to copper prices.'

Dillon blinked. 'You could say so,' he conceded.

'There have been contributions to Tshombe which we would like to see suspended in the larger interests of the United States.'

'From governmental agencies too, I heard.' Dillon replaced his spectacles on his nose. He wanted both to see and hear the reaction to this thrust. It should draw blood.

'If there were,' George replied tersely, 'they are being terminated.'

'Then I guess we can take the hint,' Dillon grunted. Privately he doubted any president's ability to control the operations of the CIA, which was almost as independent an empire as Hoover's FBI, and he was certain that Sturgess, the man who ran the PANWORLD agency in Paris, was a former CIA operative.

'Thanks,' said George calmly. 'I was sure you would see it our way.'

However, Dillon was not a man to leave empty-handed. 'Since we're talking policy,' he said, 'maybe you could give us a little guidance in another direction. Vietnam. We took over where the French left off. Is the involvement escalating?'

'Purely in an advisory capacity. Our military assistance teams are not involved in combat with the Viet Cong.'

Dillon grunted again and began drawing out more information. Wars were always of interest to Western because they could not be fought without copper in huge quantities: copper for shell cases, wiring, radios, fuses. By the time he left the Club he had decided on an exploratory trip to South East Asia. If the United States eventually became as deeply committed in fighting communism there as the French had been, the long-term contracts Western could expect would make this brief Katangan involvement look like a nursery game. He no longer minded washing his hands of it.

'I have decided to resign from the company, sir.' There was a conscious formality about Kane's statement.

James Skinner looked up. 'You don't have to stand,' he remarked coldly. 'I'm not your commanding officer. Take a seat. Well,' he went on when Kane obeyed, 'there's not a great deal to discuss, is there? We're in agreement on a course of action for once.' He flipped open a file and picked out a sheet of paper. 'We've just had the final accumulated accounting for your African adventures. We knew it was substantial, but four hundred and twenty-one thousand seven hundred and eight dollars!' He shook his head as though still unable to believe the figure. 'Four hundred and twenty-one thousand dollars! Bribes, air fares, expenses, car hire, commissions.' There was a harder edge to his voice now. 'How did you have the nerve? How? And with no return whatever.'

'It was over three and a half years.' Kane wasn't going to be browbeaten. 'It was all authorized. And Kiobo could be viable.'

'Which apparently is why Western's slush fund went on disgorging cash without their accountants appreciating the total.' He ran his finger along the paper. 'You also succeeded in placing your expenditure under a quite remarkable variety of headings. Talk about only being able to hire a Congolese Minister for the afternoon – Western are questioning whether some of your politicians exist.'

'Are you accusing me of fraud?' Kane went pale with anger. He had lavished money on many people, including Suzy, but they were all real, all genuine informants.

'Not yet.' Skinner recognized the danger of slandering a man of Kane's disposition. He would be straight off to a lawyer. 'I hope not at all. However, your removal would unquestionably have been demanded at the next board meeting. In the circumstances I accept your resignation. We will waive the normal period of notice. In fact you can leave this afternoon. Three months' salary will be paid to your bank.'

Still white-faced, Kane rose to go without attempting his temporary left-handed handshake. As he reached the door, Skinner spoke for the last time as an employer, unable to keep the rancour out of his voice. 'I gather you've been seeing Eric Ironstone recently. You should make a good pair.'

When Kane had gone, Skinner sat for some minutes cogitating. He prided himself as a judge of men and he had foreseen a great future for Kane. The man had all the apparent makings of success: a quick brain, a nose for profit, broking flair, physical resilience. Damn it, he could visualize those strong features and assertive manner dominating a boardroom in a few years' time. Even the African intrigues, though Byzantine in their complexity, smacked of brilliance. He recalled the day Kane had come to him with his enforced resignation for the Auxiliary Air Force and how he had advised disregarding the 'tinpot Air Marshal' who had demanded it. That Air Marshal must have detected a flaw in Kane's character which he himself failed to spot. He was not sure he could pinpoint it now. Did ambition blind the man to practicalities, or had IMEX and Western between them put too much within his grasp at too young an age? All the old clichés about the corrosive effects of money and power flitted through his mind. Eventually he concluded that Kane's basic defect was his ruthless self-interest. He had needlessly endangered Croft's life. Maybe if he had been more genuinely concerned for the others in his squadron, that Frampton crash would never have happened. Certainly Western would not have said goodbye to a small fortune. They had come to the end of the road with a vengeance, and in recognizing the fact Skinner felt defeated himself.

Grey cloud scudded across the Paris skyline and the last of the autumn leaves fluttered down to stick on the wet pavements of the Champs Elysées. Duclair picked his way among puddles, endeavouring to keep his slim black shoes dry. Droll, he thought, it's a year since Russell and I first came here and now I'm running errands for him. Time certainly brought its revenges. As he turned into the side street his two years' service in the heat of Katanga seemed immeasurably distant.

The building was unchanged. The lift groaned and swayed up to the third floor as before. The same attractive receptionist greeted him in the PANWORLD office. But when he asked for Sturgess she frowned.

'Mr Sturgess has been recalled to New York for consultations, sir. His colleague is out. Have you an appointment?'

'Of course.'

'I am so sorry.' She consulted a desk diary. 'There must be a mistake. No one else is here, though M. Dessenon will be back later. Can you wait?'

Reluctantly Duclair agreed. She made him coffee and, true to his eternal curiosity, he began pumping her for information. What he learnt was disconcerting. PANWORLD was opening up in Singapore but in Europe business had been slack. When Dessenon finally arrived, he was taken aback.

'You did not receive Sturgess' letter? No? Please allow me a few minutes to find the relevant papers.'

Once he was shown in, Duclair reiterated his previous written requests for spare parts for the T6s. Desson's embarrassment became acute.

'My dear Wing Commander, in Mr Sturgess' absence it

is very difficult. I do know we are encountering unforeseen problems. He has returned to America for that reason.'

Duclair was unmoved. 'You undertook to provide spare parts.' He flourished a copy of the document.

'May I refer you to paragraph eight?' Dessenon was obsequiously polite. 'It does specify, "This contract to be renewable after one year by mutual agreement." Eleven months and more have passed, Wing Commander.'

'None the less it is still in force. You remain committed to what you so charmingly describe as "the good development of our enterprise". We want that commitment honoured.' There was no mistaking the threat in Duclair's words: deliver or else.

Dessenon nervously smoothed his sleek black hair. It had been known for some of PANWORLD's less savoury clients to resort to violence if crossed, although the Belgian didn't look that sort.

'I shall telex your request to Mr Sturgess immediately. I am afraid there is no more I can do.'

'When will you have an answer?'

'Tomorrow or the next day.'

Duclair picked up his briefcase and left. He remained in Paris until the reply came in the form of a telephone call to his hotel.

'I regret PANWORLD's New York headquarters has instructed us not to renew the agreement. Spare parts for the T6 are no longer available.' In fact Dessenon sounded more apprehensive than regretful and he rang off as soon as he could decently interrupt Duclair's protests.

Bastards, Duclair said to himself, one should never trust the Anglo-Saxons. He set about transmitting the unwelcome news to Elisabethville.

The Fouga was a delight to fly. Mike had forgotten how exhilarating the power and speed of a jet could be. It was lighter to handle than the old Meteors of 699 squadron; in fact amazingly responsive. The mildest backward pressure on the control column brought the plane soaring up. Whereas gaining 3000 feet in the T6 was a grinding six minutes of labour, with the Fouga you were there in one. On his first solo from Kolwezi he was so pleased that he took it through a whole sequence of aerobatics, earning some wry comments about exhibitionism after he landed.

The period following the ceasefire had been more encouraging than his sharp encounter with Barlow led him to expect. The UN did not interfere when the gendarmerie fought off a Congolese National Army attack on the Katanga's western border. Again, the striking power of the Fougas and T6s was decisive.

In mid-November he was summoned to Elisabethville for consultations with the gendarmerie commander, now an African with the rank of general. It was a sign that his somewhat equivocal authority within the air force was recognized. But from there on the news was bad. The UN had brought in more troops and more aircraft; five Swedish Saab jet fighters and five British-built Canberra jet bombers of the Indian Air Force. The Canberra held several world speed records. As if this arrival was not serious enough, he learnt of PANWORLD's refusal to supply spares. To his dismay, the general made light of it.

'No one complained about parts in September. You have the planes. Fly them!'

In the evening he was invited to dine with Chantal and her family. Quite how much she had told her parents was not clear. However, they treated him with more respect than in recent months and he guessed she must have at least defined his intentions as being honourable, though she was still holding off answering his proposal.

'How do you see things going, Captain?' M. Berthoud asked during the meal. 'For ourselves, we don't trust this ceasefire.'

'I'm afraid I don't either,' he admitted. 'Worse still, we

can't get spares for our planes.'

'I was going to tell you about that, Mike,' Chantal cut in. 'We had an offer of military assistance yesterday.'

'You did? Where from?'

'Someone you know. Kane.'

The fork fell from Mike's fingers, struck his plate with a sharp crack and flipped to the floor, spotting the tablecloth with sauce. For a moment he gazed in astonishment at Chantal, then, muttering apologies, bent down to retrieve the implement.

'Please explain. Who is this Kane?' Mme Berthoud was doing her best to avoid looking at her stained linen, but she felt she deserved more than mere excuses.

'He .... We used to fly together,' said Mike lamely, trying to remove the mess with a clean knife. He turned back to Chantal. 'Bob Kane's not an arms dealer! What kind of game is he playing now?'

'He wants to exchange mining concessions for aid. He represents a consortium in London, so he said.'

'The Union Minière would never permit such a thing.' Mme Berthoud was scandalized. 'It's unthinkable. The British have Rhodesia, we have the Congo. That's how things will stay.'

'Well, Mama, he had introductions from a good friend of the President so Mr Tshombe received him. They had a long talk, almost an hour. But I don't think anything was agreed. The possibility was left open.'

'Is he still after Kiobo?' asked Mike.

'And Tenke.' Chantal made a face. 'I don't like him. He's too slick. But he has one very good argument. Both of those sites have been neglected by the Union Minière. When Tshombe asked my opinion afterwards, I had to say Katanga would gain a new source of mineral taxes, as well as employment.'

'As if the millions from Union Minière were not enough!' Mme Berthoud protested.

'We are going to need aircraft parts soon,' said Mike

quietly. 'Do you know what he offered?'

Chantal shook her head. 'Only that he had a source of supply and would fly things in via Brazzaville or else Rhodesia.'

'We've no ammunition problem. We took a lot off that United Nations train we hijacked and we still get plenty in through Rhodesia. It's all standard calibres anyway. But with the planes it's different. We're having to improvise already. The next thing will be cannibalizing one T6 to keep the rest flying. Do you think I could explain that to Tshombe? I don't much like Bob either, but if we have to do business with the devil, we have to.'

The next morning Chantal engineered an interview and Mike put in a strong plea for considering Kane's proposition should nothing better be found. Tshombe undertook to have it evaluated, 'if our Belgian allies are unable to help,' but he seemed confident. 'My advisers tell me the gendarmerie is more than a match for the UN. Don't worry. We shall anticipate their moves. We too can be cunning.'

For the first time it occurred to Mike that the ex-Foreign Legion advisers might be directing policy, rather than Tshombe himself.

'The debate's over at last. They've come up with a new resolution.' Margaret, trim and tidy as ever, handed Barlow a sheaf of telex messages. 'Gee,' she commented. 'That must have been quite a marathon in New York. Twelve days of speeches. Thank God I'm not a Security Council stenographer any more.'

Barlow studied the long text methodically. France and Britain, he noted, had abstained from voting. He was not surprised, this resolution of 24 November was the toughest yet. '*Strongly deprecates* the secessionist activities illegally carried out by the provincial administration of Katanga. *Authorizes* the Secretary General to take vigorous action, including the use of a requisite measure of force ... for the immediate apprehension ... of all foreign military and paramilitary personnel and political advisers not under the United Nations command. *Further requests* the Secretary General' to 'prevent the entry or return of such elements ... and also of arms, equipment of other material ....'

Barlow whistled as he finished reading. 'They went to town this time, I wouldn't call that a compromise. I'd call it marching orders.'

'Did you see U Thant's speech?' Margaret pointed it out among the papers. U Thant had taken over as acting Secretary General on 9 November. 'He promises to carry out the new mandate with vigour.'

'About time. This so-called dialogue we've had with Tshombe had been completely unproductive. You know something, Margaret? Hammarskjold's death threw me badly. But I reckon I've got over that now and I'm a stronger man for the experience.'

She glanced at him sympathetically. Her own impression had been that he was close to a nervous breakdown. 'You were pretty upset,' she agreed. 'If you can bear it, shall we hear what Radio Katanga has to say about the new resolution?'

Barlow grimaced. 'I guess we should.'

Margaret crossed to the bookshelf and switched on a small portable radio which had become an essential item of their office equipment. She did not need to tune it. The station came through resonant and tinny from the cheap set. A news summary ended. 'And now the speech to the nation of our victorious leader.' Tshombe's voice followed, flamboyant and impassioned. 'If U Thant will launch a war on our territory, not one road must remain passable, not one UN mercenary must feel himself safe in any place whatever ....'

They listened to the end of the rhetoric. 'He has some nerve calling the UN mercenaries,' Margaret commented.

'Strictly speaking the Swedes are. They're not the

regular Swedish army, just special volunteers.' Barlow always remained faithful to exact legal interpretations.

'No one here is going to love you for saying that,' she remarked crisply. 'Anyway it sounds like the fight will be on again any minute. For me, I want to see it over with.'

'So do I,' he agreed fervently. 'The whole situation is insupportable.'

Herman listened attentively to the orders Captain Jacques was giving.

'We shall establish two roadblocks, one on the airport road, one in the town. They will control the main routes between the UN headquarters and the airport. Both to be manned by gendarmerie under white command. Understood?'

The group of mercenaries assented, following closely as Jacques indicated the precise positions on a plan. They were in the gendarmerie headquarters in Elisabethville, a military complex called Camp Massart south of the city centre.

Jacques completed his orders, asked for questions, dealt with them and concluded, 'Essentially this is a test of willpower, a propaganda exercise. We are demonstrating our freedom of action, so keep your nerve. And remember, we've thrashed the UN once, we can do it again, any time we choose.'

They moved out of barracks in the evening, the trestle-like wooden barricades loaded on trucks along with barbed wire in huge coils. Once Herman found the right place it needed only five minutes to establish the roadblock, two separate barricades, each straddling two-thirds of the tarmac from opposite sides and with five yards between them. A vehicle could pass through only by slowing down to a crawl. A further ten minutes saw the trestles festooned with wire, a spare coil lying ready to be dragged across the gap. Herman dispersed his men, some out of sight, half a dozen by the barrier, rifles in hand. He himself would question the drivers. He did not have to wait long.

Soon a couple of local trucks lumbered to a halt and were duly permitted to pass. Next came a civilian car. Then Herman recognized the familiar pattern of a jeep's headlights approaching. He stepped forward, a torch in his left hand, the sub-machine-gun resting in the crook of his right arm, his finger round the trigger guard. The Luigi-Franchi was a part of himself, as familiar as the belt he buckled on every morning. It was a measure of his self-confidence that he felt no need to point it as the jeep stopped, but merely shone the torch on the occupants. They were three Swedish soldiers in blue berets and clean well-pressed uniforms.

'Destination?' demanded Herman gruffly.

'You have no right to stop a United Nations vehicle.' The officer in the front seat was calm but curt.

'I asked your destination, man. We are checking all traffic.' Herman's instructions from Jacques had been precise: show the UN they are no different from anyone else: demoralize them, but don't start a shooting match.

'This is a violation of the ceasefire agreement.' The Swede had been here many months now and knew the set-piece drill for reacting to provocation. 'I insist you let us through.'

Herman stood firm, his stocky figure a barrier in itself. 'You must tell me your destination,' he said patiently, as if addressing a child.

The officer shook his head and spoke to the driver, then said in English, 'We shall go back.' As the driver reversed the jeep the headlight beams swung along the barricade, revealing the African gendarmes beside it.

'We can't let then get away with this,' the officer shouted above the wind roar to the soldier in the rear. 'We shall have to take action.'

The next day the Swedish officer's report reached Barlow.

The same afternoon the Indian major came rushing into the office. 'Look at this!' He displayed a hand-drawn street map of Elisabethville, laying it on the desk. 'It is the mercenaries' battle planning. What more proof are we needing?'

Steve Barlow surveyed it carefully. The gridiron pattern of Elisabethville's streets was represented by thin lines. North was at the top. On the left or western side the straggling curve of the Lubumbashi river was heavily inked in, passing between the Lido and Tshombe's palace. Down the right-hand side ran the railway with the word GARE and dots showing the tunnel beneath the tracks through which ran the vital airport road. Superimposed on the plan were many tiny circles, each with three or four fainter lines radiating from it. Nearly all these circles had numerals pencilled in beside them.

'Mortar positions and their arcs of fire!' explained the major excitedly. 'See that one, T4330. Where is it pointing?'

Barlow followed his finger. Two lines ran towards the Queen Elisabeth Hospital. Then, with a cold shiver, he realized the possible significance of another, longer one. It pointed straight at the building they were in, their own UN headquarters.

'I am telling you,' insisted the major. 'This is a plan for mortar offensive. Very cunning. Using residential streets to fire from, sheltering behind innocent civilians. We must recommend immediate action by own troops before the mercenaries are implementing.'

'Let me look again.' Now that O'Brien had been replaced and a couple of others had gone, Barlow was the longest serving, most locally experienced officer in the headquarters. His opinion was often sought and carried weight. If he agreed that this was a battle plan his judgement would probably be accepted, especially since the Indians were spoiling for a chance to avenge the ignominy of September.

'It is plain to see,' prompted the major.

But why, Barlow's legal training demanded to know, should the Katangans plot to bomb their own hospital? Surely even in their wildest moments the Ultras would not do that. Futhermore, some of the lines were extraordinarily short, less than a block wide. Didn't a mortar have a minimum range as well as a maximum? The plan could be something totally different. With a sick feeling he realized that, much as he would like to believe the major's interpretation and launch the UN on a campaign to finish the mercenaries once and for all, he had to ask more questions.

'I do want Hammarskjold's death avenged,' he said grimly. Images of the Albertina's burnt-out remnants and the Secretary General's sightless corpse haunted his nights, destroying sleep. 'Don't get me wrong. Emotionally I'm with you all the way. But would they attack their own hospital?'

'The Ultras? Are you joking? Who are the patients in such a hospital, I ask you? Africans! Those French legionnaires will not be caring if a few more Africans die. They will mortar a hospital in order to be accusing the UN of murder.' The Indian slammed his fist down on the paper. 'This is a plan to strangle UN forces. We must act before they do.'

For a few moments Barlow struggled with the dictates of intellectual honesty against his own overwhelming desire for action. Logically the Indian's argument did not stand up, it was an attempt to jump the gun. 'Where did you find this plan?' he asked, knowing he was weakening.

'We are capturing from a Union Minière employee. There is mortar position shown in the Union Minière complex. Don't you know those people finance the mercenaries?'

This was undeniably true. 'OK,' he said, 'I'll go along with that. You can tell Mr Urquhart I agree your assessment.' As he spoke he knew he had made the right decision. A wave of relief left him almost dizzy. He smiled thinly at the major, 'No half-measures this time, I hope,' he said. 'U Thant has authorized removal of the roadblocks. You're no longer restricted to firing in self-defence.'

Later Urquhart, who had taken over from O'Brien barely a month before, gave the necessary authorization. A statement was issued to the press: 'With the greatest regret we have turned this over to the military. We hope there will be as little loss of civilian life as possible. But now we must carry out the terms of the mandate.'

Herman saw the Indian troops moving up and knew the roadblock was untenable. He had only a dozen gendarmes with him today and the Indians numbered over a hundred. They marched in single file along the verges, well spaced out, a jeep leading, while two trucks crawled along behind. He ordered his men to withdraw from the open area of the road and into cover by some native mud huts. A small stream ran near the huts and offered both more concealment and an emergency escape route. The rains had begun and the grass was thick and high along the watercourse.

The Indians carried out a textbook manoeuvre. Two of the platoons took up defensive positions by the roadside, while the third methodically dismantled the barricades and loaded them into the trucks. Herman studied their action through his binoculars, noticing that the same Swedish officer whom he had stopped the previous night was with them. He thought nothing of it until the Swede began gesticulating in his direction. Then he realized with a tight feeling in his gut that there was going to be a confrontation after all. He glanced round at his men, lying hidden in the grass, and gave rapid orders in Swahili. The pair with the light machine-gun shifted twenty yards, doubling with their heads down along by the watercourse to re-emerge among the huts where they could provide a concealed cross-fire at anyone approaching the rest.

Accompanied by one platoon of about thirty Indians, the Swede began walking down the slight slope towards Herman. The soldiers fanned out on either side of him, their rifles at the ready. A short distance from the huts the Swede motioned them to halt and raised a loudhailer.

'If the mercenaries surrender there will be no fighting.' His English was fluent.

The gendarmes lay concealed by the grass, rifles in their shoulders, tense. The foreign phrases meant nothing to them.

'Come and get us man,' Herman shouted back, on one knee in the cover of a bush. With the minimum of movement he took a grenade from his pouch, pulled the pin out with his teeth and held it in his massive fist, his fingers keeping the spring-loaded firing lever down.

'I give you one minute.'

Through the foliage Herman could just see the Swede standing there, his wrist held high, counting the seconds. He felt a flicker of admiration for the officer's coolness, but that was irrelevant. Calling on his men to fire, he reached back, swung his arm and lobbed the grenade with all his strength.

The machine-gun spat bullets. From its position on the flank the crew could shoot straight down the Indian line. As the grenade exploded close to the Swede a ragged but effective fusillade came from the gendarmes in the grass. Seen from the stream the Indians on the slope were skylined. They suffered for it. Eight fell and when the others saw the officer go down, struck in the chest by a jagged sliver of metal from the grenade, they faltered. Another volley from the long grass decided them. They backed away, firing spasmodically as they retreated.

Herman did not delay. He reckoned he had chanced his luck enough. He rallied his men and retreated along the watercourse, himself supporting a wounded gendarme.

An hour later Jacques had brought up a mortar team and started a bombardment of the Indians at the roadblock from the safe distance of 800 metres. Round Two of the Katangan war had begun.

On the evening of that day, 5 December, the pilots at Kolwezi, already on standby, were ordered into action. Their target was not unexpected: the UN jets on Elisabethville airport. Even so, Mike questioned it.

'Of course we can find the city at night,' he said, 'unless some joker cuts the power supply. But we can't bomb with any accuracy, not with our equipment.'

Legrand's clipped voice was harsh and distinctive even over a bad line. 'In New York the UN has authorized ground and aerial action. Get your strike in before theirs.'

Accordingly the flight of T6s took off late in the evening and droned east across the sleeping bush until the myriad lights of Elisabethville came in view on the horizon. Then Mike led the formation up to 10,000 feet, blessing the way the thunderclouds tended to weaken and vanish when the day's heat had subsided, and they throttled back and glided down, releasing their bombs as accurately as they could at the dimly visible targets before opening up the engines again and roaring away.

'We must have caught them by surprise,' he reported on his return. 'But don't count on our having destroyed much. All we can be sure of is raising a hornets' nest.'

The next day he was up at dawn, perfecting the dispersal of the planes. A call came from Elisabethville to warn that the UN jets had taken off. Inexplicably nothing happened. Then, after lunch, just as he was taxiing out to fly a mission, the attack came in. Because of his own engine's noise he never heard the jets at all until they were overhead and cannon shells were tearing into the sides of the hangars. Through the perspex he saw a pair of stubby-nosed Saabs peel off into a climbing turn, one behind the other, obviously intending to come round and strafe the airfield again. It would be suicidal to attempt a take-off. He hastily shut down the engine, turned off the fuel, then reached up and hauled the canopy back in order to climb out. As he ran for cover he heard the scream of the jets and looked round. The leading Saab was in a steep turn, about to start its attack dive. He ran some more, then threw himself on the ground. This time the ear-splitting roar seemed to envelop him and the angry whine of bullets was all around. Something exploded behind him and he felt the surge of scorching heat.

Knowing instinctively what had occurred, he stumbled to his feet and ran further, panting and sweating, to the safety of some trees on the perimeter. Once in the shadow he turned. The T6 he had just abandoned was on fire, flames gushing up from the fuselage like an obscene flower, black smoke pouring skywards. While he watched, its second fuel tank blew up. The cockpit he had been strapped into became an inferno. Was it two minutes ago, or three or four? It hardly mattered. By a split-second decision, he was still alive. He found himself trembling, his leg shaking uncontrollably in a way he had not experienced since the Frampton crash. He sank down on to the grass.

Gradually, as people realized the raid was over, activity returned to the airfield. A fire engine drove out and the crew sprayed foam on the blackened carcass of the T6. Mike walked unsteadily to the Operations Room. The windows had gone and a bullet had channelled into the blackboard, just below the Fouga's registration number. Was the Fouga next, he wondered.

When the damage was tallied they found another T6 had been hit inside a hangar, there was nothing else that mattered. But one lesson was enough. He managed to get Elisabethville on the telephone and speak to Legrand.

'We must disperse to other fields,' he insisted. 'Otherwise we'll be out of business.'

'They strafed Jadotville today. They're flying from Kamina themselves. Manono is under attack. There's heavy fighting here. What do you suggest?'

'A strip of road in the bush would do for the T6s. Anywhere with concealment.' He thought of Kiobo, then dismissed the idea as catastrophic for Father Paul.

'I'll think about it. Meanwhile we want you on immediate call. Stay put and camouflage.'

Mike hung up and resigned himself to re-thinking the protection of the aircraft. Already, after only twenty-four hours, this battle was a far cry from the triumphs of September. He thought of Chantal and cursed himself for not asking Legrand to find out if she was safe.

'Watch us and love us and for God's sake pray for us.' The pooled dispatch sent from correspondents in Elisabethville to the London office of the *New York Times* on 5 December made banner headlines in every London paper the next morning. The public was not to know that the dramatic ending was a postscript put through the telex machines in order to keep the line open longer. Besides, it caught the feeling exactly.

When Robert Kane read it in a London paper he immediately tried to book himself on a flight out. His chance had come. If he could get to Rhodesia and charter a company plane, then his plot could swing into action.

Unfortunately journalists the world over had precisely the same plan for reaching Katanga.

'We've had a rush on seats like you wouldn't believe,' the sales girl told Kane. 'And we're busy anyhow with Christmas coming. The earliest I can get you one is Sunday.' She referred to her paperwork, 'I could wait-list you for Saturday. Before then it's hopeless.' Infuriated, he opted for the wait-list. Unless he could find an alternative airline, he was losing three days. But on inquiry they all proved equally full.

By the Saturday, 9 December, the rapidly escalating

war dominated the newspapers. The UN was accused of using excessive force and not observing the Geneva Convention. In reply U Thant cited, 'Campaigns of violence, abduction of hostages, assault and battery, murder, the setting up of roadblocks, etc.,' by the gendarmerie. He also charged Union Minière with aiding the mercenaries. All in all the UN appeared unrepentant in the face of a barrage of western criticism. Moreover the British government, under pressure from Washington, had agreed to supply twenty-four half-ton bombs for the Indian Canberras.

The news made Kane even more impatient. He was frightened of losing his chance. He cabled Sendwe in Leopoldville, using guarded phrases to indicate his intentions, and went out to London airport in the evening. The girl at the check-in desk sympathized with his damaged hand and, after a tense hour's wait, allocated him an empty first-class seat. 'If anyone queries it,' she said conspiratorially, 'tell them we moved you from economy on medical grounds.' He was a good-looking man and she was pleased to help him.

The BOAC airliner deposited Kane at Salisbury at lunchtime on Sunday, well-fed and rested. He transferred to a domestic Rhodesian flight for Ndola and arrived to discover the town in a ferment of anger and apprehension. Belgian refugees were streaming in and a whole trainload of women and children was due from Elisabethville in the evening. He dumped his case at the Savoy Hotel, bribed the porter to fix him at least a share of a room, and hastened to find his principal mining contact. He knew about the companies' telephone system and he wanted to get a message to Tshombe. If his offer wasn't acceptable now, it never would be.

By Saturday night there was a homeless family sheltering in the Berthouds' villa, their children sleeping on cushions on the floor. Chantal had relinquished her room and was using the sofa. She could no longer drive to her office. Indeed, on Friday night she had slept there on a camp bed. On Saturday UN planes had strafed the Post Office, diving down out of a cloudy sky, terrorizing the city centre. Smoke hung over the town and the crump of exploding mortar bombs seemed unending. She knew the gendarmerie had several positions by the Lido. At Tshombe's Palace you could hear the whistle of the bombs as they passed high overhead. None the less she had been determined to spend Sunday with her mother and on Saturday afternoon had cautiously threaded her way back through the deserted streets, occasionally catching sight of a group of soldiers crouching by a garden wall or building. Now it was Sunday morning and her mother was semi-hysterical.

'The electricity's failed.' Mme Berthoud was on the verge of tears. 'With ten people in the house, how can we exist?'

Chantal put an arm round her. 'Don't be upset. I'll light the fire in the sitting room. We can heat something up on that.' She went outside to fetch more wood. The servants had vanished and she didn't blame them. If she had a village in the bush to flee to, she would have done the same. She brought the logs in, scrumpled up paper, laid the fire and lit it. The wood was damp from the rain and smoked furiously. For a time she was afraid it wouldn't burn. Eventually it did and she set pans of water in front to heat.

Half an hour later she had produced a satisfactory meal: coffee, boiled eggs, cold meat, the last of the bread. 'We'll pretend we're Americans,' she told the two children cheerfully. 'On Sundays they always combine breakfast and lunch.'

As they were eating there was a rumbling noise outside. Before anyone could stop her, the little girl slipped off her chair and ran to the verandah. As she opened the door there was a colossal explosion. The window at the end of the room disintegrated in a shower of glass and wood splinters. A huge and ragged hole opened in the far wall. A shell had struck clean through the house. Mme Berthoud screamed piercingly. The mother clasped her other child and pulled it down to the floor. The air was choked with dust.

'Is anyone there speaking English? Come out with your hands up.'

As they heard the shout two dark skinned Ethiopian soldiers appeared in the doorway, rifles on them.

Chantal stood up, raising her hands. 'Don't say anything, just follow me,' she whispered and led the two other women and the small boy out. On the verandah the girl was sobbing. But it was something else that made Chantal stare. Parked at an angle on the road was a massive armoured car, its main gun trained on the house, a tiny curl of black smoke still issuing from the barrel. The commander's head and shoulders protruded from the turret. A Swedish officer stood to one side. Then movement in a tree caught her attention. Straddling one of the branches was another Ethiopian, his rifle aimed at them. The Swede advanced cautiously.

'Are you all the occupants?' he demanded.

'No, my father is inside.' Chantal was so shocked she could hardly speak. She clenched her fists, digging the nails into her palms, trying to get a grip on herself.

A moment later the Ethiopians hustled her father out, threw him on the ground and began beating him with their rifle butts.

'Stop them!' screamed Mme Berthoud. 'Somebody do something, they're killing him! She launched herself at the Swede, arms flailing. Chantal leapt forward to catch her. The Swede retreated.

'Stop them,' ordered Chantal in English. 'Do you murder old people in your country?' It took her all her strength to restrain her mother.

The Swede hesitated, then shouted at the Ethiopians,

who took no notice. He shouted again and stepped towards them, revolver in hand. Reluctantly they moved away, glaring at the old man who lay inert, clutching his groin and groaning.

'I accuse you of sending smoke signals to the mercenaries,' he said. 'We saw them distinctly. You are spies.'

'We were cooking,' snapped Chantal. 'We were having breakfast. Are you mad? Look inside.' She relaxed her hold on her mother, who immediately rushed to kneel by M. Berthoud and comfort him.

'Why should I believe you?' He suspected a trap.

'Do you know Mr Barlow? He can identify us.'

'Mr Barlow? In the headquarters?'

'Who else do you think? Will you please call him on the telephone?'

Her voice was like a whip now, scornful and furious. The Swede coloured and went indoors, brandishing his revolver as though expecting an ambush. Chantal pointed at the pans in the fireplace and the debris-strewn table. 'You see. Now will you call Barlow!' She led him to the study where her father had been, the telephone on the desk.

Immediately his suspicions reasserted themselves. 'What was the man doing here? Was he telephoning?'

'He is my father. We live here. We are a family. Can you understand that?'

For a moment she was afraid the instrument would not work. The UN had done its best to put the Post Office out of action. Mercifully it functioned.

By the time Barlow arrived, Chantal had got her father to a bed. He was bleeding profusely and his left leg appeared to be broken below the knee. She confronted Barlow with his condition.

'Look what those animals have done. You must get him to hospital.'

Barlow wavered and glanced at the Swede for confirmation.

'The man was acting suspiciously,' insisted the officer, stolidly.

Barlow's expression hardened. 'This is a war situation, Miss Berthoud,' he said. 'We regret any casualties. But we have advised civilians to leave the city.' He was not going to give an inch more than he had to. The Belgians had connived to frustrate the UN's objectives for too long. They had it coming to them.

'So you beat up innocent people?' The fury was rising in her voice.

'We have to use the troops we are sent. Unfortunately these Ethiopians are from a penal battalion.'

'Mr Barlow.' She could only just keep herself under control. 'You asked me a favour not so long ago. Now I want something in return. Send away these so-called soldiers and get medical aid for my father.'

Barlow hesitated. 'I guess I can agree to that.' He was more embarrassed at the reminder of his moral debt to Chantal than at the Ethiopians' violence. 'There is one thing I can do,' he admitted 'We're organizing a refugee train for women and children. I can get your friends aboard. Your father, too, if he can travel.'

'If he can't, it's your responsibility.'

Barlow looked straight at her. He had conceded enough in return for her help back in September. 'No,' he said. 'I am not prepared to accept that. If civilians elect to remain in a war zone, it is on their own heads. Can't you nurse him during the journey?'

Chantal hit back uncompromisingly. 'No I can't. I was born here and I shall remain.' She let the words sink in, then added tautly, 'How would you feel if this had happened in Toronto, Mr Barlow?'

To his credit, Barlow blushed.

That night, alone in the damaged house, her bedroom locked, her father's revolver beneath the pillow, Chantal wished that Mike was with her. It was a lot to face by herself.

10

The Africans planting maize in the Mission gardens set aside their tools and listened with worried expressions as the drone of engines grew louder. Toiling among them to set an example Father Paul only looked up when two planes came in sight and began circling overhead. He told the labourers not to be afraid and strode quickly back towards the house, his hoe still in his hand, reaching the air strip in time to see a camouflage painted T6 land, throwing up spray as its wheels passed through pools left by the recent rain, followed by the familiar blue and white Cessna. Both swung off into the parking space near the Mission station. A couple of minutes later Mike Russell appeared, waving a greeting, and began walking down to meet him, a tall man in flying overalls close behind him.

Father Paul stopped. 'A pleasant surprise in an unpleasant period,' he said warmly. 'Not that it touches us directly, we are merely short of food. What can I do for you?'

Mike introduced his companion. 'Joe's had his Dakota impounded by the UN, so he came along to fly me back. If that's OK with you, Father.'

'You're going a little fast for me. What do you mean, if it's OK?'

'As you said, you're not affected by the war here.

Could I leave the Cessna with you until things quieten down? It's civil registered, so it should be no embarrassment. If the UN were to come, that is.'

Father Paul leant on the handle of the hoe, clasping it with both hands. His long white soutane was muddied at the hem and there were marks where his hands had brushed against it. Sweat glistened on his sunburnt forehead. He pondered the request, turning over its implications in his mind. 'To whom does the aeroplane belong?' he asked at last.

'Legally, to President Tshombe.'

'So I would be safeguarding if for him. Hmm.' He gave Mike a very straight look. 'Does it contain military equipment?'

'Only HF and VHF radios.'

'Very well. As you know we have no hangar, but we can construct a temporary shelter.' He shifted his hold on the hoe and stepped forward. 'Now, I hope you have time for some coffee. Since you're here I would like you to do something for me.' As they walked towards the house he explained. 'I am concerned about Chantal. I have heard through our Mission radio that her parents have been evacuated. She is a grown woman, I know. None the less . . . if you should be in the city.'

'Believe me,' said Mike fervently, 'I would if I could.' He looked at Joe. 'What do you think?'

'So long as we have planes to fly, we're stuck at Kolwezi.'

'She can always come here,' said Father Paul. 'Tell her that if you do see her. And pray to God this fighting does not last.'

An hour later the two pilots were threading their way through high, white clouds back to Kolwezi, Mike in the front seat flying the T6. But his routine approach call to the control went unanswered. He repeated it. Again no reply.

'Odd,' he remarked over the intercom.

'Could be they're under attack. Let's go down below this lot. At least we'll be able to see more.'

Mike eased back the throttle, adjusted the revs and dived down through a break in the cloud. In level flight the T6's big radial engine obscured a great part of the forward view, in this nose-down attitude he could see ahead properly. Suddenly, as they dropped below the cloudbase, a large jet flashed past immediately beneath. Instinctively he pulled up into the concealment of cloud.

'Bloody right,' he said to Joe. 'That was a Canberra. There's probably another with it, too.'

For a couple of minutes he flew on instruments, the inside of the cloud like thick fog, at times hiding the wingtips. A violent bump reminded him that they were in the base of a thunderhead. Then, abruptly, they came out into bright sun again and Kolwezi town lay five miles to their left with its adjacent mines, the airfield unmistakable on its outskirts. He called the tower. This time there was an agitated response.

'Negative landing. I repeat, negative landing.'

'What the hell next?' Joe commented. 'We're a sitting duck if they spot us.'

Mike put the plane into a gradual turn, scouring the dark green landscape. Beyond the town two shapes were moving, almost as dark as the ground itself, describing a wide arc.

'We must have a go,' he said. 'Even if they are three times as fast, with luck they'll be concentrating on the ground.'

'You'll never do it.'

Mike did not answer. He was assessing the chance of positioning himself above the airfield just before they reached it. He pushed on full boost. The T6's speed edged up to 125 knots.

'You're crazy,' said Joe. 'They'll run in at three hundred and sixty minimum.'

'But we have two thousand feet in hand.' As he headed

for the airfield, Mike checked the gunsight, set the compressed air selector to 'GUN' and the button on his control column to 'FIRE'. All he had to do now was line his plane ahead of the target to allow for the speed, get the Canberra accurately in the sight and press.

As he came overhead Kolwezi the Canberras had finished their turn and were heading straight for the field, one about 200 yards behind the other. A canopy glittered catching the light. Mike reckoned he was almost between them and the sun as they ran in. They'd be hard put to see him, even if they did glance up at this crucial moment when their attention would be on the ground.

The first Canberra was streaking towards the perimeter. He peeled off into a dive, hurtling down after it, his speed building rapidly to 180 knots. For a second the bomber's slim fuselage and broad wings came into sight, he squeezed the firing button and knew he had missed. Then the ground was coming up fast, forcing him to pull out of the dive. As he eased back the stick, the second Canberra passed barely 200 feet below. He fired again, thought he saw fragments of metal fly off the starboard wing, then was level behind it, the jet's slipstream rocking him violently as it escaped, climbing away steeply to vanish among the clouds.

'I'm sure you scored.' Joe sounded tense, as well he might be. 'You hit the wing.'

'Where the hell has the number one gone, though?' Mike heaved the T6 into a steep turn, scanning the horizon until he completed a full circle.

'They've scarpered.' Joe was delighted. 'We must have given them a hell of a fright.'

Mike said nothing. Short of catching a jet parked on the tarmac, he was unlikely to have as great an advantage again over such an immensely superior machine. But the best he could do had not been enough. He decided to land. It was then, focusing his attention on the airfield itself, that he appreciated the damage the Canberras had done. The main hangar was on fire, vehicles were burning, there was something all wrong with the Fouga on the hard-standing near the trees.

He made one low pass over the runway to check for obstructions, then made a tight, low circuit, landed and taxied as rapidly as safety permitted to the secondary hangar. He and Joe manhandled the plane to shelter, then made for the tower. As they reached it they realized what was amiss with the Fouga. One of the short undercarriage legs had collapsed so it rested with one wingtip on the ground, like a parked glider. Mike ran over. The perspex canopy was shattered and the instrument panel wrecked. It must have been hit by a cannon shell.

One of the Cubans came up. 'Is finish, no?' he said laconically. 'Also the one in hangar.' He looked quizzically at Mike. 'Where we go from here, Captain?'

'Miami, I should think.' Mike snapped sourly. He hadn't even flown the Fouga in action.

The official answer was not received from Legrand until evening, and Mike had to use the mining company network to obtain it since the ordinary telephone was defunct.

'All you have is one T6, correct?'

'That's right. We have nine pilots, twenty-two mechanics, three jeeps, a truck and a small stock of spares.'

'Are all the planes beyond repair?'

'Short of obtaining new major components, yes.'

'Then you bring the T6 here tomorrow. We will have a short stretch of the Kasumbalesa road prepared. Twenty kilometres south of the city approximately.' Legrand gave a map reference, which Mike scribbled down. 'You will see huts there.'

'What about the others?'

'They're in gendarmerie uniform, aren't they? Those you don't want can fight as soldiers. Send them to me.'

The orders were not well received. That night four of the Cubans stole a jeep and deserted. In the morning

Mike despatched one jeep and the truck by a cross-country route to the new landing strip, taking basic spares and ground crew. The remaining pilots left in the second jeep. He and Joe would fly the plane. In torrential rain, which reverberated on the tin roofs like machine gun fire, he went to the Operations Room for the last time. The blackboard still bore the previous day's intended missions. The bullet hole was unrepaired, fragments of glass lay on the floor. This had been his first and his last command. Whatever happened next he knew the dream was over. He found a piece of paper, printed a few words on it in uneven capitals and pinned it on the outside of the door as he left. The message read NO MILK. NO PAPERS. GONE AWAY.

As the fighting intensified, Steve Barlow found himself increasingly confused. His air force training had predicated clearly defined sides in a war, the enemy on one, you on the other. But here in Elisabethville the UN headquarters was in the centre of a city still held by the gendarmerie, despite continual bombardment and aerial strafing. Although the Katangans mortared the UN, they never attempted to storm the building. What made it even more insane was that the mercenaries unashamedly dropped into the Leo Deux for drinks, guns in hand, uniforms dishevelled, in between bouts of action. They gave interviews to the press, who were now crowded eight to a room in the hotel, and helped ferry reports out to Rhodesia. Yet the UN, with 6000 men available, seemed incapable of arresting the mere 150 whites estimated to be involved.

Meanwhile, the catalogue of alleged UN atrocities mounted. Some, he was convinced, were invented by the Katangans. But others were indisputable. Whatever the Indian major claimed, Barlow knew it was UN soldiers who had fired over thirty mortar bombs at the hospital. Worse, his own name had featured prominently in a

Belgian newspaper interview with the Berthoud family. A telex from New York had demanded a full account of the incident.

'We could be in a no-win situation,' he said wearily to Margaret. 'We're into the second week and it's still like trying to catch a bunch of eels.'

'Surely the reinforcements will fix it?' Transport planes of the US Air Force had been flying in UN troops from other parts of the Congo.

'God, I hope so.' Barlow shook his head despondently. 'What we have to do is round up Tshombe. He's the figurehead. Then they might surrender.'

'Your views certainly have shifted,' she observed.

'I was wrong before. And the UN's wrong now.' He wanted to shout at her. 'The detention of mercenaries isn't enough. We're being made fools of, Margaret, you know that. We have to break this absurd situation, break it completely and for ever.'

Tactfully she refrained from comment. 'You ought to get more sleep,' she suggested. 'No one can work the hours you've been doing. You'll crack up if you don't stop.'

'We have to finish the job. Maybe then we can relax.' How could he explain about the recurring nightmare which destroyed his rest, Hammarskjold's dead body lying near the wreckage of the Albertina, the sightless eyes reproaching his failure.

Margaret had slipped quietly out of the room. She returned with a glass of orange juice to find him staring out of the window.

'I brought a couple of aspirins too, and juice is better for you than coffee,' she said, adding hesitantly, 'There's that Englishman Kane waiting. Shall I tell him to come back later?'

'Yes .... Oh, hell, no. Give me ten minutes.' He sat down and swallowed the pills, then tried to calm himself.

Kane had spent three days in Ndola hanging about the hotel, drinking with miners and farmers in the convivial local club, waiting for messages. An initial acknowledgement had come from Tshombe's office, followed by silence. When he heard that a car was making a daily 'press run' to Elisabethville in order to file journalists' reports, he decided to make contact in person.

The driver of the car proved to be an Englishman who carried himself like a soldier, but was dressed in slacks and a brightly coloured shirt.

'If you don't mind paying your whack it should be possible,' he said affably when Kane tackled him. 'You're a freelance?'

'For a mining journal.' At least he knew the editor of one.

'You'll need a Katanga press pass, you know.'

Kane was relying on bluff. 'Does it take long?' he inquired.

'Tell you what,' the Englishman smiled as if at some obscure joke, 'we'll accredit you to the United Nations. Much simpler and needs no photograph.' He pulled his wallet out of one bulging shirt pocket and extracted a couple of large grey cards, then foraged inside the car for a portable typewriter, unzipped its case, balanced it on the car's bonnet and deftly slipped one of the cards into place. 'Right,' he said cheerfully. 'Name and details.' A minute later he handed over the completed document, which he had signed himself with a hieroglyphic scrawl. The card was headed:

OPERATION NATIONS UNIES CONGO
ONUC
CARTE DE PRESSE

The freshly inscibed signature came below the words 'Chef Service de Presse'.

'That will be five pounds for the sinking fund,' he said.

'Do you mind Rhodesian?' Kane concealed his astonishment at this bizarre transaction.

'Not at all. The barman at the Leo Deux accepts most currencies.' He gave a huge wink. 'I promise you we toast the UN appropriately on these occasions. One must honour their property.'

Despite this carefree start, the journey was slow and unpleasant. They were stopped at numerous road-blocks inside Katanga, while the last few miles saw UN troops ordering them out, searching the car and examining their papers. By the time they reached Elisabethville Kane was grateful for his newly acquired accreditation. The ravaged state of the city shocked him. A pall of smoke hung over the outskirts from a blaze in the Petro-Congo fuel storage tanks. The streets were almost deserted and strewn with the debris of fighting: walls scarred by bullets, whole houses demolished. When the car stopped outside the Leo Deux Kane asked if he could go back the next day.

'Ah,' the Englishman remarked, 'you really are doing an article.'

'What do you mean?'

'A three-day stay would mean you were writing a book. My advice, if you want to pick someone's brains, is to try Younghusband of the *Mail*. See you tomorrow around three.'

Not wanting the embarrassment of luggage, Kane had brought his shaving kit and a clean shirt in his briefcase. After discovering that reporters were sleeping on the floor in the Leo Deux, he determined to beg a bed from Steve Barlow and went to the UN offices, telling the guards he was a personal friend. After a long wait he was shown up.

His immediate impression was that the Canadian looked ten years older. The skin seemed tight over his cheekbones and there were dark pits of shadow beneath his eyes. 'What brings you here, Bob?' he asked wearily. 'We're in a sorry state right now.'

'The company wanted an on-the-spot assessment.

They're still keen on obtaining concessions.' There was no reason to tell Barlow that he no longer represented the same firm. 'Have you time to brief me on the situation?'

Barlow motioned him to a chair. 'This is what we might call Round Two,' he explained. 'Ever since Mr Urquhart announced on 5 December that we were turning this over to the military, it's become basically a question of bringing the mercenaries and the gendarmerie to heel. Take no notice of what you read in the papers.' Barlow's tone became more intense. 'It's distorted, partisan and downright malicious, most of it. Our job here is impossible within the constraints placed on us. Listen, Bob, I'll tell you something I wouldn't to any man except a friend. This is like killing a pig. The longer you take over it, the more noise it makes. It's altogether preferable to get it over with fast.'

'And can you?' This was what Kane wanted to know.

'When are you leaving?' Barlow asked, apparently changing the subject.

'Tomorrow.'

'Take my advice. Go before the evening. Well before.'

'You mean?'

'Nothing,' Barlow permitted himself a wry smile. 'We were merely talking between friends, OK? Where are you staying?'

'In the Leo Deux. I hope.'

Barlow considered this and frowned. 'You're welcome to use my sofa for one night. We work pretty late now, but I'll be going back in a couple of hours.'

Kane thanked him profusely and arranged to return. He had one all-important contact still to make.

Outside it was raining again and becoming prematurely dark as thunderclouds hid the declining sun. Kane hurried to the Leo Deux, hoping to make a telephone call. The lobby was crowded. Despite making a liberal payment to the porter, it was twenty-five minutes before he was able to try his luck.

'Sometimes it works, sometimes not,' the porter shrugged his shoulders. 'With a local number, perhaps.'

After many attempts he got through and asked for Tshombe's office. Chantal's voice came on the line, though there was a curious echoing background noise which made him assume the phone was being incompetently tapped.

'I am sorry,' she said firmly, 'It is impossible to speak to the President. He is giving no interviews.'

'You know what I'm calling about,' Kane insisted, 'You got my message. Has hc an answer?'

'He is very busy. Surely you can understand that?'

'Listen. I am here for twenty-four hours only. Can I come down in the morning?'

'You can come. I will warn the sentries. But I make no promise.'

Baffled, Kane went to the bar and killed time chatting to some journalists. There was a generally held conviction that the UN was about to make a major move.

That evening, eating an unappetizing supper with Barlow, Kane discovered what was afoot. Barlow's emotions were so pent-up that he eventually blurted out the truth at which he had earlier hinted.

'We're going in for the finish tomorrow evening. Thank God. Our troop reinforcement is complete. The Katanga air force has been destroyed. This will be the final offensive.'

'And what about Tshombe? Do you arrest him?'

'Officially, no. This operation is to restore order and expel the mercenaries. I tell you, Bob, it's mad. The orders are to negotiate with him. Sure enough, he's refusing. Next thing we know he'll vanish, just like he did back in September. If I were in charge I'd go right in and seize him, keep him under house arrest until a ceasefire was signed.' Barlow swore, a rare event for him. 'Anything less is a counter-productive farce. Anyway, one thing is for sure. We're going to throw the mercenaries out of here for good and all, Tshombe or no Tshombe.'

During the night the intermittent gunfire kept Kane awake and he lay on the sofa in his underclothes, a sheet drawn around him, brooding over his plans. It was essential for him to lure Tshombe to Kiobo. The airstrip was not far from the Rhodesian border. If the Katangan authorities went into hiding that fact would be in its favour and his scheme might succeed. But he would have to present them with a time limit.

After Kane had gone, Chantal knocked lightly on the President's study door and entered.

'That Englishman has made what he calls a final offer.' she said.

Tshombe looked up from behind his desk, his broad face troubled. 'What does the colonel think of it?' he asked.

'He doesn't see how they could provide supplies in time, though the contract would be useful in the long term. But of course he insists that Union Minière must agree.'

Tshombe sighed. 'There are so many considerations! I am inclined to sign if the situation becomes any worse. Why does he insist on our coming to Kiobo?'

'He says his English colleagues do not like the risks in the city. They can fly in safely from Rhodesia to Kiobo.' She paused. 'It is true that we can rely on Father Paul's discretion and it is most unlikely that the United Nations would be in the area. Anyhow, Kane has returned to Ndola. We can always be in touch with him there. May I make a suggestion?'

'Please.'

She dimpled. Tshombe was invariably courteous. He made her feel he valued her assistance. She outlined what she had in mind as succinctly as she could.

'Your reasoning is excellent.' He beamed at her. 'I was going to ask you to stay on if I am forced to go. We can remain in contact through the radio.' He sat contemplating her proposition for a further minute, then asked, with every indication of genuine concern, 'The risk does not worry you?'

'I think it is less for a woman.'

'Then we are in agreement.' He slid open a drawer in his desk, rummaged for a moment and brought out a small object. He stood up and handed it to her.

'A small souvenir of a most happy working partnership. It was intended for your birthday, but who knows?'

Chantal moved across to the desk and he laid the object in the palm of her hand. It was a small, delicately made gold brooch fashioned in the shape of the traditional Katanga cross.

The jeep skidded to a halt and an over-excited mercenary leapt out and ran across to Mike. 'The Swedes are attacking Camp Massart and the Ethiopians are round the Lido. Legrand wants maximum air support.'

'He knows damn well we've only one plane. Who does he want strafed first?' Mike was tired and disillusioned. The solitary T6 stood shrouded in camouflage nets beneath a group of trees. His maps were spread on a trestle table in a mud hut. Fuel had to be transferred from drums with a hand pump. He had no communications. The mechanics were utilizing the truck as a mobile workshop. A handful of gendarmes guarded the stretch of road which he was using as a runway. So far the UN had failed to notice their presence, but once they did, it would all be over.

'They've obviously launched a major offensive,' said the soldier. He was young and spoke with a South African accent. 'Legrand says give them all you've got.'

'All right. I'll have a crack at the Ethiopians. Presumably they're a threat to Tshombe's palace?'

'Too right. If he's there. Rumour is he and his staff have bugged out.'

For the thousandth time Mike wondered if Chantal was safe. In the forty-eight hours since he had flown across from Kolwezi he had been unable to go near the city. Despite his feeling that the attempt was futile, he had conscientiously laboured to organize this last-ditch air-strip.

Fifteen minutes later the T6 was being pushed out from its shelter. The bomb was already on the rack, the gun in the wing loaded with its belts of ammunition. One of the mechanics came up. 'We've had a hell of a time over the compressed air cylinders,' he said. 'But the gun should be OK. Give me a shout when you want her wound up.'

Mike climbed up into the cockpit, putting his map on the coaming in front of him and methodically going through the preliminary checks. With no starter trolley, the mechanic had to use the crank to turn the engine over. He waited until the man was ready, then thrust his arm out, the fist clenched and the thumb resolutely down.

'Switches off,' he called.

The mechanic forced the handle round, sweating until the propeller had gone through several revolutions. Then he stopped, wiped his brow and called out. 'Switches on.'

'Switches on. Contact.' Mike flipped on the two magnetos and turned his thumb prominently upwards. The mechanic pushed furiously on the handle. The propeller swung. The engine coughed, then suddenly fired and broke into a roar, smoke gushing from the exhaust. Well, at least the damn thing's started, Mike thought, adjusting the throttle. He reached up and pulled the canopy closed above him, waved to the mechanic, taxied on to the roadway and after running up the engine went quickly through the take-off checks. The less time he spent out here in the open, the better. The whole sequence of actions had a sharply defined quality about it, he was conscious of each one, unlike some occasions when everything seemed automatic. This awareness continued right through his take-off, as if this flight had a particular significance.

Once he was airborne everything speeded up. Elisabethville came in sight after three minutes, dark clouds beyond shedding a curtain of rain, and he felt the same gut apprehensiveness as he had experienced racing towards Frampton Gorge in the Meteor. The Lido was easy to locate, close to the winding river, at a point where a small series of rapids interrupted its course. West of it rose the artificial hill of a vast slag heap. As Mike circled above, squinting down, he recognized Ethiopian troops moving up from the direction of the slag heap. A group of trucks made an easy target. He dived down at them, spraying machine-gun fire in a low pass, making the soldiers dash for cover, then climbed away and repeated the attack from another direction. Again he pulled up, reckoning he had had enough ammunition for a third sustained strafing.

As he banked the plane there was a sudden hammering explosion. The gunsight in front of him disintegrated and holes appeared in the windscreen which cracked right across. For a fraction of a second he couldn't imagine what was happening. Then the shape of an F86 fighter shot past and he realized he was under attack himself. He hauled the T6 out of the turn, levelled her and tried to follow the jet, now arcing round in a wide circle to shoot him up again. He had thought about this often. The only one possible way to escape was by getting right down on the deck. He dived, the slipstream making a new and frightening noise through the shattered perspex, until he was just above the trees, then headed for the grey black slag heap, twisting and turning all the time. Maybe, just possibly, he could play hide and seek around the mound, exploiting his own slowness and manoeuvrability. He glanced in the rear-view mirror, mercifully untouched. The shark shape of the F86 was behind him. He kicked hard on the rudder, jinking the plane to the right. The F86 swept past. Its very speed meant it only had one chance at a time to shoot him down. Now it repeated its wide turn, coming round to line up on his tail, but not before he had gained the slag heap.

For perhaps four minutes Mike succeeded in keeping the man-made hill between him and the jet's diving attacks. He was just congratulating himself when the engine began running rough, coughing and stopping momentarily. He peered down at the fuel gauges. Never easy to read, they were set in an opaque quadrant near his feet. One emphatically showed empty. The engine spluttered. A fuel line must have been severed. With a sense of outrage Mike realized he was going to have to force-land the T6 and that he would be a sitting duck throughout. He glanced round for the F86. It was out of sight, presumably on the far side of the slag heap. He straightened out, heading away from the UN troops, searching for a reasonable open space, saw a patch of scrub near a road, and hurriedly assessed how he could land. With wheels retracted was the only way. The engine was barely giving him a quarter of normal power. He banked gently and lined himself up.

With 500 feet of height still to be lost, he again felt the drumming of bullets hitting the fuselage. The F86 swept overhead. He pumped down the flap by hand, let the plane sink, saw the bushes coming up as though in a nightmare, and with a great tearing and rasping thumped the T6 down on its belly. The impact threw him forward savagely in his straps. For thirty yards the aircraft careered along in a jarring, shuddering agony. The propeller tips were bent back, the smell of petrol suffused the cockpit, then the starboard wing hit a small tree, the plane pivoted like a butterfly on a pin and stopped. It needed all his strength to force the canopy back enough to get out. As he did so, the jet screamed past. He jumped down and ran for cover but it did not reappear. Evidently the pilot was satisfied. After salvaging his maps, Mike started to walk towards the road.

Two mercenaries patrolling in a jeep were spectators of the brief aerial battle. When the T6 disappeared from view they guessed it had crashed and accelerated hard in its direction. The found Mike, his face bleeding from a multitude of small cuts, limping his way to the road, clutching a map. They stopped and he leant unsteadily against the side of the vehicle.

'Can you take me to Camp Massart? I must report to Legrand.' He sounded more shaky than he knew.

'Are you joking?' One of them laughed nervously. 'The place is surrounded. Anyone in there is as good as a prisoner.'

He was interrupted by a wailing noise, which rose in intensity to a whistling shriek.

'Get down,' shouted the other soldier. As they all ducked a mortar bomb exploded fifty yards away, throwing up earth and stones with a resounding, head-stunning crump. Thirty seconds later another descended, detonating in a tree and sending splinters of wood flying.

'Let's get out of here,' exclaimed the driver. He revved the engine, Mike scrambled into the back and they jolted off towards the city just as a third bomb came down.

'The bastards must have seen us,' commented the driver.

For some minutes Mike remained slumped on the back seat. Eventually he asked them if they knew Herman.

'Herman the German, you mean, big guy with a red face? A sergeant major.'

'That's him.'

'You'll find him in the Union Minière complex. Want to go there?'

Chantal had never felt so alone in her life. Tshombe and three aides had left in the big Dodge, the boot crammed with transmitting equipment, slipping out of the city before the UN completely encircled it. Radio Katanga was on the move too, operating from a truck. As the fighting grew more bitter, with the mercenaries tenaciously clinging to the city end of the tunnel against an onslaught from the UN Irish, others in the administration followed their President's example and fled.

Although the guards remained outside the palace, the interior was a tomb, peopled only by terrified cleaning staff, Chantal herself, and two radio operators. The fighting was perilously close. A small eucalyptus wood separated the palace grounds from the river, on the far side of which the Ethiopians were wresting the grounds of the Lido from the gendarmerie. The firing, though sporadic, never ceased entirely and at times was ferocious, the rattle of machine-guns punctuated by single staccato shots which Chantal imagined must be from snipers. Several bombs had cratered the palace garden. She haunted the radio room, praying there would not be a direct hit on the building.

Late in the afternoon of the day Mike was shot down, 17 December, the message she had anticipated came through. Tshombe would meet Kane at the Kiobo Mission at midday tomorrow. The President insisted on precise details of the arms Kane would provide. He also required to be flown out to Salisbury in time to catch an evening flight to Europe. Chantal mulled over this until she remembered the President's odd insistence on being flown to Ndola in September, in spite of the town being only two hours distant. Presumably he had a new plan. However, there was nothing to indicate that he was overruling the private arrangement they had made. She summoned an escort and was driven the short distance to the Union Minière headquarters in order to telephone Kane.

On the way in she recognized Herman standing with a group of mercenaries in the courtyard.

'Hey, miss,' he called out, 'do you know who is here? Mike Russell has arrived.'

Her immediate instinct was to drop everything else and

find him. With an effort she walked calmly across to Herman, trying to suppress her pleasure, to ask where Mike was.

'He's lucky to be alive. The doc's told him to lie down for a few hours. He's in the dressing station.'

The Union Minière's dispensary had been transformed into an emergency medical centre. As soon as she had passed on the message for Kane, she hurried along to it.

'Nothing worse than cuts and shock,' the doctor said briskly. 'A night's sedated sleep will put him right. You can take him away if you like. Indeed I wish you would, we'rc getting too many serious casualties.'

In that moment, Chantal knew what she was going to do. She was going to take Mike away and look after him and marry him. It seemed absurd not to have done it before. With the realization, she found a new mood.

'I'll be back in ten minutes,' she told the doctor. 'There is one thing to organize.'

She hurried back to the courtyard, found Herman and explained that she needed an armed escort for tomorrow. Hesitant to exceed his authority, he took her to an officer, who agreed to her proposal.

'But Herman and one other are as many as I can spare. With the pilot you'll be a jeep-load. Surely the President can send some gendarmerie from closer to this place Kiobo?'

'Do you think we can break out if we are so few?'

The officer consulted his map. 'To the north-west, yes. The Irish are at the tunnel and the Gurkhas further up round the airport. But with luck you will find the Jadotville road possible.' He glanced at her, appraising her quickly. 'Can you drive?'

'Certainly I can.'

'Then take my advice. Keep the men's hands free for their guns. If you are challenged, don't stop. Let them shoot their way through.'

When she returned to the dispensary Mike was sitting

there, grinning. 'You know,' he said as she came up, 'I was supposed to be seeing that you were safe. Father Paul asked me to specially.'

'Never mind. What does it matter if I take you to the villa or you arrive by yourself? The result is the same.'

That evening she gave Mike a sedative and put him to bed, but when firing started and bombs fell close by, she crept out of her own room, not daring to put on the light, and went to him. He stirred drowsily, felt her body and put his arms around her.

'Oh, Mike, darling,' she whispered, 'I'm so frightened. And so glad.'

Barlow read the transcript in bemusement. Could it be correct?

'We are intercepting all radio traffic.' There was pride in the Indian major's voice. September was being avenged. 'This is accurate translating. But where is Kiobo? Who is Kane?'

'It's a Catholic Mission,' said Barlow, 'I've been there. And Kane,' he faltered, 'I thought Kane was in mining.'

'This man is arms dealing. Read. It is clear. Contrary to Resolution of 24 November, emphatically contrary.'

The phrase *in flagrante delicto* passed through Barlow's mind. How could Kane have had the gall to pick his brains about the UN plans and then offer Tshombe arms? It was the most flagrant double-crossing imaginable.

'We'll have to pick him and Tshombe up at the same time,' he said angrily. 'Kane we can certainly arrest. Tshombe I think I shall have to bring back here to Mr Urquhart.'

'You are wanting troops?' asked the Indian.

'Definitely. Vehicles too.' He thought about it. It was now evening. Kiobo was four hours' drive. But they must have time to prepare an ambush. If UN soldiers were in evidence Tshombe would unquestionably be warned and the pilot of Kane's charter aircraft would probably turn back without landing. He tried to visualize the airstrip at the Mission, recalling that the buildings were on one side, and that the other was uncleared bush. He explained this to the major.

'Then I am coming with you,' he said confidently. 'And I am making very careful planning, very careful indeed.'

11

The rain drummed on the roof, cascading into the storm drain alongside the house like a waterfall. In the moment of waking Mike thought he was at home in Kenya, listening to one of those torrential downpours which heralded the long rains and brought relief to the farm. Slowly he came to, the effect of the drug leaden on his mind, and realized he was in a strange room. He had not slept in a bed for many days and he felt sure Chantal had been with him. He sat up. It must have been a dream! There was no sign of her. But someone other than himself had folded his clothes on a chair. He struggled up, splashed water on his face in a basin, put on his shirt and went in search of answers, his legs and feet still bare.

The living room had a boarded up window and a gaping hole in one wall, but it was recognizably the Berthouds'. Plates clattered in the kitchen. He went through. Chantal was making coffee, the aroma welcoming him. She put down the pot and kissed him affectionately.

'How are you feeling, my love?'

He laughed. 'A little bewildered! What's going on?'

'Your aeroplane was shot down yesterday. Today we are going to Kiobo. Very soon, in fact.' She poured a cup of coffee. 'Sugar and milk? Yes?' She handed it to him. 'Don't worry, the doctor said you might suffer a little from shock. Take that back to the room and get dressed. We haven't much time.'

Yesterday's events were coming back to him now, though the contrast between the huts by the road and this comfort was still unbelievable. And Chantal had shared his bed. She certainly seemed to have accepted him. As he pulled on his trousers he decided to make no reference to it, just in case it had been a dream. He drank the coffee gratefully and by the time Herman drove up in the jeep, was fully awake.

Dawn was breaking as they left, the rain still beating down, huge drops splashing on the road, running away in muddy rivulets. Chantal drove, the three men tense. Although the jeep's canvas roof was up, they had to leave the sides open in order both to see and to fire. The windscreen itself was barely kept clear by the wipers.

'There's a small road that crosses the Lubwe river, beyond the radio station,' Chantal told them, feeling less self-assured than she sounded. 'Once we're there, I can find my way out towards Jadotville.'

Herman said nothing. He was in the front passenger seat with the Luigi Franchi on his lap, its magazine on, its mechanism cocked. He also had two grenades readily accessible.

'All kaffirs hate the rain,' commented the third mercenary, a South African called Piet. 'If we hit the Ethiopians we'll be fine. They'll have their heads down.'

Chantal went through residential side street, avoiding the radio station. Already they were getting soaked from spray and her shirt clung wetly to her exposed shoulder. She had put on the most practical clothes she could find, flat shoes, slacks and an old shirt of her father's. Her make-up and a dress were in a small leather grip tucked away in the back of the vehicle.

As she swung out of the Avenue Molemey a hundred metres or so short of the river, she was confronted by a roadblock. It consisted only of a jeep parked half across the road. A couple of UN guards stood shrouded in dank capes beside it.

'Go past on the left.' Herman shouted. 'Put your foot down, man.'

There was just room. The two guards began to raise their rifles, encumbered by the wet capes. One stepped forward.

Suddenly it occurred to Chantal that in this murk and half-light they might mistake the jeep for one of their own.

'I'm pretending to stop,' she said. 'Don't fire unless you have to.'

She slowed right down. The guards lowered their rifles, peering through the rain, hardly able to discern the figures inside the approaching vehicle. She changed into second gear. At two yards she accelerated hard, running the left wheels partly on the verge. As they jolted past both Herman and Piet opened up with their sub-machines. A shot sang past them. Then they were across the bridge and hidden by trees.

'Bloody good,' exclaimed Mike delightedly. 'You did that beautifully.'

Chantal, exhilarated, did not look round. 'Let's hope the UN are concentrating on the towns. If we can by-pass Jadotville, we should be all right.'

Five hours later, exhausted even though the others had shared the driving, she reached the Kiobo turn off. They halted in the Mission compound at 11.20 a.m. The tail of a truck was projecting from a barn. Herman recognized it immediately.

'Man,' he said with rare excitement. 'Captain Jacques must be here with the paras.'

He was right. The first person to emerge and greet them was the lean, deeply sunburnt ex-legionnaire. Mike introduced him to Chantal.

'Have you any message?' she asked. 'Is Tshombe coming?'

'He sent us ahead to secure the airstrip, that's all I know. The only message I have is that the plan is unchanged.' He chuckled. 'Father Paul is not too pleased. But I assured him we should only be around for a few hours.'

'Is he there? I must see him.' Chantal ran to the front door of the Mission house and called his name. When he appeared she embraced him warmly. 'Oh, Father, I have something tremendous to tell you.'

He smiled at her calmly. 'Then you had better come in,' he said. 'Your para-commando friends are not leaving us a great deal of time.'

'The met. is appalling.' The charter pilot showed Kane the teleprinter account of the weather in its abbreviated, aeronautical form. 'There's a massive front lying over Elisabethville.'

'Can we fly round it?' Kane suggested anxiously.

'It'll cost you. Our rates are based on direct mileages.'

'To hell with that. The aim is to get there.'

The pilot chewed this over, spent a further ten minutes poring over the weather charts, and finally delivered his opinion. He was too experienced to make promises. 'I'm prepared to try. If we don't make it you'll be charged for the flying time, OK? I shall want you to sign an indemnity to that effect.'

Kane had no option but to agree. He had enough on his mind as things were. Ironstone had failed to send out a second representative. To appear by himself would look suspicious. Futhermore, even though the pilot knew of his intention to fly on further into Congo, with Tshombe aboard, he had not dared explain that this might have to be at gunpoint. It would all depend on Tshombe's sense of direction. One area of central African bush looked much like another. Around midday the sun was at its zenith and gave no clear indication of east and west, especially not to a man seated in the shade of an aircraft cabin. He reckoned the President could be kept occupied by business discussions during the hour or so of flight. Kiobo might be near the Rhodesian border, but it was also half-way across Katanga. They would be landing at Luluabourg before Tshombe could guess anything was wrong. None the less Kane had felt the need of an assistant so acutely that, against his better judgement, he had acquired a substitute in Ndola. By chance he had met a mercenary, just expelled from Katanga by the UN, who could play the part so long as he said little, and had hastily bought him a respectable suit and shoes. The man already had a shoulder holster and a gun. Kane was playing for very high stakes and he felt the additional risk was minimal compared to the advantages.

The plane was an Aztec, twin engined with six seats and a comfortable cruising speed. But from the take-off onwards, there was little comfort on the flight. Despite the pilot's skill, they were thrown around with a violence worse than he had ever known. The mercenary was sick, spewing into a paper bag. However, they did get through the front and into calmer weather near Kolwezi. From there it was simple, following the road until Kane recognized the hills gashed by the exploration trench, and then identified the Mission. They landed at 11.55. He had anticipated a strong guard on the airstrip and was unsurprised when a group of gendarmes directed the pilot to park in front of the Mission.

Chantal came out at once. She had changed into a dress, tidied herself and now walked over to greet him with conscious formality. She distrusted Kane, but she was under orders.

'The President is on his way,' she said. 'He has authorized me to start the discussion.' She glanced at Kane's companion. 'This is your colleague from London, I presume.'

Kane began an introduction, then saw that he had lost her attention. She was staring past him, horror in her eyes. He swung round. Emerging from the bush on the far side of the airstrip, some 200 yards away, was a line of troops, rifles in hand, advancing steadily. Prominent among them was a civilian.

Steve Barlow would have preferred to bring a stronger force, but with the battle for Elisabethville reaching its climax, the most the UN Command would allocate was half a company of Ethiopians, some sixty men. Given this relative inadequacy, the Indian major had done a magnificent job of laying the ambush. The Ethiopians might lack discipline, but Barlow was astounded at their capacity for silent movement through the thorn scrub and trees which concealed their approach route to the Mission. They had lain hidden since soon after dawn. Only when the plane landed did the major give a silent signal for them to close in.

As the Ethiopians reached the edge of the clearing, Barlow saw a scurry of activity by the buildings. The gendarmes had fallen immediately into firing positions. The girl who he knew must be Chantal was hurried to safety by Father Paul, his white soutane conspicuous at any distance. Two men ran to the plane. Barlow recognized one as Kane.

The major waved his men forward, finally halting them a scant fifty yards from the aircraft, facing it in a half circle. It was the same technique as had been used with the Gurkhas at the radio station and, as then, the defenders were hemmed in by the buildings behind them.

Now that they were close Barlow recognized Mike Russell. He and a further bunch of mercenaries had appeared round a corner where a second aircraft, the Cessna, was parked. The two groups faced each other, the whites and most of the African gendarmes standing aggressively defiant. Not a word had been spoken. The sun had come out and glinted on the Cessna's wings and fuselage.

Barlow glanced sideways at the Indian, who inclined his head as if to say 'go ahead'. Making it plain that he was unarmed, he stepped out in front of the Ethiopians. He had rehearsed what he would say and he pronounced it slowly and distinctly.

'In accordance with our mandate I call on you to surrender. All that will happen to a man who surrenders is that he will be expelled from the Congo.' He turned to face Kane. 'I am arresting you, however, for attempted arms smuggling.'

There was total silence. Herman, standing next to Mike, gripped his machine-gun. Jacques scowled, wanting if possible to avoid firing the first shot. The Ethiopians fidgeted, unable to understand why they were not already shooting. The overriding lesson they had learnt from the Congo operation was that white men talked too much.

'Russell.' Barlow's voice was taut. He found the lack of response unnerving. 'I call on you to surrender.'

Mike handed his gun to Herman and moved forward, all eyes watching him. He walked very deliberately towards Barlow, but without raising his hands. He stopped right in front of the Canadian.

'I'll see you in hell first,' he said, so quietly that no one else heard it.

A look of frozen astonishment spread over the Canadian's face. This was a reaction he had never anticipated. But he knew what he had to do. He reached out to seize Mike's arm in the physical act of arrest. As he did so, Mike lashed out with his fist, catching him square on the jaw. A second later the two men were sprawled on the ground, struggling.

The Ethiopians needed no further signal. They opened fire. As the mercenaries replied with a barrage of sub-machine shots, Barlow struggled up, waving frantically. He had time to shout 'Stop!' once before a bullet hit him in the chest and he fell back on top of Mike.

By the aircraft Kane's hired man pulled his gun and joined in, dropping on to one knee by the undercarriage, taking aimed shots with his hand high. The nearest Ethiopians shifted their attention to this new target, high velocity bullets tearing into the plane's fuselage. Kane himself fell, clutching his stomach and screaming with pain.

Inside the Mission Father Paul rushed Chantal through to the safety of a back room.

Then Jacques made the break. Shouting to the group to follow him, he dashed away from the buildings and into the cover of some small trees. From there he could outflank the Ethiopians, exposed on the airstrip. As more of their number fell, their nerve broke. A few ran back to the bush they had emerged from. Seconds later they all took to their heels. Immediately Jacques began rallying his remaining para-commandos in pursuit.

Mike had lain flat throughout the brief engagement, hopelessly caught in the middle and with the weight of Barlow on top of him. Now he pushed the body away and scrambled to his feet. He was soaked in blood and examined himself incredulously. He was unhurt. The blood must be Barlow's. He looked down at the Canadian. He was unquestionably dead. The white shirt was crimson, and the side of his head was drilled through with another bullet. Mike felt the vomit rise in his throat, ran to the grass and was violently sick. In dying Barlow had saved his life.

He recovered himself, wiped his mouth, tore off the sodden shirt and took stock of what was happening. In front of the building Father Paul and Chantal were bent over a wounded man. He ran across. It was Herman, lying on his back, his breath coming in gasps, blood trickling from his mouth. Father Paul knelt in the dust, giving him absolution, the words of the ritual firm and clear. Mike looked down, not knowing what to do. Herman saw him, tried to lift his head and speak.

'Man, you . . .' he managed to say, then the effort overwhelmed him. Chantal held his hand and a flicker of a smile passed across his lips. A moment later he was consumed by a fit of choking coughs, the last one seeming to tear his whole frame apart. Again he tried to speak, his eyes staring up at Mike. Then he went limp.

Father Paul took his wrist, felt for a pulse, and said with infinate regret. 'There is nothing we can do. Let us carry him inside.'

The two men lifted his body between them and laid him on the floor where it was cool, Chantal fetching a cushion for his head.

Mike stayed with him for the half-hour until he died, trying to give some comfort to the semi-conscious man whose life, as he saw it, had been savaged by fate. By what logic did Herman's humble ambition to improve his smallholding lead to this? Barlow, of course, would have regarded him legalistically as a killer who deserved to die. But it was not as simple as that.

Herman was not the only one. Three more were dead and there were several wounded, including Kane. The other priest supervised the emergency medical care. Meanwhile Chantal found the gendarmerie radio operator and passed a brief account of events to Tshombe's command car. Soon afterwards a message came back stating baldly that the President was 'leaving for his destination by other means', and that she was to take whatever steps she thought appropriate for her own safety. As the conversation ended Jacques returned.

'We're clearing out,' he said, 'with the casualties. What about you?'

'Unless the Cessna's damaged, I think Mike will want to fly it. Let me go and see.'

She found Mike and Father Paul. 'Tshombe must be on his way to Paris,' she told them. 'In effect we have been defeated. He said before that if things went wrong we should take the Cessna to Rhodesia.' She looked at Mike, tears welling up in her eyes. 'It's over, isn't it? I know it must be but I don't want to believe it.'

Mike put his arms around her and she cried unashamedly.

'I think you should use the aircraft,' said Father Paul to him. 'One must be a realist. The UN will be back within hours.'

'Do you want to come with us?'

'No. Take Chantal to find her parents. For me, the work lies here. My vow was to serve Africa.' He paused. 'I must be truthful. That task will be easier when you soldiers of fortune have gone. Tshombe is a fine man in many respects, but this continent must find its own solutions.' He reached out a hand to Chantal, who was drying her eyes. 'Let us have a last talk before you go.'

Mike left them, ascertained that the Cessna had suffered only unimportant damage, and was then accosted by the charter pilot. The Aztec was unflyable and Kane too ill to be moved. Kane's so-called colleague was dead.

'What the hell next?' demanded the pilot. 'Who pays us?'

'Who pays any of us?' Mike snapped. 'I'll fly you out of here if you want. Count yourself lucky.' He had no time for anyone connected with Bob Kane.

An hour later they left, Mike circling the Cessna above the Mission, waggling the wings in salute as Father Paul waved below, a diminutive white figure by the brick Mission house with its clearing in the vast landscape of bush.

'So,' said Captain Zog succinctly, 'you discover time it takes and you come back.' He was standing on the tarmac at Wilson Airport, the line of planes gleaming in the sun, and was endeavouring unsuccessfully to conceal his pleasure. 'Maybe now you have girl friend you settle down, eh? Is no bad thing. You want job back too?

'You did say you'd keep it open.' Mike grinned at Chantal. 'Don't worry, he's a nice man at heart.'

'Is kind of you, is very kind.' Zog scowled unconvincingly. 'And now is four days from Christmas. I suppose first thing you ask is for holiday? I tell you something.' He slapped Mike cheerfully on the arm. 'You take Christmas this time for one reason. I know damn well your licence need renewal.' He grinned at Chantal. 'Don't worry. Once we have filled in forms is all OK. Then we keep him busy. Both of us.'

Epilogue

Eastair Safaris
Wilson Airport
Nairobi
Kenya

22 January

Richard Cox, Esq
c/o Peter Grose
Curtis Brown Ltd
1 Craven Hill
London W2

Dear Richard,

Thanks a lot for sending me the manuscript of your book. It feels odd reading about oneself like that, but neither I nor Chantal have any serious objections. She thinks she remembers you, though there were so many pressmen around in those days that she's not sure. As you must have heard, we got married soon after leaving Katanga and our boys must be about the same age as yours. They're at school in England. Although I took Kenyan nationality after Uhuru I want them to have the option. Not that this isn't still a good place to live. There was no upheaval when the old man died and business is booming. This year we're taking delivery of a Learjet so that will be one ambition satisfied at last! I'm also in charge now, as I took over from Zog when he retired last year. He sends his regards, by the way. He says don't imagine you ever fooled him. He knew you got arrested with the Cessna in Ruanda that time.

Looking back it's funny how fated the men who seemed to control our destinies were. Kennedy assassinated. Tshombe surviving to become Prime Minister of the whole Congo in 1964, deposed a year later, then kidnapped over the Med in a private jet and dying in jail in Algiers. They say the Algerians could never bring him to trial because he had committed no crime and in the end they injected air into his veins. Sendwe bit the dust too, hacked to pieces by his own Baluba near Albertville in 1964. And Hammarskjold, of course. I reckon both the inquiries into that crash exonerated us. No one really questions that the pilot quite simply came too low on his approach. The locals in Ndola have a theory that he mistook the lighting on the Kitwe road for the runway lights. It's a cruel thing to say of the dead, but it's just as well Steve Barlow wasn't around to give evidence at those inquiries.

Thinking of Steve reminds me that you're wrong about a few things. He may have thought he was responsible for Tshombe agreeing to meet Hammarskjold at Ndola, but I reckon it was the British consul who was the real man behing the scenes. The British played a much bigger role in Katanga than you seem to have realized. As for Steve himself, well, Father Paul commented that he should have been a monk. He needed a God to obey.

Of course Father Paul came to Nairobi to marry Chantal and me. He told me he never trusted Bob Kane, although he nursed him for several weeks. I used to admire Bob in the old squadron days. He was a good commanding officer in some ways. But a solid gold bastard underneath. You asked where he was now. Frankly I'm not interested. I heard he was involved in some deal in Angola. Well, the communists will have caught up with him there all right.

Oddly enough I flew a client down to Tenke not so long ago. Some American had got together an international consortium to develop it. Allegedly they invested 300 million dollars and still haven't got a single ton of copper out. Changing the Congo's name to Zaire hasn't made the Congolese any more predictable, nor renaming Katanga as Shaba! I did not enjoy going back to the old stamping ground. The chaos and corruption were appalling. There wasn't a single airport official we didn't have to bribe. The Americans are still heavily involved there. It would hardly interest people now, but I would like to know if it *was* the CIA which provided our aircraft and those Cuban pilots. I'm damn sure PANWORLD was a CIA company. It can't be a coincidence that Tshombe had exiled Cubans flying for him again in 1964. The mercenaries lasted longer than the UN in the end!

'Mercenary' is a pretty dirty word these days, but I don't regret having been involved. There was a sort of idealism among a few of us, though I admit the legionnaires were a tough bunch. That reminds me, one final point of detail. You describe a mercenary plan to seize Elisabethville. Actually you've got the wrong one. It was Colonel Faulques's orders for a defensive action which the UN got hold of in December 1961. The one you must have seen was the so-called Hammond plan, which was later. Not that it matters. As you say, it is a novel and I suppose that entitles you to bend the truth a bit.

Apologies for these rather rambling thoughts. We're so busy I've had to dictate this. Hope to see you here sometime. Send us a copy of the book when it comes out.

Yours sincerely,
M. Russell
Managing Director